A second tank was bearing down on him from the right, only eight metres away. He heard the driver step on the accelerator, then suddenly all he could see were huge caterpillar tracks moving to crush him, blocking out everything else, and the enormous, terrifying turret cannon. At that moment he knew he would never see his mother again, and he shrieked, insanely, just like those Frenchmen he had heard in his nightmares. And he saw his own blood flowing into the dirt; he felt his heart stop, his legs become paralysed. And one final time he saw into the vision-slit, glimpsed a cap badge, then tracks, just tracks, turning, turning, squelching on to take his life –

and then there was nothingness . . .

Also by Will Berthold in Sphere Books:

LEBENSBORN
DEATH'S HEAD BRIGADE
EAGLES OF THE REICH
PRINZ-ALBRECHTSTRASSE

Brotherhood of Blood

WILL BERTHOLD

Translated by Fred Taylor

SPHERE BOOKS LIMITED
30–32 Gray's Inn Road, London WC1X 8JL

First published in Great Britain by
Sphere Books Ltd 1982
First published under the title *Feldpost Nummer Unbekannt*
Copyright © 1978 by Wilhelm Goldman Verlag, München
Translation Copyright © Sphere Books Ltd 1982

Set in 9½/10½ Compugraphic Times

Printed and bound in Great Britain by
Hunt Barnard Printing Ltd., Aylesbury, Bucks.

CHAPTER ONE

They were men who had cursed and killed, feared and fought like lions, sung till their lungs burst and suffered as much as their young bodies could stand, and they had grabbed victory for the Führer. Many of them, too many, had died before they knew what it was to bed a woman. They had tramped, crawled, trucked, squirmed. They had blisters on their feet, a yawning nothingness where their brains should have been – and Paris in their pockets.

It was May 20th 1940. Spring. But there was no heady scent of blossoms in the air for these boys – only the acrid odour of cordite and death. The German Blitzkrieg had sliced through Holland, scooped up Belgium; the armoured spearheads, breaker-waves of the field-grey tide, had flooded into northern France, cutting off the French from their Tommy allies, and now they were pounding hell-for-leather towards the Channel coast.

An anti-tank unit of General Rommel's 7th Panzer Division stopped that day in a tiny village near Arras and finally leaguered for a rest, maybe for no more than a few hours. For the top brass who were directing the Blitzkrieg, the menu was tempting: surprise attacks, panzer thrusts from the flanks, burned-out bunkers and screaming Stuka raids. But those were the kind of dishes that only the tactics instructors at the War Academy really appreciated. For the conscripts, the poor bastards on the sharp end, the biggest pleasure was to stand in line for warm grub from the field kitchen . . .

'You have to look at it this way,' as Private Kleebach, the platoon's philosopher, used to tell them. 'This is better than chewing daisies . . .'

He and his sidekick Böckelmann were on sentry duty

together in front of the village school house, which had been turned into a makeshift billet.

Slowly day merged into night. And with the darkness the idyllic little village seemed tranquil and sleepy – no hint that it could well be pummelled to rubble in the morning. Its people were forbidden to leave their homes; even the German troops had been ordered to stay in their quarters. So these human beings, enemies, co-existed uneasily, physically close but separated in the iron prison of what the Nazi propagandists called those 'heroic times'.

From the other side of the line, out of the blackness where the enemy sat licking his wounds, came a gentle gust of wind that played among the leaves of the sturdy chestnut tree in the school yard. Under its spreading branches were parked the company's vehicles: four self-propelled field guns, two trucks, an armoured gun and a captured French anti-aircraft piece. In the darkness the steel monsters stood silent and immobile, like contented cows in a meadow, and somehow they were no longer objects of terror – as if they, too, had come under the spell of this peaceful place.

Machines are lucky, thought Private Gerd Kleebach. When the time comes, someone switches them off. But the human heart carries on beating, taking the strain, and the nerves don't stop tearing you ragged; you're exhausted and you can't sleep, starving and you can't face food. Like a pendulum that can't stop swinging, backwards and forwards for ever in the emptiness . . .

'Another half an hour until we get relieved,' murmured Private Böckelmann. They had known each other as kids, played in the same Berlin streets. 'You get any mail?'

'Yes,' Kleebach answered sourly. 'A letter from home . . . but three weeks old.'

'Frigging disgrace,' Böckelmann said. 'You oughta complain, for goodness' sake. Your old man's something big in the post office, isn't he?'

'No . . . he just delivers the darned letters.' Kleebach grinned. He gazed up at the sky, searching the horizon, and then gave a satisfied nod. 'Those Tommy tanks won't dare budge out of their rat-holes tomorrow. The Stukas'll keep them pinned down and out of our way.'

Then they stood side by side and stared out into the night.

Nothing moving out there. The houses, with their steep roofs and tiny windows, looked unreal and magical, like something out of a fairy tale.

'Here . . . what kind of a stretch is it to Paris?' Böckelmann asked.

'About three weeks,' his mate said with a smile.

'Stupid bugger . . . I mean, how many kilometres?'

'Three, four hundred maybe.'

'Jesus, that must be a wild city . . .'

'You'll see.'

'Jesus, I hope so,' Böckelmann said. 'And what about the crumpet, eh? Raven-haired beauties . . .'

He traced a voluptuous outline in the air with his stubby hands.

'I don't think they're exactly panting for the likes of us,' Kleebach said wryly.

'Speak for yourself. But they'll get used to us . . . don't you think?'

'Yes. Maybe.' Kleebach was suddenly distant, preoccupied.

'Yeah . . .' Böckelmann fantasised, getting into the swing of it. 'When we get to Paris . . . first I'll kip for a couple of whole days . . . then an hour in the bath, a bucket of scoff, half a barrel of red wine . . . Yeah, and then a clean shirt on my back, press the old trousers, ticket of leave in my pocket, and from then on it's Mademoiselle, voulez-vous, and all the rest . . .'

'Why not?' Kleebach muttered.

'Well, those French birds are supposed to be hot stuff.'

'So they say.'

'Oh, come on!' Böckelmann protested, goaded beyond endurance. 'I bet you could fancy some little Parisian bit . . .'

'No,' Kleebach retorted arrogantly.

His mate frowned, then laughed quietly. 'You'll get nowhere with them, because you've got no faith in yourself.'

They parted and began to pace out the regulation distances, one to the right, the other to the left.

Kleebach, little more than a boy, had been a soldier for a year and at the front for all of ten days. Those days had been enough to show him what death meant. For the rest, he was about the average, no urge to be a hero, less to be labelled coward. He was slightly built, almost skinny, supple, with a face that could have been called soft. The last ten days had

7

started to draw the features on that face tighter, etched the creases at the corners of his mouth more deeply. His baptism of fire had not been so thrilling as the war reports said it would be. A flurry of action, fear, then past . . . When it was over, he had simply changed his underpants – for the first and last time after action – and that had been that.

He was young, but experience had taught him a few things: how to make yourself invisible, how to drink neat Pernod, how to snap the identity-disc from a fallen comrade's neck, how you chucked away your ration of artificial honey without being noticed, how a soldier managed to show a maximum of devotion to duty with a minimum of effort – and how when you looked at a pretty French girl you managed to forget that it was her brothers you were shooting at . . .

The air was sweet, the evening mild. The half moon climbed higher, bathing the roofs of the buildings with its silvery light. Kleebach looked up at the Great Bear. His mother, father, and the other five Kleebachs would be gazing up at the same sky. He could feel the peace like a physical force, spreading like a blanket over the countryside, covering strongpoints, bunkers, ruins, trenches, orders . . . Somewhere in the distance a lone machine gun chattered, but it was so far away that they need not bother with it. A flare burst on the horizon; its sparks fell down among three tall poplar trees looming out of the dead-flat landscape, and for a moment they were like memorials in a graveyard, a sudden, sad image.

Kleebach looked away and up at the wads of blossom on the tree above him. In a few months there would be a rich harvest of chestnuts, but how could he know whether he would still be alive come autumn? He glanced around, taking a deep breath. Another scent. Spanish lilacs, white Spanish lilacs, his mother's favourite flower. Suddenly he was angry that the flower should waste its fragrance on a world at war.

It was then that he saw a dim light in the house opposite. The glimmer from the window was faint, but bright enough to guide an enemy shell.

'What the hell is that?' Kleebach cursed, and made to go over to the house.

Heinz Böckelmann, moving to his side, grabbed his arm. 'Hey, look there . . .'

You could only see a shadow through the curtain, a shape

8

that was the silhouette of a slim figure – a girl, and yet a woman. Two hands above a head that was dipping gently, long hair cascading, two willowy arms that suddenly swung upwards, as if grasping for something, as if in surrender.

They stood and gasped.

'Man, oh man,' Böckelmann murmured.

Then the light went out. But the two sentries could not tear their eyes from the window. They saw the curtains part and a young girl lean slightly out, as if listening for something, staring into the night. She was so close that it felt as if they could reach out and stroke her face with their hands.

The French girl noticed the two soldiers and slammed the window shut with a brutal finality.

'Get that,' said Böckelmann.

His friend said nothing.

Now it wasn't just the scent of lilacs in the air that he sensed, but spring itself. He could feel it in his finger tips, it was like a gentle pressure in his chest, like a potion that made you drunk, and it made him see war with a new bitterness. War, which was out to steal his youth – and with it his right to live, love, to dream, to kiss, experience and return another's passion.

'That was the one from the bakery ... the blonde ...' Böckelmann sighed. 'You know, the one who called the Feldwebel a filthy boche ...'

Kleebach didn't hear him. His eyes were still glued to that window, but night had already blocked out his peep-hole into another world. Two cats over the other side of the yard, though, were celebrating the glory of the senses. Clever animals, cleverer than men. They didn't give a damn for the war.

'She's twenty at the most,' Böckelmann said, getting quite excited. 'I'll tell you, she wouldn't have to ask me twice ...'

'Have you gone out of your minds?' boomed a harsh voice from the darkness.

The two privates automatically jerked to attention. They had seen the shadow, and a second later they had both recognised the voice of Hauptfeldwebel Weber.

'You arseholes!' he oathed. 'You old women! Good-for-nothing layabouts!'

Private Kleebach tried to make his report. 'Two men on . . .'

'On a Sunday frigging outing!' cut in Weber.

'Nothing new to report, Hauptfeldwebel.'

'Naturally,' the sergeant-major growled. 'Never anything from Kleebach. Always the frigging same: shooting his mouth off, because he went to High School! You're a useless cretin!' Relishing his power, he dropped his voice to a threatening whisper. 'What are you, Kleebach?'

'A . . . a useless cretin, Hauptfeldwebel,' Kleebach answered miserably.

'You learn fast,' the sergeant-major mocked, and moved on. 'When your duty's over, you report to the company commander, understood?'

'Yes, Hauptfeldwebel!' Kleebach shouted at Weber's retreating back. His vision of spring had been well and truly pissed on.

'Shit,' hissed Böckelmann, who was a creature of few words.

At last they were relieved. Their duty ended just as the cats found their way into the gutter of the house opposite. Böckelmann bent down to find himself a stone to throw, then dropped it quickly.

That was when they heard the shots.

'Alarm! Alarm!' Kleebach bellowed.

Whistles sounded, doors slammed, everyone staggered sleepily out of their billets, getting in each other's way. A man tripped and fell, three or four others stumbled over him, cursing, hauled themselves upright again, until the first orders came, bringing something like order into the chaotic game of hide-and-seek.

The night panic didn't last long. Maybe the forward sentries had really sighted an English patrol, or maybe they had been fooled by a stray dog in the hedgerow. Whatever the cause, they blasted away in the direction of the sound, and before long the enemy was firing back, suspecting a night attack. Searchlights tore at the darkness, flares exploded high above, machine guns threw deadly orange ribbons into the empty sky. Anyone would have thought that death had wings.

Just as suddenly, the silence returned. An hour after the alarm, the conscripts slouched back into their billets, eager to tear off their kit and hit the sack. They cursed the fact that it had been nothing, but maybe they were relieved, all the same . . .

Then three soldiers dragged over a bundle wrapped in canvas.

'Well, what is it now?' the company commander asked testily. He stood with his cap pushed to the back of his head, a cigarette in his mouth, his right hand on his hip. A typical go-getter, tailor-made for all-out war.

'The Feldwebel . . . Herr Oberleutnant . . .' said a lance-corporal.

The company commander went over to the bundle and leaned over the wounded man. One glance told him the situation: nothing to be done. The dying heart was pumping the last blood out of the man's arteries. Hauptfeldwebel Weber's features began to take on the look of death. His eyes became huge, pleading, and then finally the light began to go out of them. His lips twitched once more, until they too were rigid and icy-pale.

The Oberleutnant stood up. 'How the hell did this happen?' he asked.

'In the confusion . . . a spot of bad luck . . .' the lance-corporal said.

'Filthy business,' the Oberleutnant muttered, shaking his head. 'Cover him up . . . and keep your mouths shut. The rest of the company'll know about it soon enough.'

'Yes, Herr Oberleutnant!' the three of them bawled in unison.

The company commander headed for the other ranks' billets.

'Attention!' roared Böckelmann.

But the young officer motioned for them to stand easy. 'Well, how're you young warriors feeling?' he asked.

'Fine, Herr Oberleutnant,' they chorused. It was the only answer they could give.

'Then be so good as to get your heads down!' The company commander lit himself a cigarette. 'I don't know when I'll next be able to fix some sleep for you . . .'

He was about to leave the room when Private Kleebach came up to him and stood to attention. 'I was ordered to report to you, Herr Oberleutnant.'

11

'Ordered?' the officer said absently. 'By whom?'

'By Feldwebel Weber, Herr Oberleutnant.'

'But he's . . .' the officer began, then broke off, because his own tongue had come close to exceeding his own order. 'Come with me, Kleebach,' he added quickly, and took him out into the corridor of the school house. 'In trouble again?'

'Yes, Herr Oberleutnant . . . I was talking on guard duty.'

'To yourself, eh?'

'No, Herr Oberleutnant.'

'So, who were you chewing the fat with?'

Private Kleebach hesitated. His chief realised that he was trying to protect a comrade and smiled sympathetically. 'Okay,' he said. 'Guard duty's a pain in the arse.' He scratched the back of his head. 'I didn't invent it . . .' He walked back into the billet with Kleebach and nodded. 'Make yourself scarce, boy . . . and don't get caught again!'

Kleebach was still hesitating.

The officer saw it, played a bit with the identity disc that hung like a medal round his neck, and said sardonically: 'Something else . . . want to use the W.C., do we?'

'No, Herr Oberleutnant . . . permission to inform the Herr Oberleutnant that my parents are celebrating their silver wedding anniversary on June 14th . . .'

'And what can I do about that?' the officer murmured.

'I have four brothers and one sister,' Kleebach continued. 'They'll all be there on the day . . . and I'd like . . .'

'To join in the party, eh?'

'Yes, Herr Oberleutnant,' answered Kleebach, relieved, and added in a highly unmilitary fashion: 'It's not for my own sake, Herr Oberleutnant . . . but, you understand, my mother's been waiting for this, and she . . .'

'Mothers always wait,' the officer cut in tersely. 'And they're always lovely ladies . . . no, son . . .' He clapped Kleebach on the shoulder. 'All leave cancelled, order of the High Command.'

'Yes, Herr Oberleutnant,' Kleebach answered sadly.

'Kleebach,' the Oberleutnant said. 'I'm not a monster, but I can't make any exceptions. But . . . when all this palaver is over, you'll be first in line for a fast train home, got that?'

'Yes, Herr Oberleutnant.' Kleebach saluted with a snappiness that went beyond the call of duty.

In the school room, which had been cleared of desks and chairs, the light was still burning. A few soldiers were snoring loudly. Three die-hards were playing cards, a couple of super-keen types were cleaning their rifles, some were drinking red wine out of mess-tins, and others were eating tomorrow's rations, because it was better safe than sorry. Böckelmann sat in one corner playing his harmonica. A kid next to him was rubbing the ribbon of his newly-awarded Iron Cross Class II with disc, to make it look battle-stained. Kleebach sat himself down at the rickety wooden table and gave some thought to the letter he intended to write to his parents.

'Good night, mother, good night . . .' Böckelmann played softly, picking out the old sentimental song.

'Shut that racket!' someone groaned in half-sleep.

'Leave him!' said the others.

'Yes, I've caused you pain, but it'll be all right . . .' Kleebach whispered, supplying the next line. All at once he was close to her, not as embarrassed as he had always been before when he had wanted to show tenderness and had always felt inhibited, with his young boy's awkwardness, but had never managed to hide how much he felt for her and his father.

And now June 14th, the great day, was coming – the day the Kleebachs had been talking about, writing about, for months past.

Dear mother, Gerd Kleebach wrote in tidy, even script, and dear father, I have just discussed things with the Oberleutnant, and he has promised me special leave for your twenty-fifth wedding anniversary so long as we arrive in Paris in time, which is a certainty. You will have heard all the war reports and know how quickly the advance is proceeding. Things are really not too bad . . .

Gerd finished the letter and took it to the mail in the darkness. He was the last to sleep. A few hours later, the shrill notes of a noncom's whistle sounded roll-call, summoning them to a hell no soldier in that company would ever forget. At least, no soldier who survived . . .

The day was beautiful right from the start, sunny and warm, as if it had a personal interest in lightening the burden of those two dozen men in their blue uniforms at the branch post office in the West End of Berlin. They slung their bags over their shoulders and started briskly on their rounds. They knew that a whole nation had become used to waiting at the window, waiting for the postman to call.

Arthur Kleebach, postman, knew and loved the district he served. For more years than he cared to count, he had tramped up and down tenement stairs every workday. He was a thickset man of fifty, jovial and well-liked. He shared people's pleasure when he could bring them money, and they even kept their affection for him when he had to ask for it. He knew that there was an old lady who lived alone, and that you had to knock gently so that she didn't take fright, and he would wave a mother's field-post letter from a distance, to let her know her son had written from the front. He brought bills, newspapers, circulars and greetings, signs of life and notices of death. The war had raised the mail service to the great pivot of fate and human hope.

Loud marching music boomed out of the open windows on the street. Kleebach, the postman, had even got used to that. These were noisy times, perhaps great times, times that blew on the trumpet and hammered on the drum. Why not? The fanfares that came before the special reports on the radio had trouble keeping up with speed of the German forces' advance. The swastika flag flew proudly; even cautious people had become fanatics, the sceptics optimists, and those who opposed the Nazi system had begun to silently despair. Out there, an Austrian corporal was showing his generals how to run a Blitzkrieg. Today, however, he was about to suffer a kick in the teeth. In a few hours the world was going to hear about the fiasco at Arras.

Arthur Kleebach had almost finished his round. A few hours' break, and then would come the afternoon delivery. That was his routine, had been for all those years. He couldn't say how many pairs of shoes he had worn out in the course of his duties. A short while ago, he had been due for replacement by a younger man, but Kleebach had fought it, because he didn't want to be parted from 'his' people – from men and women who had become confidants, with whom he enjoyed those little chats at the door, the cheerful word as he went on his way. There were those who considered his job boring, mechanical, but for Arthur it was the most fascinating job in the world. He was at home in any apartment on his round, if only as a temporary 'guest' at the door. On the third floor of number 15 he would occasionally be offered a glass of wine, and the widow at number 21 made him a cup of coffee, whether he brought good news or bad.

Kleebach had become a connoisseur of humankind during his life as a postman. It no longer surprised him that he often got the biggest tips from people who he least suspected of generosity, or that others, to whom he was constantly delivering great mounds of mail, gave him nothing. His daily contact with his 'customers' had created relationships that came close to friendship.

Duty and family were the two poles of his life, the centres around which he revolved. He wanted nothing more, and he was content with both.

Two more houses. Kleebach stepped up his pace. Three more newspapers and two letters. He lived in his own delivery area, and today there had been nothing for him. Yesterday, though, Gerd had written, and the day before there had been a note from Fritz. They were twins, and both were serving in the western campaign, one with the army and one with the Luftwaffe. Besides them there was Thomas, the oldest, who had picked up a bullet-wound in Poland and was still recovering in the Heimat Hospital in Berlin – which meant that he, at least, was safe. After him came Alfred, nicknamed Freddy, who was also known jokingly as the 'gigolo', then Achim, a banner-bearer in the Hitler Youth, and Marion, the girl. Above all, there was Maria Kleebach, his wife, the woman who had brought the whole varied brood into the world and held them together with an iron will. Arthur Kleebach's fondest wish was that all the children should have a better life than their parents. Perhaps it was, as yet, his only unfulfilled desire.

Thomas, the philosopher, had already qualified as an engineer when he was called up. He had volunteered for half his army pay to be sent to his younger brothers and sisters. Gerhard and Fritz had sailed through their school-leaving certificates, with the help of state grants. Marion was a secretary, Achim was in the seventh grade at High School, and Freddy, who had managed his intermediate exam before leaving secondary school, would make his mark in his own way, of that his father was sure.

Kleebach walked up to another door and rang the bell. A woman in a housecoat answered.

'Good morning, Frau Birner,' he said, handing her the field-post letter. 'Bound to be from your husband . . .' he added, in answer to her unspoken question.

'Thank you,' the woman said absently, and hastily took the envelope.

Kleebach quickly went on his way. All the women looked like that, and they all snatched at the letter with the same abruptness. Their relief at his arrival at their door was always so intense that they seemed dazed.

His last mail was for the joiner's workshop next door. Just as he was returning from there, he heard a scream and saw the neighbours rushing toward's Frau Birner's house. A few moments later she came out, and he saw the pain etched in her face and knew that he had not brought her joy but pain. He had delivered the official letter, the letter that told her that her husband had died in action . . .

Head hunched between his shoulders, he trudged wearily on, not daring to think that one day he might deliver just such a letter, not to another family, another wife, but to his own.

The morning had brought sun, the clear sky an air alert. The anti-tank unit moved into position near Arras, as ordered on the previous day. The local civilians scuttled nervously into their cellars. The ground was warm, visibility good. Above them, caught in the rays of the climbing sun, aluminium glinted. Aircraft, and not German aircraft. These were British, flying over the battle-lines in frightening, ordered formation.

'Bang goes our peace and quiet,' Böckelmann moaned.

His friend Kleebach shook his head. 'What's up today?' he asked, frowning disapprovingly. For the past few weeks the German Luftwaffe had ruled the skies. The most they had got sight of had been an occasional Allied plane – and any foolhardy lone intruder had been pounced on by their Messerschmitts, to be blasted out of the clouds or seen off in double-quick time.

'Our frigging fighter-pilots are still in their beds,' Böckelmann scoffed. 'Your brother Fritz always was an idle sod.'

'Come on, he flies a Heinkel III,' Kleebach protested.

'Break it up, you two!' the company commander bawled. 'Kleebach, be so good as to stay with that junk-heap of yours!'

'Yes, Herr Oberleutnant,' Kleebach said, duly chastened. He was gun-layer on the aged French ack-ack gun that they called the 'junk-heap'. Shooting up the enemy with his own weapon had a certain poignancy to it.

Partial battle-readiness ordered. Ten a.m. They could already hear the dull roar of approaching tanks. As a precautionary measure the company commander called up the Luftwaffe to ask for Stukas. The Stukas didn't come.

'Who cares?' the officer said coolly to his men. 'We'll handle it alone . . .'

The company's heavy guns were in position in a depression to one side of the main body. There was no sign of anything yet, but the men stared at the horizon until their eyes streamed with the effort. They knew how to knock out a tank. They had practised it a hundred times in training, and had gone through the process at least a dozen times in combat. You had to keep calm, you had to summon up a bit of courage, and a lot of nerve, and after that it was child's play; let them get as close as possible, aim carefully, use the element of surprise, a direct hit, and then those square killing-machines ended up as steel coffins . . .

By just before eleven, all hell had broken loose in the section of the front to their left. And still no Stukas. And no counter-barrage from the artillery to the rear. As yet, none of the conscripts took things too much to heart. It was only about mid-day that they started to become uneasy, when word got around that the Tommies had made an armoured break-through. And now there was pandemonium to their right as well.

'All the fun of the fair,' growled the Oberleutnant. 'The balloon'll be going up any moment . . . How do you feel, Kleebach?'

'Excellent, Herr Oberleutnant.'

The company commander grinned. 'For every tank you bag, you get an extra day's leave,' he promised. 'Have we got a deal?'

'Yes, Herr Oberleutnant,' the layer answered quickly. As the officer turned, Gerd Kleebach was smiling too.

The boy felt calm. There was no trace of fear, just a faint

17

fluttering in the lower part of his gullet, where it opened up into the stomach. He chucked away a cigarette and lit another. He had three French tanks destroyed to his credit, a fourth marked as a possible. This was nothing new for him, but it still repelled him. Fear of being crushed by advancing armour wasn't the problem. What he hated was the moment when the shell left the barrel and three hundred metres away there was a sudden pillar of flame and men who were enemy soldiers – but still human beings – fried in vapourising petrol. You could hear that last scream, the scream that held all the terror and pain of this world . . . Sometimes Kleebach would wake from uneasy sleep and clap his hands to his ears, because he could still hear that animal shriek, see Frenchmen who had managed to get out of their tank running away in blind panic from the inferno, human torches. He knew they were doomed, but in those crazy, half-awake moments Kleebach wanted desperately for them to live, to prove that he wasn't the worst human being in the world, that he was only bad at killing . . .

Suddenly the roar of engines grew louder.

'They're coming from the left!' Kleebach oathed. He had been expecting them to come from straight ahead.

'So far, so bad,' muttered the loader as they hauled the gun around.

Slowly they crept nearer, just dark shadows on the landscape at first, then like a mass of sinister, giant beetles scouring the surface. Three, five, eleven, seventeen – soon there were so many that Kleebach gave up counting them. He aimed his gun at the foremost one and waited, waited for the death that he alone could bring.

'Distance nine hundred metres,' the aimer reported. 'Eight hundred and fifty . . .'

The noise intensified. The earth seemed to shake with terror. The harsh growl of the engines hacked at the men's nerves, turned their mouths to dry deserts. Anyone who didn't have to operate a gun lay down in the grass, and felt a longing to burrow down deep, as deep as possible, under the crust of the world's skin.

'Seven hundred metres.'

Plenty of time yet, Kleebach muttered to himself, trying to keep calm. He looked to his left, where Böckelmann was crouched sideways in a fox-hole that probably wouldn't cave in . . . He ran his eyes over the hollow where the big guns were waiting to catch the enemy in his flank. He looked up, because suddenly there was another noise, this time from on high. The droning silhouettes were coming in low, maybe a thousand metres. Aircraft, German dive-bombers, Junker 87s.

About time, Kleebach thought with relief. He watched out of the corner of his eye as the Stukas flipped into a loop to gauge their run-in, then picked their targets among the enemy tanks and began to swoop, slowly, almost lazily. Suddenly they dived, and those cruel noses were near-vertical to the ground; their engines began to scream, the terrifying sirens howled, and the Stukas plunged straight for their victims. The tanks zig-zagged frantically in an effort to avoid the merciless rain from heaven, but the black dots above kept coming, getting bigger all the time, louder, until the men on the ground could hear nothing but the high-pitched shriek of Stukas, Stukas. And the earth shook, until there came one huge boom and everything seemed to disintegrate.

Four Stukas had off-loaded their bombs and were turning for base to re-arm. The dive-bombers were busy today; four, five times they climbed and came back. But for the first time in the campaign they called the Blitzkrieg, the English seemed to have conjured up more tanks than the Stukas could handle. Overnight . . .

The last formations attacked. A huge, jagged crater scarred the earth where the second-foremost Tommy tank had been. Another gushed pillars of flame. A third was clanking round into retreat, belching out smoke from a gash in its side.

But the others kept on coming, grinding towards Kleebach's gun. They hadn't seen him, and they rolled on. Impassive. Roaring like beasts of prey. Merciless. Four hundred metres to go.

'Fire at will!' yelled the company commander.

Three seconds, and Kleebach sent the first shell booming, arcing towards the enemy.

'Direct hit!' roared Böckelmann, who was acting as observer.

Bang on the turret, thought Kleebach. He bit his lower lip until the blood flowed and took aim at the next. Then the smoke cleared – and the German gunners stared through red-rimmed eyes at an unbelievable sight: the stricken tank was still coming. Its turret a mass of twisted metal, it came closer, as if nothing had happened, as if they'd hit it with a paving-stone and not a heavy shell.

It's coming on blind, Kleebach realised. He pumped shell on shell at the bizarre monster.

His knees were trembling, his eyes smarted, but the range was dead on, his hand held steady, and the gun was working like a dream.

And it all did no good.

Kleebach smashed at the foremost tank, fired and fired, hit it and hit again, crazy with anger. Suddenly he had only one aim in life, one thought, one raging desire, one burning obsession: to wipe the filthy thing off the face of the earth.

Range two hundred metres.

The Tommies in the tanks didn't even feel the need to shoot. It was only now that the boys on the anti-tank guns realised that the enemy was not returning fire, and by this time they were so close that you could see the flat steel helmets of the British infantry, the vision-slits, the muzzles of the mounted guns.

To the right the heavy batteries opened up. As always, the company commander orchestrated the hail of fire. For the first time, the British were sending in tanks whose armour was too thick for the German anti-tank weapons. Not just in this position but along this entire section of the front – hundreds of tanks, some of which had already broken through and were thirty, forty kilometres behind the German lines ... The young Oberleutnant was not yet aware that the British and the French were throwing everything into the battle, had already blasted their way through in four places, or that the German High Command had been caught completely on the hop, without the air and artillery support that alone could have stopped the rot. What he did see was that his anti-tank boys would be mashed into the ground if he didn't do something fast, even if that something was crazy ...

He attacked the English from the flank, going out ahead of the other heavy guns in his command vehicle, shot the leading tank to pieces from the side, aimed at a second, drew the fire onto himself, raced like a bolting horse straight into the Tommy ranks, the cavalcade of death – before his own ammunition exploded, blowing him to kingdom come.

Four or five Tommies changed direction to deal with the other German self-propelled guns, but the main horde clanked on, heading into the anti-tank positions.

Kleebach screamed, wept, cursed, fired wildly, and trembled. Eighty metres now ... Seventy ... He stared into the mouth of the big turret-mounted cannon, and knew that any moment they would belch destruction. Jesus, he wanted to live, he wanted to hit the buggers, to be victor, to get out of here. He aimed, and knew it was futile, totally futile.

Fifty metres.

No cover. Nowhere to run. The foremost tank turned, heaving up on its tracks, and its driver slammed it into low gear. The engine's note rose to a jarring whine. That was when the men in the German anti-tank position realised that the deadly steel juggernaut wasn't even going to bother to blow them to bits. It was simply going to plough them under. And there was nothing to stop it.

The last shell whooshed through the air, exploding harmlessly between two tanks. The last, desperate throw. The Germans threw themselves to the ground, begging, whimpering, burrowing. Except Gerd Kleebach.

It was over. Kleebach stood, shoulders bent in despair. Finished. Beaten.

That was what his friend Böckelmann saw. And then he, of all people, the man who knew only too well that this was time to eat dirt, hurled himself to his feet, raced out of cover, and with two or three strides was at the tank. Hanging onto the turret like a man possessed, he fixed an explosive charge under it, then flung himself off. He was hit by machine-gun fire, lay still, then staggered to his feet and finally collapsed two metres from his trench. And the Tommy tank's turret swayed slightly, then slowly rose, and finally went up, blown away like a top-hat in the wind.

Kleebach had no time to believe in any illusion of salvation, because a second tank was bearing down on him from the right, only eight metres away. He heard the driver step on the accelerator, then suddenly all he could see were huge caterpillar tracks moving to crush him, blocking out everything else, and the enormous, terrifying turret cannon. At that moment he knew he would never see his mother again, and he shrieked, insanely, just like those Frenchmen he had heard in his nightmares. And he saw his own blood flowing into the dirt; he felt his heart stop, his legs become paralysed. And one final time he saw into the vision-slit, glimpsed a cap badge, then tracks, just tracks, turning, turning, squelching on to take his life – and then there was nothingness . . .

CHAPTER TWO

June 14th 1940, the day when the Kleebachs had walked down the aisle twenty-five years before, was the day Paris surrendered to the Germans. Like every other family in the street, they hung out flags from the windows.

Everything seemed to have conspired to smile on the family's special day: father Kleebach, who had been given the day off, had also been promoted to senior postman. Thomas, the eldest, was on convalescent leave. Freddy had managed to get hold of a fat roasting goose. Achim had taken care of the wine supply, and Marion, the youngest, had persuaded the local baker to part with a big cake, despite the shortages.

Fritz wrote often, and the day before yesterday they had received Gerd's letter, the one he had posted in the village near Arras. Father Kleebach was unaware of what it said, though, for he had left it unopened so as to provide his wife with the greatest pleasure of the whole celebration.

The Kleebachs lived in a block set back from the street on the corner of Litzenburgerstrasse and Wielandstrasse in the western part of Berlin. The celebration party took place in the front room, the one they kept for receiving guests and for 'occasions'. The table had been set, the presents were stacked on the dresser, and there were so many flowers in the corner – more flowers than they had vases for – that they threatened to take over the room.

'The goose'll soon be done to a turn,' announced Freddy, appearing from the kitchen. He was a slim, good-natured boy with curly dark hair and beautiful eyes that could break girls' hearts – and already had. 'Don't ask me how I did it – we experts have our secrets . . .' he said proudly.

'The usual method, I bet, gigolo,' Marion mocked.

Freddy looked hurt, then grinned. 'Blimey,' he said. 'I had to

23

play up to that delicatessen-owner's daughter for three whole weeks . . . wrote her letters, held her fat hand, whispered in her shell-pink ear in the moonlight.' He laughed with a hint of arrogance. 'Then finally the old goose came up with the edible kind . . .'

'Freddy, please!' Father Kleebach wagged a stern finger at his son. Almost all his children towered above him these days, but as far as he was concerned he was still the boss of the household.

Mother Kleebach shook her head. She looked at her brood, and it was as if she was seeing them for the first time. They were so different from each other. Thomas, the eldest, was so serious for a twenty-four-year-old. Then Freddy, the joker, and Achim, sitting spellbound by the radio listening to the news from conquered Paris, dead to the rest of the world.

'Man, oh man,' he enthused, turning to his mother. 'Paris in the bag . . . that's the best present you could get for your silver wedding!'

Mother Kleebach smiled quietly. She cared very little who had Paris, but she didn't want to spoil her youngest son's pleasure.

Thomas put his arm around her.

'At least the war in the west will be over soon,' he said softly. 'And Gerd and Fritz will have come through safely . . .'

His mother nodded. Achim turned the radio up to maximum volume.

'Keep that darned thing quiet, will you?' Thomas snapped. He had stopped a bullet in the Polish campaign, and he didn't need some hack radio reporter to tell him what war was like.

Father Kleebach let them be and granted himself a glass of schnaps. He felt a little thoughtful today, looking back on twenty-five years of contented marriage, a quarter-century of happiness, work, and self-sacrifice. 'This is it, then,' he said, leaning over to his wife. 'Time passes . . . would you ever have thought there'd be so many Kleebachs?'

She shook her head.

'And would you say "yes" to me again?' he asked.

'Any time,' answered Maria, and looked him straight in the eye.

She smiled, the same way she had smiled all those years ago when he had popped the question. He had taken his time wooing her, nervous that he, a minor civil servant, would be

24

refused by the daughter of a middle-class family. But she had decided that she liked him – and more – and Maria's quiet, intense strength had overcome all opposition.

'Yes,' she said now to her husband. 'I am grateful to you, Arthur . . . for everything.'

Embarrassed, he took off his spectacles and started to clean them. It had always been the same: his wife could express exactly what he felt.

In truth, the Kleebach family was a kind of voluntary matriarchy, with the mother at the centre of everything. Her children had become used to looking up to her every bit as much as their father. She had a peaceful, finely-structured face that was still handsome. Somehow the grey hairs only seemed to enhance her looks.

'He's got pimples,' Freddy told Marion teasingly. He was at his favourite sport, criticising her new boyfriend. 'And a squashed nose. You do pick 'em!'

'You gorilla!' pouted his eighteen-year-old sister, blushing scarlet.

'And he didn't even make the basic Hitler Youth Achievement Badge,' Achim chipped in solemnly, breaking off from his radio. 'You should have seen him in the gymnasium. Talk about a cripple . . .'

'He's so shy, he hardly manages to open his mouth when he's with you,' the Gigolo said.

Marion's eyes flashed. 'Unlike you,' she shot back. 'Yours is always wide open and parroting away.'

'You bet,' Freddy said, unconcerned. 'Send him along sometime . . . I'll give him some lessons in chat.'

'All right! Cut it out!' father roared, ending the fight.

'And despite it all she moons over the bloke,' Achim muttered, then caught his father's eye and shut up.

The cake stood on the dresser, waiting for the afternoon coffee. A delicately-styled heart made of glycerine contained the number 25, but the heart would be divided into only six pieces, for the seventh and eighth Kleebachs were absent: Gerd and Fritz, the twins serving with the Wehrmacht in France. There was an unspoken agreement among the rest of the family not to talk about them, but father broke it now when he went out and then came back carrying a big bouquet of Spanish lilacs.

'From Gerd,' he said simply.

'How . . . ?' his wife asked.

'He asked me to get them, and forbade anyone else to give you white lilacs.' Arthur Kleebach smiled. 'Because they're your favourite flowers . . .' he explained. Then, seeing how much the twins' absence pained her, he added quickly: 'And there's something more – a letter from Gerd . . .'

'Oh,' Maria Kleebach sighed.

'Here, your glasses, mother,' Achim said.

She gripped the envelope as if unable to decide whether to open it. Her hands were trembling – hands that were both gentle and tough, that could caress and punish. A matriarch's hands.

'Gerd . . .' she said, so softly that they hardly heard her. Just as she was about to open the letter, the door bell rang. Father Kleebach looked at the clock.

'Twelve already?' he said. 'Must be Rosenblatt . . .'

'And what does he want with us?' his wife asked, bewildered.

But their uninvited guest, the district Nazi official, was already over the threshold.

'Please come in, Herr Rosenblatt,' Arthur Kleebach said in welcome.

'Heil Hitler, Ortsgruppenleiter!' Achim bellowed, and sprang to attention.

'I don't want to disturb you,' said Party Comrade Rosenblatt before he went ahead and disturbed them.

He lived in the next-door block, and most of the time he ran around in uniform – perhaps because he was embarrassed by his Jewish-sounding name and wanted to make sure everyone knew he was pure, hundred-percent Aryan. He wasn't a bad sort compared with other Nazi worthies, but he could match any of them for sheer banality.

'Heartiest congratulations!' he blustered, shaking Maria Kleebach's hand. 'And I must tell you that I have a pleasant duty to perform.' He raised himself to his full height, treating the middle of their living room like a speaker's rostrum. 'Frau Kleebach,' he intoned. 'I have been designated to convey to you the congratulations of the Party . . . and the gratitude of our Führer . . .'

'To me?' said mother Kleebach helplessly . . .

* * *

26

Before Maria Kleebach was given the news that she was to be awarded the Mother's Merit Cross, a registered parcel arrived at the branch post office in Berlin-Charlottenburg. The workers there knew what it meant only too well when they ran an eye over the contents list: a briefcase, a watch, a ring, a few photographs and a handful of letters. These were the last, miserable belongings of a dead German soldier, and they were addressed to the Kleebachs' home on the corner of Lietzen-burgerstrasse and Wielandstrasse.

The man who had deputised for Arthur Kleebach so that he could celebrate his silver wedding made his way along the street, between the fluttering flags, past marching groups of Hitler Youth and brownshirts, on a bitter journey to deliver tragedy to a colleague's apartment . . .

Just as Party Comrade Rosenblatt, firmly established in the Kleebach's living room, was about to begin a 'brief', meaningful oration, the aroma of roasted goose filled the air and it appeared on a dish from the kitchen. The neighbour who had been helping in the kitchen was of the opinion that a medal could be pinned on a body any time, but roast poultry had to appear on the table as soon as it was done.

Because the Ortsgruppenleiter was one of those people who find it difficult to start a speech and impossible to end one, he ended up staying for the meal. He was shown by the head of the household to a place at table.

'Right then, cheers!' said father Kleebach, raising his glass.

'Oh, that smells delicious,' the party official said by way of reply. Obviously considering this the right moment, he stood up and began: 'I shall be brief . . .'

Everyone looked at him, and with their attention Party Comrade Rosenblatt fancied that he grew several inches, became incisive, masterful, the way he had always wanted to be.

'My dear Frau Kleebach,' he said loudly. 'I must apologise for encroaching on your family party. However, you must please look upon me as the representative of our great German racial community . . .'

Mother Kleebach smiled at him as she put the juiciest piece of breast meat from the goose on his plate, his due as a guest. She gave it generously, without reserve, but there was a little

27

catch in her breath as she served him, for after all he sat at their table as representative of Gerd and Fritz, her twins, who were kept from the celebration by the campaign in France.

She could see the white lilacs in the corner, set in their own vase, the finest the family possessed. When mother Kleebach saw them, it was as if Gerd was there. Gerd, who had thought of her, and who had told the others that only he could give her her favourite flowers on her silver wedding.

And then there was the letter, which her husband had carried around unopened in his pocket for two days so as to give her a surprise on this special day. She would have liked to have gone into the bedroom to read it in peace, to be alone with Gerd for a few minutes. But there was no time, and it wouldn't have been right to do it in haste.

'Every child that a German mother presents to her Führer is a battle won by the entire nation!' Rosenblatt droned on.

Mother Kleebach smiled politely, but with a hint of mockery. Actually, she had presented her children to her husband and no one else. She exchanged a fleeting look of mutual understanding with Thomas, her eldest.

Thomas sat with his arms folded on the table, and his expression seemed distant, impassive. He was broad and rugged, anything but easy-going – outwardly the most similar to her husband but a good head taller. He was a man of few words, none of them unnecessary, and seldom acted impulsively.

He's too old in his ways for a boy of his age, Maria Kleebach thought. Twenty-four. But he would go his own way, because he knew what he wanted – even if she didn't always understand what drove him. She knew that Thomas was the only one in the family who really thought seriously about politics. It had never been a subject for discussion in this house. Their father, with his simple ideas of right and wrong, had only one ambition, and that was to bring his children up to be decent human beings. Arthur Kleebach's opinion was that they could join the Nazis if they thought it right. For the rest, he just wanted them to have a better life than he had been able to have, even though, in fact, his had not been so bad. And they were good kids, honest and upright, the kind any father, particularly a civil servant, would wish for himself.

'Take pride in yourself, Frau Kleebach,' the Orts-gruppenleiter continued. 'When I look around this room, I see that you have accomplished a great task . . . You have given us five soldiers . . .' his eyes hovered for a moment on Marion, who reddened once more '. . . and assuredly a future mother, who will always look up to you . . .'

The corners of Thomas's mouth twitched. Marion quickly whipped a napkin up in front of hers. Achim, the Hitler Youth leader, seemed to be lapping up Rosenblatt's words, while Freddy, who knew what was what, fiddled noisily with his cutlery. Father Kleebach was as controlled and patient as ever.

'I shall conclude,' the Nazi official said. He reached into his pocket and then, like a conjurer producing a white dove, took out a small case made of mock leather. Out came the medal and its ribbon, and he trod with weighty steps over to Frau Kleebach. 'Hereby, at the request of the Führer, I present you with the Merit Decoration of the German Mother in Silver,' he proclaimed.

He carefully laid the ribbon round her neck and shook her hand with great emotion. She stood, more than slightly embarrassed and totally lost for words.

'Hey, how does it feel, mother?' Achim asked enthusiasti-cally, leaping over to congratulate her. But it was their neighbour, a very determined woman and very proud of her way with roast goose, who walked in at that moment and came up with the right formula 'And why's no one eating?' she asked brusquely. 'It'll all get cold . . . and I've taken so much trouble.'

'My apologies, dear lady,' Rosenblatt murmured, nodding to show that he was a man of the people and understood these things.

At last. But then the door bell rang again.

'I'll go,' father Kleebach said, and walked over to the door.

When he saw his deputy standing there, he felt a surge of fear. His colleague's solemn face seemed to bring an icy wind into their home.

'Is . . . something wrong?' he said quickly.

'Yes, Arthur, well actually . . . I mean . . . in a way . . .'

Kleebach glanced at the table and felt his head spinning, as if he was struggling to look through the blades of a plane's propeller that any moment now might come whirling down on each of those who sat at the festive meal. He saw them gazing at him, avoided their eyes, his head sank and he could find no words.

Then he glimpsed Rosenblatt's brown uniform. It had never seemed a more welcome sight, and he signalled to the official like a drowning man calling for a lifebelt.

'Can I speak to you for a moment?' he mumbled.

The two of them went out into the hall, with everyone watching them. Arthur Kleebach, the veteran postman, had realised immediately what was wrong. He had seen the small registered packet and knew only too well what was in it: a watch, a brief case, a few photographs – the last, pathetic possessions of a soldier killed in action . . . Gerd or Fritz? he thought dully. He glanced at his wife and began to wonder how he could soften this tragic blow for her, bit his lip as he saw that she was still holding Gerd's letter in her hands, as if she wanted to caress it, hold it to her.

The Ortsgruppenleiter looked distraught when he returned. The incisive, masterful leader was gone. The man who could recite all the party clichés had run out of words.

'I'm sorry . . .' he said finally, in a tiny, strained voice. 'I . . .' His courage failed.

Her eyes bored into him. Party Comrade Rosenblatt took Mother Kleebach's hand, as if he needed the support, and stuttered: 'Your son . . .'

'Gerd?' she whispered.

He nodded gravely. The sudden silence in the room was like a vacuum, dizzying and uncanny.

'He fell at Arras . . .' he said, eager to get it over quickly.

Suddenly father Kleebach appeared at her side to catch his wife as she tottered. His lips had shrunk to pale, bloodless ridges in his face. Where he tried to look comforting, supporting, there was all too clearly nothing but despair. He hoped – and feared – that Maria would cry now, let everything out . . .

Arthur Kleebach did not see Rosenblatt go. He didn't notice that the party official left out the usual 'for Führer, Folk and Fatherland' and even forgot to make the Nazi salute.

'Mother,' he said softly, and held her tight.

The wind played with the flag hung out of the open window behind her. Somewhere an ecstatic radio commentator was shouting a description of the German troops marching through the Arc de Triomphe. Down in the street, crowds were celebrating the fall of Paris.

Outside, there were only victors. In the Kleebachs' home, nothing but losers ...

'Come,' Arthur Kleebach said protectively, making to lead his wife out of the room.

Frau Kleebach leaned heavily on the table. Her eyes seemed to have turned inwards, as if seeking something. Her face showed a kind of serene pain. It was the way she must have looked twenty years before, when she brought Gerd into the world, given him life. A life she would dearly have loved to give him this second, impossible time ...

If only she weren't so chillingly calm, thought Arthur Kleebach. She was beginning to focus again, and now her face looked old and tired.

'No,' she said softly, and shook her head.

None of her children would ever forget the terrible, tortured smile that trembled on her lips at that moment.

Slowly, as if under a spell, she picked up the creased envelope from where she had dropped it in her first horror. Gerd's letter. From a dead man now.

'Please, don't ...' Kleebach said, and made to take it from her.

'No ...' she repeated.

She opened it with great care, as if it were made of flaked china. The rustle of the paper cut through everyone's nerves like a thin saw.

'Please, mother.' Father Kleebach tried again to take the letter, but it was a futile gesture.

'No,' she answered. 'I want to. Now ...'

She was quite calm and controlled as she read Gerd's last words. Slowly, because she knew now that she would have a whole lifetime to read this one letter.

'My dear mother and father,' it said. 'I have just discussed things with the Oberleutnant, and he has promised me special leave for your twenty-fifth wedding anniversary so long as we arrive in Paris in time, which is a certainty. You will have heard all the war reports and know how quickly the advance is proceeding. Things are really not too bad . . .'

The paper began to tremble in Frau Kleebach's hand, first gently, then more strongly. Her lips were moving, as if she was reading it out loud. Or perhaps she was already praying . . .

'But in case I don't make it after all,' the letter went on. 'Here are a few lines from me, so that you know I shall be with you June 14th in spirit if not in person – and that I shall be closer to you both than ever before. And to you, my dear mother, I want to put in writing the thing that's so idiotically hard to say: that we all know what you, and father too, of course, have done for us. In the future, when the war is over, we'll be able to stand together and make it all up to you as best we can . . .'

The letters seemed to flow into each other before her eyes, jumbling, standing on end, but she read on through the welling veil of tears.

'And so I thank you both and wish you all the best. I wish I could do more than just send you a pathetic bunch of flowers to remember me by. Heartfelt best wishes and kisses. Your Gerd.'

So short? Mother Kleebach thought. She was about to begin again when she saw the postscript. 'P.S. You don't need to send me anything. When I get to Paris, I shall get mother some of that famous perfume and Marion a pair of real silk stockings!'

She did not look up as she carefully slid the letter back into its envelope. Up the street a loudspeaker blared out radio speeches: 'And the Führer is with his soldiers . . . in the front line . . . He knows their worries, their hardships . . . has experienced everything in person . . .'

Maria Kleebach walked over to the flowers, slowly and with immense dignity. Her shoulders were slumped, as if the mother's medal still hanging round her neck had turned into a millstone. She slipped Gerd's last letter under the flowers, like a sacrificial offering on the altar – and then she began to weep, at last, because she had realised that her Gerd would never again give her white Spanish lilacs . . .

Arthur Kleebach took her in his arms again, and finally

succeeded in drawing her gently out of the room. As he held her and shared her despair, he made an angry, impossible vow to himself. She, his Maria, would never again receive tidings such as these.

Paris fell, and France faced military catastrophe. In the crazy confusion of those early June days, the demoralised French *poilus* had streamed south and south-west from the frontiers, in a desperate attempt to escape the remorseless armoured columns of the Wehrmacht. Inexorably, their pursuers forced them back on their own northern defensive line – and Hitler's way to Paris was open.

Since nine in the morning of June 14th 1940, the Champs Elysées echoed to the harsh tread of jackboots.

Victory in the West was assured. Where in the First World War the German army had failed, after four bloody years and a million dead, now it had gained the prize in exactly six weeks.

True, three weeks before at Arras, where Private Gerd Kleebach had met his death, things had suddenly looked very different. For a few hours, the battle had been in the balance; for the first time in the campaign the Allies had achieved a real superiority. Rommel's 7th Panzer Division had been ordered to probe south and west of the town of Arras, where strong British and French forces were still active, and then swing north. All at once the High Command had lost control, the attack had ground to a halt, and Rommel's right flank had been open as a hay-barn door. Through that gap, hundreds of British tanks had rolled, in the kind of numbers that no German had ever dreamed of. Big, heavy metal monsters, with armour so thick that the German shells bounced off them like soap-pellets.

The Allied breakthrough had succeeded, and the tank squadrons had rolled on – to Wailly, where they encountered a regiment of the Waffen-SS, and also east of Arras, straight into the German line of advance at Hanin-Broiry. The Germans, it seemed, who had achieved so much through sheer mobility, were about to be beaten at their own game.

The situation was grave. Things were starting to fall apart. Panic reports from all sections of the front, breakthrough following breakthrough.

The Stukas acted as fire brigade. They flew screaming mission after screaming mission, pouring a storm of high-explosive death down on the massed Allied armour. It was their intervention that first stabilised the situation on the right flank at Maubeuge. The Allies, it was becoming apparent, had no idea how to exploit their success. Once again, the chance to deal a decisive blow was lost in a morass of indecision and conflicts between the British and French commanders, and the element of surprise disappeared. The lightning advance slowed down, then deteriorated into a struggle for local tactical gains.

Private Böckelmann, seriously wounded in his attempt to save his friend Gerd Kleebach, had lain unconscious through the rest of the débâcle. British infantrymen had given him emergency first aid and carried him to a British field dressing-station in Arras. He was still on the operating-table when the Germans stormed the town. An English R.A.M.C. captain was acting as anaesthetist while a German medic removed shrapnel splinters from his body and cleaned out the two wounds where bullets had passed through his upper leg. The surgeon had operated without any great hope of success, but after a few days Böckelmann's tough constitution had pulled him through. By the time the Dunkirk fiasco was reaching its climax, he was out of danger.

Three hundred and fifty thousand Tommies were trapped in a German pincer on the coast. All the Wehrmacht had to do was to strike home. Hitler, as usual, hesitated.

And Göring, the fat Reich Marshal who headed the Luftwaffe, had his own axe to grind. He didn't want the army to get all the credit for this victory; he was determined that his own force would carve off a juicy slice of glory at Dunkirk. While the British Expeditionary Force prepared for 'Operation Dynamo' – the desperate plan to evacuate their entire army over the English Channel and home – Göring boasted that he would prevent the British escape with his airforce alone, without any support from the army. But for the first time in this war the Luftwaffe failed. The boys who had been able to do no wrong were suddenly cut down to size. Firstly, their bases were too far from the zone of operations. Secondly, the British Home Command took the risk of allowing hundreds of fighters to cross the Channel to cover the British embarkations and sea-crossings. Suddenly the myth of total German air superiority had been exploded – and the vain, over-confident Reich Marshal ended up with egg all over his plump face.

Whole divisions of German combat troops, ordered not to intervene, watched helplessly while the entire British Expeditionary Force was transported back home, where it was so desperately needed. British losses were comparatively small. No ordinary German soldier could understand why they had beaten the French only to let the British go free. No matter how sonorously the propaganda newsreels trumpeted the amounts of weapons and *matériel* left behind at Dunkirk, there was no disguising the fact that for Germany Dunkirk was a defeat within a victory.

So far as Böckelmann was concerned, the campaign in the West ended long before the fall of Paris. Just as the French capital was occupied by the Wehrmacht, he took his first, faltering steps out of his hospital bed. And as Pétain, the new head of the French government, signed his country's surrender in the forest of Compiègne, he took his first walk in the garden of the hospital, leaning heavily on a stick. He had become a prize exhibit, trundled out by the medics at every official inspection. But Böckelmann wasn't interested in being a medical phenomenon. He wanted transfer to a hospital at home – in Berlin.

He got his transfer in July. By the beginning of August he was fit enough to be granted a walking-out pass, and he knew that he had to use it to visit the Kleebachs in the Lietzenburgerstrasse. But Gerd's father came first to visit him in the hospital. He asked no questions, just made a request. His drawn face still showed how hard Gerd's death had hit him.

'It's not for my sake,' he told Böckelmann, slowly and painfully. 'I will adjust somehow – I have to. But my wife . . . do you understand, Heinz?'

Böckelmann nodded and stared at the floor.

'Go to her,' father Kleebach asked. 'And be gentle. Perhaps . . . perhaps! . . . it will make things easier for her when she knows . . .'

They sat together for a long time in silence. There was no need for more words; they understood each other too well.

*　　*　　*

One day in August, Heinz Böckelmann stood facing his friend's mother. She made it easier, because she gave every appearance of calm. Gerd's portrait hung on the wall behind her, beneath it the dead flowers he had sent that last day. His friend was smiling in the photograph, the smile of youth and carefree happiness. And now he would never smile – or cry – again.

'It was all over quickly . . .' he said to Frau Kleebach. 'Gerd can't have realised what was going on . . .' He had never lied more convincingly in his life, or felt less ashamed of the fact. Böckelmann was a rough-and-ready character, but nowhere near as superficial as he liked to pretend to his mates. His words were tactful, and his face showed the sadness that he himself felt.

'Stay a while,' said mother Kleebach, who had to leave the room, because it had finally got too much for her. 'And come again, won't you? Please . . .'

She had not got over Gerd's death, and never would. But she controlled herself, to make it easier for the others. It was only when she was alone that she read his letters and cried. For the rest, she had enough to worry about with her remaining five children.

Achim, the youngest boy, had been conscripted into the Labour Service. Thomas, the eldest, was with a reserve unit in Germany and would soon be off on his travels again. Marion worked as a secretary with a Berlin company. Fritz, the mad-keen flyer, had just written a letter. And Freddy had managed to swing himself a nice little job with the city administration, even though he was passed fully fit for army duty. He had no intention of being conscripted, not from cowardice but from honest conviction. He wasn't the type to plod his own path in silence, like Thomas, and nor did he have any urge to prove himself, like Achim. He had no time for dying: Freddy was greedy for life . . .

'Enjoy yourselves, kids,' he said now to Böckelmann and his sister. 'I have to go . . . still got a few jobs to do today, you know . . .' He grinned and clapped Böckelmann on the shoulder.

Böckelmann sat opposite Marion, trying to be sociable, but the picture of Gerd on the wall behind her somehow made it impossible. He forced his eyes down from the portrait and concentrated on the girl's long, auburn hair. She had cool, deep, blue eyes, too, like a mountain lake. You could get drowned in those eyes, and enjoy it ... Böckelmann cursed himself for being such a filthy-minded swine. He stood clumsily and said, 'I'll have to be going.'

Marion smiled warmly. 'But you'll come again?'

Böckelmann nodded. She's Gerd's sister, but she's grown in the last year or two, he thought. Just a short while ago she had been an awkward child, all freckles and beanpole arms and legs. And now she was a girl, almost a woman – and a darned pretty one, too ... For Christ's sake, he cursed inwardly, if only she weren't Gerd's sister!

Marion watched him with curious amusement. Then she realised that in his thoughts he was back with her brother, and she looked away. In fact, Böckelmann came and went after that time, only occasionally at first, and then almost every day. He was obviously happy that he was so welcome. For mother Kleebach he was a part of Gerd, even though the fact hurt. To father Kleebach he was a young, no-nonsense sort of boy who could have been his own son. And to Marion he became a friend – a friend who was shyer than he needed to be.

Whenever he was with her, Böckelmann felt a vague excitement, and a nagging unease when they were apart. Böckelmann had just turned twenty-one, the threshold of manhood, when he realised that he was probing new, unknown territory. The handful of survivors from his company sent him letters and cards from Paris, full of unambiguous references to the good time they were having with the mademoiselles. Böckelmann didn't give a hoot about Paris. All those dreams of *la vie en rose* by the Seine, the girls and the booze, were forgotten before they had a chance to become reality. Let his mates have their fill. They'd earned it, but he couldn't help thinking about what it had taken to get them there ...

Many was the time he sat up suddenly in the night, sweating. In his mind he was back crouched in his foxhole with the fear of death choking every nerve, desperately curling, grovelling, trying to merge with the earth ... and then he leapt up again, hurled himself and the explosive charge towards the British tank, then ran for his life, felt a blinding pain, fell ... and told himself again, I did everything

I could, Gerd . . . I could do no more . . . and I should have bought it there, too . . . and your sister Marion's so pretty, and I'm fond of her . . . maybe more than that, but you shouldn't think, wherever you are, that I'll ever forget that she's your sister . . .

Marion asked him to go out with her, and he agreed. From late summer they used the familiar 'du' form to each other. Those who saw them thought they were a 'couple', but they were not. Occasionally they would touch hands, by accident. Then they would move quickly apart, as if they had touched a live wire. That was all, but it was more than Böckelmann had ever experienced before.

Marion walked back to the military hospital with Böckelmann. His fellow-patients stood grinning at the window. Their leers left no doubt about what they thought he was getting up to.

The lance-corporal with the lung wound smacked his lips appreciatively. 'What a corker, eh?' he told the others. 'I wouldn't say no . . .'

Böckelmann just smiled thinly. They were poor, he was rich. Let them talk.

'Yeah . . . I had a red-head like that once . . .' the one with the lung wound went on. 'I'll tell you, she was crazy for it. Randy as a bitch on heat . . .'

Böckelmann made to leave, but his ward-mate wasn't going to let him off with nothing. 'Hey,' he said, almost pityingly. 'Wassa matter? Haven't you made it yet, or what?'

'Mind your own damned business!' Böckelmann rasped, squaring up to the man.

'Oh, I see . . .' the lung wound mocked. 'Waiting till she gets snapped up by some fancy officer?'

Böckelmann shrugged and turned away, bored by the empty chat. He had nothing against lung wound, who was just playing a game like they all did. A few months ago it could have been himself talking. These men are lonely, surrounded by hundreds of other men, a whole military machine, and they're lonely, he thought. They need tenderness, and instead all they can do is play the big-mouth, the stud . . .

Then the autumn came. One evening he and Marion sat on a bench in the park, watching the leaves fall. She was resting gently against him, and there was something about her that

38

worried him. An urgency. He felt it grow stronger, and felt a hotness inside him, though the evening was cool, and he took a deep breath.

Now and again, passers-by wandered across their field of vision. Among them young couples, a soldier and his girl, who, like them, could not know how long fate would leave them together.

'When will you be released from hospital?' Marion asked suddenly and with unexpected bluntness.

'In three weeks, four maybe . . .'

'And what happens then?'

'I suppose I'll be off,' he answered gloomily.

'You should make better use of your time,' Marion said, smiling.

'How's that?'

'Get yourself a proper girl, you know . . .'

'But Marion –' he protested, then fell silent. He had wanted to say, 'I've got you', but the words just wouldn't come.

They looked at each other. Marion's smile seemed to be swallowed up by the encroaching darkness, but her eyes were big and shining, tempting him, confusing him, like will-o'-the-wisps.

'Do you really like me?' Marion asked.

'How can you ask that?' he said heavily.

'Then why don't you tell me so, you . . . you stupid idiot?' she snapped.

'Because . . . because . . .'

Marion's eyes flashed. 'Get up!' she ordered.

Bockelmann was mystified, but he stood and followed her a little way under the trees. He stopped when she stopped, and faced her, slightly stooped, arms limp by his sides, happy but paralysed with indecision, like someone waiting at the gates of paradise but too nervous to step in.

'Look at me!' Marion said. 'And stop staring at that stupid tree over my shoulder!'

Her face was so close to his now that he could feel the warmth and sweetness of her breath. Her eyes were will-o'-the-wisps no longer, but stars. And Böckelmann would have given anything to be able to reach out for her. He desired, but he did not dare. Inside, he was blowing up a hurricane, but he did not move.

Until Marion put her arms round his neck and pressed herself to him, kissed him, and he suddenly realised that she wanted him. When he tasted her raw passion, he finally drew her into a full embrace that he never wanted to end. In a way he had won – but he had also lost a battle with himself . . .

CHAPTER THREE

They weren't chewing grass any more, but sand. So much Acting-Feldwebel Thomas Kleebach had established when they disembarked at Tripoli and first set foot in North Africa. The crossing from Naples had been hair-raising. The Italians might call the Mediterranean *il mare nostro*, 'our sea', but the whole stretch between Gibraltar and Malta was swarming with British planes. The wops were big-mouths.

It was 1941. Everything still pointed to a German victory, but down in the deserts of North Africa things looked bad. Thirty-three thousand determined Tommies had chased 200,000 Italians over the Egyptian border and 1,200 kilometres into Libya. Hitler had to do something to help his friend Mussolini, the *Duce*. And so he sent a single, wretched division, a token now but destined to grow into the famous Afrika Korps.

The battalion commander called together his men. Hauptmann von Klingenstein was cheerful and bullshit-free, as ever.

'Don't worry,' he announced wryly. 'I don't know what the hell's going on either. I suppose we just head off and see if we can find a few Tommies to take pot-shots at . . .' The lanky, wiry officer scratched his chin. 'And if you bag some, then you can bring me back a few English cigarettes . . . I can't smoke these blasted "special mixture" things any longer . . .'

They all roared assent.

'Kleebach,' the battalion commander said, turning to Thomas. 'You take charge of the first company . . . I've got no officers left, so you'll have to lead this bunch of has-beens . . .'

'Yes, Herr Hauptmann,' Kleebach rasped back, standing to attention.

He would soon learn, though, that correctness was out of place in Africa. The theatre of war he now had to get to know was unique. The desert was the front, and the battle-line could be ahead, in the rear, to the left or right, or even all at once. The devil knew where the enemy was at any given moment – because sure as hell no one else, from generals to privates, did.

Seven panzers motored out of camp. Their crews were happy enough with the order to action, because at least it meant that they wouldn't freeze in the cold desert night. They were even happier to be under the command of Feldwebel Kleebach, a man who rarely took a drink but never missed his target, the enemy.

Most of them were veterans, but strangers to desert warfare. They didn't even have proper tropical uniforms. First they had to fight against extremes of heat and cold, dust, thirst, scorpions, malaria, sandflies and hyenas, which crept among the corpses of their dead comrades at night. Then they had to fight against Australians, New Zealanders, Indians, South Africans and British – the whole might of the British Empire. And, last but not least, they had to contend with their highly unreliable Italian brothers-in-arms.

Feldwebel Kleebach smiled to himself as he thought of the wops. They might not be great soldiers, he pondered, but as human beings they were more successful than the Germans. They understood only too well that the most glorious victory was no good to a man if he was dead before he could enjoy it . . .

The night was pitch-dark, as if the stars wanted nothing to do with the war. The panzers travelled in file, with Kleebach at their head. He knew he could rely on his people, as they could rely on him.

'He doesn't give much bull,' an N.C.O. said of him. 'Never gives an unnecessary order, keeps dark what he has to keep dark, and won't tell you to do anything he wouldn't do himself, oh no . . .'

They drove by compass directions, by the faint green glimmer of the needle-dial. And it was all sand, nothing but sand. So far they had come across nothing but darkness and desert, but they knew that any moment they could also meet General Rommel, the 'Desert Fox', who loved to spin around the lines in his unmarked Volkswagen jeep.

The fuel-gauge indicators were hovering towards zero. There should be a fuel depot at a certain position close by. Should be.

The references on the maps were usually accurate, but all too often the petrol was missing.

They couldn't know it, but a little farther on, shrouded in darkness, sat an enemy tank unit that outnumbered their own several times to one, and Feldwebel Kleebach was leading them bang into it.

He suddenly ordered his seven panzers to halt and checked his map for the position of the fuel dump, which was still invisible in the desert.

'Bleedin' cock-up!' his driver oathed. 'Out of juice, and if we bugger around here much longer we'll end up havin' to walk back!'

'Put the lid on it!' growled Kleebach.

In fact, they were only 400 metres from the enemy, but he didn't know it. If he ordered his unit on, he was going to collide with a New Zealand tank squadron three times his own strength. If he changed course, he would by-pass the New Zealanders without their noticing, but probably end up running straight into their guns on the return trip. His orders were to simply break through up front, shoot up whatever he saw and wait. The system of the desert war was no system – a fact which proved to be Rommel's greatness, for he was a master of improvisation.

'What I'd like to know is what're we up to here?' the driver grumbled.

'Don't bother to ask me,' Kleebach said nonchalantly. 'All I know is that the C.O. needs some Tommy cigarettes, because he's had Wehrmacht special mixture up to here.'

'Great . . . and if we get shot to bits in the process?'

'Then we'll have been unlucky, won't we?'

The driver grunted. 'And they call it a "hero's death",' he muttered sarcastically.

'I didn't invent that phrase,' Kleebach said testily. He had the others report their fuel levels, even though he knew they would be close to empty. He thought quickly and decided to carry on for a few kilometres. If they failed to find petrol, then they would just have to camp out overnight in the desert and hope their own people found them before the Tommies did.

He waved the panzers forward. Four hundred metres ahead lay victory or defeat, a hero's leave or an unmarked grave. But Kleebach had no time for considerations such as those. At this moment he was no thinker any more, just a Feldwebel pure and simple. He shared with his men a sour satisfaction that, when it came to it, at least they were warm in these bloody steel boxes, not like the ones left behind.

He pressed his eye to the periscope, glimpsed a few shadows ahead. For a moment he thought his eyes were playing tricks, but then he saw the glow of a cigarette and nodded happily. He was amazed that these people had posted no perimeter sentries. Must be the fuel wagons, he thought: only a supply column would be so damned careless. He pressed on, and the other six panzers followed obediently, one after another, as the message was passed round that they had reached their goal at last. The men cheered up, because a refuelling stop meant that they would be able to open a few cans of food and stretch their legs. And they would have enough fuel for the return trip when the time came.

One hundred metres to go.

Kleebach opened his turret cover and popped his head out. He saw soldiers loafing around their tanks, smoking and strolling around in small groups. One waved to him, and it was then that Kleebach saw quite clearly that they were wearing broad, flat steel helmets . . . He ducked back inside his panzer as if he had been scalded by the night air. Tommies! Something like twenty vehicles. Tommies who had been caught on the hop but would soon realise what was going on and give his pathetic little band a taste of hell . . .

Jesus, thought Kleebach. Five seconds and we've had it. 'Watch out!' he bawled into his headphone, but his own panzer rolled on. Maybe the driver hadn't realised the situation, or maybe he was so shit-scared that he couldn't take his foot off the accelerator.

Amazingly, the Tommies still made no move. It was as if they were in a waking sleep, lulled by their own superiority. Could be they had been spoiled by fighting the Italians for too long – the wops always ran at the slightest sign of enemy opposition.

Kleebach's mouth was a small desert of its own, and he felt his skin prickle in a kind of fearful excitement. He realised he had nothing to lose, and so he acted like a fool and carried on issuing the order to advance, until the three leading panzers were heading to the left of the New Zealanders while the other four, on his instructions, were coming round in a half-circle from the right and turning in towards the enemy encampment. The Tommies had thrown their precious time away.

It was, in fact, at that moment that the New Zealanders realised that these were not the reinforcements they had been expecting, but by then it was already too late. Before they could scatter to their tanks, Feldwebel Kleebach had leapt out of his turret and landed on the sand with a loaded machine-pistol pointed straight at an astonished-looking enemy major.

'Hands up!' he bellowed in English.

The officer stared at the German as if he was a ghost, but he raised his hands, slowly realising that he had been taken for a ride by nothing more than a depleted panzer platoon.

The major shook his head and smiled with infinite bitterness.

'Please all your men down to the ground,' Kleebach said.

Four or five other panzer crew were standing by his side now, all with machine-pistols in their hands.

The New Zealand officer issued the order in a voice like teeth chewing glass. He looked so shattered that Kleebach actually felt sorry for him.

'Never mind, sir,' he said. 'Next time it might be us . . .'

He took the major's pistol and forced him to climb up into the leading German panzer.

Kleebach's men went round picking up the enemy weapons like small boys harvesting fallen apples. At first the Tommies were herded together onto a small dune, where they were guarded by four men with machine-pistols. Then they were transferred to two trucks which had been carrying cans of petrol.

The confidence-trick had succeeded without a shot being fired. The desert war had witnessed a bloodless coup, and Acting Feldwebel Kleebach had become one of its reluctant heroes.

At the moment, though, he had other things to think about. Such as how he was going to guard ninety-eight Tommies with thirty-five men and bring three trucks and seventeen fully-operational Mk II tanks back to the German lines without a disaster. Once he had diverted eight guards and two drivers to look after the Tommies, he would have only twenty-four left, and for his own panzers he needed at least one driver and one gunner each.

That left him with ten men, who had to do a very special job. One would sit next to each British driver and make sure they kept to the course he ordered. Which still left seven tanks remaining and – though it caused Kleebach great pain – he had to shoot up the seven 'Marks', praying all the time that the din and the shell-flashes didn't bring the devil's vengeance down on them from the British lines . . .

Kleebach's men had never dreamed of the likes of this, but they carried out his orders as if they did it every day. The German panzers were filled up to overflowing with British petrol, even though this meant risking damage from the foreign-grade fuel. All the time the New Zealanders kept cursing, but there were no attempts at a mass break-out. The Germans would have mown down half of them before they were swamped.

Once the surplus Marks had been thoroughly destroyed, Kleebach's driver bounced out of the ranks with a suggestion. He was of the opinion that the Greater German Wehrmacht had now received its due, and that it was time the ordinary blokes got theirs . . . And so there was a short interval while he organised the sharing-out of the captured rations and, above all, cigarettes. No point in leaving them for their headquarters troops to plunder. Everyone got a huge tin of vacuum-packed cigarettes and as much food as he wanted.

'No decent schnaps in there, worse luck,' Kleebach's driver said, grinning like a satisfied cat.

'Get a move on!' bellowed the Feldwebel.

The company set off on its return journey by the flickering light of the burning enemy tanks. The captured Marks were sent up front, each covered by their German shadows, with the trucks and Kleebach himself in the middle. Once he realised that they were not being pursued, he moved forward to the head of the column. He had been lucky up until now, but he harboured no illusions: in the chaos of the desert war, a British unit could appear out of the darkness at any moment, and then the waste material would really hit the air-conditioning. It wasn't unusual for prisoners to be captured, liberated, then captured again two or three times during the course of a night. Even if they did meet a German unit, that possibility was fraught with danger. Their comrades might see the Marks first and open fire before they realised the situation.

Kleebach hung out of his open turret, chainsmoking and scanning the horizon.

It was true that he was pleased with what had happened. But he knew it had been no more than luck, and he had no intention of getting excited.

The Afrika Korps were a law unto themselves; in actual fact they fought more for Erwin Rommel than for Adolf Hitler. As for Feldwebel Kleebach, they all left him cold. His ambition was to get that uniform off his back as soon as possible, because Thomas was a natural civilian and the only Kleebach who had political principles to back it up.

Thomas had joined the socialist youth organisation just before Hitler came to power, despite his father's opposition, had attended meetings and gone round sticking up posters. Nowadays, even he saw the whole thing as a youthful excess, part of the past. But it had done one thing: given him immunity to the blandishments of Nazi propaganda. In those pre-war years he had proved himself in his profession, and as a salary-earner had always been willing to help out when things got tight for the Kleebachs.

Then the war had come and Thomas, silent as ever, had put on a uniform, ready to take part in Hitler's war. He had no interest in medals or promotion, but his natural efficiency had quickly taken him to the rank of Acting Feldwebel, the kind of man who could be entrusted with an entire tank company on a mission such as this one.

All that ran through his mind now, and he found himself smiling at the ironies. Then came the urgent need to get his men back in one piece, and it put an end to the luxury of thought.

The tension mounted with every metre they travelled. They babbled to each other on their vehicle radios, giving each other the creeps, seeing shadows where there was nothing, hearing imaginary noises that tore at their nerve-ends, constantly jumpy that their prisoners were plotting escapes. In the end, Kleebach had to issue an order cutting down radio conversation to the bare necessities. He himself stared at his watch, praying fervently for daylight – or the Afrika Korps – to put in an appearance.

Outside his panzer, nothing moved. In an hour there would be light, quite suddenly, just as sudden as the night came, because Africa knew no twilight. When it did, Kleebach and his brood would be sitting targets, maybe no more than a few hundred metres from the enemy lines.

'Halt!' he yelled.

He had them go hull-down in the general direction of the enemy, moved into the middle of the sparse defensive circle and made his preparations. He had decided to try and make radio contact with the outside world – a big risk, but a necessary one.

No one said a word. The captured cigarettes suddenly tasted sour; even the British corned beef couldn't tempt the hungry Germans. They waited, sweating their way into the day. And there was no answer to Kleebach's radio signals. Which didn't mean that Tommy hadn't heard them ... there could be an entire armoured brigade heading this way ...

The sun burst up like a firework on the horizon, bleaching the sand and burning down on their heads. Twenty minutes they had been standing here. Twenty-five, and time passed so slowly ... Desert time was different to time in Berlin, Rome or London; it moved slow and lazy as a camel. The prisoners, meanwhile, were getting restless. They had reckoned on being freed by their comrades, but it was beginning to occur to them that a meeting with their own people could be bloodier than any link-up with the Germans.

The Tommy major sat in the crew mechanic's seat in the panzer with Kleebach, head sunk down on his chest. He had a pink tomato of a face, thin lips, and he just stared down at the floor, muttering over and over: 'Dammit! Goddammit ...'

Kleebach offered him a cigarette – one of the 'special mixtures', for he had had no time to open up a tin of the English ones.

'Forget it,' he said.

The major blew out some smoke, coughed, then chucked the barely-smoked cigarette on the floor and stamped on it. 'You manage to fight a war on that muck?' he asked.

'Dust!' someone yelled at that moment.

Kleebach swivelled the turret and took a bead on whatever was coming.

A dust-cloud. Always the first sign – and often the last ...

48

It was a huge pillar of sand, and behind it could be friend or foe, salvation or disaster, and at the most he would have a few seconds to make up his mind which it was.

Kleebach's eyes were watering. The firing straps on the panzer's cannon were damp with sweat. Sand and dust, hope and fear.

Again, the Feldwebel decided to risk everything on one roll of the dice. 'I'm heading straight for them,' he roared into his radio-microphone, prodded his driver and they raced away – to suicide or a hero's homecoming.

Two hundred metres, then 100.

Suddenly Kleebach realised that it was German panzers coming towards him. He stood up in his turret, groped around for the best thing to signal with, and his hand found the tin of British cigarettes. He grabbed it and began to wave it from side to side, catching the sun on its metal surface so that it glinted like a mirror.

'What the hell's going on over there?' Hauptmann von Klingenstein muttered.

'Could be a trap,' said his adjutant.

'Rubbish!' retorted the Hauptmann who had been wandering around with his radio o.d. for hours now. 'Jesus, that's Feldwebel Kleebach!'

The entire battalion rolled forward in formation, and its commander leapt out of his turret and ran over to Kleebach.

'What d'you think you're doing?' he growled. 'Sunday bloody driving?'

Only then did he look over towards the rest of Kleebach's unit, see the ten British tanks and begin to understand.

'Order carried out, Herr Hauptmann,' Kleebach said levelly. 'Ten British tanks of type Mark II and three trucks captured, seven tanks destroyed, ninety-five Tommies and three officers taken prisoner. No casualties. Full stock of ammunition.'

Klingenstein's jaw dropped. He shoved his cap to the back of his head and scratched his forehead in disbelief. 'Jesus,' he said. 'And we've been cruising around for hours, because those cretins from the fuel unit let 'emselves get put in the bag.'

'You can get petrol from us,' Kleebach said.

'Fantastic!' bellowed the Hauptmann, and clapped his Feldwebel on the shoulder. 'I reckon you're due for a special leave, promotion and a Knight's Cross in one go.' He reached over and plucked the tin of captured cigarettes from Kleebach's grasp.

The Feldwebel grinned. 'All that may be true, Herr Hauptmann,' he murmured. 'But I can tell you I wouldn't mind a few decent cigarettes either . . .'

As the Second World War moved into its third year, there came the first signs of a turn of the tide: the lightning victories began to be celebrated less often. The tinny fanfares of the 'special reports' on the radio could not conceal the fact that only death was winning the war now. The personal columns of the newspapers were filled with obituaries for fallen heroes, black became the fashionable colour of the moment, fear came with everyone's daily bread, families were stretched to breaking point. War filled the churches and emptied the schools . . .

There had been changes in the Kleebach family, too. Father Kleebach, who had served in the First War, was called to a medical examination and classified gvH – fit for garrison duty in the homeland. Achim, the Hitler Youth boy, had his labour service behind him and was already undergoing basic army training in a garrison town in Saxony. Fritz, the pilot, had been transferred suddenly from the West to Sicily. They had had no letters from Thomas, the oldest, for a while. Freddy, the gigolo, was becoming a stranger in his own home, and Marion, the only one still to live permanently at the house in the Lietzenburger Strasse, was causing concern to her parents. Officially she was engaged to Heinz Böckelmann, who was back at the front now. The business where she had been working as a secretary had closed, which left her with the alternatives of joining the women's auxiliary or working in a war factory.

'For goodness' sake, I'm not stupid enough to want to dirty my hands,' she pouted at her parents. She dressed smartly, the kind of girl soldiers turned and wolf-whistled at, and she didn't pretend not to be pleased by the fact.

'Are you going out again?' mother Kleebach asked.

'Why not?' Marion said defiantly.

'Who with?' asked her father.

'With friends.'

'Don't you think you ought to bring these friends of yours home some time? We'd like to meet them.'

'Oh, you're so old-fashioned,' Marion said irritably. 'Anyone would think this was the middle ages.'

'Have you answered Heinz's letter?'

'I'll do it tomorrow.'

For a moment it looked as though Arthur Kleebach would give in to his rage. Then he caught a warning glance from his wife and controlled himself, with difficulty.

'Marion,' her mother said gently. 'Don't you care for Heinz any more?'

'Nonsense,' Marion retorted, with a harshness in her voice. 'But I'm young. I can't sit at home all the time . . . twiddling my thumbs and feeling miserable . . .'

'You know he'll be waiting for a letter from you . . .'

'That's logic . . .' Marion shrugged. 'He'll be just as pleased if it arrives a day later.' She threw on her coat and pranced out.

Father Kleebach watched her out of the window. She was a picture of self-assurance, a little too elegantly dressed for wartime, but from the looks of the passers-by they appreciated it rather than resenting her.

'She's only nineteen,' said his wife, who had joined him at the window. 'And she has to go without so much that we've always enjoyed. And perhaps we're too strict with her . . .'

'Perhaps,' answered father Kleebach thoughtfully.

He was better able to deal with the boys. Marion's lust for life, which seemed to become more urgent from day to day, was alien and a little frightening. His wife was right: Marion was very young. And he feared she might be taking on too much for a girl with so little experience of life.

Otherwise, his everyday routine had not changed. Arthur Kleebach had succeeded in avoiding call-up for garrison duty, and still did his rounds twice a day through his familiar territory. He was ashamed when he passed a home without anything to offer, and pleased when he could give wives and girlfriends some sign of life from their loved ones – even though they could never know whether, like Gerd's last letter, death had moved faster than the post. A year before he had delivered one death notice a week; now the average had climbed to five or six.

The increase did nothing to lessen the personal tragedy of

those bereaved. During the course of his daily duties. Arthur Kleebach had glimpsed a hundred private hells, boundless chasms of suffering and despair. They, and his own feelings about Gerd's death, brought him to a realisation: that the true heroism in this war lay not where the medals were handed out and the speeches made, but in the quiet confines of millions of homes, millions of families.

Their concern for their sons – the four who should have been five – had become the most important thing in the Kleebachs' lives. It was worst at night. Arthur Kleebach would lie next to his wife pretending sleep, knowing that she was weeping softly into her pillow. She could not adjust to the loss of Gerd, however much she tried to conceal the fact. Then he would feel electricity run through him, a tingling on his skin, and he would realise that he was praying: God, let them come home in one piece ... not because of me. Maria has a weak heart, and she's a mother who doesn't deserve this ... And she has suffered so much already ... And she couldn't survive another Gerd ...

Maria Kleebach would sit up. 'Can't you sleep?' she would ask softly.

'It's all right. I think I need to go to the bathroom ...'

'Thomas hasn't written again,' she would say.

Then he would take her hand. The gentle pressure summed up twenty-six years together.

'I served at the front myself in the First War ... I know what it's like. When you're in action, you're so dog-tired you can hardly lift a pen ... Now, sleep well ...'

'Yes,' she would answer.

More hours would pass, hours while they lay there trying to hide from each other the fact that worry would not let them sleep ...

Thomas Kleebach had to get used to being a hero. He had become a star of the weekly newsreel even before the propaganda people knew whether he was photogenic or not. One thing was for sure as far as they were concerned: pictures of the piled-up captured material, the tanks, the ninety-eight Tommies – you could round that up to a solid hundred – were as photogenic as you could get.

While Kleebach waited at Rommel's makeshift headquarters for an interview with his general, he was discovered by the officers of the Italian liaison staff. They quickly fixed him up with the *Medaglia d'Argento al Valore Militare* – just to get in ahead of the Germans in handing out the decorations – and invited him as guest of honour to their daily victory party. This institution had nothing to do with the military situation, much more with the Italians' motto: if you have to fight a war, do it in style. So the wops had not just three separate grades of toilets – for officers, N.C.O.s and other ranks – but three lots of kitchens, and those for officers were staffed by ladies picked more for their charms than for their culinary efficiency. If the *Duce's* privileged soldiers were going to be forced to chase around the desert in the most undignified fashion, instead of having a good time on the beach at Ostia, they could at least ensure that this war business was made as pleasant as possible. The Italian army looked after its stocks of eau de cologne with as much care as its munitions.

Their German allies would keep an eye out for supply columns, eager for the assurance of more petrol for their panzers. The Italians would watch out for the bus carrying a new selection of dark-eyed *signorinas*. The German conscripts would sit up and take notice then – it was just about the only thing they envied the wops . . .

Acting Feldwebel Kleebach sat as guest of honour between grinning Italian officers, drank Chianti and ate as well as in a luxury hotel. A quick toast to the *Duce*, at which a lieutenant-colonel yawned ostentatiously, then the jazz-band started up. A German transport officer had shown the temerity to demand that these men be used as reinforcements for the gaps in the line, and the Italian general had protested violently. So they, and their instruments, had stayed to delight headquarters.

In that case, the Italians had won a victory. And so Thomas Kleebach could enjoy the music, the *vino* and, pretty soon, *amore*. He was beginning to experience a sincere admiration for their Roman allies' success in creating a lifestyle that totally ignored the war.

There were a dozen or fifteen girls in the big tent, elegant, well-groomed beauties who would have been more in place on the Via Veneto in Rome than in the middle of the North

African desert. They had been carefully chosen by men with excellent taste.

Maybe Thomas Kleebach had drunk a little too much of the smooth Chianti, but he soon felt a kind of confused arousal at the parade of seductive talent: girls with long hair that flowed down to their shoulders, girls with raven hair and flashing eyes, temptresses, ones who preferred the innocent look, ones who were voluptuous women – and knew it.

The candles cast a flickering, eerie-romantic light. It was dark outside now. Thomas Kleebach forgot everything. Outside lurked the enemy. Outside, his comrades were on guard-duty somewhere in the emptiness. Outside, hyenas howled. Outside, the Ghibili, the notorious wind of the desert, would whip up sandstorms that tore at a man's lungs and jammed his rifle, often beyond saving.

A pretty little Italian girl spoke to him. Kleebach, unable to understand a word, smiled and shook his head. Then he looked closely at the girl and felt a shiver of memory: she bore an uncanny resemblance to Luise, his first sweetheart.

The pretty *signorina* went off to see the colonel and asked him a question. The colonel answered in a stream of rapid-fire Italian, with much arm-waving, obviously describing Kleebach's triumph in battle. Kleebach realised what was going on, and for a moment he found himself marvelling that such a simple thing could be expressed in such beautiful, flowing phrases.

'*Salute!*' they all yelled, raising their glasses to him again.

He laughed. The girl came back, and he could look at her properly. The similarity to Luise was uncanny, and he couldn't help asking himself what a girl so much like Luise was doing here. He asked her name.

'Goia,' she answered.

'A pretty name.'

'You please me, German,' she said, and smiled at him with big eyes.

He still couldn't understand what she was saying, but he got the general drift. When communication occasionally broke down altogether, a young lieutenant from the South Tyrol, on the border with Austria, acted as translator. Soon they found they could do without him. Her eyes were shining with a teasing, sensuous gleam. When she smiled, two pretty dimples showed up on either side of her mouth. It was tempting, confusing.

Kleebach felt his mouth going dry, and it wasn't from the red wine. He could feel that Goia liked him, but then she seemed to like everybody. Suddenly he wanted to be alone with her.

'Why you so serious?' she asked him.

He shook his head wordlessly.

'You Germans ... always so serious, so tough ...' Goia went on. 'Everything serious for you ... even war ...'

'It's not exactly a picnic,' Kleebach growled.

'Today nix war,' she said. 'Today ...' She moved closer to him, and he felt her animal vitality, a passion he had never seen before in a woman. He felt as if he were being wrapped up in a silk cocoon of sensuality, and it felt good – even though he knew it was artificial silk.

He fled in his mind to the Wielandstrasse, to his mother and father and the other five Kleebachs, and suddenly he was back among them sitting on the frayed sofa in the living room, the one with the cushions that were always having to be mended. Then he left them and walked two floors up in the same block, to where Luise lived, the girl he had courted for so long without finding the right thing to say – until someone else came who was not so slow, who had taken Luise before Thomas had even possessed her just once. And the victor, the one who had won her, could no longer find words to say. He had been killed a year before in France.

It was my fault that Luise slipped away from me, he told himself. The old story: I think things over too much.

The same story now. He saw Goia's lips come close to him, half-parted, quivering slightly, saw her even, white teeth. He told himself she was no more than a cheap tart with a superficial resemblance to Luise that had turned his head.

'You ...' she said softly.

'You're pretty,' he answered.

Goia giggled. 'Should I be ugly?'

'No ... everything else here is ugly enough.'

'Do you despise me?' the Italian girl asked.

'No ... but ...'

'You think too much, German ...'

'I don't mean to, I really don't . . .' he said.

'You should think less, live more,' she said, brushing away a lock of his hair from his forehead. 'Just be happy that we have met each other.'

'But I am.'

'Oh no,' she said firmly. 'But you would like to be, no?'

She stood up, then leaned down towards him, her pale, smooth arms reaching out like serpents, encircling him. Serpents are treacherous and poisonous, he told himself and fought one last time against the sight, the scent, the touch of temptation.

'*Vieni*,' Goia whispered throatily. 'Come!'

And the hero was lost.

CHAPTER FOUR

General Rommel came the next day, back to his headquarters from a tour of the front. He gave Feldwebel Kleebach a brisk handshake, promoted him on the spot to a Leutnant of the Reserve, granted him three weeks' special leave in Berlin, and then called after him as he left that he would be recommending him for a Knight's Cross. The Luftwaffe, too, made a grand gesture: the newly minted Leutnant, still wearing a Feldwebel's shoulder flashes, found himself in a Ju 52 heading for Sicily as their guest. Because he knew that his brother Fritz had been stationed here for a while at an airfield nearby, he wangled a stopover and found Fritz in the vicinity of Catania.

When Thomas faced him, he felt a shiver run down his spine. For a moment it seemed as if he was facing Gerd, Fritz's twin brother. It was as if Gerd's eyes were looking at him, Gerd's voice talking. The pain was there, but he knew he would get over it. But what about his mother and father, when Fritz finally came home?

'What are you looking at me like that for?' asked Fritz.

'Long time no see,' said Thomas evasively. To cover his embarrassment he added: 'You look older.'

'Hardly surprising,' Fritz drawled. 'When it comes down to it, war's not exactly a rest cure.'

Thomas nodded.

'Yeah, I was in on the Coventry raid,' Fritz continued, 'I tell you . . . that city was well and truly blasted – and so were we!'

'Is that so?' Thomas said absently.

'Same thing here now,' Fritz said, pointing to a map on the wall of his quarters. 'Malta. In three weeks the island'll be a heap of rubble.'

He saw that his brother failed to share his optimism, shrugged and tossed his cigarette end out of the window.

Someone had a radio on outside, tuned into a military station. The foxtrot blaring out over the sunlit courtyard suddenly broke off. The Wehrmacht report of the day began. Neither of the two men bothered to listen.

'Wet your whistle,' said Fritz and pointed to a bottle of *Grappa* sitting half-empty on the table. 'The stuff tastes terrible at first, but you can get used to anything . . .'

Thomas motioned at the planes lined up under camouflage netting outside. 'Still enjoying it?' he asked.

'I don't give a damn about the war,' Fritz said. 'What interests me is flying, nothing else . . . And if the only way I get to fly is by taking part in a war, then I'll drop bombs on anyone . . . understand?'

Thomas said nothing. He gazed at the Junkers on the tarmac and wondered how many wouldn't come back from tomorrow's mission. The squadron was due to make a mass attack on Valetta, and it was no secret that the British had stuck so much anti-aircraft flak on the island that there was hardly any room for more. Malta threatened the life-line of the Afrika Korps in the Mediterranean: Thomas knew how much blood a stronghold like that could cost, and made a rough guess that something like five planes didn't come back from every mission.

Fritz laughed, and it had a hollow ring. 'Fed up with the war, eh?'

'If you like.'

'I understand your problem,' Fritz agreed. 'I'd rather be flying tourists for Lufthansa . . . but that'll only happen once all this shit's out of the way.'

Both brothers lapsed into silence. The voice on the radio echoed through the room: 'Today . . . the Fuhrer awarded Leutnant of the Reserve Thomas Kleebach, company commander in a panzer unit, with the Knight's Cross of the Iron Cross . . .'

'What!' yelled Fritz. 'Jesus!' he whooped. 'Jesus – you, of all people! How the hell did it happen?'

Before Thomas could answer, he stormed out of the room and ran along tearing open the doors of his comrades' quarters, summoning them to his personal victory celebration. Time to crack open a few bottles . . .

Once again, Thomas Kleebach found himself sitting like a stranger round a table where he was being toasted, just as he had been with those Italians in the desert. The only thing missing was Goia, the little Italian girl who looked so much like Luise. And Luise had been missing from his life not just since yesterday but for two years now. So Thomas Kleebach sat there again like a block of wood, taking no part in the party where he was the guest of honour. With bitter self-mockery, he pondered that the war for which he felt nothing was spoiling him, as Fritz had said, of all people. War had brought him home leave, an officer's shoulder-flashes, a medal round his neck, and a girl in his bed. And despite it all Thomas hated the whole damned business, which was why he sat there almost sulkily, looking older than his twenty-five years, wearing the same expression on his face as his father when old Kleebach was weighed down with the cares of the world.

The party ended quite soon. By ten in the evening the Luftwaffe men were back in their quarters, because the squadron was due for an early start in the morning. Thomas slept in his brother's room. He persuaded Fritz to scribble a few lines to his parents, something he could take with him. He rose with the dawn roll-call whistle, though his train did not leave for another two hours, and watched Fritz getting into his flying-kit.

He shook his brother's hand and murmured a meaningless farewell. What was he supposed to say at a time like this? 'Be careful'? Or 'Don't do anything silly'? Or 'It'll be all right'?

Thomas Kleebach looked once again into the eyes of Gerd, their fallen brother, saw the line of that mouth, the feature that the twins shared, and then left Fritz without another word. He watched the Junkers take off, then hitched a lift in a Kubelwagen to the railway station.

The sun was putting on a good show, lighting up a cloudless azure sky, turning the sea brilliant blue, casting a golden clock over the sand. But there were no tourists on the beach. Just the squadron of killer-planes heading over in disciplined formation towards the horizon.

The Junkers avoided a British destroyer, because they had been ordered to save themselves for Valetta. The attack was to be mounted in three waves, and Pilot Officer Kleebach was to go in with the last. His crew thought themselves lucky: by the time they went in, the British anti-aircraft batteries should have been given a good pounding.

Now that they were getting close to the target, Fritz Kleebach was no longer quite as devil-may-care as he liked to seem when he had firm ground under his feet. Now he would gladly have changed places with Thomas, who he knew would be sitting comfortably in a train heading for home. He took a gulp from his vacuum flask: coffee with Pervitin, the drug they used to keep up the Luftwaffe's spirits, give them courage – as if they needed it. The twin engines of the Junker roared smoothly and Kleebach put his plane into a banking dive. The others followed him flipping over in succession, crisply, just like an air display.

A few Spitfires approached from the east, but immediately the Messerschmitts were there too. The fighters hared around the sky while the bombers kept stubbornly, placidly on course. Behind them a column of billowing smoke tailed off and disappeared into the sea. Impossible to tell whether it had been a Spitfire or a Messerschmitt. Kleebach's Ju 88 hit an air pocket and dropped suddenly. He picked her up again, with supreme elegance and control. His instinct for flying had been apparent even at glider school, and had been refined into something approaching genius in the tough training-ground of the Luftwaffe. Fritz Kleebach had a dream, and he lived it out nearly every day: to be floating above the earth, away from everything, hovering between heaven and hell, riding the wind or defying it, with a touch of the controls harnessing the enormous power of those engines far above the dirt and suffering, the death that crawled its way across *terra firma* . . .

Malta was in sight. The plane's wings began to vibrate gently in tune with distant explosions. Kleebach's co-pilot jerked a finger at the scene below. The harbour was in flames.

'Welcome to hell, gentlemen,' Kleebach murmured.

The first wave was already on its way back to base, but then they were Heinkel IIIs, who simply dropped their bomb-loads from on high. Now it was the turn of the Ju 88s, the dive-bombers, the ones they always saved up for the toughest targets.

'Prepare to attack!' the Commodore barked tersely into his head-set. Seconds later his Ju went into a hair-raising dive.

Kleebach snatched a glance at his comrades, saw their pale faces, bloodless lips, shot them a tight smile. Then he looked down, recognised the shape of the harbour basin and pushed hard on his joy-stick. The Ju's wings scythed whistling through the air like swords. The engines rose to a scream. Blood drained from the crewmen's heads, and their hearts beat like frantic message-drums. The breath went out of their lungs, their eyes went glassy, their skin felt like leather.

Thirteen hundred feet, and the Ju's nose was pointed straight at the target with the puffball-like explosions of flak left and right. The anti-aircraft shells were falling short, but pretty soon Kleebach would be low enough to be in range. He put the thought out of his mind and simply kept the howling machine on target, luxuriating in its power, the thunder of its engines – a miracle of technology plunging into an inferno of destruction.

At the exact moment that the bomb-load was released, Kleebach wrenched his machine up, bringing its nose horizontal, then pulled the Ju into a steep climbing bank to the right. Seconds later the whole plane shook like a trapped bird; the bombs had hit target.

Now just get away, Fritz Kleebach thought, fighting against that treacherous feeling of relief that could cost an unwary pilot his life. Away. He had the worst of it behind him. Not yet twenty-one and a master of his craft, with only two missions until he was due for his silver combat-clasp.

The flak boomed angrily after the German bombers.

'Idiots!' Kleebach said contemptuously, his voice crackling over his head-set like sandpaper on wood.

The squadron regrouped. Two planes were missing. The Commodore throttled back, to give the tailenders a chance to catch up – until he realised that there were no tailenders . . . No one asked which crews had had it. That was something that they would find out soon enough when they made it back to base. All that mattered now was to get the hell out of this shit-storm . . .

'Alarm!' yelled the gunner.

But Kleebach had already spotted the Spitfires, zooming out of the sun like glistening streaks of foil. They had his Ju in their sights. But Kleebach banked at the last moment, so sharply that he threatened to ram his neighbour in formation. But he didn't, there had never been any risk of that, and he grinned confidently. Until he saw three bullet holes in his wing and he knew the Spitfires would be back for him . . .

He opened the throttles, but the blasted engines would not respond. They whined like whipped animals. The left engine began to cough. Something was badly wrong. Kleebach just about had time to hear his Commodore's radio message, bellowing for fighter cover, and then the Spitfires were on him again.

This time they came from the left. Kleebach escaped them once again, but now he was falling behind the main force. After the third attack, his left engine was in flames. A few short seconds more and his petrol tanks would go up, but Fritz Kleebach, the perfect pilot, stayed cool. He put the bomber into a near-vertical dive, in a desperate attempt to put out the fire.

The Commodore watched him from his command cabin, saw him extinguish the flames, but knew it wasn't over. The Commodore knew how hard it was going to be to pull a Ju out of a seventy-degree dive on one engine.

Now, he thought, frantically willing Kleebach to survive, seeing the bomber's wings bending up as if they had to break, the Ju making strange, awkward hops in the air, then levelling out. God, that fellow Kleebach . . . The damaged Ju was flying on slowly, too slowly, gradually and inevitably losing height, coming low over the sea. It had to ditch down – if the Tommies didn't get it first.

What a flier, thought the Commodore bitterly, and what a poor, poor devil. He tore himself away and began a second, desperate call for fighter cover . . .

Thomas, the eldest son, pierced the gloom of his family's wartime existence like a sun breaking through the early-morning mist. More important than the fanfare of publicity in the radio reports was the certainty that he was safe. His previous letters had gone down with a German troop transporter torpedoed in the Mediterranean.

He had sent a telegram from Rome telling them that he was on his way back to Berlin, but even before he could catch his train the propaganda machine had got hold of him again and passed him around like a lucky charm. By the time Goebbels's minions had finished with him, the railway line north had been put out of action by enemy bombing. Then, luckily, Thomas was offered a lift in a Luftwaffe general's personal plane.

'If you ever have to deal with the Luftwaffe and need my help,' the general told Kleebach when they parted. 'Just get in touch with me direct, Kleebach.'

'Very well, Herr General,' Thomas answered politely. Little did he know how soon he might have to take the man up on his offer.

Long awaited but unheralded, he turned up at the apartment in the Wielandstrasse. His father, resting on the sofa between delivery rounds, shot delightedly to his feet, so excited that he did up the wrong buttons on his postman's uniform. He pointed to the Knight's Cross at his son's throat and stammered: 'Congratulations!'

'What for?' Thomas said testily.

His father laughed. 'Still the same old Thomas . . . always so modest . . . I know you've got no time for bits of tinsel, but it won't do you any harm when it comes to making a career later on . . .'

Thomas drew his mother to him, overcome with emotion, 'I saw Fritz,' he said quickly. 'Here . . . a letter at last . . .'

'You were with Fritz?' Maria Kleebach said softly. 'How . . . how is he?'

'Great,' answered her eldest. 'Fit as an Olympic sprinter . . . and he's put on weight . . . You won't recognise him . . .'

'But the things he has to do down there . . . aren't they . . . dangerous?'

'So-so,' Thomas shrugged. 'Not exactly a picnic . . . but nothing compared with those dog-fights in France.'

'You're not being kind to me, are you, my son?'

'Of course not, mother.'

'Then why doesn't he write to me more often?'

'Well, you know how it is,' Thomas said. 'Our Fritz never would put pen to paper, idle kid . . .'

'See, mother,' father Kleebach chipped in, 'You're always worrying needlessly.'

Freddy, the gigolo, had also been granted special leave, because his brother had become a war hero. Achim, the Hitler Youth leader, had written delightedly – and foolishly – home: 'Thank God, all this will soon be over.'

Heinz Böckelmann, friend of the dead Gerd and also Marion's fiancé, was also home on leave. He was slowly getting used to the idea that Marion too was due for conscription as a woman auxiliary in the Wehrmacht. He took her into her office in the morning and fetched her after work, and in between he moped. With father Kleebach's quiet support Bockelmann tried to prepare the ground for an early marriage, but Marion always answered: 'In wartime? No! I want to do it properly . . . honeymoon in sunny Italy, all the trimmings.'

'After all, they're still both very young,' her mother would say, smoothing down the ruffled feathers.

Thomas was already sick of being stared at on the street like a circus animal because of his Knight's Cross, and so he wore civilian clothes almost all the time. Otherwise he spent the majority of leave quietly at home. Happy as mother Kleebach was to see him, she would have preferred her eldest to be a little more relaxed. He turned down invitations to visit relatives, sat most of the day in the corner reading. His mother cooked all his favourite dishes, so long as she could get the ingredients, but he scarcely seemed to notice. His mother realised what was missing in his life and asked him carefully, a whole week after he had arrived: 'Have you seen Luise?'.

'No.'

'Perhaps you should go and see her, just once . . .'

Thomas looked up reluctantly from his book.

'She gets so lonely,' his mother said. 'Since her husband . . . joined the fallen.'

'I'm sure we shall bump into each other,' Thomas growled.

He would not have had far to go. Luise lived in the same building, two storeys higher, and had done for many years. She had been Thomas's first love – if his tongue-tied, gauche courtship can be honoured with that description. When she married someone else, he had been forced to put her out of his mind. And when the other man was killed in action, Thomas had dared not dwell on the fact that Luise was a free woman again. He had not seen her on his last leave, and mother Kleebach feared that he would ignore her again this time.

In the end an air-raid alert achieved what all Maria Kleebach's gentle urging had failed to bring about. All the tenants in the building had to pile down into the cellar, and there suddenly, almost guiltily, Thomas and Luise stood face to face, crammed in among the rest of their neighbours.

'You haven't changed,' she said.

'Neither have you,' he answered. Thomas could hardly bear

to look at her. But he had seen enough to realise that she was more mature, more womanly, but every bit as pretty as the teenager he had known.

'Thomas . . .' she said, almost embarrassed.

'Yes?'

'Would you like to come round sometime?'

'If you like,' he answered.

'I'd like it.'

He nodded and said nothing more. The first time, he seemed to go reluctantly. Soon, though, he was out almost every night, never saying where he was going. His parents smiled knowingly to each other.

And so he sat at Luise's side, the way he had many years before. They each had a glass of wine before them on the low table, and the radio played romantic music into the cosy room.

'Do you really resent me for . . . you know . . .' she began.

'What?' Thomas said.

'For . . . not waiting for you . . .'

'No,' he said. His voice was hard. Perhaps he had once hated her for it, and maybe blamed himself as well. Soon it had all merged into a dull feeling of disappointment.

Neither of them spoke. Their eyes met slowly, and Luise smiled. Thomas realised that he was fidgeting with his hands – he was fighting with his own shadow. He still couldn't find the words.

A blind man could have seen what Luise felt for him, but Thomas could not, dare not, because that would have meant hope and the threat of a second disappointment. Time had taught him to never build castles in the air.

I'll talk about it tomorrow, he told himself, and postponed it again, even though he knew his days on leave were numbered . . .

The training company to which Achim, the youngest Kleebach, belonged, was sprawled face-down in the mud, just where it was thickest. The recruits were forced to wear gas masks, ungainly, uncomfortable, that made them look like bedraggled elephants. Sweat was pouring out from under their helmets, their tunics were covered in filth. They panted painfully, near to exhaustion, but there was no mercy: anyone who didn't crawl fast enough through the sodden slime got a kick up the backside from their instructor.

It was the twelfth and last week of their basic training. From a practical point of view it was intended to raise the eighteen-year-olds to a peak of physical fitness, and psychologically it was supposed to make them eager to get away from home duties. In a week the camp would be spitting young recruits out to the front. Only the instructors would remain, ready to start moulding new cannon fodder.

'Up!' yelled the Feldwebel in charge. He had a voice that hissed like a fire extinguisher, with the result that the recruits had named him after one, the 'Minimax' brand.

Now he had decided he had done enough shouting. He reached for his whistle. They had arrived at a huge, deep puddle, and this was his big moment.

'Get in there!' he ordered. 'When you're at the front, you'll be going through twenty of these buggers a day, and no excuses!'

The Feldwebel stood by and made certain that every one of them ended up soaked to the skin. Even that, though, wasn't enough.

Then he had them line up in three ranks. 'Oh, so this is all too nasty for your tender sensibilities, is it?' he roared. Three soldiers were put on report on the spot, another ten reserved for fire-watch, and the whole company confined to barracks.

The Feldwebel devoted the rest of the morning to rifle-practice and field training – down, roll forward, back again, up, down . . . He glimpsed their company commander approaching and decided it was time to really give them hell.

'Gas masks on!' he ordered. 'Forward at the double!'

They stumbled on like obedient robots, stepping over some poor swine who had collapsed in the dirt.

'Sing!' the Feldwebel shrieked. Feebly, panting and swaying as they tried to keep up the pace, the boys moaned: 'It's so fine to be a soldier . . .'

'Halt! Gas masks off!' He looked along the rows of faces, checking for signs of defiance. 'I see lovely pale faces,' he gloated. 'Soft as silk, peaches and cream . . . get in a circle!'

They fought to re-form.

The Feldwebel bided his time, then pointed at the mud.

'Help yourselves, gentlemen!' he said, smirking at his own wonderful joke.

They bent and clawed at the filthy earth, then rubbed it into their faces, good and hard like he had taught them.

'And what is that, Kleebach?' the Feldwebel shouted.

'Camouflage, Herr Feldwebel!' Achim answered obediently.

The unit filed back to their hut.

'Company will report for meal in two minutes!' the corporal bawled.

As planned, they didn't make it in time. With fiendish ingenuity, the Feldwebel ordered a nail-inspection, after a morning spent grovelling in the mud. The resourceful Achim cleaned his with a fork. He had no intention of being picked out for retribution. He accepted the brutality, because he intended to become the perfect soldier. Others might festoon their lockers with pictures of naked girls, but he brightened his up with the latest party slogans. Since he had been told that his brother had won the Knight's Cross, he was determined to get one too, and with oak leaves into the bargain. He longed for recognition, and when the others threw themselves exhausted onto their bunks he forced himself to stay awake and read the Fuhrer's speeches. Achim was the perfect young product of the Nazi system, where kids were fed slogans like cod-liver oil until they were in their blood.

The next day he reported to the commander's office.

'Well, Kleebach?' the Oberleutnant said, pacing round him.

'Gunner Kleebach reporting!' Achim bellowed, standing stiffly to attention.

'I can see that, my dear fellow,' the officer said amiably.

'Permission to express a request, Herr Oberleutnant.'

'A request?' the company commander asked, amused. He lit a cigarette and raised his eyebrows. He was a great advocate of subtlety in training methods – which meant that he left others to do the shouting for him. He regarded his Feldwebel as a dumb-ox peasant who when he was called up would doubtless have not been able to tell the latrine from a coal-hole, but he gave him a free hand. On a good day the Oberleutnant could be filled with bonhomie, but on a bad one he could give those boys a tougher time than all Greater Germany's Feldwebels put together.

Now he stared at Kleebach and moved closer. 'May I?'

'Yes, Herr Oberleutnant.'

The officer brushed an invisible speck of dust from the recruit's tunic. 'Stand easy,' he said then. He tossed his burning cigarette at Achim's feet. The recruit immediately bent down and put it in the ash tray.

'And who ordered you to do that?' the officer hissed.

'Orders of the Feldwebel!' Kleebach bellowed. 'Three days close arrest for burning cigarette ends!'

'Are you suggesting that I should be put in the glasshouse?' the Oberleutnant asked with a superior smile.

'No, Herr Oberleutnant.'

'All right. Then what do you want?'

'My brother is a bearer of the Knight's Cross,' Achim began haltingly.

'I bow to that.'

'I request transfer into my brother's panzer company.'

'Want an easy life, eh?'

'No, Herr Oberleutnant. I wish to prove myself.'

The company commander pondered long and thoroughly, then came to a decision. After all, the boy was very keen.

'Very well,' he said finally. 'I'm no sadist, and I'd hate to stand in the way of a cosy family reunion . . . I'll put it through the proper channels . . . Now clear off!'

Kleebach stood stoutly to attention yet again, then turned to go.

'Just a minute!' the officer called after him. 'Be so good as to report me to the Feldwebel for that cigarette end!' He grinned, savouring the crestfallen look on Achim's face. 'And that's an order!'

Thirty seconds later the trainee gunner carried out that command.

'Are you pulling my leg?' the Feldwebel said in a dangerously gentle voice, narrowing his eyes. 'Kleebach,' he continued. 'As a lesson in dealing with your superiors, I'll give you another order. When you're dismissed this evening you can polish all the N.C.O.s' shit-houses, every one of 'em . . . till you can see your face in them. Understood?'

'Yes, Herr Feldwebel,' Achim answered, shut the door behind him, and felt happy. He had, after all, got what he wanted.

*   *   *

The Nazi psychologists had decided that death-notices could no longer be left to postmen. With cold precision they had established new rules. They made bleak reading, but for father Kleebach they meant some release from his burdens:

'OKW – AZ: B 31 t AWA/WVW (III). Subject: The informing of relatives of members of the Wehrmacht killed, died, or missing on active service. The Fuhrer desires that such information be communicated in first place and in his own handwriting by the commander of the individual's unit, but that the above should be delivered by the appropriate official of the National Socialist Workers' Party . . .

Hereto the following instructions 33/42 and 77/42 of the Party Chancellery:

1. It is of decisive importance that the notice of fallen or missing personnel be delivered to the relatives in a suitably tactful fashion. The individual official must assume responsibility for selecting the form and manner most appropriate to this purpose.

2. The communication is under all circumstances to be made in an inconspicuous fashion. To this end civilian clothes may, if necessary, be worn.

3. It is unnecessary for the Ortsgruppenleiter or his deputy to make the communication in all cases. The official should rather select an individual from his local Party branch who is suited to the particular circumstances of the case, the conditions being that the individual must be absolutely politically reliable, have served himself as a soldier, and above all enjoy the confidence and trust of the family of the casualty. If the communication is to be made to a woman, then it is permitted for a member of the Women's Section to accompany the Party member . . .

For the Reich Chancellor & Führer (signed) Bormann, Reichsleiter.'

These days Arthur Kleebach received the notice of death in a plain envelope, which he handed over to the local Party office. He had got out of the habit of counting up the numbers of dead from the weight of the packages he had to deliver.

Party Comrade Rosenblatt had become a pathetic figure to Kleebach. He had aged a lot, and it needed no more than a hint from Martin Bormann for him to change into civilian clothes.

Once people had grinned when they saw his mustard-brown uniform; now their hearts beat faster when he came up to them in that ominous dark suit. And the Ortsgruppenleiter, like almost everyone else, had his worries. His only son was serving at the front.

'That's it then,' Arthur Kleebach said on this day, turning to leave the Party offices as soon as possible. He was already at the door when Rosenblatt called him back.

Tense, like a sinister shadow, the official came up to him. He tried to say something, could not. And father Kleebach felt instinctively at that moment that the war had robbed him a second time. He stood as if paralysed, hands hanging limply by his sides, and waited for Rosenblatt to say what he had to say.

Kleebach learned that his son Fritz, brother of the dead Gerd, had been posted missing.

In that moment the simple, shy postman lost control. It was all too much. He made the crazy decision that his wife and his family must never know the tragic news, whatever the cost to himself or anyone else . . .

Arthur Kleebach walked home slowly, bent like an old man. He trod the hard concrete of the pavement like a man wading through a swamp, seeing, hearing nothing. He felt as if every burden of this world had been heaped on his shoulders.

They had been waiting for him at home for some time. He was already half an hour late home from work, and it was the kind of thing that people noticed, because his life was founded on punctuality, order in the trivial as well as the important things. His life was about caring and happiness, love and security. And now war had reached into that private world for the second time.

Two girls hurried round the street corner.

Kleebach almost bumped into them. 'Sorry,' he murmured.

'It's all right,' the girl answered.

'He did that deliberately,' the other hissed as they walked on. 'Old misery-guts . . .'

Arthur Kleebach heard but did not understand,. He stood for a moment and gazed absently after the two girls.

'The Leutnant is so charming,' one was saying. 'And imagine, he says he wants to marry me.'

'Martin?'

'No . . , Gerd,' her girlfriend answered with a laugh.

Gerd . . . father Kleebach thought. Gerd was dead, lying somewhere in northern France under a wooden cross, perhaps with a steel helmet above it if they had been able to spare one. At least they had plenty of wood. Gerd, he thought. The first blow, and how hard it had struck Maria, his wife. She would never get over it, never, and there was her weak heart, that quiet bravery and the way she faked sleep at nights. Sons might win wars, but a mother was always the loser.

And now Fritz, the other twin. Missing with engine failure a hundred feet above the sea. His comrades had seen him crash. Not even a wooden cross, thought Arthur Kleebach.

But he was not concerned with his own pain, even though Fritz was part of his world of love and sacrifice, the world which he had worked so hard to create and defend. Yes, it hurt, but the hurt was for Fritz's fragile mother. He was absolutely certain that she would never survive this second, terrible blow.

The small, shy man, who had lost control, did not ask himself whether he was entitled to lie to his wife. He knew he had to. He could not bring himself to become the executioner, the man who snuffed out Maria's will to live.

Next corner. Two streets to go. Flags were hanging from the windows again, right down to street level. A swastika banner brushed against Kleebach's face, and he swept the flag aside with an unthinking motion of the arm. A woman passed him, pushing an eleven-year-old boy in a wheelchair. A congenital spinal condition. He knew the people.

How wonderful, Arthur Kleebach thought for one desperate moment, if all his boys had been crippled at birth, unfit for dying . . .'

He was breathing heavily. His face seemed unhealthily grey, his skin like old parchment. In a couple of minutes he would be standing in the kitchen, lifting the lid off the cooking-pot and sniffing the supper, father home from work and spreading good humour through the house. Maybe the famous actor, Heinrich George, could manage that kind of thing on the stage, but Arthur Kleebach was no thespian, and his life wasn't a piece of theatre.

He stood at the door of the apartment. His key was in his pocket, but he rang the doorbell to give himself more precious time. Downstairs in the hall he had met a soldier on crutches

71

who had lost his left leg in France. If only they had just taken Fritz's leg too, his father thought savagely. At least he would be alive, and his mother and I would love him just as much.

He stood face to face with Maria, still pale but feeling a little more in control.

'Aren't you well?' she asked.

'I don't know,' he said as casually as he could. 'Must have been something I ate.'

'Have a schnaps,' shouted Thomas from the living room.

'Best not to,' his father answered with a forced smile. 'You know I've got a weak head.'

'Eat a plate of soup, at least.'

'Yes,' he said, nodding, and sat down at the table.

Maria ladelled out some soup, then looked sidelong at him. 'Still no letter from Fritz?' she asked.

'No,' Arthur Kleebach said angrily. 'When that lazy son of mine comes home on leave I'll sort him out!' he blustered. 'Leaving us to worry for so long!'

His wife nodded sadly.

'I'll give him something to remember,' Kleebach growled, looking away to the window. 'He's not too·big for that yet . . .'

'Come, come . . .' his wife twittered.

Arthur Kleebach ate as if the food tasted good. 'Thomas,' he said, turning to his eldest son. 'Now you see what it's like at home . . . this eternal waiting . . . Please write to us as often as you can when you're back out there.'

'Even if it's only a couple of lines,' Maria Kleebach said.

'You can rely on me,' Thomas said. He got up and smoked a cigarette half way through the meal, because he didn't know why but he had a sick feeling in his own stomach . . .

CHAPTER FIVE

The old steamer that was supposed to be taking them across the Mediterranean looked as if it could sink itself without any help from the Allies. A 5,000 ton senior citizen of the sea, it had been saved from the breaker's yard by the war and got ready for a fate that would probably amount to the same in the end. The steamer that had once hauled bananas over from the West Indies now took cargoes of cannon-fodder for Hitler.

'I hope the moths haven't had too good a go at her.' muttered Achim, the Hitler Youth leader, as he dragged eighty pounds of pack up the gangway. Otherwise he was happy – on his way to the Afrika Korps to join his own brother's company, to serve with an outfit led by a Knight's Cross holder.

The sun shone brightly on a bright blue sea. There was a salty tang in the air, and a hint also of longing and of adventure. The German conscripts, they soon found out, were travelling fifth class, packed together in the lower decks like canned meat, so tight that they could hardly fall over.

'Like ruddy sardines,' Achim told his mate.

The other private nodded gloomily. 'At least sardines can swim if it comes to it,' he said.

'I can too,' retorted Achim proudly.

His mate grimaced. 'Not as far as Benghazi.'

They were part of a German convoy taking reinforcements from Naples and Sicily to North Africa. They crept through the Mediterranean like thieves in the night, and still lost two-thirds of their ships . . . The Italians proudly called the Med 'our sea', *il mare nostro*, but they forgot Gibraltar and Malta. The two British outposts, with their airfields and naval bases, were more than a thousand miles apart, but they turned the sea between them into a happy hunting-ground, and made sure that Rommel's reinforcements sweated before they set foot in Libya.

Achim Kleebach was with the last group to board, and so he was able to stay up on deck just a few yards from an anti-aircraft gun. 'Hey, sailor!' he yelled to one of the gunners, grinning with elation. 'Question: What's red, lies out on the deck and sleeps all day long?'

The gunner made a sign that clearly indicated his lack of interest and his contempt for the questioner's mental soundness.

'A flak gun,' Achim mocked.

The rest of them paid no attention. Their thoughts were elsewhere: some still in the Italian whorehouses, others dreaming of home, and the cautious ones checking the lifejackets, which most of them had never seen before in their young lives.

An hour later the lead ships left the harbour, with an Italian destroyer in the vanguard flanked by two ageing escort vessels, and in the middle four overfilled transporters that had long since seen better days. Visibility was good, the sea calm with almost no swell. Silver ripples shimmered gently across the surface. Sea-gulls followed the ships until the Italian mainland was just a thin blurred line on the horizon. The men perched on their packs and made themselves as comfortable as they could.

'Shit!' oathed Achim's comrade. 'Thirst is worse than a nagging wife, I'll tell you.'

Achim grinned. 'How would you know? Been married?' he asked the nineteen-year-old by his side.

'Well, no,' his mate admitted, preening himself. 'But almost . . . as good as engaged . . . man, she was something . . .'

He said a lot more, for more than an hour. He talked his throat dry and his mouth to parchment. Then they were given a bottle of beer to every two men. It was lukewarm, but better than nothing. They took turns with the bottle.

'Siesta?' said Achim afterwards, lying back on his belongings.

'This hero of the fatherland could do with a playmate,' his comrade started up again. 'Right now a nice dark wop piece'd go down really well . . .'

'Don't you ever stop your fantasies?'

'Yeah, one like yesterday. You should have come with us, you bloody fool. Man, those girls . . .'

74

'What for? It's always the same,' Achim said lazily, doing his best to seem superior. First rule: never admit you're a virgin . . .

An Oberleutnant forced his way through onto the upper deck. He saw that most of the soldiers had taken off their life jackets because of the heat and cursed them roundly.

'Put those damned things back on!' he bellowed.

But the order went unobeyed – not least because the Oberleutnant also wasn't wearing a life jacket.

'Those Italian girls,' Achim's mate droned on. 'Flavia, one of them was called. They've got paprika in their blood, Jesus, hot stuff . . .'

'Take cover!' someone shouted. Very funny. Until they realised it was no joke.

Cursing, the men on the upper deck tumbled over each other. Achim crawled under his pack and said to his comrade with a grin: 'Wake me up when it's all over.'

The English formation flew over at altitude and got the measure of the convoy. The Tommies waited until the destroyer, which had opened fire wildly and far too soon, was off to the left. The frigates would be no danger, and the heavy-laden transporters could be ignored. By the time the enemy planes came in for their first attack, the German convoy was dangerously dispersed.

They howled in from behind. Spitfires scudding over at 700 feet.

The anti-aircraft guns opened up. But the English were diving with wing guns letting go with all they had. The second Spitfire came over, the third, fourth, fifth . . . Silver streams across the deck, pearls of death that couldn't miss.

The rear deck got the worst of the strafing. Achim Kleebach was crouched on the other side of the ship. In the panic he had become separated from his gear, and all he could do was to hug the deck, trying to make himself as small and flat as a cockroach. He risked a glance at the sky. Two Spitfires still to come, he thought with a rush of hope. Only two; it would soon be over. He pressed himself against the planks again and felt a raging hatred for the lucky soldiers down below, who would be playing cards, finishing their beer, while up here they were dealing out 'hero's deaths' in the sunshine.

When the last Spitfire had climbed away, they could hear

the moans and screams of the wounded, see the river of blood that was washing over the planks.

'That was nothing,' the flak gunner said comfortingly. 'They'll be back in no time.'

A Feldwebel had been cut in half by a machine-gun burst, right across the stomach. A young soldier who had been lying next to him saw the blood, the open guts, and suddenly leapt to his feet and started to race across the deck like someone running amok, springing straight over dead and wounded men.

He tripped over a man's head that had been torn from his body, stared around wildly, then without more ado shrieked and leapt over board.

The screams of the wounded were blood-chilling, inhuman. Hundreds of pairs of hands groped for men who had survived unharmed, pleading and clawing for support, for life.

'Come on!' yelled an officer. 'Let's have some air! Throw the dead over board!'

Achim worked like an automaton. He was heaving his fourth over the rail when he realised that the man was not dead, only wounded. He stared after the falling body in horror. It was too late . . .

'Come on! Get on with it!' his mate bellowed.

The Spitfires came again, this time from the right. In those first moments the helpless human targets on the open deck were almost relieved that the howl of engines blocked out the terrible sounds of suffering. This time Achim was right in the middle of it all, but he was lucky. The stairways leading up top were in chaos. The soldiers on the lower decks had lost their nerve and were trying to get out into the open, while their comrades on the upper decks were trying to get down into cover. Seething concentrations of men were forming at the exits, and the Spitfires did not miss their chance.

Suddenly, after a few minutes, the fighters broke off their attack.

'Jesus!' moaned the flak gunner. 'We're in for the real shit now . . .'

Achim didn't believe him. He looked around at the panorama of hell, the dying, the shattered limbs and bodies, and despite everything he felt only relief. He stood there and laughed, loudly, hysterically, insanely, until a comrade kicked him hard in the backside and brought him back to his senses.

Death had cleared the decks. They had air now. More than half of the men who had started their journey up top and almost all the packs and equipment had been heaved overboard.

'There they come!' someone yelled.

Again tiny silver darts scudded across the sea, so low it seemed that they must be dragging their tails in the water. These were Swordfish. Torpedo planes. Suddenly they seemed to stop and hover, but Achim understood nothing until he saw the foamy trail being cut through the waves, heading straight for their ship.

'Move out!' an officer screamed. 'To the other side!'

Kleebach obeyed, swept along in the crush, feeling and thinking nothing, instinctively flailing with his arms to help clear a way through the stumbling, cursing mass until he reached the far rail. At that moment the torpedo smashed into the other side of the hull, piercing the outer skin, tearing the engine room to bits and finally exploding with a dull roar. The old tub of a transporter was finished. Maybe two minutes until she went down.

'All men overboard!' Achim heard, and didn't wait a second. He didn't even look for a life-jacket. All he wanted to do was hit the sea. At the last moment someone grabbed him and held him back. He had been about to leap right into the middle of a blazing patch of oil. He looked down for an instant, slack-jawed with shock, and heard screams that curdled his blood in his veins.

Then he jumped, pushing off from the rail as hard as he could to give himself a good start away from the sinking ship, plunged into the sea and struck out in powerful strokes. He was breathing like a stirrup pump, and the salt water was goading his eyes, and as he swam he realised that the men on the upper deck who had survived had been the lucky ones. The others, crammed in down between the decks, would go down to the bottom with the rats . . .

Achim did not look round. To the right and left, men trod water. Others rained down from the ship. One went under, came up once more, then drowned just a few feet from him. Another just lay on his back with arms outstretched, not moving, doing absolutely nothing, but staying afloat. He had kept on his life jacket. At that moment, Achim would have gladly torn it from his body.

The raging urge to survive, to live, seemed to double the boy's strength. After twenty minutes in the water he saw a small life raft with many too many men clinging to it. The weight pulled it down. Waves washed over it, but one side rose again.

Achim, his face contorted with effort, swam closer, and saw that at least four survivors were hanging on to a life belt as if grasping life.

A Feldwebel saw him approaching, pulled himself up and shouted: 'Clear off . . . there's already . . .' His head bobbed under for the last time, and his last words, too, were dragged under the waves.

This was not the picture of noble comradeship that he had been fed since he was a child, but Achim understood only too well that comradeship was a luxury now. What mattered was getting to that life belt . . . He was a strong lad, and he used every ounce of power to reach out and grab the legs of one of the survivors. From now on that man would have to carry double the wait – and fight for his place with five other pairs of hands on the tiny rubber ring.

The man lashed out and hit Achim in the stomach. The boy from the Hitler Youth didn't feel it. He looked over to the other side and saw a man let go of the ring and go under, and he sensed no fear, only relief, for that meant one less hanging on, more chance for the rest. The man whose legs he was clutching made another attempt to shake him off, but Achim was as tough as his victim. And there were other survivors making for the last hope of safety. Everyone knew that they would all be condemned to death if any more men tried to cling to the life belt and overloaded it. Those that had strength left defended themselves brutally, with all their animal instincts, hacking at neighbours' faces and hands as hard as they could again and again. It was every man for himself, the ancient truth that they never admitted in the propaganda reports.

They pummelled and punched and murdered comrades. And the name of the inhuman game was survival.

Achim saw what was going on, hesitated, then shut his eyes and cursed himself for a pansy. He took a deep breath, manhandled himself forward onto the other man's back, and put every ounce of his final will to live in a savage blow with the flat of his hand across the side of the man's temples. It was a ju-jitsu blow that he had learned long ago in the Hitler Youth, and it worked: the man went rigid. Achim grinned stupidly and watched as the other let go of the life belt, then grabbed for the security of the ring. It was then that the waves tossed the man to one side and Achim saw his face for the first time. Savage satisfaction gave way to horror: he had killed his own comrade. His mate would never see another Flavia, never boast of another girl again . . .

Seven hours later a German U-boat fished the life belt out of the water. Five men were still clinging grimly to it, among them Achim Kleebach.

Panzer Leutnant Thomas Kleebach's leave came to an end. It had been a strange time. The young officer, a man among men and – though he still wouldn't admit the fact – a decorated war hero, usually went in for frontal assaults on his targets. Now, though, he was wracked by indecision. The target this time was different: her name was Luise, she lived two storeys up in the apartment block, and she had been his teenage sweetheart.

When he wasn't around his parents' apartment, he was at Luise's place. Like today. He had brought flowers, dark-red roses, which he handed over to her with something close to embarrassment. He had been waiting a long time; now he was determined to make the leap into the unknown.

They sat side by side in the comfortable little flat. They hadn't been out together once, because they just wanted to be alone and undisturbed, able to talk as they wished over a bottle of wine and some gentle music from the radio.

'Everything all right at home?' Luise asked.

'Oh, you know the way things are,' Thomas said. 'Mother simply hasn't got over Gerd's death . . . but at the moment I'm more worried about father.'

'Your father?' Luise said incredulously. 'He's always the tower of strength.'

'Yes . . . but the last ten days he's changed. The worst thing is that he knows I know but won't talk about it.'

'Perhaps he has trouble at work.'

'I don't think so. I know him too well.'

'Then maybe you're just imagining things, Thomas.'

'I hope so.'

They sat as always, starting off with little secret looks and then holding each other's eyes more directly. Luise liked the way he talked, and the way he knew when to be silent. Most of all, though, she liked the way Thomas looked at her: his frank gaze expressed the way he felt about her more than a thousand words. Those eyes of his were dreamer's eyes, but somehow sober, tender and yet cool. Eyes that caressed her – in place of the hands that did not dare . . .

'When does your train leave?' she asked, though she knew full well.

'In three days,' he answered.

'So soon?'

'Yes.'

She lay back among the cushions. She was petite and curly-haired, with a turned-up nose and a pointed chin. The overall impression was of energy and sensuality, strength without dominance.

'And when will you come back?'

'I don't know.'

'But you will come back?' Luise pressed.

'I don't know about that either.'

'But I . . .'

'You . . . ?'

'I can feel it . . . people feel it when . . .'

'When they what?' he said quickly.

'When they care for someone, and fear for them.'

'Luise . . .' he began.

'Yes?'

'I'd like to . . .' The words dried up like water in sand.

'What would you like?' Luise sat up and moved her face closer to his. Her eyes were so close that he felt as if he could drown in them. Thomas could see that her lips were quivering slightly. He felt dizzy, and noticed that his arm had gone numb and cold, as if it had fallen asleep. He turned away, looked at the clock on the mantlepiece, and gave himself another ten minutes before he would ask Luise to be his wife.

She smiled. She had understood, and she was happy and perhaps a little amused. She was his, whether he said the words or not, and she knew it. He needed a woman like her, someone who could stop him from being too serious, who could remind him that there were pleasures in life as well as duties.

Luise crossed her legs with a rustle of nylon, smiled coquettishly and lit a cigarette, which she put in Thomas's mouth. He drew deeply on the smoke and she could see he was already trying to find the words that would put her into his arms. She decided to help.

'Thomas,' she said. 'How old are you?'

'Twenty-five.'

'And turning into a bit of a hermit . . .'

'Maybe.'

'But you're a soldier,' she continued. 'Soldiers have girls . . . maybe more than one . . . Have you ever loved a woman?'

'I don't know,' he sighed. 'Perhaps one . . .'

'And what was she like?' Luise asked, though she knew very well.

'As pretty as you.'

'And where is she now?'

Thomas shook his head miserably.

'And why didn't you and she get together?' Luise probed.

'Because . . . because I was too slow . . .'

'And why?'

'Goddamned war!' he growled, and stood up.

And so another evening ended with no progress. But Luise was patient. She could wait. She didn't force the issue. But she used all the feminine tricks that have existed since Eve, chose her sexiest clothes, her best make-up, learned to listen and coax, could be serious or flirtatious, though she had no intention of seducing Thomas – only making him hers.

Two days to go. They sat closer together. Her shoulder pressed against his a little more insistently. They spoke even less and came closer, and Thomas could feel longing in his skin, in his limbs, right to his finger-tips. He felt it when he looked at Luise, and he knew she wanted him too. Suddenly it happened. Her lips opened and he leaned over her. She kissed him, and then reached almost violently to bring him to her, pressing his body against hers, stroking his hair, caressing, urging . . .

Suddenly Thomas tore himself free.

His face was grim, his body tensed. Luise stopped smiling. She followed his eyes, knowing instinctively what the problem was. On the wall hung a portrait of her dead husband, and

Thomas was staring at it with agony in his eyes. Luise knew that he had to fight this battle alone. She was not superficial; the dead man had meant a lot to her, and still did, but she was too young and too full of life to devote herself to a cult of death. The shadow of his life and death would always be with her, but she did not intend to let it cast a gloom through the rest of her days.

'Yes,' Thomas said with difficulty. 'You understand . . . It's not jealousy, nothing like that . . . But he died. He was killed in this damned war . . .' He got to his feet and punched the air in frustration. 'Who knows whether any of us will survive this senseless slaughter?' Thomas almost choked on his words. 'And I won't . . . I won't get what I want through another man's death . . .'

'Thomas,' Luise said softly. She rose and went to his side. 'I knew him well,' she began. 'Very well. And I know he would think differently if he could see us now.'

'No!' Thomas barked.

Luise realised that she was going to have to give a helping hand, even if it meant forcing the issue. She went slowly over to the picture of her dead husband, looked at it thoughtfully, then with great care took it off the wall. She did not let Thomas out of her eye for a second. His face showed his inner torment as he stared at the place on the wall where the picture had been, a square of paler-coloured wall where the surface had been protected.

'Sure,' Thomas said wearily, and pointed to the patch on the wall. 'Wounds heal . . . but the scars are always with us . . .'

Both of them knew now that with only two days left they would never lay the ghost that stood between them . . .

The next morning Thomas Kleebach sat opposite his mother at the breakfast table. He could see that she wanted something from him, and he waited patiently for her to summon up the courage to ask.

'Tell me, Thomas,' she began hesitantly. 'That . . . thing . . . gives you some influence, doesn't it?' She meant the Knight's Cross.

'Maybe.'

'Didn't you have a lift with some Luftwaffe general on your way home?'

'Yes. So what?' he said absently.

'Your father,' Maria Kleebach said. 'He's obviously worried that we haven't heard from Fritz for so long. We have to do something . . . Why don't you put on your lovely medal, go to this general and ask about Fritz . . . ?' She tried to seem light-hearted, but he could see that she was in deadly earnest.

'All right,' he said simply. 'I'll give it a try.'

The Feldwebel on the reception desk at Luftwaffe headquarters stood to attention when he saw Thomas walk into the room. A Knight's Cross was a passport to anywhere in Germany. It opened the door to the general's office like a magic key.

'Ah, it's you,' the general said. 'Want a transfer to our outfit?'

Thomas shook his head and smiled. 'No . . . the Herr General was kind enough . . . when we were in his aeroplane . . . to . . .'

'Jesus, come straight out with it,' the general guffawed. 'I stand by my word, even if I was drunk . . . on the subject of which . . .' He rummaged around in a desk drawer, fished out a bottle of cognac and poured large measures into two glasses. 'Cheers, my dear fellow!'

'Prost, Herr General!'

'So. What can I do for you?' the air force man asked with a comfortable smile.

Thomas gave him the number of his brother's squadron and the name of his air field in Sicily. 'I know you're a busy man, Herr General,' he said. 'But it's my parents . . .'

'No trouble. Won't take a minute.' The general pressed a button, and when a general presses a button it means that information can be found about any obscure airman or soldier, no matter how far away . . .

The general sat under a big portrait of Reich Marshal Goring. They wore the same uniform, but that was where the resemblance ended. The general had a thin face and a body like whipcord, and when he smiled there was none of the smugness and self-satisfaction of the fat Reich Marshal.

Thomas Kleebach sat opposite him. He had offered to withdraw while the general's underlings ferreted out the information, but the general would have none of it.

'Stay here, my dear fellow,' he said. 'It's a pleasure to sit with a combat man.' He smiled wryly and gestured at a folder that lay on the desk in front of him. 'Red tape, a load of shit! Production shortfalls, casualty figures, petrol shortages. Do you know what I really am? I'm no general,' he explained with a sour grimace. 'I'm a blasted official receiver, a liquidator of the Luftwaffe!'

He spoke to the young Leutnant as one soldier to another. In between they drank cognac, another glass and another, though it was still before mid-day. They drank not for pleasure, but to keep the war at bay.

An adjutant walked in and glanced at the general in a way that made it clear he wanted to talk to him alone.

'Just a moment,' the general growled. He pointed to the bottle. 'Help yourself, Kleebach, while I'm away.'

A minute later he came back and walked over to the window, where he stood for a while staring out, hands behind his back. Then he turned round. 'Kleebach,' he said, his voice heavy. 'You are a soldier and an officer, aren't you?'

'Yes, Herr General,' Thomas answered. The surface of his skin had gone cold as ice.

'It's a bastard of a thing to have to say, but I'm not one of these people who beats around the bush . . . Your brother is missing, Kleebach.'

'Missing?' Thomas echoed dully.

The general did not take his eyes off him. 'Have another cognac,' he said, and reached quickly for the bottle himself, as if he had just as great a need. 'It happened after a bomber mission over Malta . . . Engine on fire, down in the drink . . . Understand?'

'Yes, Herr General.'

'I'm sorry,' the other man said. 'Bloody sorry . . . not just for you or him, but for all those boys . . .'

'There's no hope?' Thomas whispered.

The general came over to him. From his face Thomas could see that red stripes and fancy epaulettes hadn't robbed this man of his humanity. He put his hands on the young Leutnant's shoulders.

'Jesus, Kleebach,' he said gently. 'Don't be a fool.' He let go and paced the room. 'Let's not gild our lily . . . Maybe the crew bought it during the shootout . . . Maybe when the plane hit the sea . . . but even if they had the devil's own luck, you have to imagine what it's like going down four hundred fathoms in a tin can like that . . . At that depth, the water's like cement . . .' He lit a cigarette with such violence that he had to strike a second match. 'And even if the wreck survived intact, you have to understand what the water pressure's like, pushing down and inwards . . . None of those poor buggers will have made it out . . .'

Thomas downed his cognac. 'So my brother Fritz must be considered . . . killed in action?' he asked.

'Missing, Kleebach,' the general retorted. 'Tell your parents that he's missing, for goodness' sake, no more than that. Everything else is just between us, all right?'

Kleebach nodded.

The general extended his hand. His grip as they shook was firm and sincere. In a moment he was going to have to turn back to those anonymous casualty reports, and maybe he was relieved. Better a hundred of nameless dead men than one whose brother stood in the room with him, the general thought bitterly. The calculation was in no way cynical, just necessary for his own sanity.

When Thomas was already at the door, the general called him back just once more. 'One more thing, Kleebach,' he said thoughtfully. 'I don't understand . . . the notification went off from your brother's unit three weeks ago, and was filed a week later with us. You should have been informed some time ago. That's not quite right . . . If nothing else works in our glorious Greater Germany, at least the post office is still operating.'

Thomas finally found himself out on the street, a street like any of the ones his father had trudged through a fortnight before after hearing the news about Fritz. He walked absently in the direction of Western Berlin, shoulders hunched, so preoccupied that he failed to notice people staring at his Knight's Cross and forgot to return soldiers' salutes. And he came to the same decision as his father had: that he would keep the worst of the news from his family, as the general had advised.

He went into a bar.

'You don't look too cheerful,' the owner said. 'But I'm honoured . . .' he added and poured Thomas a schnaps on the house. 'Leave almost over, eh?'

'Yes,' Thomas answered vaguely.

'Girl trouble?'

Thomas said nothing to that.

'Blimey, a chap like you! Don't let it get you down . . . go straight to it!' He jabbed a finger at the Knight's Cross. 'Just like you did when you got that!'

At last the bar owner realised that he wasn't going to get anywhere with Thomas. He poured him another double, then put the top carefully back on the schnaps bottle.

Far from clouding Thomas's mind, the schnaps seemed to sharpen his wits. He found that he could think clearly and precisely. 'Something's not right,' the general had said. Two weeks before? And why had his father changed so much since then? It was also true that his father was the one who delivered all their letters . . .

Suddenly he found his suspicions turning into certainties. It's nonsense, he told himself, but it did no good. After all, hadn't he been intending to keep quiet about the news? My God, he thought, and felt his spine tingle. 'Give me another schnaps!' he said, turning to the bar owner.

The good-natured man chuckled knowingly. 'Right you are,' he said. 'Now you'll have some lead in your pencil. You go and see that girl of yours and tell her hello from old Otto Schulze . . .'

Thomas drank up, paid and left. If he hurried he would be able to intercept his father on his morning round. He had to be sure, and if he was right he intended to make certain that his father didn't have to carry a terrible burden alone.

He walked quickly and met his father two streets from home.

'Hello, you stay-at-home!' Arthur Kleebach called out when he saw him. 'Finally decided to come out and see the world?'

'Yes,' Thomas muttered. 'I have to talk to you.'

'Now?'

'Yes.'

'Here?'

'Yes.'

'Three more, then I'm finished,' his father said.

Thomas did not leave his side. Father Kleebach felt fear growing. He knew something was about to happen, and he took his time in finishing his round. But finally he was ready.

They went into a small café.

'So what's wrong?' asked Arthur Kleebach, as casually as he could.

'I've just come from the Luftwaffe headquarters,' began Thomas.

'And?'

'Mother sent me there.' Thomas kept his eyes on his father.

'And why did she do that?' Arthur Kleebach said hoarsely.

'She wanted me to ask about Fritz.'

'I see.' His father stared into his coffee cup, then raised it to his lips, slowly and mechanically, spilling a little. It tasted like acid, like the cup of suffering.

'Father . . .' Thomas said. He was finding it hard. Arthur Kleebach stared at his eldest with agony in his eyes. 'Did you know?' Thomas asked.

'Yes.'

'And you didn't . . . pass on the news?'

'That's right.'

'Why?' Thomas asked, and immediately felt ashamed of the question.

Neither of them could meet the other's gaze. They looked at the dirty table cloth, the grubby curtains, the unwashed glasses, and at the soldiers in the corner, busy trying to drink themselves silly by lunchtime. Anywhere but at each other.

'More coffee, sir?' the waitress coaxed.

Neither of them seemed to hear her. She stomped off, complaining loudly to anyone who would listen: 'Big-heads! A few bits of tinsel on their jackets and they think they don't have to answer a civil question!'

'You know that your mother is very ill,' Arthur Kleebach said, quietly breaking the silence.

'Yes.'

'We have to protect her . . . do you understand that, my boy?'

'Yes, father.'

'At least as long as there's still . . . hope for Fritz,' he said wearily. 'After all, he's only been posted missing.'

'Just missing,' Thomas repeated in a broken voice.

The silence returned, a kind of complicity between the pair of them. Dying is nothing, Thomas thought sourly. You had to be able to lie as well. Maybe it was more important, more necessary. These days everything was lies: the whole war was a lie, from the slanted propaganda to the lyrical tributes to the dead, the cheap fanfares to victory . . . But the bastards who thought up those lies found the work easy. How difficult it was for himself and his father . . .

Arthur Kleebach looked imploringly at his son.

'Father,' Thomas said very softly. 'I understand you, believe me . . . But you can't do it, you won't get away with it, do you realise that?'

'No,' his father answered harshly.

'More than that, you can't destroy yourself like this . . . mother needs you more than ever now that we're all away from home.' He looked straight at his father and added firmly: 'You're going to kill yourself, and I won't let you.'

Arthur Kleebach returned Thomas's gaze, and his son felt a spurt of fear at the power of his eyes. It was like seeing someone for the first time. That power was fascinating, shattering, the massive energy of total despair.

'In a few minutes a special report from the battlefront,' the voice on the radio loudspeaker blared. The café's staff gathered round the set.

Father Kleebach got to his feet and tossed some money onto the table. Thomas followed him quickly. They made good their escape before the trumpets sounded for yet another 'special report'.

They walked side by side in silence. Suddenly father Kleebach stopped dead in his tracks. 'Are you going to tell mother?' he said challengingly. 'Can you bring yourself to do it?' The look he cast at Thomas was merciless, penetrating, brooked no excuses. The older man was conscious of his superiority, the fact that Thomas would have to give in.

'Thomas,' he said quietly, as if talking to a child. 'I hate lies . . . I brought you all up to do the same, and believe me it wasn't easy . . .'

They walked on slowly towards home.

'And today I ask you . . . beg you with all my heart . . . to lie, Thomas. As well as you are able, because you must . . .'

. Thomas looked straight ahead, impassive.

'You must lie like a professional,' his father said. 'Will you promise me that?'

Thomas made no answer. His father seized him by the arm. 'All right,' Thomas said reluctantly. At that moment he wished himself thousands of miles away from Berlin, in North Africa, right in the middle of the desert war, in hell among the filth and the blood. Anywhere but here.

The boat scudded over its entire length, sending out wide
All right, Bernd, he said, relieved. At last! Somewhere,
perhaps hundreds of miles away from them, in Heinz
Achim slept in the muddle of the heart was, in bed against the
hub and the blood. Anywhere but here.

CHAPTER SIX

From the south the scirocco breathed its scorching, enervating way over the Mediterranean. Over the choppy surface of the sea crept a shadow. It was night, and the U-boat scudded over the waves on half-power. It had reached the the agreed spot but there was no sign of the promised British convoy. The captain was busy on the radio, where he was hearing from base that there would be no wolf-pack attack tonight. The other three U-boats had been withdrawn.

'Operate as you see fit,' the Admiral ordered.

'Right,' the captain told his first officer of the watch. He was checking his position on the chart in his cabin: he was in the correct spot all right, which was just about the only part of this damned box of tricks that hadn't been fouled up.

'How are our shipwrecked heroes?' he asked.

'Dead to the world. They don't even know how lucky they were. Sleeping like babies . . .'

The captain nodded absently. 'Probably from Convoy A × 27. Not much to show, eh?'

Just then, Achim Kleebach, the Hitler Youth leader, came gradually back to consciousness. His head ached, his eyes wouldn't focus. It was like having the mother and father of all hangovers. His whole body trembled in time with the roll of the sea. He clawed himself upright with difficulty and realised that he was in a hammock hanging directly above a torpedo. The light was dim. Suddenly a sailor leaned over Achim, a man with a face the colour and texture of cured leather.

'Where . . .?' croaked Kleebach. 'What's going on?'

'You're in the clear,' the U-boat man said with a grin. 'Get some more sleep, mate!'

Achim felt pins and needles in his upper arms. His hands were balled into tight fists, so that he could hardly prise his fingers apart. Suddenly he was back hanging onto that lifebelt and fighting against the waves and the wind and against other men who were trying to pitch him into the sea . . . He was spitting salt water again, going blind with the effort – and he knew that not only his arms were seizing up but so was his mind.

He forced himself to sit up. He found that he could open up his right hand, and he stared dully at the swelling on its side . . . Now he was no longer on this U-boat but at a Hitler Youth camp in the forest, and the adult instructor was saying with a grin: 'A good clean chop with the side of your hand there . . . and the other fellow's out for the count.' The instructor had been right. Achim Kleebach knew it, because he had put his best friend out for the count . . .

His features were convulsed with the pain of it. Every muscle in his body ached. He would have gladly changed places with the man he had killed with a 'good clean chop', but now it was too late – for both of them.

A sailor put a flask of rum to his lips and Achim swallowed it greedily. The liquid ran out of the corners of his mouth and down his chest, and it tasted of blood. Achim spat out the blood, but he couldn't rid himself of that taste.

Four of the survivors were still alive. They had been dragged aboard and collapsed like wet bundles of rags. Scarcely one of them had still possessed the strength to realise that he had been saved. A Feldwebel died after being hauled from the water. After that the captain had ordered the others to be slapped around the face until they showed signs of life. Maybe he had been right, maybe wrong, but then a U-boat captain has to be a jack of all trades, from psychiatrist to engineer, from radio ham to surgeon.

The dead man was dropped back overboard and the other four were taken below. Achim Kleebach learned all that only now. Under any other circumstances he would have considered a trip on a U-boat as a treat, a thrill. Now, exhausted and wracked by self-loathing, he stared glassily into space.

Achim Kleebach glimpsed the captain coming through the hatchway, recognised him by his white cap, hauled himself clumsily to his feet and caught the back of his head sharply against the bulkhead. He stumbled straight into the young commander's arms.

'Take it easy,' he said with a laugh. 'You're not on the barrack-square now.'

'Yes, captain . . .'

'How are you?' the captain said. 'Feel up to coming onto the bridge?' He pointed to a bottle of schnaps. 'Take a mouthful of that, take a deep breath . . . Plenty of time to chew the fat later.'

Achim stared at the captain fixedly with wide-open eyes. Without realising it he had begun to hero-worship. Then he caught himself examining the naval officer's hand. It's not swollen, he thought bitterly, and you're a swine who'll never be a man like him . . .

'Had a hard time, eh?' the captain growled.

Kleebach nodded like a civilian. 'Pretty bad, captain. And what happens next?'

The officer smiled wolfishly. 'First you'll learn to swim . . . then how to fear.' He handed Achim a cigarette. 'Do you know who the other three are?' he said.

'No, captain.'

'Have a quiet smoke, then give us your personal details,' the officer said by way of conclusion. 'If we happen to end up near the North African coast, we'll drop you off . . . Otherwise you'll get a luxury cruise, free, gratis and for nothing . . .' He realised that Achim wanted to say something else and clapped him on the shoulder. 'Problem?' he asked.

'Captain,' the boy said hesitantly. 'My parents in Berlin . . . would it be possible . . . I mean, the radio . . . ?'

'No,' the officer said flatly. 'Love's a wonderful thing, but I'm not prepared to bring half the British Mediterranean fleet down on my neck for your sake, kid . . .'

Three days later, the young commander did just that. It had nothing to do with love, but with duty, or at least what he saw as his duty. He had spotted a lightly-guarded British convoy carrying tanks for Cairo. The big ships moved slowly, and the German U-boat followed them patiently, pursuing them for hours at a safe distance. The captain intended to go into the attack at twilight.

Half an hour to go. Tension built up aboard the submarine, a physical force humming through men's minds and bodies. The crewmen were lucky; they were at action stations, with instruments and weapons to check. The four 'tourists', as they had been nicknamed, could only cool their heels.

'Absolute silence on board!' the captain ordered. 'We're going into the attack!'

The order was superfluous. Even with the whine of the electric motors, every man there could hear his own breathing. Half-crouched, Achim leaned against the bulkhead and watched the torpedo from under his hammock being released and prepared for action. From then on he sensed fear creeping up his spine, paralysing him. Crew members had to dig him in the ribs to get him to move about.

'Don't piss in your pants, mate!' a sailor said, tossing him a life-saver.

'How does it work?' Achim asked shrilly.

'No time,' the man growled. 'Do what everyone else does . . . It's a load of crap, anyway . . . If a depth-charge gets us, the damned thing'll do you no good . . . and if we make it you won't need it.'

'Then why do we have it?' Achim yelled at the retreating sailor.

'To calm your nerves,' the man said, and carried on. 'Keep your trap shut now . . . think of that girl of yours at home!'

Achim had no girl. But fear made him obedient and pliable as a child, a child who's always promising to be better tomorrow . . .

On the bridge the attack was being prepared with icy precision. And below decks Achim Kleebach searched frantically through his eighteen-year-old soul for a girl. He rummaged desperately through his past. Not one girl . . . He had failed his first test, and it had cost his comrade his life. Now, at the second, no more than a bystander, there was terror in his face and shit in his pants.

A girl, he thought feverishly.

Yes, Irene at his dancing lessons. Before he had only seen her as a BdM* leader in a black skirt and a white blouse . . . and suddenly she was no longer a young Amazon but a seventeen-year-old beauty in built-up heels, in a dark,

* Translator's note: "League of German Girls". The female equivalent, the Hitler Youth

93

tight dress cut low at the neck, with lipstick on her mouth and expectant eyes. Irene. Soft and tempting.

And there he, Achim, had stood, wooden and clumsy. The worst dancer in the class.

'One, two, change,' the teacher said, tapping him in the chest. 'You must be supple, graceful!' he added. 'You're not stomping down the street now, you know; you're supposed to be gliding across the floor. Go on, and loosen those muscles! You're like a clockwork toy, boy!'

For the first time, Achim wasn't top of the class. He had always been the best, on the sports field, in school, at political education classes. He hated the dancing teacher for it, and he hated that girl Irene, who was smiling down at him so contemptuously. At that moment he hated everything that had nothing to do with the Party, and it was for the Party he wanted to live and, if need be, die . . .

'Torpedoes one to four go!' the captain ordered.

The torpedoes left their tubes with a gentle motion that scarcely disturbed the boat's motion. They hissed through the water towards the target, four at once, because the captain had decided to offload an entire tube.

'Fifty-five seconds to target,' a monotone voice announced.

Everyone stared at the control dial. The needle was leaping like a mountain goat. Soon there were ten seconds to go, ten seconds of life or death.

Achim noticed nothing. His features were contorted with terror, his whole body rigid. But he was talking to himself, as never before, and he was drawing Irene to him, brushing his lips against hers, feeling her breath in his nostrils, and a force was rising in him, so strong and fiery that he wanted to forget the Movement, the Party, and just stroke Irene's hair, betray his Fuhrer.

'A direct hit! Port side!' the voice bellowed, no longer so calm.

They all felt the shudder of the explosion, or at least believed they had. The captain nodded happily, but was not yet completely satisfied. He ordered the torpedo team to reload and called: 'Full speed ahead!'

He hung on to the convoy like a limpet, a tick on an ungainly animal's hide. He dived under a searching British frigate and came up in one piece. He saw one burning freighter packed with tanks go down, and he looked for the next one. The Tommies were zig-zagging wildly. He avoided them and lurked to one side. The next two torpedoes missed, but the third hit home and crippled another freighter.

More! The commander hunted the crippled convoy stubbornly all night and into the day. Come the daylight, the massive surface superiority of the British would start to tell, and the captain would have to think more about saving his hide than the luxury of more tonnage to his credit.

Four hours later the second freighter was finally sunk too, but the main part of the convoy had got away. The German U-boat had been hit by one of the escort destroyers, had dived to 400 feet, and was involved in desperate manoeuvres to survive the depth-charge attack that had to come.

The first exploded to starboard, but not deep enough. Between explosions it was quiet, deathly quiet . . . And during one of those pauses they heard a gentle clicking sound, as if tiny stones were being pitched against the steel hull. At that moment even the foul-mouthed sailor who had chewed Achim off reached for his life-saver.

'Holy mother,' he moaned. 'They've found us, the swine . . .' He gulped in a breath of air, the deepest breath Achim had ever seen a man take. He shut his eyes, but that didn't shut out the vision of what was happening on the surface, the two frigates and the destroyer, the hunters, above. He saw them cruising closer, heard the new depth-reading coming up on their sounding instruments, and knew they would be setting the charges to the right depth . . .

A hit to the right. The U-boat rocked to the left. Above. The boat dropped, so violently that a cable whipped down from the bulkhead and across Achim's shoulders.

'No!' the boy shrieked, and leapt to his feet. But he didn't get far. The force of the next explosion sent him flying left and he landed on top of a motionless crewman.

An explosion beneath them. The U-boat was punched back upwards and see-sawed violently in the water. Then came the next.

Finished. Silence. The chief engineer righted the boat, got it level at the second attempt. The crewmen stood up and stared at each other.

More clicking noises.

Second batch. The next wave. More depth-charges. How many of the goddamned things did they have on board? Enough for ten U-boats, and one would do ... A direct hit came, slicing through the outer skin. And then came the water, flooding, increasing all the time. Water. The victor, the bloody victor ...

Another explosion. A second later, Achim looked into the eyes of the sailor. The lids were twitching in time to the reverberations like flickering danger-signals.

Irene, Achim thought, and crouched small. Irene, he thought with a stubborn lust. In those few minutes on the hinge of fate he had recognised a yawning gap in his life that would never be bridged.

The next depth-charge exploded closer to the U-boat than any of the others, hurling the crew against each other like windfall apples in a storm. Heads cracked against the steel bulkheads. The lights went out. Someone screamed, another laughed hysterically, most of them stayed absolutely quiet. The U-boat men were aware that they had survived even this latest onslaught.

But Achim Kleebach had no such experience. He was out of control, insane with fear, and he wanted out. Out of this prison that would take him down with it, tear him apart.

He howled and screamed, lashed out wildly, lost his life-saver. He couldn't even think of Irene any more. Five, six sets of fists pummelled him to the ground.

It was the end for him. He let his head sink between his hands and he thought of his mother. That was when the remnants of his reason went. He jumped up again. 'Let me out of here!' he whimpered. 'I want to live!' He tripped over a torpedo. 'Mother!' he yelled. 'Gerd is dead ...'

The next charge struck towards the stern. Another miss, but it threw the boat around and sent Achim hurtling against the sailor. Achim saw those predator's lips and the wild eyes, and his hands, searching for a hold, clamped like a trap and closed round the throat of the sailor, who punched wildly in self-defence.

'Mother,' Achim moaned. 'Mother. And Gerd ...'

The next explosion threw the sailor and Achim apart. From now on the Hitler Youth boy cowered on the deck, whining like a tiny baby. Gone the courage he had sought so proudly, gone all rational awareness, with madness approaching, he waited for the next depth-charge, and the next, the explosions that would go on for ever . . .

It was a grey day, and the station was grimy. The air hung thick with soot; people wiped flecks out of their eyes like tears. A drunk bellowed at the ticket collector. Two military policemen checked the papers of a young private. A stray dog ran by, without a document to his name, and stood idly in front of a freight car from which bags of field post were being unloaded. Fate, weighed up and sorted by the bundle.

Nearby a soldier climbed into a carriage, returning to the front of his own free will because his wife had betrayed him with another man. A few yards away an officer returning home threw himself into his mother's arms. A young couple, at the end of their honeymoon, wandered silently along the platform. And between them a man wearing a red cap prepared to blow his whistles and send another leave train into the great world outside.

This was the everyday stuff of war: trains arriving, trains leaving – only people were always there . . .

Panzer Leutnant Thomas Kleebach leaned out of the window of his compartment. Luise stood on the platform between his parents. He had asked all three of them to stay at home, but they had insisted on coming: his mother because she wanted to stay with him until the last moment, his father because he could not leave his wife, and Luise because she had something else to say to him.

Thomas looked at his watch. They were a minute late already, and because of those tearful, never-ending sixty seconds he hated the station master, the guard, the driver, the entire damned state railways system.

His mother came up to the window. She was trying to speak, but all she could do was cry. To the watching Thomas it seemed as if her eyes were more glazed, her hair greyer than ever before.

'Come back, my boy,' she said, like a prayer.

'Of course I will,' he answered quickly.

His mother nodded.

'It'll take me a fortnight to get back to my unit,' Thomas

said with forced jollity. 'By the time I arrive down there in Africa, the war will be over.'

'It seems to be going full swing,' said his father, then looked away.

Thomas had met his eye for just a second. Then his father had avoided contact. To his shame, the young officer was relieved to have the last few days of his leave behind him. He knew that his father had started a lie that would break the man – and there was nothing he could do about it.

His mother waved, and she and Arthur Kleebach moved back two or three paces. Now Thomas had only Luise to contend with. She was beautiful and pale, sad and self-controlled in a pretty, tight-fitting dress and jacket. At that moment Thomas would have been prepared to leap the tragic, invisible barrier between them, forget the patch that had stayed on the wall when she had removed the picture of her dead husband.

'I love you . . .' Luise murmured softly, to four men at once, for three other soldiers were fighting to get space at the window behind Thomas to wave one last farewell to their close ones.

'Lu . . . ise,' he answered, moved, overwhelmed.

Then the whistle blew. The train juddered and was moving laboriously. Another bump and a shudder. The couplings clanked together, the wheels began to turn, and sparks showered gently onto the station platform. Thomas gripped the edge of the window so tightly that his knuckles turned as white as his mother's face. He saw her, then Luise, then his father, three faces that stayed with him until they were tiny featureless blobs and the train was racing . . .

Thomas slammed the window and turned away. His eyes met those of the other three soldiers in the compartment. No one said anything.

The Kleebach parents did not speak for several minutes.

'Luise,' Maria said then, with infinite tenderness. 'Are you fond of our Thomas, despite everything?'

'Much more than that,' the young woman answered simply.

'He must come back,' Frau Kleebach said, as if to herself.

Luise took her arm gently and steered her back through the station. The father walked behind the two women, nodding as he went, as if still telling himself what a fine man his eldest boy had turned into. He didn't know whether to feel relief or anxiety. To the last he had feared that Thomas might break his promise. Now that problem was out of the way, he was overwhelmed by another fear that made the first seem insignificant and selfish. Come back, he thought, and even as the words ran through his mind he knew that there were hundreds around praying in the same way – prayers that for many, he knew, would be in vain.

Thomas sat in the train compartment staring blankly into space, a veil over his eyes, his feelings. Underneath the expressionless face, the frosty calm, something was boiling within him, so fiercely that it seemed it would burst. His old dislike for war had turned into a raging hate that infected him down to his every pore. It made him strong and unreasoning, and it would need some outlet if it wasn't to choke him. Gerd dead, he thought. Fritz missing. His mother with a weak heart. His father imprisoned in a lie. He on the way back to the front, and Achim already on transfer somewhere . . . and all because of the ancient slogan, the wisdom of the armchair warrior that had been beaten into them at school, screamed at them from loudspeakers: 'Praise be to what makes us hard!'

Praised be what makes an end of this, he rephrased it in his mind. What makes an end of this damned war . . .

A day's stopover in Rome. On to Naples. A wait for a troop transporter. Then again a stroke of what some might call luck: a lift in a Ju 52, and a smooth flight over. Safe landing in North Africa, with a Kubelwagen standing ready to take the Leutnant to his unit.

General Rommel was impatiently at work on his offensive. The desert war needed men like Kleebach, needed men and equipment, crazy, lost characters, the damned and the death-happy. The desert was hot, and between the sand hills the blood evaporated quickly, very quickly.

Two days after leaving Berlin, Thomas Kleebach reached his unit. So far as his men were concerned, he was the same man they respected, though there were those who suspected that he had changed. He shook each of them by the hand, had a word for everyone before he moved on to the next.

'Major von Klingenstein bought it,' the Feldwebel told him. 'He didn't even get a chance to smoke his English cigarettes.'

'Pity.'

'Oberleutnant Hammer is dead, too.'

'Not quite such a pity . . . and otherwise?'

'In all, four officers and twenty-seven other ranks dead,' the Feldwebel growled. 'Fourteen wounded.'

'Reinforcements?'

'Eight panzers and forty men.'

'And where are they?' asked Kleebach.

'At the bottom of the Mediterranean,' the N.C.O. said bitterly. 'The whole frigging issue. All that arrived was the transfer papers.'

Thomas Kleebach shrugged and slouched off to his make-shift command-post. A new offensive, he mused. What was the point? If they captured Tobruk, they'd have to have Cairo, after Cairo, Damascus, and maybe after that Tehran . . . two steps forward, one step back, two steps . . . The only victors would be the sores on their feet, the malaria in their blood, and the jackals out there in the desert . . .

Then he sat at his desk and stared into space, thinking of his parents, of Luise, and he told himself that he would write to them today. If he was lucky, his little sign of life wouldn't get lost in the great and glorious chaos of the offensive.

'Here,' announced the Feldwebel, who had followed Kleebach to the command post. He slapped a wad of papers down on the desk. 'Our proud reinforcements . . . God help 'em . . .'

Thomas grunted. 'And what happens now?'

'There's another convoy due out of Naples. Maybe it'll get through.'

'And if not,' Kleebach growled, 'then I suppose we start making bows and arrows.'

The Feldwebel thought for a moment, wracking his brains for a way of cheering up the Leutnant's homecoming, then remembered and clapped himself on the forehead. 'Jesus, Herr Leutnant,' he boomed. 'We kept a couple of captured bottles of whisky for you.'

'Bring it here!' answered Thomas. He might not be a great drinker under usual circumstances, but these were not usual. He lit a cigarette and stared at the pile of papers in front of him, the documents that were everything that remained of forty soldiers. He felt panic as he pondered whether he would be responsible for writing to the families of those forty men, then decided that the navy must be.

God, didn't one of them survive?

He leafed quickly through the names. Names, nothing but names, meaningless to him, eighteen-year-olds fresh from basic training, boys he had never clapped eyes on. Ah, here was a veteran, an old man of nineteen. 'Pfeiffer,' he read absently, then 'Bergmann', 'Huber', 'Müller', 'Triebenbach', 'Kuntze', 'Obermaier', then . . .

He was reading his own name: Kleebach . . . K for kitchen, L for louse, E for egg, egg again, B for Bertha, A for Anton, C for Caesar, H for . . . No more spelling out.

It was then that he realised that his youngest brother, Achim, had gone down with the transporter . . .

His cigarette burned his index finger; he did not feel it. Slowly, with the heaviness born of despair, he got to his feet. He stumbled over to the window like a sleepwalker and saw three soldiers silhouetted against the wall of a tent, playing skat.

'Nothing to show,' one said.

No, nothing, thought the Leutnant, and turned back, shoulders hunched, his face pale and empty. For a few crazy moments he looked at his pistol holster and wondered whether it wouldn't be so much better, so much easier, if . . .

He took hold of the chair for support and saw the whisky. He tore the cap from the bottle like a farmer wringing a chicken's neck and gulped greedily at the stale-tasting, luke-warm liquid. He stopped, stared at the label. *White Horse*. Then he tipped the whole lot down his throat, and suddenly he could hear ghostly voices in his brain, singing louder and louder, crazier by the moment, an old folk song he had heard once when they were all together on a family outing: 'At the White Horse Inn on the Wolfgangsee . . . At the White Horse Inn on the Wolfgangsee . . .'

By the time he had finished the first bottle, what had been a quartet had turned into a hideous, booming choir of millions, millions of men without faces . . .

He was sprawled on his camp bed, hands behind his head, with the second bottle open beside him, when the Feldwebel entered and reported: 'The new commander has arrived, Herr Leutnant . . . Major von Klingenstein's replacement. I request the Herr Leutnant's orders . . .'

Kleebach nodded gravely. 'The new . . . the comman –

commandant . . . is to . . . give my kindest regards to General Lommel . . . Rommel . . . And . . .' he stood up and took a few unsteady steps round the tent. 'The new password is . . . is . . . Heil Hitler!'

The Feldwebel grinned from ear to ear.

Leutnant Kleebach stopped in front of the official photograph of the Fuhrer on the wall of the tent, and there was nothing very flattering in the look he gave his commander-in-chief. In fact, if the man had been there himself in the flesh, instead of on cheap paper, the magazine of Kleebach's service pistol would have been empty in about three seconds flat.

'Ah . . . Herr Leutnant,' the Feldwebel said carefully. 'What do you want me to report to the new commanding officer?'

Thomas gave the matter some thought. 'Tell him,' he said then. 'That I am drunk as a skunk.' He lay himself back on his camp bed with his face to the wall . . .

It took five minutes after the explosion of the last depth charge for the U-boat crewmen to be sure that the attack was finally over. They got hesitantly to their feet and looked round as if they were seeing each other for the first time. When another fifteen minutes had passed without incident, the captain had some music put on the p.a. and handed out rations of rum.

The men felt the heat down below. Their lungs filled deep with stale air. But they didn't smell the sweat and the oil and the shit; to them it was as sweet as the first breath of spring.

This grey wolf of the sea had been blessed with something more important than all the courage and devotion to duty in the world: luck. The U-boat had escaped from the trap. Again. One more time . . .

The cigarettes tasted good again, and tongues no longer felt like dried-out leathers. The sailor who had stumbled into Achim Kleebach laid his life-saver contemptuously away again, and the Hitler Youth leader started to rehearse the story of his miraculous salvation, ready to tell his parents every . . . well, almost every . . . detail. He was so glad to be alive that he could no longer even feel the swelling on his hand.

The U-boat was out of the worst. From now on there was no more talk of attack, just of escape. The captain was a sly fox and a tough operator. He calculated that the British would be looking for him in the northern theatre of operations and so he sloped off on a southerly course.

The steel shark surfaced at nightfall. Suddenly the air smelled of land, of a coast nearby. The commander saw his chance of getting rid of the four burdensome 'tourists', that quartet of hungry mouths, and decided to put them ashore in a rubber dinghy. He hugged the coast and studied it with his telescope. The night was misty and cold, and his farewell to the four of them was short and to the point.

'Okay, you heroes,' the captain said, shaking each by the hand. He had broken radio silence to report his action; so close to the large military concentrations on land, there was little chance of him betraying his boat.

The captain tried to hurry things along, but there were still delays, since most of the crewmen wanted to send letters to home via the four lucky survivors.

Then it got under way, and everything went quickly. Achim stood with his comrades on the soil of Africa for the first time, heard his first jackal bark, and felt the chill of the desert night. The captain had given them rough directions, and so they followed the route into the night. Somewhere, sometime later, they stumbled across two men on guard duty, and recognised German helmets.

'Hey, mate!' Achim yelled.

The soldier whipped round, his machine-pistol at the ready.

The four of them ran towards him with wide-open arms. They ended up being herded over to the command post with hands above their heads. The officer of the watch, who had no intention of taking any risks, reported their arrival to the Military Police. The M.P.s who turned up to fetch them treated them as, at the least, deserters, if not enemy saboteurs.

One more interrogation, and the four of them were in the clear. While they were finishing their explanations, the U-boat's message had been decoded, confirming everything. A transport officer took them over then. 'Aha,' he said sardonically. 'The reinforcements from Convoy A × 27. The general will pinch himself to see if he's dreaming.'

The four survivors were rewarded with new kit and forty-eight hours' leave in the headquarters zone.

The story of their rescue had travelled the rounds and given them a degree of fame. After all, sinkings were commonplace, but you rarely met survivors. They had to shake hundreds of hands, drink dozens of glasses of schnaps. The temporary glory of those few days cured Achim Kleebach of any stupid, morbid thoughts of morality. He was a great man, everyone he met told him so. He didn't think of the swelling on his hand at all.

He knew nothing of Africa, but he thought that he cut a dash in the khaki uniform. And everything else was a revelation. He saw soldiers saluting officers in the most unbelievably sloppy fashion and not getting chewed out. He saw men sunbathing in their Kubelwagens, heard no N.C.O.s' whistles, no recruits eating sand, and he was impressed – even though discipline was perhaps a little too lax for his taste . . .

His most joyous find, though, was the bathing beach, which he didn't discover until the second day. Half the rear head-quarters was sand by the sea, under a blazing sky, just like those idyllic postcards from the Mediterranean. Achim wanted to go off to the left, but the other three were hanging around the entrance to the right-hand side. Their reasons were pretty soon clear: three girls in flesh-revealing swimsuits were lying sunning themselves on the sand, as if this wasn't the North African theatre of war but the Cote d'Azur.

The four of them stalked the girls cautiously.

'Must be female Wehrmacht auxiliaries,' said one.

'Officers only,' growled Achim knowingly.

'But I bet they know what it's for.'

They had the whole day ahead of them, the sand was hot, the water heavy with salt. Achim allowed the waves to carry him, and this time he needed no life-belt. He dived and surfaced, floated on his back and let the warm waves splash over him. He stayed longer in the water than the others, and did not hear them shouting from the beach.

Then he became aware of a disturbance in the water and saw one of the three girls, the redhead, surface just by him. He smiled at her, flopped over and swam off in pursuit. Achim had always been embarrassed with girls, but being in the water made things easier. He could always duck under when words failed him.

He was maybe a couple of metres behind her.

The redhead turned nonchalantly, without breaking her stroke. 'Do you want something?' she asked.

'No,' he answered.

She laughed. 'Then why are you hanging on to me like a limpet?'

'Because . . . because . . .'

She started to swim back towards the beach, and he followed her. They reached the shallows together and stood up. The girl's swimsuit clung to her firm, high-breasted body like a second skin. She stripped off her bathing-cap and shook her long hair free. To Achim Kleebach she was a dream, like nothing he had ever seen before, sensual and . . . almost animal. The girl stood with her hands on her hips and looked at him in amusement. 'You like what you see?' she said.

'Yes,' was all he could say. Suddenly he realised that he was afraid.

'I can see that.' She cast an eye over his pale skin and asked: 'You haven't been here long, have you?'

'No,' the Hitler Youth leader answered. 'Actually . . . I just landed from a U-boat . . .'

'Really?' the girl said. 'I haven't heard that one before.'

'Yes. From that hell . . . and this paradise here . . . I can't believe it.'

'Take it easy, little warrior,' she said, made to go, then lingered just long enough.

Achim drank in the envious looks of the other three, and it gave him the courage. He'd show them. 'May I . . . accompany you?' he asked stiffly.

'Do you always ask so many questions?'

'No . . . yes . . . Are you from the army, too?'

'No, the Luftwaffe,' the redhead said. This boy was fun, in a naïve sort of way. She was ten years or so older than he, and she had been long enough with the forces to know her way around. She had so many officers hanging around that it was getting slightly tedious.

On the beach she sat down on her towel. Achim, uncertain what to do, stood over her.

'Come on,' said the redhead.

He sat in the sand.

She giggled. 'No, not there . . . on the towel, hero of the fatherland.'

'Thank you,' he mumbled nervously and moved forward until he was perched on the outermost edge.

'Not much experience with women, I see?'

'Almost . . . almost none,' Achim admitted, and could feel himself blushing.'

'Well, there's a time for everything,' the Luftwaffe auxiliary said with a laugh.

'Would you perhaps be willing to help me out?' he said.

She pouted teasingly. 'That depends.'

'Depends on what?'

'On what you've got to offer.'

'Try me . . .' Achim said, suddenly bold.

'Perhaps,' she answered, and lay back on the towel.

She shut her eyes against the sun. Achim made his way forward slowly, inch by inch; she noticed him, and smiled. He touched her arm, quivering with anxious excitement.

'You won't get far that way, young man,' the redhead countered coolly.

She saw her two friends approaching, shaking their heads in disapproval.

'Makes a change,' the redhead grinned, and signalled to the other two Luftwaffe girls to disappear.

For Achim, the next hour was a dream, and in the evening it turned into a fairytale fantasy. The girl was at a loose end, just as he was. And she knew all the bars, and all the other possibilities in the headquarters zone.

After dinner they switched to the familiar 'du' when they talked, after a kiss to seal the friendship. The kiss turned Achim hot and cold, and it gave the readhead, Ingrid, a foretaste that she clearly wanted to follow with a main dish. Then they began to drink. The Hitler Youth leader moderately, she like an old hand.

Then, suddenly, it was night, and she snuggled close to him, because she was cold. And then they stood, wondering what happened next, and Ingrid suggested that they go back to her place. Maybe it wasn't even her place, but Achim asked no questions. He had been hot right from the start, and the drink had brought him to fever-pitch.

'Sit down,' she told him when they got to her room. She fiddled with the dial of the radio.

'Yes,' he said. 'Imagine ... the way that tanker went up ... three hundred feet in the air when the torpedo hit ...'

'Come on, give it a rest!'

He sat in silence for a moment, tongue-tied. 'It's good to be with you,' he said then. 'But after all, we can't forget the war entirely ...'

The Luftwaffe girl said nothing, just lay down on the couch with a glass in her hand, humming gently to herself. He looked into his own glass and said: 'Imagine, my brother's got a Knight's Cross ... and I'm joining his unit ...'

'Sure. Very nice.'

'I'll get myself an Iron Cross First Class, you can bet on it.'

'Not tonight, you won't,' the readhead said sarcastically. 'Here, come and sit beside me ...'

Achim obeyed like a dog on a lead. 'I'm not going to be outdone by Thomas,' he continued. 'You're doing your duty, too ... like the Führer who leads our struggle ...'

'Leave all that crap,' Ingrid pouted. She took his hand and led it gently over the contours of her face until the fingers were resting on her full lips. She noticed that he didn't know what to do next, and she smiled, then squirmed close to him. He asked her if she had a boyfriend.

'No,' she said. 'I've been saving myself up for you.'

'I'm all alone, too,' he answered.

'God, you're like nobody else I've ever met,' the girl said with feeling. She sat up slightly, took a swig from her glass, then lay back again, enjoying his fumbling hands and excited panting of his breath. He was staring at her legs now. Well, they weren't that bad, she told herself.

Achim unbuttoned his tunic, and she drew him down on top of her. She felt him freeze up, and decided this was starting to be a bore.

'What exactly do you get up to here?' Achim began again.

'Hot days, cold nights,' she answered. 'And when a boy like you turns up, I think to myself that I'd rather be down at the registry office, making a good girl of myself ...'

He kissed her forehead, her eyes, her neck, great fawning eyes looking down on her. She was the most beautiful woman he had ever seen. The problem was that he hadn't known any others. He asked himself what his mother would say if he brought home a girl years older than himself and decided that she would understand, because she always did. He could feel a nervous sickness in the pit of his stomach, and thought fleetingly: any minute now I'm going to feel a slap from that dancing teacher . . .

'I . . . I love you,' Achim said. At last.

Ingrid smiled.

'Believe me,' he assured her.

She nodded.

'Even though I'm just an ordinary soldier,' he went on. 'But I'll make something of myself, I'll prove I'm the right material . . . first the Iron Cross, and then in a year or so I'll get a commission . . .'

'That's a long time to wait for a bit of fun,' the readhead said, gazing ironically up towards heaven.

'You now. Then . . . you know . . . as a real man, as an old soldier . . . as a National Socialist . . .'

The Luftwaffe girl had suddenly had enough. She shoved the boy off her and sat up, eyes blazing with contempt. 'I'll tell *you* something,' she snarled. 'Clear off out of here!'

He stood looking at her vacantly.

'Well, what are you waiting for?' she asked coldly.

Achim obeyed, not even staying long enough to button up his tunic. Cursing, he walked round in circles for hours, terrified that he would meet the other three somewhere.

He had only been a soldier for four months, but he knew what kind of a story he had to make up for his mates in the morning . . .

The Kleebach parents were on their way home from the cinema. The film had been enjoyable enough, but Arthur Kleebach had spent most of the time casting sidelong glances at his wife. He had known that he had to take her mind off things, and so he had exerted gentle pressure until she had agreed on this evening out.

Now they were heading home, back to the worries and cares. By the time they got to the corner of Wielandstrasse and Lietzenburgerstrasse they could both feel things closing in on them again. For weeks now the likeable postman had known that Fritz was posted missing, and no letters had come. The lies had had to get bigger and more convincing, the hopes had become fainter.

They met the Ortsgruppenleiter in front of the house. He looked tired and drawn, and his jovial greeting had an air of hollowness.

'I'm glad to have caught you,' he said. 'I have a request . . .'

'Let's not stand out on the street,' Frau Kleebach suggested politely. 'Do come up to the apartment, Herr Rosenblatt.'

They walked up together. 'The situation is that we're holding a social for wounded soldiers,' the official explained when they were sat down in the living room. 'If you have a book you don't need, or something else that would make a present . . .'

Mother Kleebach thought for a while. Thomas had left a few packets of cigarettes behind when he had gone back from his leave, so that his parents could barter them for provisions. But now, of course, they were all alone, and they were all right for food, and surely her eldest son would have approved the cigarettes going to the wounded.

She gave him a packet.

'Oh,' said Party Comrade Rosenblatt. 'Cigarettes. Twenty, and English at that . . .'

'My son captured them in North Africa,' father Kleebach explained. He offered the official one from an opened pack.

Rosenblatt smoked appreciatively. 'They taste good,' he said. 'Once the war's over, we won't be smoking this "special mixture" stuff any more . . .' He was so eager to enjoy the cigarette that he swallowed some smoke and went into a short fit of coughing. 'And how is life otherwise, Frau Kleebach?' he asked then with smooth professional concern.

'Well,' she answered. 'You know how it is . . . when you have four boys away at the war . . .'

Arthur Kleebach froze. He turned away and stared out of the window, unable to look for a moment.

'Three have written lately,' Maria continued with a sad smile. 'But we haven't heard from Fritz for weeks now.'

The Ortsgruppenleiter looked at her strangely.

'Fritz?' he said. 'Is that the flier?'

'But of course . . .'

'But he's the one who . . .' Rosenblatt's gaze flitted over to Arthur Kleebach. The father was desperately signalling to the bemused official.

The silence was tense, unreal. A few seconds. A few

heartbeats. And only one of the three in the room knew what it was really about. It was all over, Arthur Kleebach thought; any minute now the lie he had created to protect the woman he loved would be exploded . . . Suddenly he felt a terrible emptiness, the emptiness of a beaten man.

'Oh yes,' Maria Kleebach said quietly to Party Comrade Rosenblatt. 'You must know our Fritz?' She smiled painfully. 'We're the only people who could tell him apart from Gerd . . . they were so alike . . . and we haven't heard from him for six weeks now . . . no letters, not a single line . . .'

She fell silent and looked down at the carpet. Rosenblatt cleared his throat uncomfortably. He caught Arthur Kleebach's eye and slowly began to understand the conspiratorial gestures, the harshness in the man's manner. Their eyes met for a few seconds, and Kleebach nodded. He knew that the moment of danger had passed, and that Rosenblatt was not going to betray him.

'Wait a minute,' Arthur Kleebach said in a taut voice. 'If it's for our boys at the front . . .' He spoke with difficulty, almost panting with the effort. 'I've got a couple of cigars somewhere . . .'

He went to a small table in the corner, found a pack with three in it and handed over the cigars to the Ortsgruppenleiter. Rosenblatt paled as he took them, like a nervous housebreaker, and smiled foolishly. He knew that Kleebach was trying to change the subject.

'And I must talk to you about something, Ortsgruppenleiter,' Kleebach said quickly. 'Maria,' he asked with a forced jollity. 'How about making us a quick cup of coffee?'

Even she could see by now that something was amiss. She gazed at him oddly but without reproach. Maria was not a suspicious woman, but she was sensitive enough to recognise the strange tension that seemed to afflict her husband more and more lately. 'Of course,' she said simply, and disappeared into the kitchen.

The two men waited until the door was shut behind her.

'You . . .' Party Comrade Rosenblatt began angrily.

'Not here,' Kleebach snapped. 'Please,' he added in a whisper.

'So your wife knows nothing about the fact that he's been posted missing?'

110

Arthur Kleebach nodded.

'I can't tolerate that,' the Ortsgruppenleiter said. 'Most irregular . . .' He couldn't bear to look the other man in the eye.

'I'm asking you to.'

The official nodded mechanically. He was as eager to postpone the evil hour as Kleebach. The pair of them sat in tense silence, drank real coffee, a rare delicacy in wartime, but neither of them was in the mood to appreciate it.

'Mother,' Arthur Kleebach announced afterwards. 'I'm going to walk with Herr Rosenblatt for a bit . . . I need a little fresh air . . .' He hurried the official out of the apartment without waiting for an answer.

On the stairs Rosenblatt's self-pity boiled up into anger. 'I won't tolerate this under any circumstances,' he barked.

'Psst!' answered Kleebach.

Rosenblatt continued regardless. 'I am responsible for the correct communication of news of missing members of the Wehrmacht,' he said primly.

'Well, you gave me the news in the correct way.'

'Good heavens, Kleebach,' Rosenblatt retorted when they reached the street. 'Be reasonable . . . I have to face the women, mothers, relatives, every day.' His voice rose to a shrill squeak. 'Do you think I enjoy it?' he moaned. 'No,' he added, supplying his own answer. 'It is a duty . . . a duty that I wish would go to blazes!'

They walked side by side. Their shapes were swallowed up in the darkness, occasionally given ghostly life by the dim light of the emergency lamps that were the only guide in the blackout.

'If you can't bring yourself to tell her, I'll do it,' Rosenblatt said.

Arthur Kleebach made no answer.

'As gently as possible,' the official added.

'No,' Kleebach retorted. 'Fritz has only been posted missing . . . There is still hope. Maybe I am clutching at straws, but at least give me a chance.'

'Missing,' the Ortsgruppenleiter echoed miserably, shaking his head. He had been intending to be hard with this man, but once again he couldn't bear to meet his gaze.

Kleebach continued. 'Two angina attacks in one week not so long ago . . . I know how things are with Maria, and I will not allow anyone to . . .'

Rosenblatt's hand was fiddling with his tie as if it were a noose around his neck. 'Kleebach,' he cut in. 'You can't go on like this. It's not possible . . . One day your wife will find out, and then . . .'

Silence again.

'Have you no human feelings?' Kleebach said.

'I can't help you . . . I shall have to report the matter . . .'

They stood staring at each other in the dull light, the mist of an autumn night. The light was enough for Rosenblatt to feel terror, because he could see the hard glint of fanaticism in Kleebach's face. This man was prepared to countenance anything to get what he wanted, without thought of the consequences.

'Give me time!' Kleebach growled threateningly.

The Ortsgruppenleiter hung his head in despair. Once he had been an official of a great, pulsating political movement; now he was no more than a herald of misery. Even 'final victory' had become a matter almost of indifference to him. He had begun secretly to hate the 'glorious era,' which he had once believed in. 'Kleebach,' he stuttered. 'I'll give you three weeks. But this must stay between us alone. If you let a word of it out to anyone else, then I'm finished . . .'

Kleebach nodded. Three weeks, he thought. Three weeks! He savoured it; it was as sweet to him as a stay of execution for a murderer. In truth what he had achieved was miserable enough, but he could not help feeling a warm glow of gratitude as he shook Rosenblatt by the hand.

He walked back to the apartment block quickly and with purpose, but he did not go upstairs. Instead, he stood in the yard and looked around cautiously. No one was in sight, and so he made his way to what had been the garage, which he had fitted out as a workshop. It was his hobby to tinker and make things. For some days now, though, he had been tinkering with something quite terrifying: he had been practising copying his son's handwriting . . . He had spent his time shaping letters and sentences in Fritz's style, spelling out the thoughts and desires of a son he knew in his heart must be dead. He knew too that this was sacrilege, but he pushed the thought out of his mind. Whenever doubts came, all he could see in his mind's eye was Maria's sad face when he came home from his round empty-handed. Lately he had seen her waiting at the window, watching, seeing from the way he came home whether there was anything from Fritz today . . .

Arthur Kleebach sat behind a locked door at a joiner's bench with an old school book of Fritz's open beside him, checking letters and practising forging them. He had improved his version of the capital 'R'; the sweep of the 'P' was still faulty – there was a youthful impetuousness in it that he could not wholly imitate. But Kleebach had been using every free moment to practise, and by now he felt he was good enough to make up a convincing fake.

Now he had a sheet of writing-paper in front of him and was tracing out a whole letter: 'My dear parents . . . I have just come back from a mission. Everything went well, and I'm still a little tense, so I hope you will excuse my bad handwriting. I shall write you a proper letter soon, but for the moment please put up with these few lines, just to show that you need not worry about your son . . .'

Arthur Kleebach could feel a sickness in the pit of his stomach; he fought to keep his hand from shaking. The letters seemed to blur together in the flickering candle light. He rubbed his eyes, then checked over what he had written before adding: 'In my thoughts I am always with you, and I shall be back soon. Your Fritz.'

The 'letter' was finished. And so was Arthur Kleebach. His head sank slowly into his hands, and at last he allowed himself the luxury of crying, weeping in great spasms. He waited a few minutes afterwards until the tears had gone, wiped his face, and then went to Maria.

He spent the next morning in a state of feverish tension. He finished his round fifteen minutes earlier than usual. He had practised what had to come next a hundred times.

Maria was watching him from the window, and Arthur Kleebach waved to her from a distance. He hurried up the stairs and saw her waiting at the open door of the apartment, with an incredulous smile on her face.

'Yes,' he panted. 'I've already opened the letter . . .'

Maria took the folded sheet, and as she read her hands were shaking. Kleebach stood with his arm round her shoulders, gazing at her anxiously. But she was much too happy to be suspicious. She read the letter again and again, while the lunch

113

burned on the stove, and he stood beside her, paralysed by the enormity of what he had done.

But when he looked at the tears of joy in Maria's eyes, he knew that he had been right, sacrilege or not . . .

CHAPTER SEVEN

Panzer Leutnant Thomas Kleebach reported to his new commander, and his first glance told him that they were not going to get on. Major Schreyvogel looked like a giant hacked out of stone; he spoke in clipped sentences, and what he said was larded with political slogans. The reputation which had come on ahead of him was that he had been an official of the Hitler Youth and a disciplinarian – both rare qualities in Rommel's army.

'So. You are the hero of the regiment?' the new commander greeted him with a twisted smile.

'As the Herr Major wishes,' Leutnant Kleebach answered coolly.

'Kindly leave off this addressing superiors in the third person,' Major Schreyvogel snapped. 'In my outfit we'll have none of that feudal crap, understood?'

'Yes, Herr Major.'

The commander lit up without offering Thomas a cigarette. He looked him up and down, and feasted his eyes on the Knight's Cross. It seemed to cause him some disturbance. 'Of course, I've got nothing against officers who earn their rank through guts,' he said. 'But I'm not sure whether you have enough experience to lead a company.' He exhaled some smoke, and it was like a spit in the eye. 'Don't misunderstand me, Kleebach . . . I'd be the last to detract from the glory of what you did . . . But I have been considering whether it might not be a good idea for me to send you to officers' academy for tactical training . . .'

Thomas Kleebach smiled with something close to pity for the man. 'Herr Major,' he answered slowly. 'The tactics needed in this war can't be learned at any academy.'

Major Schreyvogel snorted. 'I see,' he said acidly. 'You supped in wisdom with your mother's milk, did you?'

An ordinance officer brought in a folder of paperwork. The commander simply left Kleebach standing in front of him while he read through the documents. It was some time before he lifted his head and looked at him again. 'Eight or ten days and the balloon's going to go up here ... It goes without saying that I expect my outfit to be the first to march into Cairo.'

'Yes, Herr Major,' Kleebach answered tersely, and thought: cretin! He thought of the barriers between here and Cairo, of Sollum, Tobruk, the fortifications at El Alamein. He thought of the vast distances, the thousand-mile supply-lines. And he knew that this novice would run out of bravado at about the same time as he ran out of petrol.

'Until something happens, keep your people busy!' Schreyvogel ordered. 'They must not get soft ... tell me, what do you actually do with your company?'

'If there's nothing going on, the usual ... occupational therapy, Herr Major.'

'No such thing in an outfit of mine,' Schreyvogel snarled. 'Nobody takes it easy, gentlemen! Drill! Training! Hard graft!' He paused for breath, then added: 'And along with that, some theoretical education ... the Party's programme, the Jewish question, and so on ... Kleebach, I expect to report what you're doing in that direction!'

'Yes, Herr Major,' Kleebach answered, stood to attention and ducked out of the tent, fighting to suppress his loathing.

He drove his own Kubelwagen back to where his company was camped. The Feldwebel greeted him with a wry smile.

'Well, how was it?' he asked.

'If he carries on at the front the same way he behaves here, he won't live to draw his pension,' Kleebach said grimly.

'We live in hope,' retorted the Feldwebel.

'I didn't hear that.'

'I know, sir.'

Then he took the Leutnant aside and led him over to where the carefully-camouflaged new panzers were waiting, like packages under the Christmas tree.

'Any replacement crews on the way? Or do these things drive themselves?' Kleebach asked.

116

'There's a truckload of reinforcements on their way ... forty-two men. Straight from the barrel, you might say, or rather from the training-camp.'

'Good,' said Kleebach. 'Send me the new boys ... one by one.'

He went to his tent and waited. It was his way to welcome each recruit to the company individually, size every man up and get to know his face. This time, Thomas was going through the trivial routine with exaggerated care, because he needed to give himself a diversion. He didn't want to think of Gerd, or Fritz, or Achim, or of his parents, who were slowly being bled of their children ...

He was glad when the first ones arrived, shook each by the hand, had a private word with every one, and took his time. The seventh man he met stuck out in some way; he was a big boy with dark hair and sad eyes.

'Private Trautmann,' he reported.

'Take a seat,' said the Leutnant, and busied himself with the man's papers. 'I see you've been a soldier for four years and you're still a private?'

'Yes, Herr Leutnant.'

'Come on,' Thomas said with a laugh. 'Don't be afraid to speak ... Had a hard time from somebody?'

Private Trautmann said nothing, just stared at the floor. There was something tormented about the man.

'So what's the problem?'

Trautmann took a deep breath. 'My mother is Jewish.'

'Oh,' Thomas said, appalled. He had wandered over to the entrance of the tent while the conversation was going on. Now he stared out at the sand, wondering what to say next.

'As a half-Jew I cannot win promotion, Herr Leutnant,' Trautmann said.

Thomas turned round quickly. 'There are no half-Jews in my company,' he growled. 'Only soldiers ... got that?'

'Yes, sir.'

'So we'll keep it to ourselves,' Kleebach said, and reached out to shake the recruit's hand. 'It's no one else's business.'

Trautmann stood up and saluted. Kleebach gestured for him to be dismissed. The man's eyes were like those of a whipped dog . . . He cursed thoroughly, took a swallow of schnaps, and called for the next one. He was still rummaging through the papers on his desk, with his back to the entrance, when the next entered, grinning.

'Gunner Achim Kleebach!' he bellowed.

Thomas span round, and for a few moments he stared at the arrival in complete disbelief, unable to credit that this wasn't a dream or a desert mirage.

'Jesus,' he croaked. Then he went over to the boy and threw his arms around him, holding him so tight that he felt as though he must be hurting him. He took a step back. 'You . . .' he said.

'A slight detour,' Achim chuckled. 'First we got sunk . . . then came a U-boat attack . . . a spot of leave – terrific girl, I'll tell you – and here I am . . .'

Leutnant Kleebach stuck his head out of the tent and told the others to clear off for a while. The Feldwebel had, in fact, known all along that his brother was among the new recruits, and had co-operated in giving the Leutnant a surprise.

Thomas turned back and saw that his brother was looking at him almost ecstatically. 'What's up?' he asked with a laugh.

'The . . . the Knight's Cross . . .' Achim said, overcome with admiration. 'You of all people . . . I mean, you've wiped away the dishonour.'

'What dishonour?'

Achim smiled. 'Come on, it's forgiven and forgotten.'

'Look, what are you actually talking about?'

The boy lowered his voice. 'You know . . . all those years ago . . . Your time with the Red youth movement . . .'

'I see.' Thomas looked away and shrugged slowly.

Then Achim told him all about how he had secured a transfer to his brother's unit, and when he had finished he said: 'I don't want you to treat me any differently to the others . . . and I ask you to give me a chance to prove myself as soon as possible . . . maybe a raiding-party or something . . .'

Thomas frowned. Now that he had got over the first delight at seeing his brother alive, he realised that this situation placed a terrible responsibility on his shoulders. He could see his mother's face, hear her words: 'I can rely on you, Thomas, can't I? You'll look after my youngest. I'm so glad he's under your wing . . .'

Thomas poured out two glasses of schnaps and handed one to Achim, his face solemn, almost sad.

Achim noticed it and asked, 'What's the problem?'

'Fritz has been reported missing,' Thomas answered heavily, looking him straight in the eye.

'Fritz?' Achim said. Suddenly his young face was pale with fear, and his breath came in short gasps.

'Yes. Mother doesn't know it yet. Father is keeping it from her.'

'My God,' the boy murmured. 'That's terrible.'

Thomas nodded drily.

'But, I mean, when the first pain is gone, when she's had time to think about it, mother can at least be proud . . .' Achim stuttered.

'Proud of what?' asked Thomas, in a voice that could have sawn through glass.

'Well, that he bravely . . .'

'Idiot!'

'Our patriotic struggle . . .'

'Shut your trap!'

Achim's face was flushed with anger. 'That's not the spirit that won you your Knight's Cross!' he whined.

'Get out of my sight!'

'Thomas,' Achim said coaxingly. 'The thing with Fritz hurts me too . . . but it's not just a matter of one of us . . .'

'What is it then?'

'Well, what's important is the whole . . . the Führer and Greater Germany.'

'You won't get far with that shit in my company,' Thomas answered coldly. Then he clapped the boy on the shoulder. 'We'll talk more tonight. I must get on with seeing the others . . .'

'Very well, Herr Leutnant,' Achim barked, drawing himself to attention.

Thomas watched his younger brother march away with mixed feelings. He was glad to have the boy with him, but he was also grimly determined to turn this automaton into a human being, a creature of flesh and blood, and above all with an ability to think for himself . . .

* * *

During those early months of 1941, the Afrika Korps still looked like a paper army, a convenient fiction to comfort the Italians for the loss of their North African empire, a gesture of German good will. The battle for North Africa seemed over. The Italians had lost time, territory, whole armies, and vital sources of drinking water so essential to desert warfare. General Wavell's British forces stood on the Syrte river, drawing breath before the final push to Tripoli that would throw the last Italian into the Mediterranean Sea. It would be a matter of days, it seemed.

Hitler could not spare substantial forces, but he wanted to give the *Duce* some sign of his friendship, and so he sent a young, untried general and two incomplete divisions. On 12th February 1941 General Rommel landed in Tripoli and realised the full extent of the disaster. A trained tactician would have been content to hold the city and wait for reinforcements. Rommel, however, was no cautious theoretician. He was gifted and he was ambitious, and he decided there and then that he would throw the British out of Cyrenaica.

As far as the British were concerned, the Afrika Korps was at first no more than a trivial rumour. Then the German commander brought a secret weapon into play: bluff. A column of panzers, anti-aircraft guns and motor-cycle units set out along the Via Balbia, the solitary tarred road along the coast, heading towards the old Turkish fort of El Agheila. Armoured infantry units secured the right flank, while to the left the British saw only a huge panzer column that Rommel seemed to have spirited out of the empty desert like a magician. By the time the British saw through the trick, Agheila had fallen, and the gate to Tripolitania had become Germany's springboard into Cyrenaica – and Egypt. German reinforcements poured along the 800-kilometre long coast road, the *Littoreana*. The British, who had been forced to send their élite units to Greece, saw themselves confronted with a German offensive of serious proportions, largely because of Rommel's inspired deception.

They poured back towards Egypt. A British general issued an order of the day in which he told his men that the Germans were no supermen; it didn't stop the panic, as General Gambier-Parry found out ten days later when he was taken prisoner by the same Germans.

Rommel, the Desert Fox, had soon become a legend to friend and foe alike. He harried the fleeing Tommies like all the hounds of hell, and told his men: 'Keep close to the enemy and make a lot of dust, boys. Dust saves ammunition . . .'

He drove on without waiting for reinforcements, living from hand to mouth, until Argedabia fell, where there were huge stocks of weapons, vehicles, ammunition, food and water that the English had had no time to destroy. The Desert Fox chased blindly on, and the enemy retreated in terror. In order to win a decisive victory in Cyrenaica, he had to drive from Agedabia over the Musus and through the desert to Mechilli, a 300-kilometre stretch where there was only thirst for company. He had no reliable maps, there were no natural features to guide him, and the Italians who had lived there as colonists told him that it was impossible. But like Hannibal, who crossed the Alps in ancient times, Rommel and his army broke through to Tmimi, while a simultaneous German attack from Benghazi came up the coast.

Kleebach's unit was the spearhead of the 21st Panzer Division. They drove by compass and luck, without a tree or a blade of grass in sight, just occasional deserted mud huts. The air was like boiling soup. They rode on through the Dschebel wind, through sandstorms. Thomas Kleebach's panzer was the first to roll through the pass towards Mechilli . . .

On April 8th, after a short, bloody battle, Mechilli fell, along with huge quantities of captured matériel. The highland region of Barce was now in German hands, clearing the way into eastern Marmarica.

Onward. The lightning victories followed each other: on April 9th, Bardia; on April 13th, Sollum. The British launched massive counter-attacks, but the Afrika Korps rolled relentlessly on. They stormed towards Tobruk and met their first setback. Rommel had underestimated the defensive capacity of the fortress, which could be supplied by the British from the sea.

Though Tobruk remained in British hands, the Afrika Korps stood almost at the Egyptian border. Kleebach's panzer company had always been in the vanguard, always in the thick of the fighting, often way ahead of the German thrust, rolling, blasting, day and night. They got to the Halfaya pass covered in glory, with the loss of eleven men. Now that the war of movement had turned into a grim, bloody slogging-match, the Panzer troops had some leisure. They were put into reserve as a 'fire brigade' to counter any surprise enemy attacks. Leutnant Thomas Kleebach commanded more captured enemy vehicles than German-made ones; he had petrol, cigarettes and cans of provisions, and above all he had the satisfied feeling of having brought his boys through the worst without serious loss. So far.

His unit had leaguered behind the bizarre barbed-wire barrier that ran the length of the Egyptian border, originally put up by the Italians as a defence against bands of Bedouin brigands that operated across the frontier. Today at dawn, two captured scout cars were to be sent through a gap in the wire on a reconnaissance mission. And even before Kleebach could ask for volunteers, his own brother, Achim, had reported for the mission.

Thomas hesitated. Then he shrugged resignedly.

Four a.m. The sun would soon be rising, and the Leutnant said his farewells to his men. Achim was due to travel in Trautmann's vehicle, a heavy captured British monster on which only the badge had been changed. Private Trautmann, now an experienced driver, knew its ways well, and Unteroffizier Ehrlich – motto: 'Ehrlich can keep it up till the Tommies go home' – was the company's most seasoned patrol-leader.

'Ready?' Thomas asked.

Ehrlich nodded, tossed his cigarette to the ground and carefully kicked sand over it. The Leutnant shook him by the hand, and they looked at each other for a moment, neither saying a word. They understood each other anyway: there was a silent plea in the company commander's face for his brother to come back safely. Kleebach clapped Achim on the shoulder.

'Good hunting,' he said.

'No sweat,' grinned Achim.

Thomas Kleebach gazed after the two vehicles and shook his head. Their mission was in some ways contrary to the usual rules of desert warfare; it could be easy or it could kill them all, depending on what they met out there. The first vehicle rolled off to the left, Trautmann's armoured scout car to the right in a miles-long arc that should bring them together again at their target, then back again by the shortest, quickest route.

They went through the gap in the wire still under cover of darkness. The company commander stared at the horizon, waiting. No sound. No sudden eruption of enemy flares. The start, at least, had gone off safely, he decided with relief. According to yesterday's air reconnaissance reports, the area they were due to patrol was clear of the enemy, though British radio traffic during the night indicated that the enemy was moving troops up. It could be a sign that the long-awaited British offensive was in preparation; Rommel, too, was marshalling his forces, and it could only be a matter of days before one side or the other made their move.

Suddenly the sun exploded above the horizon, bathing the pale sand in its light. Daylight brought heat and thirst. Achim leaned sleepily on his machine-gun. The excitement he had felt when they had started out had turned into weary boredom. The Hitler Youth leader had been through his first campaign without seeing much action. But he had seen enough to know that it was different to be part of a formation attacking an enemy in the open to cowering on the deck of a packed troop-transporter being shot down like a defenceless dog. It was better, too, than sitting in a U-boat, a helpless spectator to convoy warfare. Better than counting depth charges, waiting for the next to tear the fragile shell of the boat apart . . . Here in the desert he had a vehicle to ride in and a weapon in his hand. And right at this moment, drunk with the feel of victory and inexperienced enough to enjoy it to the full, Achim felt ready to take on the whole British Army.

'Where are the bastards, then?' he asked gruffly.

'You'll see 'em soon enough,' said Unteroffizier Ehrlich.

Trautmann kept himself to himself, gazing with intense concentration at the featureless sand, trying to distinguish thorn bushes from flak positions.

'There!' Achim said, and waved wildly at the heat-haze. He saw dark flecks, and began to count them off out loud.

The Unteroffizier by his side just laughed contemptuously. 'The heat's getting to you, boy,' he said, tapping his forehead. He handed Achim a bottle of lukewarm tea. 'Have a sip of that. That'll take a load off your mind.'

Ehrlich yawned, despite the pep pills he had taken before they set out. He had a bad feeling. They had been under way for two hours or more, heading straight through enemy-held territory, and they hadn't seen a single Tommy. That, he knew, meant that they must have passed maybe dozens of British forward positions without realising it.

'Deeper into the shit,' he muttered.

'What?' Achim asked lazily.

'Nothing.' Ehrlich glanced at Trautmann, who nodded acknowledgment.

Maybe they've mistaken us for Tommies, Ehrlich thought, searching for comfort. No wonder: they were in a captured enemy vehicle, a situation that was common in this war and sometimes deadly. The Afrika Korps often used British vehicles, and both sides' soldiers wore khaki shorts. Even pretty close up, it was hard to tell a flat Tommy helmet from a German one. All right by me, mused Unteroffizier Ehrlich. But somehow he couldn't shake off that vague gut feeling that something was about to go terribly wrong . . .

Five kilometres to go to the rendezvous. The scout car moved out in a sharp curve to the left again, its engine screaming, wheels chewing the drifting sand. Achim was thrown about the cab, but he managed to doze with his eyes open. In his day dream he saw his brother Thomas handing him an Iron Cross, the decoration that would be his passport to all the girls he could handle on his next leave. It was time he got himself a girl or two, after all. Fair or dark, or maybe redhead? It didn't matter, he decided. Main thing was that she had all the right equipment.

Driver Trautmann had more than just good eyesight; he possessed instinct. And so he started to drive more slowly. Ehrlich noticed it, said nothing, but kept a sharp lookout through the windscreen. Within seconds he recognised the British infantry position beyond the dunes, but before he could give any orders Trautmann was already driving straight at it. If they have armour-piercing artillery, we've had it, thought Ehrlich dimly.

Then Ehrlich's 200 mm cannon was spraying shells among the Tommies. Achim froze for a moment, then whirled his machine-gun round, aiming into the trenches. He saw an enemy infantryman rise to throw a grenade and cut him down with a short burst.

The British were firing back, but their rifles could make no impression on the scout car's heavy armour. Achim crouched in the steel shelter, laughing crazily.

The whole massacre lasted no more than sixty seconds. Just before they reached the infantry position, Trautmann wrenched the wheel round and took the scout car side-on to the trenches, giving his comrades a perfect field of fire. All Achim and the Unteroffizier had to do was keep shooting, pouring death among the near-defenceless Tommies. Achim saw twitching, writhing figures, staring, fear-crazed eyes, saw men fall like squirming live ninepins. Every shot a winner. The enemy had no chance, maybe a few seconds to prepare for death. A few lost their nerve and leapt out of their trenches.

'Poor bastards,' muttered Ehrlich, and mowed them down. His face was pale with disgust at the business of death. If only they could defend themselves, he thought, anything but just sit there and be slaughtered like cattle. He saw one raise his head too far above the sand and pulled off a quick shot. No problem. He was grateful that he couldn't see the results of his handiwork because of the billowing smoke drifting across the position.

Eighty metres to go. Another jumped up and pulled the pin from a hand grenade. Achim caught him before he could throw it; a seam of machine-gun bullets sliced the Tommy to the ground, where he kicked like a doll and lay still. The grenade exploded in the British trench. Another four or five dead, Achim calculated wildly. The laughter had gone from him. He was biting his lips until the blood ran. He could smell blood, feel the machine-gun growing moist in his hands. He saw men's last terrors, their last, desperate desire to live, but he carried on sowing death, killing in bulk, by rote, and stopped only when, to his horror, he found himself shooting at men who had their hands raised in surrender . . .

The scout car reached the other side of the British position.

'Right. Let's get out of here!' Ehrlich bawled.

Trautmann ground the gears down until the din drowned the roar of the engine, and the vehicle shot away. Suddenly Achim felt drained and miserable. He had never seen death from so close-up. Until then, shooting had been an anonymous thing, a mechanical exercise, but now he dared not turn round and look at what they had just left. A dozen men, at the most, could have survived the rain of death on the Tommy trenches.

'Home!' Ehrlich roared. Orders carried out, he thought, and now we piss back to camp double-quick.

They didn't get far.

There were shapes on the shimmering horizon, squat, dark flecks travelling from precisely the direction they had to take to reach their own lines. Ehrlich and Trautmann both realised what they were: not thorn bushes this time, or tricks of the light, or. mirages, but six or eight British tanks, probably summoned by radio by the infantrymen who had survived the one-sided battle.

Only Achim, the Hitler Youth boy, had not yet noticed the sudden danger. He was sitting with his head on his chest by his machine-gun and staring at his hands. They were shaking. The boy was struggling to put the thought out of his mind that those hands had just killed or maimed twenty or thirty of his fellow human beings. He had set out this day to beat the enemy, to deal death – but not to see that death from close quarters, the blood, the torn sinews and the guts and the fear in those crazed, inhuman, pleading faces.

Trautmann braked so sharply that the scout car skidded in the sand, hurling Achim upright and over against the armour plating. The driver slammed into reverse gear and stepped on the accelerator to take them away from the threatening shapes closing in from the distance. The wheels span a few times, then suddenly bit the sand, and the armoured car shot back so abruptly that Achim was thrown sideways, this time cracking his head against another part of the steel shell. Trautmann did a half-circle, then changed into forward gear, making the vehicle scream like a wounded animal. Then all they could do was go hell for leather and wait – for the flashes on the horizon, the shells, the shrapnel, the deadly spurts in the sand. If the Tommies had seen them – they had probably been sent hunting after the German patrol – then the scout car's only chance was to use its speed.

Nothing happened.

Unteroffizier Ehrlich expelled all the breath from his lungs in a long sigh that was like a locomotive letting off steam. 'That's that . . .' he growled.

The scout car had been forced to take a completely new course and instead of heading home they were moving in the opposite direction, deep into enemy territory. Ehrlich didn't doubt that the Tommies would be looking for them, searching for a needle in their haystack. But needles had it all going for them, he thought bitterly, because they could bury themselves in the sand, away from the anti-tank guns.

'What's the petrol situation?' he asked, glancing at the fuel gauge.

'We might make it,' Private Trautmann said, without much optimism in his voice.

'Then head left!' the patrol commander ordered.

Trautmann made a sour face, then hauled the wheel round and drove with shoulders hunched. He knew just as well as Ehrlich that they were taking a big risk by passing the enemy tanks side-on.

They were sweaty with tension. The heat seemed to take all the air out of their lungs. Their eyes were red with sand-dust.

Still nothing happened. Unteroffizier Ehrlich gripped the 200 mm cannon with both hands and bounced in time with the engine as if he were trying to urge the scout car on like an old horse. Trautmann crouched over his steering wheel, back arched, while the boy Achim knew that same fear he had felt back in the U-boat, the fear of the helpless victim . . . And then, just when it looked as though they had made it, all hell broke loose.

Guns spat flame on the horizon. Four, five shells exploded in front of the scout car, which pitched up on two wheels, dropped down again and rolled on uncertainly. More explosions. A hit on the turret. Trautmann accelerated. More . . . maybe the worst was over . . .

'Stupid bastards!' Ehrlich yelled, getting to his feet, while the vehicle careened wildly towards a British anti-tank gun. He saw it too late. The first shell exploded five yards behind them, the second scored a direct hit up top, hurling Ehrlich on top of the boy with tremendous force. Achim pushed him away and scrambled up.

Trautmann drove like a man possessed. He zig-zagged at full

speed in a weird race where the prize was life or death.

A shell detonating to their left almost bowled the scout car over. The next bounced the front wheels up, making the vehicle rear like a frightened horse before a fence.

Trautmann swung left, then sharp right, ducking among the shells. He seemed nerveless, a driving machine, and he was taking them through the lethal anti-tank fire like a master – or the luckiest man alive . . .

Achim Kleebach was to realise that afterwards, but for the moment he was staring slack-jawed at Unteroffizier Ehrlich. A piece of shrapnel had torn open an artery in the N.C.O.'s neck, and now it was pumping blood in spurts to the beat of Ehrlich's heart. His tunic was crimson with fresh lifeblood, and there was nausea rising in Achim's gorge. He croaked: 'Stop! What do I do?'

The driver didn't hear him. Trautmann was drawing on his last reserves of strength and concentration to drag them out of the jaws of death. They had covered another few hundred yards when, without turning his head, he bellowed: 'Bandage him up!'

'He's bleeding all over me!' the boy whined. Then, finally, he took out his first aid kit and gingerly wound a bandage round the wounded man's neck. Within seconds it was seeped in blood.

'Stop!' Achim yelled desperately.

The anti-tank fire was falling short of them now. Trautmann slowed down for a moment and looked at Ehrlich over one shoulder. The N.C.O.'s lips were twitching feebly, his eyes were great saucers of suffering. 'Leave it . . . I'm a goner . . .' Ehrlich whispered.

'But we can't just . . .' Achim said.

'You can make a report to the Führer,' Trautmann retorted acidly and spat out into the sand.

The shattered scout car picked up speed again.

Achim had taken the dying Unteroffizier in his arms. His last bandage was already bloody beyond use. He saw blood pouring onto his own tunic and gently layed Ehrlich away. He watched the N.C.O.'s struggle against death, noticing how the features seemed to dissolve in on themselves. Then his nostrils told him that fear had reached Ehrlich's bowels . . . Achim crawled as far away as he could and made himself small, which was good, because the enemy tanks had come close again and the first shell tore away the turret like a hat blown away by the wind.

Trautmann forced the scout car on for another few yards, until another shell hit the engine. He saw the flames, slammed on the brakes and screamed: 'Out!'

He took time out to give the terror-stricken Achim a smack in the ribs, then leapt full length out onto the sand. Achim followed him blindly, rolled, smashed his leg against something and hobbled up into a crouch. He couldn't run.

Trautmann saw him, ran back two yards, heaved him up onto one shoulder and stumbled away from the vehicle. Just in time he hit the sand, dragging Achim with him. Another second and the petrol tank went up, with a roar of exploding fuel and a shower of tiny, white-hot fragments of metal.

The Tommies had seen the explosion. They rolled cautiously towards the burning wreck, while Trautmann desperately dragged Achim farther away, hauling him under the arm-pits like a sack of coal. Perhaps the British didn't see them, or maybe they let them go, knowing that two wounded men alone in this desert would die of heat and thirst and be food for the hyenas before the next sun rose.

By the time the first Mark II had reached the site, Trautmann and Achim had collapsed in a heap four or five hundred yards away.

'My foot . . .' the Hitler Youth leader whimpered. 'And I'm so thirsty . . .'

Trautmann turned round to see if the British were after them. Then he nodded. They were being left alone.

Achim's terror slowly subsided, and he began to be able to think again. 'What . . . what happens now?' he asked.

'We die of thirst,' the driver said coldly.

Achim gazed at the water bottle dangling from his comrade's belt and his eyes became greedy.

'Where's yours?' Trautmann said.

'In . . . in the vehicle . . . Give me some . . .'

'Later.'

They could hear the sound of engines starting up again. The British tanks were heading off, and the pair of them were alone in the arid wilderness and the sand dunes. Not a tree, not a branch, not a suspicion of shade. Nothing but sand, thirst, sun, flies, and hundreds of scarab beetles, crawling all round them . . . Not another human being, even an enemy, and their minds dulled by the heat, imagining mirages, strange noises to their left, right, behind – including the cruel sound of water, cool, flowing water . . .

Ehrlich was lucky, Achim Kleebach thought. At that moment he envied the Unteroffizier his quick death. He forced himself to stand.

'Here,' Trautmann said, handing him the water bottle. 'Two swallows each.'

The Hitler Youth leader nodded. He gulped eagerly at the precious liquid. He had taken four swallows when the other man prised the bottle out of his hands.

'How long can we hold out for?' Achim moaned thickly.

'We'll make it through the night, probably. Another twenty-four hours, and you can kiss your arse goodbye.'

'Don't leave me,' Achim pleaded. 'My foot . . .'

'I won't. Don't worry,' Trautmann said. He took two carefully-measured gulps out of the bottle, carefully put the stopper back and shook it to gauge how much they had left. Half-full.

'You're a real mate,' Achim said. 'If you weren't, you'd . . .'

'Don't give me that crap,' Trautmann growled, close to anger.

They went off into a shallow sleep, a sleep wild with bad dreams. But Trautmann awoke to a droning noise, blinked and saw a shadow in the sky. Shade, he thought longingly, and then realised that it was a Fieseler Storch light plane, and that it was circling over the wreckage of the scout car. He saw his chance, stood, collapsed, succeeded the second time, and waved his arms crazily. For a moment it seemed as if the silver shadow was preparing to fly off, but then he saw that the crew had spotted him. But he still waved crazily, waved and waved until he crashed unconscious into the sand . . .

Panzer Leutnant Thomas Kleebach lay sprawled on the burning sand. There was shade aplenty, as much water as he could want, but for two hours now he had known that the patrol was overdue, and he didn't give a damn about the heat. Achim was out there, he thought, filled with self-loathing, and he could do nothing about it. The crews of the two patrol vehicles would be prisoners of the British if they were lucky, and if not they would die of thirst in the boundless sea of sand.

He had asked the crew of a short-range reconnaissance plane to keep an eye out for his lost men, without daring to hope too much. He had finally forced himself to lie on the sand after wandering through the camp aimlessly. Whenever he had come across a group of men from his company, all conversation had ceased. He knew what that meant: they too had given up hope.

'Herr Leutnant!'

Thomas sat up and saw a signals private loping across the sand towards him clutching a piece of paper.

'A report from the Fieseler Storch!' the man panted, handing him the paper.

Thomas grabbed it. It gave precise co-ordinates, and from that moment on he acted like a machine, cold-blooded and without feeling. Two columns of trucks were sent off to the right and the left, with orders to trace arcs in the desert and kick up as much dust as possible. With luck, the British would mistake them for panzer squadrons and would move in to investigate in strength. The moment they made contact with the enemy the trucks were to pull back and make their way to another spot to repeat the charade. Thomas Kleebach himself took two Kubelwagen jeeps and drove straight through the middle, powering towards the position that the reconnaissance plane had given him.

Leutnant Kleebach acted on his own initiative, without consulting his commander. He would have done exactly the same even if his own brother had not been among the missing men, but that wasn't something he could bear to think about at this moment.

They raced through the desert, driving by compass mark, not bothering to look left or right. Kleebach did his own navigating. They went on for two hours, hearing firing behind, as expected. Please God no casualties from the diversion, he thought, keeping his eyes glued to his field glasses. Shimmering heat. Endless nothing. And finally – luck . . .

The Leutnant tore off his binoculars and gave them to someone else to take a look, just in case he had been mistaken. The driver stepped on the gas.

Thomas leapt from the moving Kubelwagen, sprinted over and recognised Trautmann and Achim unconscious on the sand. Both of them would never know anything about their rescue from first hand. He ordered the second Kubelwagen to go and search the wreck of the scout car. They recovered the corpse of Unteroffizier Ehrlich, which had been hurled thirty yards by the force of the explosion.

He returned to his company during the late afternoon. They had lost only one captured truck, which had developed engine trouble and had to be left behind, plus two wounded, who were glad to be heading for home.

The two men they had rescued recovered quickly. Trautmann awoke to see the smiling face of his commander. The driver took water in moderate amounts, and insisted on pausing between swallows.

'Get some rest,' Thomas told him. Trautmann was experienced, knew not to overload his parched system. The driver wanted to submit a report there and then, but Thomas refused. 'Later,' he said.

He went off to his tent and found the battalion commander waiting for him with a face like thunder.

'What the hell's been going on here?' bellowed Major Schreyvogel.

Thomas did not flinch. 'Two men were posted missing, then located. I ordered them to be brought back to our lines, Herr Major.'

'And for that you send in half a frigging company?'

'Volunteers only, Herr Major . . .'

'And without consulting me at any point?' the major spluttered.

'Everything depended on speed,' Leutnant Kleebach answered coolly. 'Would you have had me leave them to rot?'

Schreyvogel's anger seemed to have given way to a dangerous calm. He stared venomously at the junior officer. 'We shall discuss this some other time,' he said, and stormed out of the tent.

Thomas watched him go, smiling and unconcerned. For the first time since God knows when, he had got a kick out of this war today. He could feel pleasure and relief in him like a physical release.

Then Trautmann insisted on reporting.

'Back on your pins already?' Thomas asked.

'Yes, Herr Leutnant.' Trautmann gave a thorough description of the disaster that had befallen the reconnaissance party.

'And Gunner Kleebach?' Thomas enquired with a grin.

'He hurt his foot while escaping from the vehicle,' Trautmann answered. He said nothing about how he had risked his own life by dragging Achim away from the burning scout car, but Thomas could see that something of that kind had happened.

'And how was he during the rest of the action?'

Trautmann smiled sourly. 'Well, you know,' he said at last. 'He hasn't seen much before now . . . still a bit wet behind the ears . . .'

'I see,' the Leutnant commented solemnly. 'Without you, he . . .'

'We were lucky,' Trautmann interrupted. 'And so were you, sir.'

Thomas took a couple of steps towards him, his face suddenly serious and concerned. 'Trautmann, have you had any letters from home?' he asked.

'Yes, sir,' said the driver flatly, but his eyes were evasive, almost fearful.

'Everything all right?'

'Yes, Herr Leutnant.'

'Your mother as well?' Thomas probed carefully.

'Yes,' answered the driver, fighting to keep himself under control. As a 'half-aryan' he was forced to die for a system that persecuted his mother. History would see it as a bitter irony. To this man, now, it was a double measure of suffering.

Trautmann's and the officer's eyes met for a long moment, and the look they exchanged said more than any words could. Kleebach could see the conflict within this brave soldier, and he knew that even if Trautmann survived the desert bloodbath he would never know if he had a mother to go home to at the end.

'Go and get some kip,' Thomas said wearily. 'You are excused duties until further notice.'

'Yes, Herr Leutnant,' said Trautmann mechanically, but there was something distant in his eyes still, and it was several moments before he collected himself sufficiently to salute and leave.

An hour later, Achim reported to his brother.

Thomas smiled, but it did not quite reach his eyes. 'Here,' he murmured and tossed a letter onto the desk between them. 'From home . . . read it first . . .' Then he left his brother alone with their mother's letter for a moment.

When Thomas came back into the tent, Achim had finished reading. 'I can see things are no picnic at home, either,' he said.

Thomas nodded. 'Would have been even worse if things had gone wrong today . . .'

'It wasn't that bad,' Achim retorted cockily.

Thomas stared at him with ill-concealed contempt. 'I can see you haven't learnt much.'

'What do you mean?' snapped the boy.

'You still don't know what it's all about.'

'It's all about victory!'

Thomas Kleebach shrugged. He could have pressed on, but he was still too relieved that his brother had survived to give in to anger.

Achim, though, had no intention of leaving it at that. 'How many missions do you have to complete with your outfit before you get the Iron Cross Second Class?' he asked aggressively.

'Get yourself some rest and keep your mouth shut!' Thomas grated.

'I'm not tired.'

'Is that so?' Thomas said slowly. 'You're still fresh . . . fine. I'm glad you don't feel the need to rest, because everyone else involved in today's business does.' He walked up to Achim until their faces were inches apart and continued: 'In that case, you can get a shovel and prepare a hole for us to put Unteroffizier Ehrlich in . . .'

'Very well, Herr Leutnant,' the Hitler Youth leader gulped. He crept out of the tent with his tail between his legs. That swine of a brother, he thought, had given him the order so as to put the fear of God into him . . . Well, dear Thomas would get a surprise or two before this war was over . . . a cruel surprise or two . . .

For now, however, the cruel surprise was on Achim. The corpse of Unteroffizier Ehrlich was lying on the sand covered by a tarpaulin, and it was some time before the boy could summon the courage to touch it.

When he did, the dead man was not a pretty or a romantic sight. Ehrlich's right arm had been torn off by the explosion; the face had begun to turn black, and the upper lip curled back so that the teeth were exposed in a hideous grin. Swarms of flies buzzed around the body, and as Achim stood staring down at the dead man there was a moment when he really felt fear that one day it could be him lying in the sand . . . He saw the left eye, still open, and it seemed to be staring at him with a feverish fierceness, as giving a final warning, a warning from a dead friend. Achim would have liked to have run, but he forced himself to stay and ducked to rummage under the corpse's tunic for Ehrlich's identity disc.

His fingers touched cold flesh and the warm metal of the tag. Achim fought back nausea, and his hatred for Thomas gave him the strength to break the tag from its chain, though he had to shut his eyes as he did it, and not open them again until he had slipped the flat metal identity disc into his pocket like a stolen five-mark piece.

'Give it to me,' said Thomas, who had come up behind him to watch.

Achim obeyed as if in a dream. The Leutnant looked calmly down at the dead man. 'One of the best,' he said. 'Doesn't look too nice now, eh?'

'No,' the boy said through clenched teeth.

Thomas nodded.

'One dumb stray shell,' he continued, as if he were discussing the weather. 'And we could be lying there, just like that . . .'

Suddenly it was too much for Achim. He felt bile rising in his gorge, took two or three faltering steps, bent over and threw up noisily into the sand.

'Take a damned good look at that!' Thomas said, spinning him round. 'Who's that?'

'Unteroffizier Ehrlich,' the Hitler Youth boy whimpered.

'Right . . . and apart from that, he's the end product of a heroic death.'

Thomas took him by the arm and led him to one side. 'Good,' he murmured. 'Now you must collect a whole heap of stones, or the hyenas will dig our friend Ehrlich up . . .' Then he let his brother go and walked off without looking back.

For a few moments Thomas Kleebach felt content with the lesson he had taught his brother. Then the satisfaction drained from him as he realised that he was going to have to write a letter to the dead man's family tonight. It just went to show that there were no good days in a war . . .

CHAPTER EIGHT

Marion Kleebach, the family's youngest, looked up from her typewriter and gazed longingly through the grimy window-pane of the Army H.Q. building in Berlin.

Outside an early summer day beckoned. The sun shone, children played noisily, and couples walked arm in arm along the streets. But she sat day in and day out at her desk and added up lists of socks for the Wehrmacht, overshoes, artificial honey . . .

'Are you doing overtime again?' asked Erika, the girl she shared an office with. There was a hint of sarcastic superiority in the other woman's voice; Erika believed in having a good time.

'What else is there to do?' Marion answered.

Erika laughed. 'If you don't know, I can't tell you . . .'

'What do you mean?'

'You go out just once with Captain Schneider, and you'll understand.'

'With him? Ugh!' Marion said sourly. She was the youngest and the prettiest of the auxiliary girls, a mature woman now but still somehow a child. Most of the officers had written her off as a hopeless case. In truth, she was bitter at the world – not at Heinz Böckelmann, her dead brother's friend and her fiancé, whom she hadn't seen for a year, but at the war that kept him away from her. Since his last leave she had been forced to concentrate her feelings in letters, and though she still liked Heinz, with time he had become a vague idea. Which was why she was sitting now, miserable and resentful, in this office, and doing the work of other girls who preferred to chase staff officers.

'Cigarette?' Erika asked.

'Thanks,' said Marion, and gave up trying to work.

Erika was also engaged to a private serving with the Wehrmacht, but that didn't stop her from enjoying herself. She was only a little older than Marion, with a seductive smile and a mouth that spoke of experience. Her uniform was cut for effect rather than military correctness, accentuating the generous curves of her statuesque figure.

'This life's bad enough,' Erika said. 'Why make it more boring than it need be?'

'That's my affair.'

'You'll be nineteen soon . . . and you're no nun, are you?'

'I am what I am.'

'But everyone's got to enjoy themselves sometime.'

'Not the way you do,' Marion answered firmly.

There had been no shortage of offers. The trouble was that the officers, mostly attached to the Reserve Army, were all married men, and could not hide the fact, no matter how much they tried to act the Romeo. They cheated on their wives with girls who then cheated on them, and so the merry-go-round went on . . . And the war was their big excuse. They had been lucky enough to be posted to headquarters in Berlin, and the motto was: if the others have to die, we might as well live while we can . . .

'I'd like to go dancing again, though,' Marion said.

Erika coolly blew a smoke ring. 'Then come out with me tonight,' she coaxed.

'Where?'

'A big villa . . . handsome men . . . plenty to eat and drink, anything you want . . .'

Marion looked at her suspiciously. 'And what happens afterwards?'

'Nothing,' Erika said. 'Nothing you don't want to happen. Don't be stupid . . . no one's forcing you to do anything.'

Marion shook her head. She had no desire to get involved with Erika's murky friends. All she wanted was to be with Heinz. Of course she liked to go out now and again, for a little dance, maybe a flirt; her fiancé would have nothing against that.

Erika shot her a sidelong, encouraging glance.

Marion hesitated. 'Do they really . . . dance . . .?' she asked.

'And how . . . hot music, the kind you don't hear every day.'

'Really . . . dancing?'

'As much as you like . . . and with whom you like.' Erika pursed her lips. 'Well?'

'Perhaps . . . another time . . .'

'Rubbish!' her friend hissed. 'But as you like . . . I'm just trying to help you, but if you don't want help . . .'

Marion thought it over for the space of half a cigarette, then squashed the butt firmly in the ashtray and said almost violently: 'All right . . . I'll take a look . . . But I'm not getting involved in anything funny . . . and you'd better believe me!'

'Oh, I believe you,' Erika said sardonically. She flashed Marion a satisfied smile, because Marion didn't know that the captain had promised her five bottles of champagne and five pairs of black market silk stockings if she succeeded in persuading Marion to go to one of his orgies at the villa . . .

The time had come when father Kleebach was at the end of his tether. Ortsgruppenleiter Rosenblatt's ultimatum had almost expired, the big lie he had told was threatening to strangle him, and he had already written another forged letter. He had decided that the truth must out, even if it killed him, because there was no alternative. Then came the day when the mild-mannered postal official lost his head again.

When he got his bundle of letters to deliver that morning, he had looked through them quickly, as was his habit. He had suddenly come across a post card, and he had stared at it for a long time, and as he stared the colour of his face had changed so dramatically that colleagues had rushed over, fearing that Kleebach had suffered a heart attack.

Arthur Kleebach, panting, had warded off all offers of help, then had buttoned up his delivery bag and fled from the building. He had headed straight to his own apartment by the shortest route, still puce in the face, with wondering passers-by staring after him. He almost ran the whole way, forgetting the stitch in his side that reminded him that he was fifty-one years old, as if the miracle that had just occurred had also magically affected his body. He leapt up the stairs two at a time and rang the door bell. When his wife came to the door and looked at him in horrified astonishment, all he could do was grin foolishly. 'Here,' he stammered, and thrust the postcard at Maria.

'What . . . what's this?' she asked nervously.

'Read it, mother . . . read it,' he wheezed, and forced into her hand the postcard from the Red Cross that told them that Fritz, the flier, was in an English P.O.W. camp.

Maria Kleebach leaned against the door frame for support, took one last fearful glance at her near-hysterical husband, and then ran her eyes over the card. At first she felt panic: Red Cross meant hospitals, she thought, and she could almost smell the carbolic, see the surgeon in his clinical mask, bending over Fritz with his scalpel ready to hack . . .

'No, mother. Don't you understand?' Arthur Kleebach said, reading her expression. 'Fritz has been taken prisoner by the English. He's safe . . .'

The sudden noise outside the Kleebachs' apartment was beginning to attract attention. Doors on the landing opened and neighbours peered out. The landing was filled with the everyday smells of the block.

'England?' Maria answered vaguely. 'But they might . . .'

'No! He'll be very well treated!' her husband shouted. 'The English are fair. They're gentlemen . . .'

Keep the noise down . . . Maria thought automatically now that the crisis was over and respectability was important again. She took her husband gently by the arm and pulled him in through the door.

They stood gazing at each other. The hand that held the card was trembling slightly. Maria had understood, was relieved, but now came the doubts.

'But he wrote to us a few days ago from Sicily,' she said. 'If this is a mistake . . .'

'You know how unreliable the field post is these days,' Arthur Kleebach said quickly, realising that he would have to be careful not to let the whole lie out after the danger was over, after the nightmare of the last few weeks had been evaporated by the miraculous news. And he, Arthur Kleebach, the quiet little postal official, had been right. He had been harder than Thomas and cleverer than Party Comrade Rosenblatt – and stronger than his own nerves.

No, this had been no miracle, he thought, just the result of faith. With the burden removed from his shoulders, he suddenly felt superhuman, almost drunk with elation. He would have liked to have gone and thrown open the window and shouted out to the world: Listen everyone, I was right and nobody else; me, alone, and Fritz is alive! I always knew it. It was you smart-ass sceptics who doubted he was safe . . .

'But we won't see him again for a long time,' Maria whispered.

'No, we won't,' Arthur Kleebach answered, a little more sober now. 'But at least we'll know that he's alive, that things are all right with him, that nothing can happen to him, nothing at all . . .'

His wife smiled sadly. Her mind could see the reason of what Arthur said, but in her heart she knew she would never be happy again until she witnessed her surviving twin's return, safe and sound. 'But I wonder how it happened?' she asked, to cover her inner turmoil.

Arthur Kleebach shook his head . . .

Even he could not know the truth that lay between the lines of the all-too-brief message on the postcard. He could not know how Fritz, the man who flew out of love, had pulled off one final tour de force, how he had struggled against all hope to save himself and the rest of the crew, on one engine and a few metres above the sea, with his wings shot to ribbons, water beneath him and looming up ahead. The sea . . . at that speed the water had the force of concrete when a plane hit it – and not the firm, smooth safety of a runway but an unyielding, cruel hardness like a brick wall . . .

Not even a glance at his comrades, paralysed with terror in the cabin beside and behind him. He opened the throttles again for a last, desperate bid to gain height. What Fritz Kleebach, the perfect pilot, showed that day was more than you learnt at flying school. The engine screamed in pain, then choked. Misfire. The tattered wings swished through the air like giant scythes of death. Grim reapers . . . Soon it would be over, finished. At 300 kilometres an hour, maybe more, and with no more shots in Fritz's locker. The end would come in a shattering collision and emptiness, an end each man would meet alone, terribly alone, knowing it was final, senseless.

Still Fritz Kleebach did not give up. His hands gripped the control column with savage determination, and he held the flying wreck above the water. God, the sea was calm, almost like a huge, still pool. Scarcely any swell. Azure and deep, merciless and limitless and hard . . .

They lost more height. Twenty metres. Another thirty to go to death. A last bellow of the engines. And the pilot fought and fought, with a strange, fixed smile on his face. He knew he would never regain height, so the only solution was to make distance, wrench the plummeting Junker's nose up and keep her on an even keel and going, however slowly. Pull her up again and again.

The radio operator had already closed his eyes. He had seen what Fritz was trying to do, and his feverish admiration for the pilot's cold-blooded stubbornness kept him from going insane during those last, paralysing seconds . . .

They hit the water in a crunching fountain of spray and the plane fell apart like an over-ripe pumpkin smashed against stone. The first man was treading water. The second was dead, the sparks. The radio operator had been crushed when they hit the water. One other struggled gasping and splashing out of the swirling wreckage: Fritz Kleebach.

His life-saver worked perfectly, inflating on contact with the water as it was meant to do. But where was the fourth man? Gone without trace. Maybe gone down with the tail section, trapped and unable to get out in time. Holy shit . . .

Fritz's brain worked like a machine. Breathe. Swim. Survive. Fight exhaustion. Strike out. Spit out the water, the damned salt water, because salt burned you, made you thirsty, tired, sapped your brain, gave you red, crazy eyes like an animal's. He had to hold on and not give up, and then maybe, just maybe . . .

The hours passed in a dream, and the dream was merciless. Time had no shape, it was nothing. The two survivors could not keep together. They bobbed away from each other, unable to find the strength to fight the waves, and drifted miles apart. For Fritz Kleebach there was nothing to see or hear. Just a cruel sun, blinding him and torturing his eyeballs, worse than the salt. He hated the sun. He hated the salt. He hated the water. He hated the frigging war . . .

He had to hold on, survive. He had to get home to his mother, father, Thomas, Achim, Freddy and Marion. One feeble stroke for mother, a kick in the water for father, head up for Thomas, a splash to the side for Freddy, breathe out for Achim, another stroke for Marion. Again. Again and again.

Hope was gone, but who cared? He did not give up. He kept on.

Half-way through the afternoon a British coastal patrol picked up the drifting flier, his body numb and close to unconsciousness. He had swallowed a lot of water, a lot too much. The Tommies beat him with wet towels, shook him and knelt on him until finally he threw up. They continued the treatment, and he spat out a pool of salt water mixed with vomit. Then came the first cigarette. A1 English blend, and even in his weakened state it tasted out of this world . . .

That was how Fritz Kleebach ended up in British captivity, how he survived and flourished, because he received expert care, good food and medicines. He sent a card to Berlin, but it failed to arrive. The cargo ship was sunk. Then he was shipped off to England on a convoy via Gibraltar and experienced a U-boat alert in the Atlantic, complete with exploding torpedoes, ships going down all around him. That really would have been a sick joke: to be killed by a German attack at the last moment . . .

He made it. From an English port he was taken to a camp in Scotland to join thousands of other German P.O.W.s, most of whom were glad to be out of the war, a few who were embittered, longing to rejoin the fight. From there he was transferred back across the Atlantic to Canada, but before that he managed to send a message home through the International Red Cross in Switzerland.

Arthur Kleebach could only guess at all that, but his overwhelming sense of relief turned him into a clown. He drank a glass of schnaps and smoked one of his choicest hoarded cigars. Maria had a drink too; she had not wanted to, but Arthur forced it down her. He would have liked to have danced her round the room, or everything at once with her: cry, pray, laugh . . .

Then he took his postbag and went off to distribute his morning's bundle of fate, good and bad news. Today he excused himself for being late and for the foolish grin on his face, saying: 'You know . . . it's just that I've heard that my son Fritz, who had been posted missing, is all right . . .'

Many congratulated him, others simply smiled, and others

still could only shake their heads, inured to one man's joy by the burden of their own suffering . . .

At the time that the news of their brother Fritz's capture reached Thomas and Achim Kleebach in North Africa, the war there was still in uneasy stalemate, a calm before yet another storm. The panzer company remained on constant alert, and the soldiers' free time was filled with guard duties, inspections and lectures on the correct 'world view'. The new battalion commander, Major Schreyvogel, was particularly keen on the last-mentioned, but then he was one of those who had worn uniform when he was a civilian.

Today's lecture subject: the Jewish Question.

Leutnant Thomas Kleebach stood by and watched as the Feldwebel gave out the orders for the day. When they got to the part about the lecture, some of the men grinned, others whispered behind their hands, and the rest, already made apathetic by the heat, stared dully ahead. They were lined up in ranks three deep, counting the hours until evening, waiting for the war to have its fill of corpses.

The evening would come. The end of the war was another thing entirely.

'So who's going to give us this lecture?' the Feldwebel asked sardonically. 'Who's going to volunteer?'

There was silence. Then one man slowly raised his hand. It was Achim Kleebach, the Hitler Youth leader.

'Report afterwards to the company commander,' the Feldwebel said without a flicker of emotion, then dismissed the company.

Gunner Kleebach marched up to his brother and stood to attention.

'Come with me,' said Thomas.

They walked off across the sand together.

'You again, eh?' the Leutnant said. 'Always have to be in on the act . . .'

'And what's wrong with that?' the boy growled.

Thomas shrugged his shoulders. 'And where does your wordly wisdom come from?' he asked.

Achim smiled proudly. 'I have been schooled in the principles of National Socialism.'

144

'If you say so,' Thomas muttered with open contempt. 'You're excused duties this afternoon to prepare the thing.'

Thomas stalked off.

'That won't be necessary!' his brother called after him.

The arrogance in the boy's voice brought Thomas spinning round to face him, his features set in a snarl of derision.

'Fine, Gunner Kleebach,' he snapped. 'Then be so good as to report for kitchen duties.'

Achim stared miserably at his brother's retreating back. The constant fights with Thomas fed his hatred and provided the rest of the company with entertainment. The weird duel between the two brothers had long become a feature of the unit, and Achim was particularly bitter that the overwhelming majority of his comrades were on the Leutnant's side. No guts, he thought. A bunch of shirkers, moronic civilians in uniform, no real commitment to the Führer and Greater Germany . . .

He peeled potatoes that afternoon with savage single-mindedness, as if he were scalping the enemies of the Fuhrer. He managed to cut his finger in the process, and the kitchen sergeant kicked him out with a flea in his ear. 'Next time, tell the Leutnant to send me a chimpanzee!' he bawled. 'Piss off and see if you can unscramble your pea-brain before tonight, boy!'

Then came Achim's big moment.

The company were seated in a semi-circle and Achim stood out front, as he had always dreamed he would. He could feel everyone's eyes on him – which was true, because most of them had mastered the soldier's trick of sleeping with their eyes open. Achim took a deep breath and launched off into a rag-bag recital of party clichés, speaking in a sonorous tone that he had copied from the newsreels.

'The Jew,' he intoned solemnly. 'The Jew is the historic enemy of our people . . . he is devious and stubborn. He uses his financial power to cause chaos in our nation . . . the Führer alone has been prepared to take him on and liberate our Greater Germany from the semitic poison . . .'

He gazed along the rows of comrades before him. Most were dozing quietly. One was imagining what it would be like to commit a variety of outrageous sexual acts with a female auxiliary he had seen at battalion headquarters. The man next to him was composing a letter home in his mind. A third was waiting for the sardines he had eaten that afternoon to take effect. He had left the opened tin out in the broiling sun all day in the hope that the result might give him jaundice, because being ill was better than this goddamned hero's existence.

Finally Achim found himself meeting one man's eyes. They belonged to Private Trautmann, who had saved his life a few weeks previously. Trautmann seemed to be the only one who was giving the speaker the attention he deserved; his eyes glistened, and his mouth was set in melancholy concentration. At least Trautmann wasn't as dumb as the others, Achim thought. Encouraged, he raised his voice and continued: 'The Nuremberg race laws have halted the Jew's biological sabotage of our people . . . There will be no corruption of our nordic racial purity in future . . .'

Someone at the back was snoring loudly and with great precision. Several men were staring longingly at their watches. At the moment, they couldn't care about anything less than the 'Jewish Question', but the Hitler Youth leader pressed on:

'A particular danger is the semitic infiltration of our cultural life . . . with his usual skill the Jew succeeded in gaining leading positions in this area, and thus ensuring the debasement of our music, our literature, even our language . . . But under the National Socialist . . .'

Unnoticed by Achim, his brother had wandered in and was standing to one side, smoking a cigarette and watching the proceedings impassively.

'Not so fast,' Thomas interrupted suddenly. 'Let's have an example, please!'

Caught off balance, Achim wracked his brains wildly and blurted: 'Lessing!' he said. The eighteenth-century poet's name sounded vaguely Jewish.

'Lessing was a pure Aryan!' someone drawled from the back. There was laughter, and men began to pay attention, because now that their commander was here it looked as though things might liven up.

'Mendelssohn,' Achim stuttered.

'We were talking about literature. He was a composer!' someone bellowed.

'Ludwig Börne and Heinrich Heine,' Achim said, frantically

trying to find firm ground. One obscure poet, one famous, but it would have to do. 'This so-called literature we sent to the fire in 1933, as rubbish unworthy of the new Germany . . .'

Straight out of *Der Stürmer* from start to finish, thought Thomas, but for the moment he held his tongue, waiting for his brother to dig his own trap and fall into it. Two sentences later, he cut in again.

'I'm still waiting for a proper example of precisely how this corruption took place,' he said coldly. 'Let's take the example of Heinrich Heine, because he's probably the best-known.'

'Yes,' Achim answered nervously. 'There it's clearest.'

'What?'

'The poison . . .'

'To which particular work of his are you referring, Gunner Kleebach?' asked the Leutnant.

'Er . . . All of them . . .'

'Crap,' Thomas retorted drily. 'Come on, I'm fed up with hearing a load of vague flannel. Give us a concrete example.'

'I haven't read anything by Heine,' the boy admitted, reddening. His brother had driven him straight into a corner.

Thomas sighed. 'If I had known how unprepared you were, Kleebach, I wouldn't have let you give the lecture . . .' he said amid broad grins from the rest of the company. 'This is nothing but a fraud.'

Achim turned scarlet as an embarrassed virgin, and he knew it was happening, which made it all the worse.

'Is there by any chance someone here who has actually read Heine?' the company commander said, taking over the role of the teacher.

'Yes, sir,' someone at the back said and stood up.

It was Trautmann. Thomas Kleebach recognised him and felt horror rise within him. He realised that he had gone too far. Christ, he should have made sure the driver was on guard duty or something, he thought, but it was too late.

'*Travel Scenes,*' Trautmann began to recite. '*Germany, A Winter's Tale . . .* the *Book of Le Grand . . .* These works deal with . . .'

'That's good enough,' the Leutnant interrupted with a nervous smile. Then, still grinning, he turned back to his brother. 'Take note, Kleebach: you can only fight an enemy when you know him. Kindly continue – so long as you have something worthwhile to tell us . . .'

Achim stared at his comrade, Trautmann, with hate-filled confusion. He saw the man sit down again, hunched and sad-faced, and exchange a glance with Thomas. But Achim, the Hitler Youth leader, read no meaning into the driver's expression. All he knew was that Trautmann was a good soldier, a friend who had dragged him out of the burning scout car, hauled him through the desert and shared his water-bottle with him, then found the strength to signal to the Fieseler Storch . . . Sure, he might know more about Heine than Achim did, but who cared? It was all just Jewish shit anyway . . .

'The National Socialist Movement and Jewry are irreconcilable enemies,' he stumbled on, raising his voice. 'This war will end with the destruction of one or the other . . . We're only half-way, but we are in no doubt about the final aim . . .'

He looked back at his comrades and saw faces that were smiling, indifferent, amused, half-asleep. Then he met the sad eyes of Private Trautmann. Thomas was beckoning frantically to the driver, but Trautmann could not see, or chose not to see.

Achim took a deep breath and almost bellowed out the climax of his tirade: 'There must be no sentimentality! No pity! The final solution is in progress, and it must mean extermination! This applies to every individual, because each Jew is a danger, be it grown man, woman, old or young . . . We'll liquidate the lot of them!'

The Leutnant felt sick at the poison he heard coming from his own brother's lips. He made to stop the lecture, because he could see the wild despair on Trautmann's face, a despair that cut through to his heart and soul. Before Thomas could intervene, though, the driver stood up slowly and moved with heavy steps towards the astonished Achim.

'What do you want?' the boy said, wide-eyed with sudden fear.

'I want to know something,' Trautmann hissed between clenched teeth. 'This liquidation . . . Does it apply to my mother, too?'

'What do you mean . . . ?'

'She is Jewish,' Trautmann told him, in a voice like iron filings.

A terrible hush descended over the tent. Trautmann was breathing heavily. Achim said nothing, but the driver forced himself to continue: 'Yes . . . she's a Jewess . . . And today I got a letter that told me she'd been arrested . . . and now . . .' His voice screwed itself up to a scream. 'Now she's going to be liquidated!'

'But . . .' Achim moaned helplessly.

Trautmann's features were contorted into a tragic mask of terror. 'And that's what I'm supposed to risk my neck for,' he continued heavily. Then he finally lost control and his eyes were those of a madman. 'For you . . . for you swine!' he bellowed, his face only inches from the stuttering Achim's. 'I've had enough! It's over!'

'Trautmann . . .' Thomas said softly, stepping over to the driver, his face pleading. Trautmann saw him, saw the last kindness this world would ever show him, and stood for a few moments as if petrified, staring down at the ground. Then he tore himself free and stormed out past Achim and into the desert night.

'Lecture over!' the Leutnant ordered and looked at his brother with a coldness that had lost its irony. 'Go on . . . fetch Trautmann back immediately and bring him to me!'

As they were streaming out of the tent, they heard a single, thin – sounding shot, and everyone looked at each other in horror. Then men began to run in the direction of the shot as fast as they could.

The night was pitch-dark. They had to fetch torches and search with those, ignoring the blackout order. Shouts echoed through the desert silence until finally someone stumbled over something in the sand, hidden by the blackness. The man cursed, scrambled to his feet, and recognised Trautmann. One clawed hand still held the pistol with which he had shot himself through the temple.

'Here!' the soldier yelled. 'Here . . . here!'

Within seconds several men, including Thomas Kleebach, were standing around the corpse of Driver Trautmann. The

149

Leutnant crouched over him to feel the pulse while his men gazed at him with grim supplication, as if they were hoping he somehow had the power through rank to turn back the clock and bring Trautmann back to life.

The dead man's left hand was outstretched, almost in surrender. His face was contorted, ugly, the lips parted in what could have been passion but was obviously a final silent scream of torment. In the flickering light of the torch they could see the man's teeth, perfect and ghostly-white, almost obscene in their health and evidence of youth.

Without taking his eyes from the dead man, Thomas told an Unteroffizier: 'Fetch my brother here!'

Achim, the Hitler Youth leader, came slowly, with nothing of his usual arrogant bounce. He crept towards the party surrounding the corpse, and men moved aside quietly to let him pass. The boy stared straight ahead, unable to look at his comrades, but he saw Trautmann soon enough, and then he fell to his knees and began to blubber. Through his tears he heard Thomas reciting his own pitiless words back to him: 'No sentimentality ... it must mean extermination ... grown men, women, old or young ...'

'But I didn't know!' Achim howled convulsively. 'I didn't want ... Trautmann! Trautmann!' he screamed. 'My God, Trautmann ... I didn't mean ... I didn't mean your mother ... !'

No one spoke. Men who had been angry turned away sadly, for rage at Achim had turned to pity.

Thomas Kleebach walked slowly away, and as he made his way back to his tent he could still hear the sound of Achim weeping out among the dunes. He realised that he too could find no real anger in his heart, that he would have liked to have taken the boy in his arms and comforted him. After all, he would always be tortured by the hideous suspicion that his own negligence had been just as responsible for Trautmann's death as Achim's stupid 'lecture' ...

Freddy Kleebach, the one they called the gigolo, stood in front of his boss in the Berlin supply-barracks. His chief was a Hauptmann of the Reserve with a face the colour of an over-ripe peach, and he listened happily while the smiling Kleebach

150

delivered his report. The gigolo had long been mixed up with all kinds of shady deals, like the Hauptmann, and had just got the lot of them out of a tight corner through some neat footwork. Freddy basked in the approval of the man behind the desk.

'Jesus, Kleebach,' the officer said with mingled relief and admiration. 'The shit could really have hit the fan ... If I hadn't had you to sort it out ...'

Freddy grinned modestly. The barracks were big, and a long way from the front, and by now he gave the orders to the officers rather than the other way round.

'I can only ask myself,' his boss continued. 'How can I pay you back?'

The gigolo shrugged.

The Hauptmann stood up and looked thoughtful. 'You're not interested in a career, so I suppose you wouldn't want promotion?'

'Thank you, no, Herr Hauptmann,' Freddy answered quickly. He was doing very well where he was – all the goodies and none of the responsibility.

His boss wandered round the room. Until an hour before, when Freddy had saved his bacon, he had been preparing to face a court martial. Now he could relax and wander through his empire, gazing at the stocks of Champagne, the crates of chocolate and cigarettes, ignoring the fawning underlings, and knowing that he was himself again – a man who had learned that you could live better in war than in peace if you got in the right place at the right time ...

'Kleebach,' he said, coming to a halt. He fixed Freddy with one beady eye. 'I shall take it upon myself to bring you up in the world ... Do you possess a decent civilian suit?'

'Of course.'

'And I don't need to give you a lecture on keeping your mouth shut.'

'Certainly not, Herr Hauptmann.'

'Good,' the officer murmured with a jovial smile. 'Then tonight ... I know a house in Dahlem ...' he ran his tongue over his lips suggestively. 'And you'll get to know it too.'

'I thank you, sir,' said Freddy, saluting and turning to go.

'You ought to see the girls!' his boss called after him. 'Young and frisky, and you don't need to ask 'em twice!' He laughed throatily. 'Just your types, eh, Kleebach?'

First Freddy went home to change. He looked himself over in the mirror and straightened the tie that matched his well-cut suit. Sure enough, he was looking at a real lady-killer, the kind of man who hardly needed to be pimped for by a broken-down old lecher like the Hauptmann, but then who was going to turn down an invitation like that?

'Going out again?' his mother asked anxiously.

'It's too quiet here for me,' he laughed. 'But I'd almost forgotten . . .' He strolled over to where his briefcase was dumped on a chair and fished out several packets of cigarettes, a pound of butter and a bottle of wine. 'Have a nice day!' he said, and produced his *pièce de résistance*, a quarter-pound of real coffee. 'No rubbish . . . and how are the family heroes?'

'You've read Achim and Thomas's latest letter,' his father answered. 'I suppose you'll be staying in Berlin?'

'You can rely on it!' Freddy chortled.

Arthur Kleebach had to smile. Even he, the stern father, couldn't resist his charming rogue of a son. Freddy wasn't interested in dying; he wanted to live. He didn't intend to be promoted or 'prove himself', like Achim, and he had no desire for a Knight's Cross like Thomas, and above all he was determined not to end up like Gerd . . .

The aroma of real coffee wafted in from the kitchen.

'Tell me, how do you actually get hold of these marvellous things?' his father asked.

The gigolo smiled nonchalantly. 'At our place they sit there by the ton. Everyone helps themselves to a little sample every now and again.'

'Don't do anything silly, boy.'

'No chance,' Freddy retorted. His face became almost serious. 'It's your generation who did the silly things . . . you and your darned politics . . .'

'Please, Freddy.'

'Don't get me wrong, father . . . but we're the ones who have to ride the shit-storm.' He laughed contemptuously. 'But don't worry. I'm an expert!'

He gulped down his coffee, because he was in a hurry as usual. He walked to the Hauptmann's apartment, and from there they went by car to Dahlem. Freddy had already heard rumours of the villa there and the delights it contained.

His boss had his own key to the building. On the ground floor there was booze, while the girls were waiting upstairs. Freddy heard a gaggle of shrill voices from the bottom of the stairs and acknowledged the captain's smile approvingly.

'Wait here a minute, old boy,' the officer chuckled. 'First let's have a few drinks to get in the mood.'

A bar had been set up in the living room, with a pretty blonde serving the drinks. She jerked a thumb at the first floor. 'They're well under way up there,' she said suggestively.

Freddy drank cognac, while the Hauptmann chose champagne. Upstairs they were dancing to blaring jazz music. Otherwise everything was subdued in the house: the light, the laughter, the conversations, the coming and going. From time to time a girl would come tripping down the stairs to fetch a bottle of something, and the Hauptmann would stumble over for a swift paw at the goods. But the girls only seemed to have eyes for Freddy, and his boss was starting to regret having brought him along.

'I'm going upstairs now,' the blonde at the bar said, and took the gigolo's hand. 'Why don't you come with me, soldier?'

Freddy lost no time in putting his arm round her. She stopped and he kissed her, breathing in the subtle scent of her perfume. 'Chanel Number Five,' he observed knowledgably.

'For a number one man,' she said, making her intentions quite clear.

'Not hard to be that with all these old wrecks around,' Freddy said wryly.

'Easy for you to say that. They have to come up with . . . presents. You get everything for free.'

'Everything?'

'Later,' the blonde said, and pranced off up the stairs ahead of him.

On the first floor they were greeted with loud squeals of delight. The room looked like a Roman orgy in full swing, with couples writhing on the parquet floor, others behind sofas and tables. Most of the girls were already the worse for drink. Freddy stood amazed, hardly able to take it all in. 'Hello, kids!' he yelled with an enormous grin. 'Let's have a good time.

Enjoy your war, because the peace is going to be far worse . . . !'

That got a thunder of applause. Suddenly he was the centre of the party, the rooster in the hen-coop, surrounded by half-a-dozen eager girls. He sprawled on a sofa with a whoop and took some champagne with him, drinking flamboyantly straight from the bottle.

He was still gulping down champagne when he saw the girl coming slowly out of the next-door room, and suddenly he choked and the wine ran down over his collar and tie. I must be crazy, he thought wildly, then looked again. The girl was Marion, the baby of the family.

A dancing couple blocked his view for a moment, so he had time to recover and doubt his own eyes again. What would Marion be doing here? She would be home by now, tucked up in bed and probably dreaming about dear old Heinz, her fiancé . . .

Somewhere near the entrance Hauptmann suddenly let go of his partner in the middle of a dance. She crashed against a small table and sent the glasses flying. Several shattered on the floor, covering it with alcohol and splinters. The man leaned over his girl, his eyes wet with tears – of laughter.

'Broken glass is lucky!' someone shouted, and began to hurl bottles and glasses against the wall.

Freddy walked over to join the onlookers, but the girl with the uncanny resemblance to Marion had disappeared.

'Who was that?' he asked the blonde from the bar.

'Fancied her, did you? Prefer redheads to blondes?'

'You're kidding . . . but who is she?' the gigolo said harshly.

'I don't know,' the blonde pouted. 'She's only been here a few times . . . belongs to a major . . .'

'Which major?'

The girl from the bar grinned lewdly. 'Who cares? All staff officers look alike to me.'

Freddy Kleebach went out into the corridor to look, but there was no sign of the redhaired girl. He stood there for a moment, undecided, then went to the next door. The blonde followed him, unasked. Somewhere close by, a drunk was screaming over and over again: 'Take me . . . I'm yours!'

'Let me go!' a girl's voice snapped.

154

The gigolo threw open the door and turned on the light, but the room stayed in darkness. Someone had taken out the light bulb.

The girl from the bar took Freddy's arm and pulled him back out of the room. 'You won't get far here with that kind of thing,' she complained. 'First law in this house is: mind your own business.'

'Speak for yourself,' he growled.

He could see no sign of the girl, and so he went back to the big room and decided to really let rip.

'That's the way,' the blonde said approvingly.

He drank and he drank, but the taste was getting bitter. Usually he liked this kind of place – he had been to a few others – but tonight it all repelled him. The schnaps was giving him a fat head, and the forced jollity and frantic activity all around him got on his nerves. He stood like a pillar of stone, and wherever he looked he could see nothing but bloated, drunken faces, wandering hands, hear heavy breathing and greedy pants of simulated passion.

Someone tried to dance the boogaloo sitting down, until he cracked his head against the wall and cursed to high heaven. The entire room broke up with mocking laughter. Freddy's boss, the Hauptmann, lurched up to him and asked: 'Well, isn't it just like I promised?'

'Sure, sir,' Freddy muttered.

'Then don't stand around like a sack of potatoes, old boy!' The officer leered at the blonde from the bar, then back at Freddy. 'Get in there, go on!'

Freddy nodded and moved off to another part of the room, where he was swallowed up by a swarm of other girls. The blonde pushed them away and declared: 'Leave him, he's mine!'

'Let him make his own mind up!' shrilled a dark-haired girl who couldn't have been more than twenty.

The others stared at the gigolo expectantly.

'One's as good as the other,' he growled, and he was telling the truth.

The party was going with a swing in the other rooms, too. Chairs were being thrown about, and there was a broken window. To listen, you would have thought the villa was about to go up like a volcano.

'What's up with you?' the blonde asked.

Freddy shrugged moodily. 'I don't know . . . just fed up.'

'Too much to drink . . .' the blonde commented.

'No, too little,' he told her, and reached for another bottle. Champagne again. Freddy had no taste for the stuff, but he insisted on drinking the most expensive thing on offer. His host tonight was the quartermaster of the Greater German Wehrmacht, even if the gentleman concerned was totally oblivious of the fact.

He let himself be led to a sofa. The blonde wrapped herself round him and began to paw nervously at his neck like a bitch on heat. At first he just stared into space, but soon he forced himself to respond, for form's sake, and started up his usual chat.

'I can see you're not exactly made of wood,' he murmured with a lecherous grin.

'You can bet on that, soldier.'

'You been here often before?'

The girl grimaced and lit a cigarette. 'Where else is there to go in this darned war?' She pouted defiantly. 'Got something against it?'

'Not at all,' Freddy answered.

'You're here, too,' she said.

He nodded, already losing interest.

'And I'm glad you are,' the blonde added.

Freddy grunted. 'What's your name, then?'

She wrinkled her pert nose in embarrassment. 'Malwine,' she told him. 'My parents couldn't think of anything better . . . an aunt called that was my godparent, and she had a bit of money . . . you know how it is.'

The gigolo was summing her up now. She was a well-built girl, with a knowing mouth, eyes that seemed older than the face. She was pretty, all right, and he would have no problems, because she was easy. Easy as falling off a log . . .

The blonde handed him another brimming glass.

Freddy drank quickly and greedily. 'You've got me eating out of your hand.'

'That's a good beginning.'

'And how does it go on?' he asked.

The blonde chuckled throatily. 'That's up to you.'

'You need not fear on that score,' Freddy answered, grinning.

'I didn't think so.' Malwine crushed out her cigarette in the ashtray with an air of decision. 'Coming with me?'

'Where?'

'We'll find somewhere . . . this place is big enough.'

'Why not?'

She leaned against him as they walked across the room, partly to be close and partly because she could hardly stand. They tried to sneak out without being noticed, but they hadn't reckoned with the dark-haired girl who had made a play for Freddy earlier. 'I'll be timing you!' she called after them.

Malwine stuck out her tongue at her rival. She and Freddy made their way up to the second floor, and she pointed to the doors to their left. They stood and listened for a moment, trying to make out if any rooms were unoccupied. The jazz music downstairs made distinctions impossible.

The blonde opened a door cautiously. Freddy followed slowly. While she felt for the light switch, she turned to him and put one finger to her lips. He nodded.

The light came on suddenly, dazzling them. A couple were on the bed, and they separated hastily. At first Freddy saw only the man. A uniform with a major's shoulder-flashes was hanging over a chair.

'Idiot!' the officer snarled.

But now Freddy had seen the half-dressed girl, and he knew for certain who she was and what she had been doing. It was Marion, and she looked as though she was hoping the earth would swallow her up.

'Come on. Let's go,' Malwine whispered.

But Freddy wasn't listening.

'You bitch!' he yelled, launching himself at Marion. 'You whore!'

'Who the hell do you think you are?' the major hissed.

The gigolo shoved him aside, dragged Marion upright and slapped her face.

The incident was soon the talk of the party. Within moments the corridor was crowded with guests eager to see what was happening in the major's love nest. They saw Marion cowering on the sofa with her brother still looming over her.

'Get yourself decent!' Freddy bawled. 'You're coming with me! This minute!'

'I see the party's hotting up,' someone called out, and they all laughed at the major, caught in the act and unsure of how to react.

'Stupid jealousy,' someone else said.

A Leutnant was almost splitting his sides with laughing. 'What a surprise!' he chuckled. 'You come to an orgy and meet your girlfriend!'

Freddy Kleebach had no intention of sparing his sister. He took her roughly by the arm and pulled her up from the sofa, not giving a damn for the onlookers. Marion hesitated for an instant, but one look at Freddy's pale, cold eyes was enough. She followed him like a lamb. This met with general disapproval, and the spectators started to criticise.

'You can't do that here,' one officer protested loudly.

'Who brought this creep here?' a girl asked contemptuously.

Freddy's chief appeared. 'Kleebach,' he mumbled drunkenly. 'I didn't expect you to behave like this . . . You're not to come here again, understood?'

'Absolutely, Herr Hauptmann!' Freddy growled, almost spitting in the man's face. Then he took Marion's hand and dragged her downstairs. He waited until she had found her coat, then left with her. They walked from Dahlem to Charlottenburg, through Berlin in the blackout, and all the time he said not a word. At first Marion was still sobbing, but then she subsided into silence as well. At last she said timidly: 'But . . . it was my first time there . . . I didn't know . . .'

She was lying, Freddy thought, and felt shame for his family that his sister had fallen so low. What he didn't think was that without men like him it wouldn't have happened in the first place.

'Please,' she begged, halting and turning to face him. 'At least you can keep quiet about it at home . . . Father would . . .'

He shook his head and walked on, pulling his sister with him. She was wearing high heels and was rapidly becoming incapable of walking, but Freddy didn't care.

'No,' he said after a while. 'Father doesn't need to know that his daughter's a tart.' He was walking two or three feet in front

158

of her, staring straight ahead and speaking as if to himself. 'But Heinz will. If no one tells him, then I will!'

At first Marion was relieved, because she could not know that she would never be able to talk Freddy out of his promise – or what it would lead to . . .

CHAPTER NINE

On June 22nd 1941, Hitler found himself another war: in
Russia. It was true that the invasion in the East was thousands
of miles from the desert battle, but soon the Afrika Korps began
to feel the effect of it.

The Second Air Fleet, which had provided some protection
for supply convoys until then, was 'temporarily' transferred to
the new Russian Front. That meant open season for the British
Navy and a dramatic deterioration in the supply of munitions
and fuel for Rommel's army.

Exploiting the situation, the British left their fixed positions on November 18th 1941 and began their second counter-
offensive, attacking in overwhelmingly superior force. Tobruk
was relieved on December 10th, and by Christmas they had
taken Benghazi. The Germans' withdrawal was not quite as
headlong as their advance in the spring, but on January 2nd
1942 they surrendered Bardia, and sixteen days later the Italian
troops left behind in Sollum ran up the white flag. The remains
of the Afrika Korps conducted a fighting retreat to El Agheila.
The body-count: 13,000 Germans, 20,000 Italians, and 17,000
British.

Kleebach's panzer company was kept in constant contact
with the enemy throughout the retreat, and as long as
ammunition and fuel was available, they assumed their usual
role of 'fire brigade'. They had lost half their panzers. The men
were exhausted and half-starved. What had once been Major
Schreyvogel's battalion was now hardly above the strength of a
full company.

On one occasion, Thomas and his unit were in British
captivity for two hours. A nomadic motor-cycle light artillery
unit that had been wandering behind the lines for a couple of
days got them out of that one.

Now Thomas Kleebach had the pleasure of attending a situation conference with Major Schreyvogel. The situation was shitty, and the amount of conferring that would do any good was pretty limited. The best order anyone could have given would have been: run like hell until you get to the El Agheila Line . . . Shells were still exploding all round the officers, and most of the discussions took place from a crouching position in the sand.

'Now to you, Kleebach,' the commander rasped. His finger hovered above a blood-streak that had stained the map. 'A Flak unit has been cut off here . . . You'll get them out, and then follow us.'

'With what, Herr Major?' the young Leutnant asked coldly.

'With what you've got.'

'Four panzers and a couple of captured vehicles,' said Kleebach.

'Well?'

'It's crazy, Herr Major.'

'I don't give a shit about that. Or do you want to discuss it with a court martial? I'll . . .'

The rest of Schreyvogel's words were lost in the deafening howl of shells, and for one instant then Kleebach wished with all his heart that the Tommies would send one over onto the major, even if it got himself too.

'Clear off,' said the commander, without even wishing him luck.

The amount of luck this particular suicide mission would need to succeed just didn't exist in the world, Thomas thought bitterly.

He drove back to his unit. 'Right,' he bellowed at his Feldwebel. 'Helmets off and get praying.'

His brother Achim watched him with something near pity. The last few months had taught him some lessons. Since Trautmann's death, for which he still blamed himself, he had become much quieter. Even his desire to get on had cooled, because he had realised that in the desert you got promotion automatically – whether you wanted it or not. Apart from that, he was fighting a private war against the sand-flies, which seemed to pick on him personally and tormented him day and night.

'You can stay out of this,' Thomas said.

But the boy had answered simply: 'My place is with you. At least until this spot of bother's over.'

The sun was furnace-hot, dazzling, roasting the eyeballs and scorching the sand, as what was left of Kleebach's panzer company felt its way forward, probing for a gap in the British line of advance. Their mission: to rescue a Flak unit that had probably long since fired its last shell and surrendered.

At first, though, the four panzers, using up the last of their petrol, got further than the Leutnant would have expected. They had been spotted by enemy reconnaissance planes a while ago, but the Tommies – out of pity or arrogant self-assurance – had not bothered with the pathetic little band.

Thomas Kleebach sighted a mass of tanks on the horizon, at least brigade strength, and ordered his panzers to move to the right and out of their way.

'If we carry on farting about like this, we're going to end up where we started,' his driver growled.

Kleebach shrugged indifferently. All he felt was hatred for this war that sent him and his brave boys to near-certain slaughter, and the commander who handed out crazy orders with such cold-blooded cruelty. The most insane thing of all, of course, was the fact that he carried out pointless orders again and again, yesterday, today, and tomorrow, and would do so until the day came when a well-aimed anti-tank shell put an end to the whole bloody farce . . .

When more British tanks showed up on his right flank, Leutnant Kleebach made one last attempt to break off the mission. He sent a radio message to battalion headquarters: 'Am faced with strong British forces, outnumbered at least ten to one. Further advance hopeless.'

He was not optimistic, and sure enough the reply came back from Major Schreyvogel:

'Kindly carry out your orders.'

They crawled on across the sand for another half an hour, and then they were finally stopped. Enemy tanks on three sides. The British had decided to put an end to the game. An explosion nearby filled Thomas's panzer with the acrid smell of cordite. He ordered his gunner to return fire, and seconds later came a jet of flame in the distance. Direct hit, he thought dully, but so what? There were so many Tommies everywhere, rolling towards them like fat, dark beetles in the sand, and they were heading straight towards them, firing as they went. Christ, they must think these poor Jerries had taken leave of their senses. A direct hit on one of his own vehicles to the left. The panzer was torn apart like a tin can, and Thomas just had time to be sure that it wasn't his brother's crew that had bought it before his turn came. Suddenly the engine was on fire, and within seconds the munition would catch and go up.

He threw back the hatch in the turret and roared: 'Everybody out!'

The radio operator made it. The panic-stricken driver crunched his head against the solid steel of the interior armour and collapsed. Thomas, finding the strength somewhere, managed to haul him brutally up and threw him onto the sand. The man stumbled, came to his senses, and staggered off away from the panzer. Then Thomas jumped, covered twenty metres, until he was caught by a string of machine-gun bullets and was hurled headlong like a drunk being thrown out of a bar to lie spreadeagled and motionless on the sand.

A few seconds later, the two luckier members of the command panzer's crew reached the safety of the armoured car and climbed aboard. The deputy company commander, a senior Feldwebel, ordered the men to cease firing and radioed the armoured car to disengage.

Achim Kleebach, the Hitler Youth leader, sat in the Feldwebel's panzer, knowing that his brother was lying badly wounded, if not dead, outside on the sand. The knowledge pushed him over the edge. 'Stop!' he yelled at the Feldwebel. 'You can't just get out . . .'

'Shut your mouth.'

The boy stared at him for a moment, then suddenly he reached out and his hands were encircling the N.C.O.s throat and squeezing, squeezing. He pressed until the man's eyes rolled in agony, then he let him go and screamed at the driver: 'Stop, or . . .'

The driver, terrified, took his foot from the accelerator. The boy thrust open the hatchway and launched himself blindly out into the inferno. To his left and right machine-guns hacked great arcs of death in the smooth sand, but he didn't care. He saw tanks rolling towards him from every direction, and just kept on running straight into their guns.

He was a man running amok. He had found that combination of desperation and insane courage that led to so many spectacular acts in war, the kind that had no sense in terms of destroying the enemy, only in saving human life. Achim had no time to think of the fact that he was hazarding his own skin; he was out to fetch his brother, the man he loved and hated, because he wanted to spare his mother and father yet more suffering, another black-bordered letter – without considering that it would be even worse for his parents if they lost two sons at once . . .

The panzer Achim had jumped from was under heavy fire, and the driver was zig-zagging to avoid the shells. But the boy's example had lent the driver a bit of crazy courage, too. He refused to follow the others, who had got away, and drove around in a wide circle, constantly repassing the original spot so that the boy would stand at least a faint chance of getting back.

With a final burst of speed Achim reached his brother and hurled himself down into the dust beside him. No hesitation. Grimacing, he swung Thomas over his shoulder in a fireman's lift and began to stagger back without a thought of cover. The driver had seen him, and had no intention of deserting him now. Offering a sitting target to the enemy, he accelerated straight towards Achim and slammed on the brakes a few feet from the boy. The pair of them heaved Thomas up through the turret. Then there was no more pushing their luck. The message was: *Karbid*, which in Afrika Korps language meant step on it . . .

The panzer had made maybe twenty metres when two or three fat shells exploded exactly where it had been seconds before. The British were closing in slowly and cautiously; they had been fooled by Rommel more times than they could count, and they suspected a trap. The Tommies' indecision saved the remains of the company.

Achim crouched, bent over his brother. Thomas looked pretty bad. He was unconscious but whimpering faintly, and his uniform hung in bloody tatters from his shattered body. Blood was pouring over his face, he was bleeding from his shoulder and right thigh. The boy worked feverishly to clean the wounds. The forehead looked dramatic, but was only a flesh wound. He managed to stop the bleeding in the shoulder with a wad of bandages, but the thigh wound was more serious; the first bandage he tied was dripping red before he had secured it. He piled on the bandages on the thigh, tight as he could, his face pleading and, though he didn't know it, a prayer in his heart that said: Dear God, let him live. Not for me, but for mother and . . .

A searing pain brought Thomas to the edge of consciousness. He tried to sit up, slumped back and peered around with eyes that were wild and bright with fever. He recognised Achim, tried to smile, and lost consciousness again.

After ten kilometres the panzer ran out of petrol. The crew climbed out and set the vehicle alight. They took turns to carry Thomas on the march through the desert, and they were lucky. A German rear column picked them up, and half an hour later they were dropped at a mobile hospital.

They carried their wounded commander into the station, where a medical officer leaned over him. 'What do you think you're doing, bringing me corpses?' he snarled, straightening up and peering at Achim. There was fire in the boy's eyes. The medic shrugged defensively. 'Sorry. But I could do without this kind of case. We have enough trouble dealing with the walking wounded . . .'

Achim refused to move away from the stretcher.

'All right. You can clear off now!' the overworked doctor snapped.

'He's my brother,' Achim murmured simply.

The medic paused, shook his head, then clapped the boy on the shoulder. 'I'll do what I can.' He tried to smile. 'Now get out of here, son. We don't need an audience, all right?'

Achim was overwhelmed by gratitude. Only afterwards did he begin to feel a rising, raging anger against the battalion commander who was responsible for the whole deadly fiasco. He decided that he would tell Schreyvogel to his face, and damn the consequences. As it turned out, he never got the chance, because Major Schreyvogel was beyond his reach. He too had driven into an enemy trap, but he had preferred a P.O.W. camp to the dangers of a breakout . . .

The mobile hospital was wedged in among a mass of vehicles. New wounded were being brought in every minute and given what first aid was available. There was no time for surgery, because first the hospital had to be taken *out* of the immediate battle zone. Four men died during the trip to the rear, a hellish journey where the roar of the engine was drowned by the moans and screams of the wounded. At last the hospital halted and they set up the operating tent. The M.O. decided which cases were to be dealt with first – a sequence which could mean life or death for the men waiting for treatment . . .

Thomas Kleebach was fortunate enough to be towards the top of the list.

'Let's get on with it,' the medic growled at his orderly-Feldwebel. 'Get me some morphium.'

'Where from?' the N.C.O. drawled.

'Then Evipan will do, you idiot!'

'We're out of that, too.'

The surgeon cursed, then ordered them to hand out Barbera, oily Italian red wine, to the wounded.

'Drink, children, drink!' the Feldwebel bellowed, holding aloft a billy-can swimming with the dark wine. 'This stuff'll save your souls, and the state's paying for it!'

Most of them obeyed eagerly, even greedily, and those who couldn't drink themselves were helped, like Thomas Kleebach.

'Don't be timid,' the Feldwebel proclaimed. 'Come on, children, drink, drink, drink!'

They got a few aspirin to supplement the wine. The first to be carted off to the operating tent waved to the others drunkenly, and there was a ripple of laughter from the rest. Then they heard the piercing, blood-chilling shriek from the tent, and that killed the hilarity.

Thomas Kleebach was next. He glimpsed the man in the white gown through a fog of wine and pain, heard him reciting: 'Bullet in the shoulder, flesh wound in the head, shrapnel in upper thigh . . . Here goes nothing . . . forceps . . .'

The surgeon stared down at the wounded man.

'Can you understand what I'm saying?'

Thomas nodded painfully.

'I'm going to have to take some shrapnel fragments out,' the medic said. 'Not the pleasantest thing in the world for you . . . or for me . . . Keep your teeth well clenched . . .'

Three men held Thomas down while the medic took out the first fragment. The Leutnant bit deep into his lower lip until the blood flowed, but he made no sound. The screams he could hear were coming from a neighbouring tent, where another surgeon was operating. In this place there was no escape from those screams, no doors to shut them out. The sounds of animal agony cut through the waiting woundeds' minds as cruelly as any surgeon's knife, chilling their bones, turning their blood to ice.

'Any moment,' the medic said after the third fragment. By the time he had taken out the fourth, he was beginning to realise that there were five and more.

'Shit,' he oathed, and stared at his patient in irritated astonishment. Why didn't the bastard pass out? He took his Feldwebel to one side and handed him an orthopaedic hammer.

'Don't do it too hard,' he said. 'Or you'll crack the bugger's skull.'

'Got that, sir,' the Feldwebel murmured, and stepped round behind the man on the operating table.

'Scalpel!' the M.O. yelled to his assistant. He leant forward over the Leutnant. 'This won't take long,' he coaxed, and a moment later the Feldwebel, following orders, brought the hammer down on Thomas Kleebach's head. In the last resort, a brutal anaesthetic . . .

Thomas Kleebach survived, and his brother Achim went back to the front. On January 21st 1942, Rommel returned to the offensive for the last time. He recaptured Benghazi and by February 7th was at El Gazala. There was a temporary set-back at Bir Hacheim. By that time, Thomas Kleebach was already in a military hospital in Berlin.

The British Eighth Army was cut in two, with one part taking refuge in the port of Tobruk.

Tobruk fell, and for his victory Rommel was rewarded with the rank of Field Marshal. A day later the Desert Fox reached the Egyptian border once more, having decisively defeated the Eighth Army and taken 25,000 prisoners. He moved quickly into Egypt, taking Sollum and the fortress of Mersa Matruh. Only exhaustion brought his forces to a halt a few days later. A British counter-attack on the line of El Alamein was repelled.

Then, despite the glittering victories, came the end in the desert. General Montgomery, the new British commander, launched a counter-offensive, 'Operation Lightfoot' – later to be known as the Battle of El Alamein – and was helped by the landing of an Anglo-American force in French North Africa to the west. Eisenhower, with a fleet of 500 ships, landed in Morocco and Algeria, forcing the Afrika Korps to fight a two-front war; Rommel found himself in the jaws of a trap. On May 7th 1943 Tunis and Bizerta were lost, and on May 13th the last German forces surrendered on the Cape Bon Peninsula.

Achim Kleebach was not there to witness defeat. He had been awarded the Iron Cross Second Class for saving Thomas's life. It was the recognition he had always craved, but by the time he got it he was far more delighted with a postcard from his brother to tell him that Thomas was recovering in Berlin.

Achim's problem with sand-flies became so serious that he was declared unfit for service with the Afrika Korps and for a while transferred back to garrison duties in Saxony. An officer training course followed. In the autumn of 1942 he was posted to a newly-formed regiment due to join the Sixth Army in its victorious march to the Volga river in Russia. Their final destination: a city called Stalingrad. About that time, Lance-Corporal Heinz Böckelmann, Marion Kleebach's fiancé, arrived in Berlin. This wasn't the long leave that he had been dreaming of for the past two years – since his unit was being transferred from the Eastern Front to the west and he lived in Berlin, his commander had granted him a two-day pass – but those forty-eight hours were like a glimpse of heaven to him.

He made a duty visit to his mother, then rushed round to the Lietzenburger Strasse a few streets away. There he paid his respects to the Kleebach parents and talked to Thomas, who was still on convalescent leave.

Finally he made for Marion's office. When he got close, he stopped in front of a telephone box, then decided against ringing up. He would surprise her, enjoy the look on her face when he turned up. At twenty-one, he knew exactly what he wanted. He had known loneliness in a hundred variations, seen every face of death, and he was grateful to have come out of it alive. Because of his mother, and above all because of Marion. During those days and nights of hell at the front he had shared every dream, every thought, every hope with her in his mind.

He walked so quickly that passers-by looked at him strangely. He rushed past a young officer without saluting, was called back, but the officer dismissed him without saying anything. He had seen the Iron Cross Class II, the close-combat clasp, the Russia Medal – the one they called the 'Frozen Meat Award' – on the young lance-corporal's tunic, and he had forgiven him a technical lapse. Böckelmann paced up and down in front of the Headquarters building when he arrived, still asking himself whether he should really just walk in and surprise her, and then decided to go ahead. Within minutes he was standing in her office.

Disappointment. There was a girl in a garish green pullover sitting at one of the desks, heavily made-up and looking at him through hostile, cynical eyes.

'What do you want here?' she asked baldly.

'I'd like to see Fräulein Kleebach,' said Böckelmann.

'That's not possible now . . .'

'She's my fiancé.'

'I see,' the girl in the bilious green sweater said, and looked him up and down with an ironical smile. 'The famous boyfriend . . . this is a surprise.'

'It's supposed to be.'

At that moment Marion came back into the room. She saw Heinz Böckelmann and froze in the doorway, more horrified than delighted. But the young soldier was too overjoyed at the meeting to be warned by her reaction.

'You?' she hissed.

'Sure.'

'Just out of the blue?'

'Aren't you pleased?' he asked, wondering if he dared kiss her here in the office.

'Yes . . . of course . . .' She looked at her watch. 'But I don't finish work for another three hours . . . You should have written to me . . .'

'I was given stopover leave . . . I still didn't know even yesterday that . . .'

'Shall I ask the boss?' the other girl chipped in.

'I'll do it myself,' Marion said a little too quickly, obviously pleased to postpone things. She came back a few minutes later, nodded impassively at Heinz, picked up her coat and said: 'Come on.'

He walked by her side, slowly realising that there was something odd about her, but he put it down to the fact that they hadn't seen each other for so long. It was always difficult at the beginning.

'Where are we going?' she asked.

He looked at her with a puzzled frown. 'Well . . . to my place . . . or to your parents . . .'

She walked on in silence, snatching glances at Heinz from time to time. So Freddy hadn't told him anything, she thought. It would be best if she got her version in first, and as quickly as possible.

Marion stopped at the entrance to a small café, dragged the bemused Heinz inside, and ordered an acorn coffee. She stirred her cup absently with a spoon, though it was a long time since sugar had been available.

'Look, what's wrong with you?' Heinz asked.

She shrugged. 'I have to talk to you.'

'Here?'

'It will do.'

'Has something happened?' he said hoarsely.

She nodded and looked away. He was staring morosely down at the table cloth.

'Something to do with us?'

'Yes,' Marion murmured.

He lifted his head with a jerk. His face was pale and expressionless. 'Another man?' he probed.

Marion avoided his eyes again. I'm stupid, she thought. I should be talking to Freddy instead of Heinz. After all, nothing more had happened since the incident at the villa in Dahlem, and the gigolo of all people ought to be tolerant of other people's peccadillos . . .

But there was something else. She loathed herself for it, but now all she could feel for Heinz, this boy who adored her, was pity and nothing more. His fumbling for words irritated her, that and his threadbare, commonplace uniform, his cropped hair, and the way he behaved like a clumsy farm-boy.

'Yes and no,' she said at last.

'Do you love him?'

'Love?' She laughed harshly, and there was something dishonest in her voice. 'I don't think you've got any idea what it means always having to sit around waiting for the mail, spending your whole youth like a widow in mourning.'

Böckelmann nodded heavily. 'You're wrong. In this war we all have to.'

'All of us?' she said. 'Not all . . . There are people who have a good time, even in the middle of a war.'

Heinz frowned. 'Black marketeers maybe.'

'Maybe,' Marion said, grinding out her cigarette. 'But I went with one a few weeks ago . . . Don't look so damned hurt! I wanted to live a little, not just . . .'

Böckelmann could feel a pain coming on in his forehead. He stroked his temples, but it would not go away. He could see Marion opposite him, his Marion, and he could imagine her in the arms of some fat profiteer. He could imagine their panting breath, the smiles of complicity, and he could see them drinking champagne and turning down the lights . . .

'I get the picture,' he muttered between clenched teeth.

She leaned forward and stared at him, her face contorted with something close to hatred. 'And if you want to know, I don't regret it, not a moment of it! I'd do it again if I got the chance.'

'You'd do it again,' Heinz echoed slowly. It was his turn to put his cigarette out. 'Then everything's over between us?'

'Everything,' Marion agreed.

The boy sitting opposite her could sense that something didn't fit, even if he couldn't exactly understand. Every word she had spoken had hit him like a bullet in the head. Then he saw Marion's restless hands, the torment behind that stubborn face, and he knew she was unhappy. He dimly realised that he had a chance to keep her. The real question was: did he want to?

'And what do your parents have to say about all this?' he said lamely.

'Why should I care about them?' she countered. 'Everyone's got their own life to live.'

'And I suppose what it does to me . . . that's nothing to you.'

Now Marion was really looking at him for the first time, and her eyes were begging for something. 'No,' she said almost inaudibly. She hung her head. 'I'm sorry,' she went on. 'For your sake . . .' She hesitated, reached for her handbag and stood up. 'You're a good man, Heinz . . .' she murmured, then

171

gazed at him again for two or three seconds, waiting. He said nothing. She turned on her heel and walked out.

Böckelmann followed her with his eyes, but in his mind he was already alone. It did not occur to him that he had to follow Marion now if he wanted to keep her despite everything. He sat there as if rooted to the spot, but his brain was seething. At first he was stunned, then miserable, and at the end he was possessed by a raging fury such as he had never known before . . .

CHAPTER TEN

Achim Kleebach, the youngest son, was now almost twenty and no longer a Hitler Youth boy. He had been promoted to officer cadet and commanded a platoon in Russia, like thousands of other boys – not old enough to live, but ripe for death. The officer academy had wiped away the effects of his experiences in the desert and restored some of his old enthusiasm. Achim was no longer quite so keen for promotion – but he was still ready to give all for his beloved Führer.

Even in the East. It was the cold he had to face now, not the desert heat; here the sun didn't parch the land, but the rain and the mist soaked it; and a soldier chewed grass again, not sand. Yesterday eleven men had died, today so far only four – but then you didn't count your chickens . . .

The panzer spearhead's headlong advance had been brought to a temporary halt. Ahead and on their left flank they were confronted by marshy steppe, useless terrain that nevertheless had been paid for in blood. The previous day's dead still lay bloated and rotting in the stagnant pools and hollows, their lifeless eyes staring up an endless sky. When the wind got up and swirled the mud around, the corpses moved, and you could have sworn the dead men were pleading for their lives . . .

A breeze from the east dispersed the grey clouds, and a leaden sun shed its light over the landscape: over the hordes of flies, the scavenging marsh-birds, the rotting remains of horses and the floating dead. Their faces were still black. Tomorrow they would turn liverish and yellow and start to disintegrate.

There were no sand-flies any more. This time it was lice: dozens, hundreds, a whole army of lice, allied with armies of bugs and regiments of rats. Achim had been sent home from Africa because of the sand-flies. No one got sent home from Russia for anything.

'Maybe the wind'll change,' said Unteroffizier Hanselmann, the burly platoon sergeant and as hard a case as you were likely to meet even in Russia.

'That's the least of my worries,' Achim answered bitterly.

He had long accumulated enough combat experience to be given a proper commission, but that meant another course in Germany, and the Russian Front was not about to release him. For months now he had been in the forefront of the advancing German steamroller, riding in his panzer, sometimes forced to march on foot or travel in a bone-bruising horse-drawn cart. Their engines were at the end of their lives, their gun-barrels were rusting, their bodies were exhausted and their nerves shot to hell. In Russia Achim had seen nothing but blood and rubble, ruins and corpses, and peasants begging for their lives. He had passed by zones controlled by extermination-squads that killed everything that moved, and he had seen but not understood. When they halted they dug foxholes and then graves, always graves. Sometimes a hundred, two hundred at a time. The work lost its terror, and they no longer took much care to see whether a dead Russian or two had worked their way in among the German corpses.

Finally the mountains of dead had become too much for them, and they had simply piled the bodies on top of each other and poured petrol on the heaps. The blazes had brought the wrath of the Russian big guns, the 'Stalin Organs', down on the hapless burial parties. Then, of course, someone had to bury them . . .

But most of the really shitty work fell to the infantry who followed the armour. The panzer boys were still the élite, with orders to race blindly onward, heading towards the place that the Führer had marked on his pretty map in Berlin: Stalingrad, the main industrial and communications centre of the Volga region.

'If the mist comes down harder, we'll have to try and bring some of them back,' Achim said, jerking a thumb at the marshland and the dead.

'Why?' growled Unteroffizier Hanselmann.

'How would you like to rot out there?' Achim asked, shocked.

'Dead is dead,' Hanselmann murmured. 'They're not feeling any pain . . . and we could do with a rest.'

'Bastard!' Achim Kleebach muttered, but without much

174

passion. He had nothing against the N.C.O., whose cold-blooded courage had proved itself in plenty of tight corners. If he admitted the truth, he would have been terrified to carry out his own order.

Most of the battalion had carried on to the right in an attempt to penetrate the Russian front line. Kleebach's platoon had been left behind to guard the flank and wait for the mobile workshop to repair some of the badly-needed assault vehicles.

'If you let the Russians through,' his commander had told Achim. 'Then we'll have them up our arse, and you don't need ten fingers to count up what that'll mean. Can I rely on you, Kleebach?'

'Yes, Herr Major,' Achim had responded with a carefully-calculated indifference that had become his trademark.

Even if you counted the possibility that the Russians might attack, it was clear that the platoon had been lucky to get the chance of a breather. You couldn't rely on the Russians not turning up, of course, and so they had put together a rough defensive system, but since the previous day they had enjoyed peace. The only problem was the mud, but they were used to that. It came up to your knees, and even if you dug it out and chucked it over the side of the trench, more came sliding down. The mud was one weapon that the Russians could bring to bear free, gratis and for nothing.

Achim Kleebach wandered along the trench. He was in sole command of the flank-guard, but the pleasure he felt in the responsibility was limited. The front seemed almost unnaturally quiet. As he looked out over the marshes, all he could see was the arm of a dead Russian waving mockingly in the wind, like a greeting from an old friend.

Kleebach had plenty of ammunition but no anti-tank weapons. In any case, armour-piercing shells would not be needed, because no Soviet T 34 would be able to cross that terrain without sinking into the swamp. Achim had ordered the heavy machine-gun to be set up in good cover at a carefully-chosen spot half-way along the trench that provided a good field of fire over the marshland. Apart from that, he had two light machine-guns, a captured Soviet mortar, a few machine-pistols and a big stock of grenades. Weapons were the only riches these poor bastards had . . .

The thin September sun slunk back behind the clouds. The soldiers spread tarpaulins over the mud and laid themselves down. The mist was getting thicker. Achim reinforced his sentries, because he had no intention of taking chances, even though an attack in force was out of the question. You couldn't bring many men through the marsh – patrol strength at the most, hit and run. Their own left flank was guarded by an allied unit, Italians or Rumanians. Achim hoped to God it wasn't the wops, still under the influence of his experiences in the desert. He would soon learn all about the Rumanians . . .

He yawned, lit a cigarette and pondered on when he was due for his next leave. Two of the five men ahead of him on the rota had been killed in the past few days. Goes on like this, I'll be on my way, he thought sourly.

Suddenly one of the foremost sentries open fire. The sleeping soldiers in the foxholes scrambled to their feet and stared blearily at the marsh. Nothing to be seen, except little Sawitzky in his nickel-framed glasses, splashing around in the bog like a pregnant duck.

'Have you gone out of your frigging mind?' Achim bellowed.

'Over there . . .' the boy pointed. Achim followed the direction of his outstretched arm. Two swamp-cranes were fluttering around a corpse, momentarily frightened by the shot. Gradually they settled back to tearing choice morsels from the flesh.

'I can't stand it . . . that was Gerber . . . he was my friend . . .' the boy stuttered.

Achim felt the bile rise in his throat. He snapped his fingers at three men nearby. 'Fetch him here!' he ordered.

'For Christ's sake,' a corporal complained.

'Watch your mouth!'

The three men looked accusingly at little Sawitzky, who had brought all this on them.

'Let me go,' the boy said.

Achim shrugged. 'All right. But shift your arses!'

The rest of them carried on dozing.

The approaching evening was cold and damp. The men's soaked uniforms grew stiff and heavy against their raw skins. Even the lice didn't like it: they stopped biting, and the shattered soldiers could stop scratching for a change.

Achim Kleebach crouched down next to Unteroffizier

Hanselmann, slapping his hands together to keep the circulation going. 'Crock of shit,' he said.

'This is nothing,' the Unteroffizier said solemnly. 'You wait until the winter comes . . . this is sheer luxury by comparison.'

'I'd like to be in Africa now,' said Achim.

Hanselmann sighed. 'And I'd like to be at home. The wife's expecting a kid.'

'She doesn't need you any more, then,' Achim joked.

But the sergeant wasn't listening. He was away from the night, the mist and the cold, back at home in his cosy front room. There was a kettle on the stove, the radio was playing, and he could hear the click of his wife's knitting-needles. From the next room came a quavering wail. 'Ah, he's hungry again,' Frau Hanselmann said and smiled at him. 'Always wants his food, just like his daddy . . .'

With difficulty the sergeant managed to tear himself 3,000 kilometres back to the front. 'Yeah. Minus twenty-five, thirty,' he drawled. 'And then the bastards come at you, and you try to pick up your rifle . . . and your hands are rigid as iron, and you think you'll snap off your fingers if you touch the trigger . . . and if you don't do it fast enough, then you don't just freeze, you go cold . . . cold for ever . . .'

'Give it a rest!' Achim grunted. 'Once we get to Stalingrad, there'll be houses, apartments, stoves, schnaps, women . . . That's worth thinking about.'

Hanselmann shook his head gloomily. 'You'll get a surprise,' he muttered. 'You won't even want to take a shit any more, I'm telling you . . .'

'Go and check up on your section,' the platoon commander hissed, hustling him out of the foxhole.

'One good thing about a Russian winter, though,' the sergeant said as he set off. 'At least you can give yourselves a good dose of frostbite and end up in hospital.'

The previous year, in the terrible winter of 1941, the best the Unteroffizier had managed was second-degree frostbite near Moscow. He had got a caved-in nose to show for that, as well as his 'Frozen Meat Award'. Except for four weeks home leave, Hanselmann had served on the Eastern Front from the first day. On June 22nd 1941 he had crossed the River Beirbrza near Lipsk and gone with advance almost to the gates of

Moscow, had been through the Blitzkrieg and on to the war of the freezing feet ... In those days he had believed that the war would be over in the East when – not if – Hitler's armies reached the Ural mountains. He had lost those illusions well before they got to Stalingrad. Now he hated the Führer just like he hated the bugs, the lice, the rats, the Russians, the cold and the mud. Despite everything, he carried on, always clear-headed and reliable, because it was the only way he stood a chance of getting back to his Elizabeth and their baby.

Towards midnight the autumn frost reached its coldest point. The mud in the foxholes had gone thick and sticky, without freezing, making the surface even more treacherous. They had built a makeshift bunker in the middle of the position, covered with straw, and there those not on guard duty lay, sprawled against, even on top of each other, huddled together for warmth. The closeness of these men was about survival, had nothing to do with whether they liked each other; they had been forced to depend on each other – and that was what they called 'comradeship', a tough, unsentimental feeling that bore no relation to the phrase they had been spoon-fed with by the propagandists since childhood.

Achim Kleebach found it impossible to sleep. He crept outside. There was a half-moon, but you could catch no more than fleeting glimpses of it between the thick banks of cloud. Occasionally a star would appear, but there was nothing romantic about it, no friendly twinkle; much more the single, unblinking eye of the sadistic voyeur staring down on a thousand miles of suffering.

He met the men coming off sentry duty, gave them a few words of encouragement, then inspected the forward guard positions. Things were as quiet as he could have hoped for, nothing to be seen except the drifting, cloying fog that swirled over the flat landscape like a gossamer shroud. The east wind whistled gently and sadly over the isolated German position.

Achim went back to the bunker and lay down. He breathed in the fetid odour of comradeship. It was the smell of bowels and fear, the sickly scent of decayed dreams.

He still could not sleep, because his brain was supplying new dreams. He saw in his mind a sunlit Stalingrad with broad avenues, and he was strolling there, deloused and in a fresh uniform, a Leutnant now and with his leave ticket in his pocket. And he thought: it was worth it, after all. The Führer had his victory, he was off back to Berlin to see his parents, be the wonder of the neighbourhood, not yet twenty and already a war hero. A war hero who had survived, who would remember the unlucky ones on memorial days, and who had his life in front of him . . .

At last he dozed off. He was supposed to be woken at six a.m., but Unteroffizier Hanselmann let him sleep on. It wasn't until the curtain of mist was lifting and the first Russian infantrymen became visible on the other side of the marsh that he decided to raise his commander, but by that time the Russian artillery had done it for him.

The barrage from the Soviet side was wild and ill-directed. The first shells howled into the swamp, while the next lot whizzed high over the German position.

'Good morning, boys,' Achim yawned ostentatiously. He grinned and squatted down next to the heavy machine-gun to inspect the steppe through his field-glasses. The gunner looked enquiringly at him, but Achim shook his head. 'They can't be serious,' he said. 'Must just be recovering their dead.'

The picture looked different when he began to count the Russians: twenty, thirty, fifty . . . a platoon, maybe even company strength . . . or a frigging battalion . . .

'They're crazy!' Achim hissed, and ducked along the connecting trench to Unteroffizier Hanselmann. 'What do you make of that?' he asked.

Hanselmann scratched his chin. 'Could be some crazy Commissar trying to make a point,' he growled. 'Just let 'em come and we'll sort the buggers out.'

'It's nothing but suicide!' Achim yelled, and raced off back to his lookout by the machine-gun. So long as he kept his nerve, he told himself, nothing, but absolutely nothing, could happen to him and his men. Whoever had ordered the attack on the other side belonged in front of a court martial. What the boy could not know was that it was all bluff, a bluff where the stakes were high and deadly . . .

After Marion had gone, Heinz Böckelmann sat for a long time like a statue. It must have been almost an hour until he found the strength to get up and leave the café. He wandered through the city like a blind man, aimlessly, unmanned by

179

shame – shame for Marion, and loathing for himself for having let it all happen. At least his mother would know nothing of it, and in the morning he was due to rejoin his unit and be shipped off to another part of the war. After that, everything would look after itself. Heinz walked until his feet were sore and his head was spinning, from the Tiergarten to Kreuzberg and south again; stooped, his arms hanging limply by his side. He saw thousands of faces, and they meant nothing. He was bawled at by a Feldwebel in the street, but he just stood there and took it, understanding none of it. He collided with a woman on a corner and made no apology.

Finally he found himself standing in front of an apartment block that seemed familiar, and for the first time he started to regain his senses. Of course, he thought: Kretschmeier, his old school friend, lived here. His friend had been attacked by polio as a child, and his disability had saved him from conscription into the Wehrmacht.

Heinz stumbled up the stairs and looked for the name-plate. He almost turned back, then his finger was on the bell-push and it was too late to change his mind.

Kretschmeier was at home. 'You?' he said. 'This is very sudden.'

'Maybe.'

'Why the visit?'

'We were friends at school, weren't we?' Böckelmann said defiantly.

'Sure . . . of course,' answered Kretschmeier, and ushered him in.

He stared around the apartment.

'Do you need something?' his boyhood friend asked.

Böckelmann forced a smile. 'Yes. Schnaps . . . any available?'

'Of course. Round the corner.'

Kretschmeier looked at Heinz's worn, haunted face and realised what this man must have been through. In that moment he was glad to be a cripple.

'But you can get rid of that damned uniform,' he said then, limping over to a wardrobe in the corner of the room. He tossed Heinz some civilian clothes. They fitted after a fashion; in wartime no one looked too closely.

Then they set off. One bar. Another. Drinking doubles like there was no tomorrow . . .

At first Heinz drank silently, but the alcohol loosened his tongue after a while and he started to tell about his experiences at the front, something he had never done with anyone else but Kretschmeier. And they moved on to another bar, and another, though they had had more than enough.

Finally they landed up in a narrow street where the doorways and the corners were filled with the city's creatures of the night: women with tired faces, eager eyes, swinging key-rings and charging high prices.

Heinz hunched his shoulders and walked on through a gauntlet of whores. Suddenly a shadow stepped out and in the light of a street lamp he saw a dark-haired woman with slits for eyes, a come-to-bed smile on her bright-painted lips, and through his drunken haze he imagined that Marion, his Marion, would look just like that in a few years' time. He suddenly opened up the bag he was carrying, walked up to the astonished women and hurled a bundle of ration packages at her feet. Then he spat in her face and stumbled on . . .

It was ten in the morning, the wind was chasing the clouds eastwards, and the sun looked down helplessly on the savage panorama below. On the far side of the marshy steppe, streaming out of the shelter of a pine thicket, several hundred Russian soldiers advanced to certain death. They had been drilled to do just that, to offer their lives attacking a patch of swamp that was worthless – except that it was part of their homeland.

Officer Cadet Achim Kleebach crouched silently by the heavy machine-gun and took another incredulous look through his field glasses. He shook his head, because what was happening out there was way beyond his military experience. The Russian artillery was aiming with more accuracy now, but still falling short of the German position.

The advancing Ivans would take at least twenty minutes to cross the swamp, and for that entire time they would offer perfect targets. Achim knew it, and it gave him a bad feeling, though he knew too that he would give the order to fire, because for Christ's sake this was war and there was no time for chivalry.

He put down his field glasses, rose and dashed ducking along the connecting trench to give his men some last-minute encouragement. To a last man they were staring at the insane advance wide-eyed, laughing and shaking their heads in disbelief.

Sawitzky, the little private with the glasses, was the only one who was bothering to take aim at the Russians, even though they were still out of range. Achim smacked him between the shoulder-blades with the flat of his hand, and the boy spun round, his earnest face contorted with fear.

'Don't piss your trousers before it's due, son,' Achim grinned.

'But there's at least three hundred Ivans out there,' Sawitzky stuttered, his eyes still glued to the scene in the swamp.

'So what?'

'There's only fifty, maybe sixty of us . . .'

Kleebach took Sawitzky's rifle from the rim of the trench, removed the magazine and the bolt, and asked calmly: 'How many parts has the soldier's bride?'

'Seven,' Sawitzky responded, parroting the old training-camp catechism.

'Very good,' said Achim, with all the cynical authority of a man twelve months older than the little private. 'And now, sonny, to give you something to occupy your mind, you will take this rifle apart three times and each time put it together again.'

'But . . .'

'That's an order! And you'll stick with me and I'll watch every move, you arsehole!'

It made Achim feel good to prove his coolness in front of his men. Now the Russians had opened up with mortars. The advancing Soviet infantry were still a kilometre away. Though they were meeting with no opposition, they were making slow progress; every time the poor bastards took a step their legs sank in up to the knees.

'Like a bunch of goddamned flamingoes,' Achim said harshly. 'Hey, listen here!' he yelled out, cupping his hands to his mouth. 'No one fire until I give the order . . . we'll let 'em come as close as possible, and then we can play Hindenburg. This'll be our battle of the Masurian Lakes!'

Unteroffizier Hanselmann grunted to himself. If only the boy wouldn't shoot his mouth off, he thought. He was in charge of the group round the machine-gun on the left flank. Any bloody fool could see that as soon as they opened fire the Russkies would drown like rats trying to take cover.

'Understood?' Kleebach roared.

A few of the men made acknowledgment. The rest didn't bother, because they knew more about this kind of warfare than any teenage cadet-officer.

'Take cover!' someone yelled.

But everyone else had seen it too: a couple of heavily-armoured Soviet Ilyushin IIs were swooping down like huge hawks, and within seconds they had picked out the German position and gone into a steep attacking dive. The men below went headlong, heard the staccato rattle of wing-mounted machine-guns and waited for the screams of the maimed and the dying. Then silence. The Germans slowly raised their heads and looked around in astonishment. The Ilyushins had managed to miss.

'Today's our lucky day,' said Achim Kleebach.

'Wait a minute!' Sawitzky muttered, still staring intently skywards.

They both hit the bottom of the trench together, because the enemy dive-bombers were coming in again.

This time the Ilyushins dropped light bombs that made a lot of noise and kicked up a lot of smoke, but when the alarm was over Achim's platoon had still suffered no losses. The two Soviet planes banked and flew off, as if they had finished their quota for that day. There could be no question of their fearing the German Messerschmitts, because air cover from the Luftwaffe was a long-lost myth as far as the average Wehrmacht infantryman was concerned.

'Jesus, who hasn't had a go at us yet?' Achim bellowed contemptuously at the departing Ilyushins. He checked the swamp and saw that the Russians there were not yet in range. 'Those bastards want to die in their beds,' he chuckled, then glanced along the trench. 'Everything all right?'

No casualties. It was a joke. Until Private Mühlwein's mate said: 'Here, your coat's a bit of a mess.'

'Don't talk shit,' growled the plump, good-natured Mecklenburger. Then he looked and found himself staring at his own bloodstained trousers. The realisation dawned that, without realising it, he'd been served with an A 1 send-me-home number, a beautiful flesh wound in the arse. 'Christ!' he screamed in delight and leapt to his feet, laughing out loud. 'It's my frigging birthday!' They had trouble stopping him from dropping his pants on the spot and showing the wound in his behind to his comrade, who at the moment had other things on his mind.

The Russians were 700 metres away. Their uniforms were the colour of mud, hardly distinguishable from the swamp. Most of the Ivans wore steel helmets, which made them look like a swarm of turtles bobbing in the slime.

A few were moaning protests, but they were forced forward. A Russian second leutnant drove them on, waving his arms wildly and bawling harsh orders and threats.

'I'll get that bastard first,' oathed Achim Kleebach, setting down his field glasses and aiming along the bead of his own rifle, trying out the range and lightly playing with the trigger. It was tempting to squeeze it the whole way and be done with it, but he sneaked a glance at Unteroffizier Hanselmann to his left and realised that the best thing would be to follow what the veteran N.C.O. did. The platoon's sergeant would fire at exactly the right moment, not a second earlier or later. Waiting for Hanselmann to make his move, Achim spared the Russian second leutnant. A temporary reprieve.

Five hundred metres.

Hanselmann, the swine, was still calmly smoking a cigarette.

Four hundred and fifty metres.

Hanselmann carefully ground his cigarette into the mud, as if he had all the time in the world. He took over the machinegun himself, pressed the stock firmly against his shoulder, and waited.

Four hundred metres.

Hanselmann fired his first burst, and for the rest of the platoon it was like being released from a spell. His deceptively casual sweep brought down the foremost dozen Russians even before they could hit cover. They heard screams and frantic commands as the Soviets writhed in the mud of the swamp, which swallowed the corpses and the wounded like a predator. Russians went head over heels, floundering up to their necks, but they had to keep their heads above to breathe. Big enough targets . . .

It took just over a minute to wipe out the first wave. The Russians hardly fired a shot. The mortar in the rear stepped up its barrage, but it did the men in the swamp not a shred of good. The next lot of attackers clambered over the dead, using them like duckboards, and came on with their heads bowed and the look of men who knew they were bound to die.

The swamp echoed to the sound of splintering wood, shrieks of agony, howling bullets, curses and panic-stricken orders. To Achim's left Hanselmann had taken a terrible toll, mowing the Ivans down in carefully-calculated, economical bursts. So far he hadn't even had to change the barrel of his machine-gun.

Achim hit the second leutnant, but the Russian staggered up again and came on, and while Kleebach was still taking aim he was scythed down by machine-gun fire, sent sprawling backwards into the glutinous marsh. Achim watched him sinking slowly into the mud and yelled in childish disappointment: 'You bastards! He was mine!'

It was a savage, unequal battle. The Russians died like cattle, with no chance to retaliate. Bloody criminal, thought Achim, to send men into a battleground like this, just send them to slaughter. He had no time to wonder if he would ever have to carry out a similar order – but there was a moment for everything . . .

He had no time to theorise because suddenly he heard a yell and whipped round. Impossible . . . He stared in slack-jawed astonishment and let precious seconds pass, because from behind, from the heart of the German lines, were coming more Russians. Fifty, more, who knew? And they were coming on quickly, with grim determination, because there was no mud on their boots, no slime clinging to their uniforms.

In that bitter fraction of a second of realisation, Achim realised that the Russians in the swamp had been sacrificed to divert attention from a breakthrough on the flank, where the Italians or Rumanians had collapsed yet again at the first sight of an Ivan attack.

He snapped the machine-gun round and mowed down the first rank of the advancing shock-troops, maybe a hundred metres from the German trench. But there were more behind, howling with the scent of victory and revenge, their faces greedy for Nazi blood. They were coming on in text-book style, spread out, running and rolling, one covering while the other moved over the ground. You could kill three and a fourth was there, still getting closer, until you could see every detail on their faces, begin to know the man you had to kill.

Now even the Ivans in the swamp were making progress in what had turned into a miniature two-front war. Unteroffizier Hanselmann, closest to them, was forced to change the barrel of his machine-gun at last; he had his hands full, and had to leave the rest of the platoon to their own devices. But he saw the situation even before Kleebach's new orders reached him, and determined to keep at least the rear free.

The platoon defended itself as best it could, but the new attack couldn't be beaten off. The Russians came forward with uncanny precision and coolness, ignoring their losses; everywhere Achim looked he saw Soviets running, storming on, firing as they ran, yelling the Muzhik soldiers terrifying 'hurr-ah!'. Pretty soon Achim was no longer fighting to secure the panzers' flank; he was fighting for his bare existence ... and incidentally, if he died, then the Ivans would have gained a bridgehead right through the middle of the German advance to Stalingrad, and then the foremost spearheads would be cut off and the rest would be bloody chaos ...

He saw a big Russian infantryman with a cannister on his back and froze. There was nothing Achim hated or feared like a flame-thrower. He slapped a fresh magazine into the machine-gun and brought the man down.

But other Russians carried cannisters ...

Because the machine-gun had been set up to cover the swamp, with no time to change its position in the face of the new attack, there was a 'dead corner', where it couldn't reach. The Russians had realised the fact quickly, maybe twenty or thirty seconds before Kleebach, and they were using the advantage to flood through.

Achim offered a prayer that the boys down there were on their toes, but then he saw the searing crimson tide of flame and heard the chilling screams of his incinerated comrades and knew that they had caught the crew of the other machine-gun, leaving the trench to the right totally exposed. And the Ivans came on directly towards him now, working their way from the right. Within seconds they were in the trench and ducking along. Others were coming head-on, realising that they had the Germans exactly where they wanted them. It would be hand-to-hand against overwhelming force. The finish. Within minutes yesterday's foxhole would be today's graveyard . . .

Achim managed to scythe down the first three with his machine-pistol. Then he realised that it was pointless to stay in cover; he could see the gleaming bayonets of the attackers and knew he had to get out of the confined space before a grenade or a blade finished him off.

He scrambled up out of the foxhole, followed by the others, then dealt with another two Soviets, crouched firing from the hip on the rim of the trench. A grenade settled the next bunch before he reached for his entrenching-tool for the pitiless hand-to-hand struggle to come.

Achim saw a huge Ivan with a heavy peasant's face swiping at Sawitzky with a rifle butt, swung his entrenching-tool and hacked into the man's neck. He toppled like a felled tree-trunk. A second later little Sawitzky returned the compliment, bringing down another Russian with a pistol shot before the Red infantryman could bury his bayonet in Kleebach's back.

Achim lunged at the next, swinging wildly around him. He smashed a face in with the shaft, then moved on to the man behind him, blindly, like a crazed animal, and brought him down just as the Russian pulled the pin on a grenade. Achim booted the grenade back like a football straight into the bunch of attackers ahead, then hurled himself to the ground just in time. There were screams of panic, a deafening explosion, a shower of mud and fragments, and Achim was on his feet again, bawling encouragement to men who were fighting like berserkers with the final, insane strength of despair. But it had to be the end; all he could think was: how could it last so long . . .?

Suddenly he could breathe freely; a miracle! Yet again, it turned out, Unteroffizier Hanselmann had saved them. The sergeant, who always knew what to do, had seen the blind spot, let the Russians come on at first. Then he had left the Ivans in the swamp to their own devices and swung round his machine-gun, aiming straight at the Russians round Achim. Once he had dealt with them, he had a free field of fire at the Russians on the flank, who had left cover to try a frontal assault. The slaughter there was horrific, but Hanselmann kept at his grim work of reaping just long enough before he turned his attention back to the Russians staggering out of the swamp.

Within seconds the entire battlefield had gone ghostly quiet. Unteroffizier Hanselmann stood up and walked slowly over to view the damage. The platoon's survivors scarcely came up to section strength, excluding the wounded. To the left, where the Soviets had used the flame-throwers, there were only corpses, unidentifiable, blacked dolls, stripped of flesh and charred, with only hideous-white teeth to show that these had once been living human beings.

The Russians were piled up in front and behind the German position, sprawled over each other in a wall of death. Beneath and beside that wall were scattered a few comrades, and Hanselmann inspected them for signs of life. No chance for friend or enemy here. Many of the dead were still grasping at the mud with claw-like fingers, in one final spasmodic, hopeless attempt to keep contact with the earth and life.

Little Sawitzky was cowering in his foxhole, tears streaming down his face, senselessly stripping and rebuilding his rifle, over and over again . . . A few others were moving among the wounded, bandaging them up, and Achim Kleebach wandered in a daze among visions of purgatory, still astonished that he was alive.

He stopped and stared down in horror at one man, who had been pinned to the ground with a bayonet, because he recognised the contorted face of Mühlwein, the Mecklenburger who had got his send-me-home wound before the attack, and he saw too that the man was still moving feebly. Achim knelt down beside Mühlwein, gently pushed a folded-over piece of canvas under the man's head and waited for him to scream. But the plump private was past that.

His eyes fluttered open and he made an effort to speak. Achim tried to stop him, but the Mecklenburger's will to live, fuelled by his joy at the send-me-home wound, was insanely strong. He smiled up at Achim, his eyes glinting feverishly. 'They'll – send me – home,' he croaked. 'Will you take – me – to the hospital, sir?' Blood was dribbling out of his mouth with each word, running down his chin and down his neck, dripping onto the grass.

'You bet,' Achim lied softly. 'We'll bandage you up. You'll

188

be off in no time. A nice comfy train home . . . relax . . . be happy . . .'

'Oh – I – am –' the dying man said painfully. His body was stiff in premonition of death, but his face was alive, and would live on for a few seconds that seemed like an eternity, cheating death with the maniac power of self-deception. For merciful God's sake, die, thought Achim.

But Mühlwein was not ready. 'E-r-ika,' he mumbled. 'My – girl – she promised if –'

'Don't talk,' Achim whispered.

'We – were – conned . . .' Mühlwein's words were becoming indistinct. There was no more blood coming out of his mouth, no more left in his veins, but Mühlwein struggled on. His glazed eyes were fixed on that wound that would get him home to his girl, his ticket to Erika . . .

'W-water . . .' he moaned thickly.

'Give it to him,' said Unteroffizier Hanselmann, who had come up quietly behind Achim.

The platoon commander shook his head stubbornly.

'It'll all be over in a minute,' the sergeant growled. 'Pull that bloody bayonet out!'

'No!' Achim said heavily.

Whether or not he pulled the bayonet out of the man's body, plump, jolly Mühlwein was going to die a miserable death, and Achim had no intention of helping it along. The next second he regretted it, because the dying man tried to sit up with his last strength and saw the steel shaft rammed through his stomach, and the lunatic smile died on his face as he finally realised that he had no send-me-home wound after all . . .

'E-r-ika . . .' Mühlwein croaked in agony, his last illusion smashed. And then it was over.

Unteroffizier Hanselmann leaned over and carefully pulled the bayonet out of the man's stomach, then peered at the bloodstained blade for several moments, as if visiting a curse on the butcher who had done for Mühlwein. Suddenly he dropped it and turned away to help with burying the dead, without another word. They dug graves until they had to jump back in their foxholes, because the Russians were massing for their third attack . . .

*   *   *

Lance-Corporal Heinz Böckelmann left the train in Cologne to be greeted by the lullaby of 1942: air-raid sirens. He nodded to himself without particular concern, as if he had expected little else, and stared indifferently at the mass of people who were scrambling panic-stricken towards the entrance to the shelter.

He had come to Cologne, where he was due to rejoin his unit, a day early. There had been nothing to keep him in Berlin, not even his mother. The glittering capital of the Reich had become the graveyard of his hopes since he had learned of Marion's infidelity.

A patrol of M.P.s bawled at him to get into the nearest cellar, and he obeyed mechanically. Down below he was a member of a classless society, the society of fear: exhausted workers, young mothers dandling screaming children on their knees, a drunk, and the air-raid warden, who slammed home the bolt on the steel door to the shelter as if it would keep out the rain of destruction. The raid got under way and the cellar shook, and the eyes of the people down there flickered in time with the exploding bombs and the plaster falling from the walls and ceiling. The emergency lighting went off and on, off and on, almost hypnotically. They could hear the dull crump of the flak and the roar of the bombs. Six, seven nearby. They hunched down. Böckelmann was the only one who felt no fear. It left him cold, indifferent; he didn't give a shit . . .

As the R.A.F. came over the second time, he was dreaming again of that dark side-street in Berlin, tasting the bile in his mouth, walking past those whores. He had dreamed of getting out of this uniform, making something of himself, loving Marion and living with her as man and wife, and now he could see her, too, as a whore with a worn-out body and a hard face and a bunch of keys jingling in her hand. He could feel the hammering in his head again, and he began to breathe heavily, until he realised that it was the bombs and that they were coming down all around the shelter.

The light went out for good, and there were shrieks of terror in the shelter. The flak fire was getting heavier. The next attack came, and the bombs rained down on the city by the Rhine, indiscriminate in their destruction of all life below: women, children, the old, for Christ's sake dogs, cats, canaries . . .

At last it was over.

Heinz Böckelmann was in a hurry to get out, though there was no bed waiting for him above. He left the shelter and went out into the cold night air, raising his collar against the wind. He saw the glint of flame in the night sky, and reached the bombed house two minutes later. The building had been hit by an incendiary, and was already a complete inferno. The fire brigade had arrived, given up any hope of anybody living through that, and confined itself to keeping the blaze away from the nearby houses.

Heinz reached the barrier in the street and was quickly roped in by the reserve officer in charge to help with the clearing work. He was wheeling over a barrow of sand when he heard a scream. He and several others span round and stared in horror at the burning house.

Another shriek, high-pitched and agonised.

'A child,' someone said.

'Would you friggin' believe it?' another oathed. 'Selfish bastards clear off to the shelter and leave a kid behind . . .'

Heinz heard it through a fog. He gazed upwards vaguely, and suddenly one of the rescue crew laughed. On the sill of a shattered window on the first storey cowered a terrified cat, with flames licking round it. It was shrieking like a child.

Just a cat. Nothing but a cat. But Heinz Böckelmann felt himself overwhelmed by a crazy determination. It was lunacy to go into that house, but he had survived far worse situations, risked his neck countless times to kill other human beings. He felt a bizarre relief as his befuddled brain told him: it would be so much better to go to hell for a cat than to capture a stupid goddamned foxhole or hill . . .

He dashed towards the house. A few rescuers tried to stop him, but then they saw the look in his eyes and stepped back. He ran in between collapsing walls and cracking doors, sticking a handkerchief over his mouth against the choking smoke. He covered a few yards, looking for the cat, but half-way up the stairs the whole floor collapsed. A balcony came down on top of him, with great chunks of white-hot plaster, and he was buried. Before unconsciousness came, he had time to think that it was all over, and to feel an intense relief.

He didn't hear the harsh voice that roared: 'Come on, let's get that idiot out of there!'

That same night, Berlin had been saved the fire. In fact, in the Reich capital it was raining. Big drops beat a tattoo against the roof tiles. A high wind blew shadows flitting around the room. The bells of the nearby Memorial Church sounded midnight, ushering in Thomas Kleebach's last hours at home.

He sat up in bed and looked at Luise.

There had been no more barriers between them this time; the shadow had gone. Suddenly it had been natural and obvious, and they had no longer hidden their feelings. Time was a major factor: they had four weeks, and the twenty-eighth day was about to dawn. Thomas Kleebach climbed carefully out of bed, padded over the window and shut it. He moved in total silence, but he could sense that Luise was smiling at him from the bed. He saw her eyes shining, and he lay down again in her arms and held her so tightly that it hurt. How could he see enough of Luise? Three weeks before they had married, in the same church that was signalling midnight and stealing their time from them . . .

'How long can this war go on?' Luise whispered.

'I don't know.'

'The main thing is that you don't have to go back to Africa, isn't it?' she said. 'Perhaps the situation isn't quite so bad in Russia . . .'

'Maybe,' he answered tersely. 'Go to sleep now.'

He waited until Luise was breathing regularly and peacefully. These nights before return to the war were commonplace to him now, but this was the worst. He thought wildly of sneaking off before it was light, but he knew he couldn't bring himself to do it. A train whistle sounded over at the Zoo Station. That same day an engine like that would be taking him almost 3,000 kilometres away from Luise and his parents, 3,000 kilometres through the minefields, the partisan-held areas, the endless expanses of a vast country that only Hitler, a political idiot, would have thought he could conquer.

His thoughts had passed over the glorious advance, and were concentrating on the retreat, when he noticed that Luise was awake again, and that she was breathing hard and crying. 'Luise . . .' he said gently.

'I'm so afraid,' she stuttered. 'So terribly afraid . . .'

Then the clock on the church tower struck one, the first hour of the new day and the seventh-last of his convalescent leave . . .

CHAPTER ELEVEN

The headlong advance rolled on – towards disaster. Hitler wanted Stalingrad at any price – and the price was the 300,000 men, mainly from the Sixth Army, who had been ordered from the Führer's headquarters on 23rd July 1942 to conquer the Volga Basin and the Batum-Baku oilfields. The Führer had learned nothing from the previous winter's fiasco, when his armies had over-extended themselves in the drive towards Moscow, and he shouted down his generals' half-hearted objections. As always, they gave in to Hitler in the end, and so became his accomplices in the greatest military tragedy in the history of war: Stalingrad . . .

Achim Kleebach's platoon marched in the heart of the advance. They had held off the third Russian attack across the swamp long enough to be relieved by reinforcements pushing up from the German main force. A short while later, most of the vehicles had been given a clean bill of health by the repair workshop, and so Kleebach's unit – or what was left of it – had rejoined the spearhead, rolling on past the infantry, the corpses and the ruins, in a day-and-night desperate advance towards Stalingrad.

The Southern Army was divided into two. Army Group A headed off down towards the Caucasus and the precious oilfields, while Army Group B, made up of the Sixth Army, the Fourth Panzer Army, units of the Second Army, and a scattering of Hungarian, Rumanian and Italian regiments, struck out beyond the Don to the river Volga north of Stalingrad. There were bloody battles in the suburbs of the city, centred on the 'Red Barricade' and 'Red October' factories. The Soviets were defending Stalingrad with an unheard-of ferocity. The Sixth Army advanced slowly from strongpoint to strongpoint, even house to house, hindered by poor supply-lines and increased partisan activity. A further complication was that the entire railway system from Rostov onwards had to be changed over to German track gauge. But the Wehrmacht fought on, and painfully conquered two-thirds of Stalingrad. The Russians, though, held on stubbornly to their lifeline, a bridgehead across the Volga, and by the time the winter came the battle had degenerated into savage trench-warfare.

The munition situation deteriorated. Often no rations were delivered to the forward positions. German positions were inadequately fortified because of lack of materials. The soldiers were forced to find their own provisions where they could in the desolated terrain. Hitler was well aware of the supply problems, but Reich Marshal Goering promised his Führer that the Luftwaffe would be able to supply the Sixth Army from the air. It was true that he had also, in 1940, promised that no enemy bomber would ever defile the soil of the Reich, but that was obviously one mistake that Hitler had let slip his mind.

Kleebach's platoon survived the slaughter of the battle for the 'Dzerzhinksi' factory complex and dug itself into the rubble to wait for the next advance. Their panzers had long been claimed for another part of the front; now the crews were fighting as no more than humble infantrymen.

The night was damp and cold. If heaven still had any stars to show, she was keeping them hidden. Two days previously, Achim's men had lost control and eaten their iron rations, and since then they had starved. They had learned what it was like to have a vacuum in your stomach, an empty space where your brain should be, and Russia up to the eyeballs. What they didn't know was that they were still only on the lowest rung of the ladder of suffering, that after hunger came horror, and after horror came freezing, and after freezing death arrived as a release.

Even Achim found it hard to hide his misery. Nothing had come of his dreams of a sunlit stroll through Stalingrad; he was far from broad avenues, he had forgotten what a proper uniform was like, and he had seen no girls that were worth turning round for since what seemed like an eternity. When he stood up, he had to hang on to something to keep his balance, for hunger makes a man dizzy and weakens his limbs. Nevertheless, his platoon had had things relatively easy: during the course of the bloody house-to-house fighting they had looted a liquor store and a turnip-patch. The raw root vegetables gave them indigestion, and their empty, ulcerous stomachs brought the vodka straight up again, but they drank to the last bottle, ate to the last turnip, and they would fight to the last shot . . .

They were too exhausted to speak, even too apathetic to curse. Even Unteroffizier Hanselmann, the old Russia hand, was a shadow of his former self. No one thought of home any more, or even of the horror of war, but only ever of food. They dreamt of hot, steaming potatoes, of roast meat, thick, glutinous puddings, bread smeared with artificial honey, and even the turnips, though their cramped, shrunken stomachs could no longer cope with them, had become a delicacy to be hoarded. This, though, was only a trial, a modest dress rehearsal. They had not yet experienced the slow, pitiless, choking, killing hunger of the months to come . . .

Achim Kleebach was inspecting his forward sentries. He decided to give the left-hand ones a miss rather than exhaust himself further. His mouth was so dried out that even when he imagined the most delicious menu he could no longer raise an ounce of saliva.

'I told you what it would be like,' said Hanselmann bitterly, as if the young officer was personally responsible for this bottomless pit of hunger. 'It's not enough to die here . . . you have to starve as well.'

'Shut your mouth,' snarled Achim, but it came out as a feeble wheezing sound.

Up ahead a flare burst and cast light over a dead horse. It was almost rotted away, but four men from the platoon had bought it trying to bring it in that afternoon.

No sound. The Russians were sticking to their own holes. These were no longer the same, pathetic Ivans who had surrendered in their hundreds of thousands in the summer of '41, who had fought an unequal battle with antiquated weapons and inadequate equipment, who had often been forced into the attack by their commissars at gun-point. The horror of the German extermination-squads and the Nazis' treatment of Russian civilians had turned them, if not into loyal communists, at least into fierce patriots, and nowadays they fought with the most terrible weapon of all: hatred. They had also learned one or two tricks of psychological warfare, as Kleebach's platoon was about to find out this very night.

The wind changed suddenly, wafting over direct from the Russian lines. The Germans stared into the darkness, but their eyes were not probing the enemy positions. They were being drawn to the dead horse like iron filings to a magnet . . .

'I'll have another try,' Achim said. 'Who's coming with me?'

No one made a move.

'When there's food around, you'll all be waiting in line, licking your chops,' the officer snarled. 'But you won't get a scrap from me!' His eyes were crazed with hunger. 'I'll eat the whole damned thing . . . all on my own!'

He made as if to launch himself over the top of the trench, but he collapsed back almost immediately. Three men grabbed him and threw him out of the foxhole. Achim crawled silently through no man's land, cautiously at first, then throwing everything to the winds, because he saw, not death ahead of him, but just meat, meat, sweet horse meat.

The Ivans must have been watching him for a long time, but they held their fire. When he was less than five metres from the cadaver, two searchlights came on from the Russian side and their beam was exactly over the mangled horse, and it stayed there for minutes. Back in the German foxholes they could could not shoot at the lights for fear of wasting precious ammunition. Achim waited. Another few minutes. Then he got to his feet and walked slowly back to his comrades, bolt upright, completely indifferent to danger.

Yet again the Russians let him go. The boy rolled over the edge of the trench and hit the ground like a sack of potatoes, his face a mask of despair but his eyes still wild and greedy.

'Those swine!' he grated. 'They're playing with us . . .' He spared them the rest. The men in his trench knew exactly what the Russians were doing.

Things were still absolutely quiet. Uncannily. Even the machine-guns farther up the line were taking a break. Now they could not only feel the wind, they could smell it.

'Pea soup,' said Unteroffizier Hanselmann, raising his head to sniff the air. 'Peas with potatoes and ham . . . Jesus.'

They stared across to the enemy lines, hollow-eyed, and for that long moment their hatred was stronger than apathy. They would have put their lives in the balance for a pot full of pea soup if they had thought that an attack would stand the slightest chance. They crouched together in the freezing mud, and they ate every bite of that food along with the enemy . . .

Achim's head sunk between his hands; he had to bite his lip to stop himself from weeping. In his mind he was back in his mother's kitchen, and she was cooking his favourite dish. The table was covered with a clean white cloth, the one they brought out for the big occasions at home. And he chewed and chewed at the food, savouring every mouthful, his eyes fixed on the rest of the meal, the delights to come, losing himself in a dream – until he realised that he wasn't in his mother's kitchen in Berlin but in the cold kitchen at Stalingrad, where the thought of food was just another face of hell.

He heard a sound and glanced to his left. It was Sawitzky. The little man with the nickel glasses was chewing, almost silently, but hunger had sharpened Achim's senses. He crept up behind him, then grabbed his hand before it could go up to Sawitzky's mouth again, and his fingers wrenched a half of a raw potato out of his grip. The others, seeing what was going on, lunged at the little man. Two held him down and the others searched his pockets, where they found another one and a half mouldy potatoes. The five of them wolfed down the food.

'You're a bastard!' Achim hissed. 'No sense of comradeship!' The rest was lost in his eager chewing of his booty.

Little Sawitzky cried like a child. Not because of his officer's reproof, but because of the potatoes that had gone for ever.

Suddenly a loudspeaker started up on the other side of the lines, so close that it seemed to be only a few metres from the German foxhole.

'Listen!' shouted a Russian voice in unaccented, if slightly over-precise German. 'Soldiers of the Wehrmacht, do not be stupid! Throw away your weapons and come to us! We are not fighting against you, but against Hitler, who at this moment is sitting well-fed in his bunker while you are driven to the slaughter like animals . . . Come to us! Have no fear! The fascists lie! You will be decently treated and given first-class food!'

'Sons-of-bitches!' croaked Achim. He grabbed his machine-pistol and stumbled to his feet, looking for the loudspeaker, but he saw nothing.

Then, still from the other side, drifting on the wind, came

the tune, beautifully arranged in four-four time, tender, tempting, seductive, of the song, 'My Homeland, Your Stars . . .' The volume on the speaker was turned up so that it could be heard all along the line, bringing home-sickness to join hunger.

'Stars that light me in this distant place . . .'

Pea soup. That tune. Four-four time. And hunger. Pea soup. Illusion. But home. Eat. Mother. Hunger. Pea soup. Wives. And a voice:

'The heavens shine down like a carpet of diamonds . . .'

The recording faded away and the propaganda announcer came back: 'If you want to go home, then put up your hands and come to us! If you long for your wives, then all you have to do is to surrender! Then you will see them again . . . And tonight the menu is pea soup . . . Pea – soup – pea . . .' the speaker repeated the syllables as if counting each delicious green pea individually. The echo bounced off the shattered factory walls and back in among the warren of trenches and foxholes, tormenting the men's senses, raising their hunger to a raging madness. 'Pea . . . soup . . . pea . . .'

They clapped their hands over their ears to shut it out, bit their lips with the effort until the blood flowed.

'They'll do for us,' moaned Unteroffizier Hanselmann. 'I swear it, they'll . . .'

A new recorded tune, but the same old smell of soup.

The illusion was so powerful that little Sawitzky had to grip the edge of the trench and throw up into no man's land, as if he had overeaten.

'Don't be so mistrustful, comrades,' the loudspeaker voice said comfortably. 'If you don't believe us, send a man over to us . . . with ten billy-cans . . . Listen: we're offering ten billy-cans full, brimming full of pea soup . . . pea soup . . .'

It was Unteroffizier Hanselmann, of all people, who cracked first. 'I'm going to take the bastards up on that!' he panted, and leapt to his feet, snatching at mess-tins from the surrounding trench . . .

The injured man came to his senses quite slowly, as if after a road accident or a major operation. He could feel pain, and hear voices, and he began to try to work out where he was.

The air was fetid, but he did not yet know that it was the stale atmosphere of an overheated hospital room.

Böckelmann's head was buried under a thick wad of bandages which left only his mouth and nose free. He looked to the outside world like some bizarre creature from outer space, but that also he did not yet know. Opposite him on the wall was a painting of the Führer in oils, but Böckelmann could not see it.

The pain seemed to ebb for a few moments, granting him time to get his bearings. He remembered the burning house, the scream of a child, the one that turned out to be a cat, the way he had rushed in because without Marion he didn't care any more, and then the fight against the smoke, the searing heat, the masonry collapsing everywhere, the crunch and . . . nothing . . .

Looks like I'm alive, Heinz thought coolly, and began to wonder what had happened to the cat . . .

He was breathing with difficulty. Something was pressing against his chest cavity. Ribs, he pondered, broken or crushed. Then he was able to make out three voices in the room, heard laughter that had nothing to do with him, a dreamlike sound filtered through the mask of bandages.

'Well . . . I'll tell you . . .' one soldier with a thick, gravelly voice was saying. 'This Hauptmann, fat bastard, doles out punishment to me . . . he says I've got to go and help his wife tidy the house . . .'

'And?'

'Like I always say,' the thick voice went on with a chuckle. 'Blondes give you what the redheads promise . . . Anyway, I reports to the chief's apartment, and there she is . . . in a swimsuit, legs up to her arm-pits and well-stacked . . .'

'How old?'

'Thirty at the most . . . and I looks at her and I can't believe what I'm seeing . . . I gets a load of those come-to-bed eyes and I wonders how that dumb officer managed to find a girl like her . . . "What do you want?" she asks me in this smokey voice . . .'

'And you in fatigues?'

'Yeah,' said the thick voice. 'Dear lady, I says, what I want isn't important . . . I want to know what you want . . . where are the carpets for me to beat, for instance? And I'll tell you,

200

that vixen locks the door behind me and we goes upstairs with her following me so close I can hear her panting . . . And then she points to the load of rubbishy velour or whatever on the floor there, and she grins . . . And off we go . . .'

'You're making this up!'

'Cross my heart,' the thick voice said, hurt. Then he sighed. 'Easy . . . but then of course I still had two legs in those days . . .'

Heinz Böckelmann quickly ran a hand over his body, sudden panic welling up within him, and was relieved to discover that he seemed to have all his arms and legs intact. The effort sent him off into unconsciousness again, and he didn't wake up until the army doctor arrived on his rounds.

'How are we then?' soothed the M.O.

'Oh, we're absolutely fine,' Böckelmann said sarcastically. He could still see nothing through the bandages, but he could smell expensive eau-de-cologne.

'The main thing is that you've still got your sense of humour,' the M.O. said. He stood for a moment in his long white gown with jack boots peeking out of the bottom and seemed to be weighing up how frank he could be.

Heinz asked the question for him. 'And how are things with me, sir?' he said.

'You were very lucky,' the doctor answered. 'You were just about buried alive, but a few struts from the balcony protected your head until they could get you out . . .'

'So what state am I in now?'

'Oh, we dealt with the smoke-poisoning pretty effectively,' the M.O. said carefully, beginning with the good news. 'The lacerations will hurt, but no more than that . . . We'll sort out the fracture in your ankle . . .' He stopped abruptly, and Heinz, who was already getting used to using his ears to 'see' for him, realised that something was being left unsaid.

'And what about my head?'

'I'm afraid things don't look so good there,' the M.O. admitted. 'Burns in the face.' He laughed nervously. 'Lucky you can't see yourself at the moment . . .'

'Burns?' Böckelmann echoed, remembering comrades so disfigured that you couldn't bear to look at them.

'Never fear,' said the doctor with a forced joviality. 'Once the skin has healed, we'll do a little operation . . . You'll be prettier than ever, I promise you . . .'

The injured man said nothing.

'Thank modern medical science for that,' the doctor continued. 'We call it a transplant . . . we take a bit of skin from your thigh and plant it in your face . . . no one will be able to tell . . .'

Heinz Böckelmann still said nothing, just listened as the doctor prattled on. He's lying, he thought. It was strange how you could still tell the falseness in a man even when your eyes were bandaged up. His hands felt his face, tried to probe the eye sockets but felt nothing. The whole area was strangely furry, felt dead.

'Now, my dear chap,' he heard the M.O. saying to the man with the thick voice. 'Now you'll be doing a bit of physical therapy . . . Then we'll measure you for a prosthetic leg . . . Don't get too depressed . . . Soon you'll be able to run like a greyhound again, and if you've got the energy you can go skiing . . .'

'Skiing was the last thing I was thinking of . . .' murmured the patient.

Böckelmann drifted off into another exhausted sleep before the M.O.'s visit was over. Over the next few days he gained strength quickly, too quickly for the nurse, whose pitying gaze he could not see.

'This is terrible,' he complained. 'Having this stuff over your head. And the stubble's making me sore . . . when can I have a shave, sister?'

'You can have the bandage off in a few days,' she said quietly.

The others in the ward broke off their conversation and things went deadly quiet. The other three, even though they knew they would live their lives out as cripples, were glad that they weren't Böckelmann – and they prayed they would be out of the hospital before the nurse took off those bandages.

The nurse went to see the M.O. 'We have to do something with Böckelmann,' she said. 'He's getting restless . . .'

The doctor swore under his breath.

'He can be moved . . .' the sergeant orderly suggested.

'I see,' the M.O. said. 'You mean we cart him off from Cologne and dump him in a hospital in Berlin? . . . Not a bad idea, old boy; we're short of beds anyway ... What's the situation with his family?'

The sergeant looked through Böckelmann's pay-book, searching for the page that mentioned next of kin. 'Mother's still alive ... Berlin-Charlottenburg ... And there, he's got a fiancée, a Marion Kleebach ...' he read quickly. 'Berlin-West, Lietzenburgerstrasse ...'

'All right,' the M.O. decided. 'Inform the family – as discreetly as possible. And have Böckelmann transferred immediately, before there's trouble ... What is it?' he barked, seeing an orderly standing to attention in the doorway.

'Unteroffizier Güsswein has ...'

'Has what?'

'Passed on ...' the orderly said uncomfortably.

'And what can I do about that?' rasped the M.O., accidentally kicking his desk with one foot.

'Hopeless case, anyway,' agreed the sergeant.

'Always the ruddy prophet, eh?' the doctor said. 'Get out of my sight!' He stared vaguely at the retreating sergeant, who was telling the orderly: 'One good thing. It means another bed free ...'

Alone again, the M.O. immersed himself in some case notes. For a moment he considered whether, if he were given the choice, he would rather die or go blind ... And because he couldn't make his mind up, he rang up his girl friend and made a date to go to the cinema that evening.

With the wild-eyed Unteroffizier Hanselmann trailing mess-tins, all ready to climb up out of the foxhole, Achim Kleebach found the strength to do something about it. He released the safety-catch on his machine-pistol and lurched threateningly towards the Unteroffizier. 'Are you out of your mind?' he yelled.

'Yes, sir!' Hanselmann retorted. 'I'm out of my mind.'

'They'll kill you.'

'Let 'em.'

'It's a trap!' Achim shrieked, overcome with fury.

'I'm hungry.'

'I hereby order you to remain here!'

Hanselmann shrugged. 'Kiss my arse.'

Achim levelled his machine-pistol at the Unteroffizier again. 'I'll shoot if you leave this trench!' he hissed.

'Then do it,' Hanselmann said. 'Suits me . . .'

The sergeant clambered calmly out of the trench and the others handed up the mess-tins. He walked slowly, a little unsteadily at first, then upright and determined in the direction of the Russian lines. He jangled the mess-tins together so that at least they could hear him coming. Then he stopped, cupped one hand to his mouth and bellowed: 'Listen, you Ivans . . . I'm coming . . . coming . . . coming . . .'

He took a few hesitant steps, and then suddenly the Russians decided to light his way for him. When the searchlight beam caught him, Hanselmann instinctively went to hit the dirt, but he managed to restrain himself. He followed the light, moving carefully like a man on a tightrope, not moving to the left or right, along the beam and direct towards the Russian position.

The rest of the platoon followed his progress with horrified fascination. Any moment now they would hear the shots, they thought. Any moment now they would mow him down, in a pile of blood among the mess-tins, and at least the poor sod wouldn't be hungry any more . . .

'Amen . . .' whispered little Sawitzky.

It was the moment when Hanselmann reached the Russian lines. The searchlight went out, and the whole front was quiet, terrifyingly quiet.

Ridiculous, thought Kleebach, and loathed himself for not having the guts to bring Hanselmann down when he had the chance. Stupid to fall for a simple-minded piece of propaganda.

Ten minutes later the loudspeaker crackled into life once more. 'German comrades,' the voice announced. 'In a moment, Unteroffizier Hanselmann will be returning . . . with ten mess-tins full to the brim . . . If you're still hungry, come over to us . . . Our kitchen is open all night . . .'

Marching music. The searchlight again. From under its beam came a shadow that soon took on the shape of Hanselmann. His bulky, stooping figure was instantly recognisable, and he was walking proudly and without hesitation in time to the music, carrying – it was enough to drive them out of their minds – ten mess-tins heavy with soup, five in each hand. He was a hundred metres from the German positions. Eighty. Sixty. So close that they could see the stupid grin on his face.

They swung their weapons round, sure that the attack had to come soon, hoping even as they did so that when the trouble started the Unteroffizier wouldn't drop the mess-tins in panic. After all, some of it would be recoverable later, for sure . . .

But he carried on walking, led on by the beam of the searchlight, until he was only five metres from the foxhole. Then the light went out and it was darker than ever. Hanselmann let himself be guided gently down into the trench, where he presented his booty to the astonished Achim Kleebach. 'So,' he said, pointing to the steaming soup. 'Your good health . . . you can have it all . . . I ate my fill over on the other side.'

He took one of the mess-tins and gently pressed it into Achim's hand. For a moment he looked as though he was about to throw the soup into the officer's face, then he slowly and meticulously removed the mess-tin again and set it down. They were almost starving, but they attacked the food in something close to disciplined fashion. Three men to each mess-tin, a spoonful each in turn. Their faces were still incredulous, wondering; they forced down the first mouthfuls as if they were poison. But who cared? At least it was something to fill your stomach . . .

But it wasn't poison. It was just as they had been promised, cooked as well as at Aschinger's restaurant at home in Berlin, dish of the day: peas, water, ham, a pinch of salt, potatoes . . .

The mess-tins were emptied to the last morsel. And a little was left for Achim Kleebach. He resisted, standing stoney-faced in the corner, for another half an hour, with all their eyes on him. Then he fell on his portion like an animal, and he bolted it down so quickly that he could hardly breathe at the end of it. His face mirrored hunger and shame, and the fact that hunger had won out.

The next day, twelve hours after Hanselmann's crazy trip to the Russian lines, rations reached the front line at last. But before the two drivers reached Kleebach's platoon, there were a pair of real defectors to the Russians . . .

Russia welcomed Panzer Leutnant Thomas Kleebach as only

it knew how: with vodka and vermin, with the croaking of carrion crows, with muddy streets, with the howling of wolves, distant shooting from partisans, with marshes and an endless, endless landscape, with its pale light and screamed orders, fear and confusion.

He sat slumped in the corner of an officers' compartment in the train, only bothering to look out through the wooden blinds every hour or two. The view was always the same. He sat there and let himself be carried three thousand kilometres towards a bleak horizon, knowing that the way back would be hard – if it came at all.

When the train arrived at Kalatsch, they were suddenly in the combat zone. There were rumours of a Russian break-through. In fact, the train in which the Leutnant sat was one of the last to reach Stalingrad before it was cut off. And Thomas knew instinctively that he was one of 300,000 men caught in a merciless trap.

Thomas Kleebach took command of a company in Colonel Tollsdorf's task force, and with that he became duty-bound to send his men to the slaughter. At first he was horrified, but then he realised that was all Stalingrad had to offer. The city was lost, and there was only death left to think about. The cold and hunger were deadlier enemies than the Russians, and later came dysentery, which gripped almost all of the German defenders and weakened them so much that they could no longer make it to the latrine. They fought in their own shit, and they died in it.

Kleebach's company, still half-intact, was holding a for-gotten position somewhere in the north-east of the city. They had no idea why they were fighting, and still less why they were still alive. They had butchered the last horse ten days before and shared out a piece to each man in the unit.

Leutnant Thomas Kleebach was probably the only man in his company who understood the full extent of the catastrophe and allowed himself no hope – which made it all the easier to lie to the others. Their situation was no better than that of any other unit in the Stalingrad pocket, but the men looked up to their commander as a miracle-worker. Like all the others, they got words in place of rations. Three hundred thousand soldiers relied on being relieved by General Manstein, without believing in it; the men under Kleebach believed in it without relying on it, under the spell of a man who they knew would share their fate along with his last piece of bread. All Thomas could do was keep his men sane until it was over – today, tomorrow, or whenever . . .

Since November 23rd 1942 the city's lifeline had been cut. The Russians had made a breakthrough and isolated the Sixth Army in Stalingrad. The pocket was still big enough to be viable, and the Russians' hold on their newly-conquered territory was still tenuous enough for men to believe that General Manstein would be able to smash a way through for his newly-formed Army Group Don to relieve the city. But Manstein's counter-attack ground to a halt forty-eight kilometres from the edge of the pocket. Now there was only one chance: a skilfully-engineered breakout in full force. Hitler forbade von Paulus, the commander in Stalingrad, to consider such an idea, continuing to promise that his forces would be relieved. Instead the Soviet offensive that had been resumed on December 6th rolled on westwards, smashing the Eighth Italian Army, and Manstein, instead of helping von Paulus, was forced to plug more gaps to avoid another Stalingrad. By Christmas the fate of those 300,000 men was as good as sealed.

The exhausted defenders could no longer wield pick-axes to dig in, and in any case the tools could hardly penetrate the frozen ground. So they had to make do with the primitive strongpoints constructed during the summer, and the ammunition shortage became a famine. Suicide started to become widespread. The city had to be supplied solely from the air, while all the time the Russians hammered at the pocket, whittling it away until finally the Sixth Army was crammed into the tiny area around the city itself.

The advance airfields, where supplies were flown in to the desperate defenders, fell into the hands of the Red Army one by one until only the Pitomnik field was still held by the Germans. Pitomnik became the savage crucible of hope and hunger, the hinge of fate for thousands of men. Soon they were no longer fighting the Russians but each other, killing for a morsel of bread. The walking wounded trampled over their comrades laid out on stretchers in their eagerness to reach the evacuation planes, and the German flak guns were turned on hunger-crazed bands of looters from their own side. Temperatures reached minus twenty-eight centigrade, and Hitler's much-vaunted 'racial community' hit rock-bottom. It was the saga of Pitomnik, the horror-story of Stalingrad.

Thomas Kleebach and his men stared up at the sky. The Junkers were coming into land, low over the steppe, hopping and weaving like panic-stricken crows to avoid the Russian anti-aircraft fire. All the time the poor swine on the ground peered up, filled with hate for the pilots who risked their lives for them five times a day and died like flies. At least the Luftwaffe men had the illusion of freedom, the means of escape . . . Yes, their eyes were glued to those Junker transporters, pinpoints of feverish greed in their hollow sockets; they looked up at those silver wings, and if their arms had been long enough they would have torn the planes down from the sky there and then, sliced open their steel bellies and gulped down boxes of provisions whole. They would have thrown away their carbines, forgotten the Russians, and just stuffed themselves until they choked, until their stomachs convulsed and they died a hero's death in the only fight worth fighting any more: the battle for a full stomach . . .

Two Junkers were shot down, three made it. Thomas found himself drooling with anticipation, just like every one of his men. He could see the crates of ham, salami, canned food, hard-tack and chocolate being hurled out of the doors in the Junkers' bellies, straight down onto the ground, bouncing once then rolling. The ration cases lay there then between the maimed and the frostbitten masses there on the field, and the men from the special salvage squads had the job of getting it all in. If those men were seen slipping something into their own pockets, then they were shot on the spot in the beam of a searchlight to frighten off the others. It happened to at least twenty men a day. In Stalingrad, terror had so many faces: why not die with a full belly?

When hunger began to dissolve the bonds of discipline, discipline tried to use hunger as an ally. Von Paulus no longer called his men to arms against the Russians but to the field kitchens. Only those who were prepared to fight got a portion of thin soup. The rations varied from day to day: yesterday thirty-seven peas per man, today forty-one. And four men spent the whole day doling out rations, counting each pea individually . . . Thus Goering's mannah from heaven was divided up, counted, weighed and found wanting. And the men were no longer fighting for their filthy rat-holes, or for the chance to see their homes again, or against the Russians, and especially not for Hitler; they were fighting for something worthwhile: for a dollop of watery soup, even if it only gave you dysentery.

'Herr Leutnant,' said Unteroffizier Putzke, shambling up to the company commander.

Thomas Kleebach could see by the man's distraught expression that some new face of terror had arrived, and for safety's sake he led him to one side. The Unteroffizier had ginger hair and a thin face that tapered down to a pointed chin, an appearance that had once led to his being nicknamed 'carrot-head'. No one found the name funny any more . . . Nothing to do with food was funny . . .

'What's up?' Thomas asked.

'Here,' Putzke murmured, jabbing a finger at the entrance to a ruined cellar.

They went together down the crumbling steps, and Thomas strained to see in the half-darkness. An iron girder had been exposed between two shattered walls, and from the girder hung the lanky figure of Private Maier on the end of a rope. Maier was as cold, as stiff, and as dead as von Paulus's latest proclamation to his troops.

'Our first suicide . . .' muttered Kleebach.

'But not the last,' said Putzke grimly.

Thomas nodded. In Stalingrad there were days when suicide accounted for more men than the Russians. He had been able to stop the disease from spreading to his own unit so far, but obviously they were no longer immune.

'Who found him?' he asked.

'I did.'

'Who else knows about it?'

'No one.'

'Good. Then, Putzke, I suggest you keep your mouth shut!'

'Why?' Carrot-head hissed defiantly.

Thomas could read the open rebellion in the Unteroffizier's exhausted face, and it saddened him. A waste of energy.

'Yeah, he's the only one,' Putzke continued heavily. 'The only one who's had the guts and the brains so far to put an end to it . . . or do you want to argue with me?'

'How should I know?' said Thomas, hoping to gloss things over and reason with the man later.

'Just look,' carrot-head said. 'Look at that long purple tongue, the grin on the bastard's face . . .' He was breathing hard, swaying slightly. 'The bugger's laughing at us! And he's right, because . . .'

The Leutnant took Putzke by the hand and led him up out of the dank cellar. He glanced at him from the side. There was something wrong with the man, and had been since their last mail delivery. Putzke had always been a quiet, capable man, and now this business with the suicide seemed to be working him up into a frenzy.

'Something wrong?' he said gently. 'At home?'

Carrot-head shrugged gloomily and sat down on a pile of stones. Thomas joined him, took a battered cigarette out of his pocket, carefully broke it in half and handed one bit to Putzke.

The Unteroffizier lit up gratefully, then exhaled the smoke for a long moment. 'Yeah,' he said at last, still unable to meet Thomas's eye. 'Everything's marvellous at home . . . Great! Couldn't be better! . . . Sister's snuffed it in an air raid, mother's in hospital, dad's all on his own . . . And my old lady . . . well . . .' He forced out the words that had been festering in his mind for the past few days. 'Well . . . she's sitting pretty in the Luftwaffe convalescent home at Kitzbühel . . . with some young bastard of a Luftwaffe officer . . .'

'Bit too much all at once,' Thomas agreed, nodding sympathy. 'But maybe it'll sort itself out . . .'

All he could manage were verbal bromides. What else was there? He thought of Luise and his parents, and he compared his own home life with Putzke's, and in a way he envied the Unteroffizier every bit as much as carrot-head had envied Maier. It was a damned sight easier to die when no one cared about you . . .

'That frigging whore . . . that bitch!' Putzke chewed at the words. 'I'd like to get home just for ten minutes . . . to sort that cow out . . . That's all I ask . . .'

'Come on. Sounds like you're lucky to be rid of her,' said Thomas, realising he had to be cruel. He clapped Putzke on the shoulder and left him. You had to shut out thoughts of home, forget it. The best you could do here was stand in line and wait patiently for death, with as much humanity and dignity as you could muster. To do that, you had to forget . . .

He had been back in his ramshackle command post for only a few minutes when a sentry yelled: 'Oberst Tollsdorf!'

The task force's commander arrived alone, as was his habit. You could see him from a way off, easily distinguishable, a tall, rangy figure, with his hawk-like face and hunched shoulders. He wandered slowly through the rubble in casual contempt for death and the Russians, a fine target, his cap shoved back on his head and a pipe in his mouth and an expression of mild distaste for the corpses, the ruins, the filth and the rats that scuttled round his feet. He wore a shabby leather greatcoat and a pipe in his mouth that was rarely lit. It went perfectly with his cold smile as he nodded to the soldiers cowering in their trenches and asked: 'How's it going?'

No one answered.

'None too talkative today, I see,' the colonel barked. Then he strolled over to Leutnant Kleebach, who simply nodded to him and asked wryly: 'Come to bring me some rations, Herr Oberst? Or maybe some ammunition?'

'You're joking,' the Oberst growled. Then he grinned, a gesture with little humour in it. He rummaged in the pockets of his coat, fished something out and handed it to Thomas. 'I've brought you promotion to Oberleutnant, Kleebach,' he murmured with mock solemnity. The package contained new one-star epaulettes, and God alone knew where Tollsdorf had dredged them up from.

Thomas's taste for the macabre had dwindled to zero. 'And what the hell good are they to me?' he asked testily.

Tollsdorf shrugged. 'As far as I'm concerned, you can boil the damned things up for dinner,' he said. The smile faded on his lips as he stared around the lunar landscape surrounding the dugouts and over towards the Russian lines. He grimaced. 'Pity, Kleebach,' he sighed. 'I'd like to have left you and your bunch of desperadoes here . . . but I need you for a special assignment . . . to keep order, as a sort of police . . . Don't look so scared, kid . . .' He put his unlit pipe away in his pocket, took out a cigarette, broke it in the middle, and after some hesitation handed the slightly smaller half to the newly-promoted Oberleutnant. 'Celebration,' he grinned. 'I don't know how you do it, Kleebach. You're in the same shit as the rest of us, but somehow your blokes are still halfways decent . . .'

Thomas shook his head. 'I try to give them hope.'

'That's what we all try to do.'

'Then maybe I'm a better liar,' Thomas snapped.

'Maybe,' said the Oberst, unperturbed. 'Pity it's a bit late for a career in the Propaganda Ministry . . . Anyway, when guard duty's over I want you and your weary warriors to report to my headquarters.' Then he tipped the peak of his cap, stood up and wandered out of the bunker. He paused in the open, offering a clear target for the Russians, but they refused to oblige him. He shrugged his shoulders and walked slowly on.

The sentries were due to be relieved in an hour. The guards from the right flank reported back first, but the ones on the left had to be replaced to cover their withdrawal.

'Putzke!' Kleebach yelled.

But the Unteroffizier had disappeared without asking leave.

'Where's he gone?' Thomas asked an orderly-room private in the corner.

The man shrugged indifferently. 'How the hell am I supposed to know? He cleared off.' An exhausted gesture in the direction of the ruined cellar.

The Oberleutnant had a decision to make, because he knew what the gesture meant. He fought against a wave of despair. After all, what did it matter? Why shouldn't carrot-head shoot himself or string himself up rather than starve or freeze? None of them were going to make it, none of them stood a chance, so maybe it was better to get it over as soon as possible . . . He knew he wasn't leading a company of fighting men any more, just a ragged bunch of candidates for a hero's death, and if one of them wanted to get there a bit earlier, it was up to him . . . Then he pulled himself together, because if he didn't he knew his men would fall apart too. Maybe the Junkers would get through again, he thought feverishly, maybe they'd get the wounded out, maybe they'd survive the war in a Russian P.O.W. camp, and maybe one of those who did would be Unteroffizier Putzke . . .

He went carefully over to the cellar entrance, pushed the door gently on its rusty hinges and inched down the stairs until his eyes had accustomed themselves to the darkness. He heard a sound to his right, followed it and saw carrot-head.

The Unteroffizier was standing a few yards away, and his face was red with effort and determination. For a moment Kleebach stared in fascinated horror.

Putzke had taken off his battledress tunic, rolled up his shirtsleeves, and had tied a piece of rag round his left arm, which lay outstretched and bare on a flat chunk of masonry, like meat on a butcher's slab. He was searching his arm for the right place, and it was now that Thomas realised that the Unteroffizier intended to maim himself. He could see him raising a jagged iron bar in his right hand . . . Kleebach made to move but found he was rooted to the spot, and in a second it was too late. Carrot-head swung the bar down on the spot next to the rag, bit back a shriek, sunk to his knees then rose again slowly, flexing his left arm. Putzke's face fell, covered in tears of pain. He hadn't hit hard enough.

'What in God's name are you doing?' hissed Thomas.

Unteroffizier Putzke swung round, wild-eyed with agony and fear. 'Report me! Haul me up in front of a court-martial! That'd be a pleasure, compared with . . .'

'Don't shout so loud,' Thomas answered calmly.

'I want to go home,' the man grated, his face contorted into a mask of hate. 'I'll get that bitch . . .'

Suddenly Thomas Kleebach felt raw fear, an emotion he had almost forgotten in Stalingrad, and it had nothing to do with danger. They all wanted to go home, but it was love that drew them, not hate; none of them had yet found the terrible, inhuman strength to buy themselves the chance of a ticket home with an act of self-mutilation. So was hate the strongest human emotion? Kleebach asked himself, and the thought frightened him. Then his brain started to work. He could see that Putzke couldn't be helped, and that from now on he would be a one-man force for chaos and despair in the company.

'I've got to!' carrot-head shrieked. 'I will . . . and I don't care how . . . !'

'And if you're stuck here with a shattered arm?'

'That's my business,' snarled the Unteroffizier. He raised the bar again, ignoring his commander.

Kleebach could see that the man was unhinged, that he would try again and again, maybe with an axe next time, or a rope. His lips tightened with decision, his eyes went cold.

'Turn round!' he said, stepping forward and snatching the iron bar from Putzke.

Carrot-head stared at him in blank incomprehension.

Thomas took his arm and laid it back on the hunk of masonry. A few seconds later the iron bar crashed down on the man's arm, severing the elbow joint with one crushing blow. Putzke collapsed onto his knees, rose slowly. His lower lip was running with blood, but his agonised face was radiant with joy when he realised that his arm was finished, useless.

'I'll report it to the field hospital . . . you were trapped under falling masonry,' the Oberleutnant said icily, then walked out of the cellar without looking back. He wasted no time feeling guilt for having helped a man maim himself; he didn't even know why he had followed that sudden impulse. One man had bought himself the chance of getting out, and he had bought it dear. That was his choice, anyone's choice. In any case, that shattered arm would only get Putzke as far as Voroponovo, where hundreds of other wounded men were crammed into unheated railway carriages waiting for transport out, until they died of cold and their corpses were thrown out of the windows by the orderlies to make way for more, more waiting their turn to die without hope, finally without illusions . . .

CHAPTER TWELVE

Achim Kleebach's platoon, reduced once again to a fraction of its nominal strength, had dug itself in not far from the open space they called the 'Square of the Fallen', the place by the airfield where they dropped the supplies – and ran firing-parties round the clock. He leapt to his feet along with the remnants of his men when they heard the low growl of approaching planes, and their hunger seemed to suddenly sharpen, form a strangling knot in their stomachs, and they gazed upwards salivating, waiting for the searchlight and the Russian flak, hoping wildly that one of those Junkers would be shot down in just the right spot, and come crashing down right by their position so that they could smash their way in and help themselves . . .

'Listen to that!' said Unteroffizier Hanselmann. 'It's crazy sitting here waiting for them to dish out half a frigging biscuit and a handful of beans . . . I'll take a couple of the boys and get something organised.'

'You're kidding,' Achim rasped, jerking a thumb in the direction of the 'Square of the Fallen'. 'Another hour and they're due to shoot another batch of looters.'

'Looters!' Hanselmann echoed contemptuously. 'That's what they call 'em, is it? I'll tell you: I'd rather go to hell on a full belly than an empty one . . . What d'you reckon, Sawitzky?'

The little man nodded solemnly. Even his patched-together nickel-framed glasses seemed to glint hungrily.

Achim Kleebach, Unteroffizier Hanselmann and Sawitzky were the last three survivors of a unit that had been re-formed four times, reinforced five times. Most of the replacements were killed, starved or frozen to death before they could get to know their faces or even their names.

'Right. You game?' the sergeant pressed.

'You won't get away with it,' Achim said wearily, looking

back upwards with longing and greed in his young face. The Junkers were coming closer.

'Count me in,' said Sawitzky, getting to his feet.

'You don't stand a chance,' Achim repeated.

Unteroffizier Hanselmann laughed humourlessly. 'That's what you think,' he croaked. 'But you've got no brains, no more than those poor bastards who end up out there every evening . . .' He sliced at his own throat in a vivid illustration of the fate the looters were about to meet in an hour. 'Trouble is, the stupid arseholes just launch themselves at the stuff like wild beasts . . .'

'And you?' Achim mocked.

'We'll do it differently,' the sergeant said. 'A real military operation. Covering fire and all . . .' He nodded to Sawitzky and another of the volunteers. 'You make for the goodies and grab as much as you can, as quickly as you can . . . and if someone tries to stop you . . .' He grinned evilly, and there was real hatred in his eyes. 'Then I'll sort them out with my little machine-gun . . . We'll see how many try it once one bastard's got his . . .'

The sergeant looked around. 'They don't come better than me!'

The next moment the Russian searchlights were alight and the first of the Junkers was opening its doors to swoop down and drop the supplies.

'Let's go,' ordered Hanselmann. The others followed him dumbly.

They went at a run. They had maybe 600 metres to cover, and most likely they would be mown down by the first guard post they came across, or arrested and handed over to the next execution squad, or be sent in with the other suicide candidates in the next doomed counter-attack. But the whole platoon stared after them, and anyone, including Achim, who could still summon up a spark of hope, prayed that they would get back. And they hated their comrades, because they knew that if they made it they would help themselves to some on the way back, instead of saving it all and sharing it out equally according to the rules of the comradeship that they had learned at school . . .

Six or seven Junkers came in. One was shot down, but the others made it. The Luftwaffe was lucky today. The search-lights were switched off. Somewhere a machine-gun chattered.

Could be a Russian patrol, could be tonight's executions. The men with Achim were relying on good old Unteroffizier Hanselmann.

After an hour even the most optimistic had given him up for lost, and after another thirty minutes they had forgotten him. The fact that they'd get nothing to eat again today was worse than a hundred dead comrades – and the fact that the three had raised their hopes made them bastards as well as failures.

Then they heard stumbling steps. They shook off the cold, the apathy and crawled out like timid, frozen rabbits to see what was happening. It was a miracle. There was the sergeant, the big man, and suddenly they didn't give a shit if the Russians came, because between Hanselmann and the private behind him was slung a huge side of ham wrapped in tinfoil, which they were carrying like a dead stuck pig, grinning all over their faces like weekend hunters after a lucky kill. One of them was missing, Sawitzky, but the others were so hungry that they couldn't count to three; they could just see that meat, which the Unteroffizier was already slicing up into thirteen choice hunks and handing out.

'There you are,' he said. 'Enough for everybody ... at least for today. Don't stuff yourselves too quick, or you'll puke the goodies straight back up again ...'

But no one paid any attention. They bolted the ham down, threw up, grabbed another piece, and no one asked whether it had cost blood, or whether Hanselmann had used his gun, or how they had done it. Sawitzky was completely forgotten for the moment. They ate until they could no longer force it down, until their stomachs were convulsed with cramp ...

They were happy, and Hanselmann was the hero of the day. If it had been up to them, they would have sent off to the Führer for a Knight's Cross for good old Unteroffizier Hanselmann. They were not repelled by the way he wolfed down his food, by the sliver of fat hanging out of the corner of his mouth as he chewed, and when he announced: 'From now on, we do this every night,' it became a clarion-call, the only ideal they were prepared to follow to the death ...

'Yeah ...' the Unteroffizier said at last. 'Pity about Sawitzky ... the bastards nabbed him and shot him straight away.' He shrugged his shoulders. 'Nothing we could do . . . but in Stalingrad one man for a side of ham ain't a bad exchange . . .'

Suddenly a few men looked guilty. They had full bellies now, and so they could feel something for little Sawitzky again. This had been his wake, and they asked themselves whether it had been worth it, but they never got a chance to decide because the next day they were transferred to Pitomnik Airfield on guard duties, with the job of covering the loading of the wounded into transporter planes . . .

Oberleutnant Kleebach was wounded for the third time, and it happened quite undramatically. The whistle of a shell while he was mustering his company one morning, they all hit the dirt, and Thomas was the only one who didn't get up again. A sliver of shrapnel had caught him on the hip and opened up a wound in his side.

He was bandaged up and taken off to the dressing-station at Otorvanovka, which consisted of four houses and three mud huts and was dangerously close to the front line. All around the hospital the dead were laid out in rows. The orderlies simply laid the wounded down on the ground next to the dying. No one paid any attention to the dead, and no one lifted a finger for the wounded. The drugs had all been used up, the buildings were in flames, and anyone who had frozen to death yesterday was liable to be a heap of ashes today.

Thomas Kleebach was lucky, because just short of Otorvanovka the stretcher-bearers were directed off to another station. He was unconscious, already in a high fever, and he was lucky again that they didn't just drop him and leave him in the mud to die alone.

The detour took them to a hospital manned by twenty doctors in a ruined department store. The doctors had no drugs, and they had worked until their hands were scarred and swollen. They tore bandages from the dead to use on the living, because there was no choice but to risk cross-infection and gangrene except when they could tear the linings out of the men's coats and use that as bandages instead . . .

The situation was hopeless. The army doctors, surrounded by mountains of dead, had to admit that their efforts were completely futile. A man given surgery one day would die within hours of cold out in the frozen corridors because there was no room in the wards, and a man whose limb was successfully amputated would die three days later of hunger because no one gave him any food.

The little food that the Luftwaffe managed to fly in, suffering terrible losses in planes and aircrew, went first and foremost to the military police, who were responsible for maintaining what they called 'order'. Because regulations were regulations, and you had to have order, so that Stalingrad, in the words of the Wehrmacht report, could 'fight to the last bullet'. They would fight to the last bullet because Hitler said so . . .

The madness was complete. And in Stalingrad's last real hospital, in a burned-out store, they didn't even possess a Red Cross flag. Hundreds of wounded flooded in every day, carried in and dumped where the stretcher-bearers could find a square foot of space, and an M.O. would come and examine every new arrival. He would look down into that pale, pleading face and he would do what he could, even though he knew that was just prolonging one more private agony.

The day was dark and misty, like every other day. Even the sky over Stalingrad seemed to be made of ice, until suddenly the horizon would light up with flame and spit fire, and the shells would greedily search among the stinking ruins for a sign of life. The clouds of cordite, the dim light of day were all the same, indistinguishable, uniform: grey, field-grey . . .

Shells screamed over the last German hospital in the shattered department store. An explosion close by the huge ruin sent plaster showering down from the ceiling and onto the face of Oberleutnant Thomas Kleebach. He felt nothing. He was unconscious. The pustulating wound in his hip had been bandaged up with the filthy, louse-infested lining from his greatcoat, and the doctor who had treated him didn't know whether gangrene or cold would kill him first.

The shells were landing closer to the department store every minute. The walls of the storage basements where the wounded lay trembled as if in an earthquake. Senior M.O. Dr Münemann had spent most of the day hoping that the next rain of shells would bring down the whole filthy place on top of him, and his nineteen exhausted doctors, and the screaming wounded, and the orderlies who were constantly bringing in more stretchers, tossing new cases down at his feet like cats bringing mice to their masters. He felt more like an undertaker than a doctor, a healer; he had nothing left but the skills of his hands, and they were so frostbitten now that he could hardly hold a scalpel.

The Senior M.O. stood up, shook his head wearily and stared out of the window. There had been a lull in the fighting. Twenty-four below zero was enough to deter anyone. There was sporadic fire from the Russian machine-gun nests on the edge of the pocket, but then maybe the Ivans were only keeping it up so that they could warm their hands on the barrels.

Dr Münemann turned round painfully, moving only his trunk, because his feet were numb, immobile. He couldn't feel his toes, hadn't been able to for days now, and he could hardly shift without stepping on a wounded man. This room had once been the haberdashery department; then it had become a padre's office; now it was a mortuary. The story of Stalingrad.

'No more!' he bellowed at the orderlies for the tenth time that day. He would have carried on shouting, but once was enough to exhaust him. He was breathing heavily.

'Herr Doctor,' said an orderly timidly. 'Where are we supposed to put them?'

'I couldn't care less,' barked Münemann. As a student he had learned to honour his calling, as a practising physician he had made it a reality, and in Stalingrad he had come to loath it. 'It's all just going through the motions, isn't it?' He pointed to the stretchers. 'Take them out into the corridor.'

'No room, sir.'

'Then outside, in front of the building.'

'Can't do that,' murmured one of his assistants. 'We put out sixty or so yesterday to wait for treatment. Almost every man jack froze to death.'

'Frozen, eh?' Münemann paused thoughtfully. He seemed to be talking quietly to himself. Then he nodded grimly.

'Just a moment,' he said, lifting his leg painfully to step over Thomas Kleebach. He slowly made his way out into the corridor, where the wounded were stacked like corpses in a huge mass grave, living and dead alike, and went through to the big double doors, which had been barred and heaped up with bales of straw in a futile attempt to keep out the cold. He ordered them to be opened and stared out onto the open space in front of the hospital, where the orderlies were busy piling the frozen corpses like stacks of loaves. Minus twenty-four, thought the Senior M.O. And he had no drugs, no pills, no morphium, no chance of doing anything for these men . . .

Or maybe he had.

He scraped together what was left of his staff, the survivors and those who still listened to orders. The junior doctors heard what he had to say, and at first they thought he was crazy, then a genius, first a murderer, then an angel of mercy.

'I've got the answer,' he announced. 'We open all the doors, fill the corridors with the hopeless cases.' He smiled humourlessly at the irony of his own words. As if any of the wounded had a chance . . . 'Understood?'

They all murmured assent.

'Most of them will freeze to death anyway,' he explained, as solemnly and matter-of-factly as a schoolmaster. 'If we give them a push, we're doing them a favour. Just don't argue with me . . .'

The Senior M.O.'s new 'system' brought some kind of order into the bloody, moaning, screaming, writhing, pathetic universe of suffering. The doors were opened and the icy wind let in to play on the dying, and they smiled and thought one last time of home before the cold sent them into a gentle, final sleep; and Dr Münemann, taking full responsibility for the solution, walked past them and told himself a hundred times, like a priest saying Hail Marys, that to die of cold was the most pleasant death. A man noticed nothing, he dreamed, he felt nothing, not even the cold, and then he was filled with warmth, and then it was all over . . .

The doctor's main task now was to establish whether a patient had died. Any who had were immediately carried outside and replaced with a living man.

It was Oberleutnant Kleebach's turn. He was third on the right near the big double doors. He was still unconscious, and in two or three hours at the most he would be joining the mountain of corpses behind the building . . .

Suddenly the department store had gone quiet. The doctors could move again. The cold had given them a breathing-space. Despite everything, they moved silently, for fear of robbing the men in the corridors of their last illusions. Several of the doctors would have gladly lain down beside them to die, but their turn had not yet come.

A short while later, jackboots echoed in the corridor. Someone was coming who made no attempt to be silent. An officer stomped in through the doors as carelessly as if he had been out for a stroll on the Kurfürstendamm in Berlin. He was tall and thin, and his narrow hawklike face craned up out of a battered leather greatcoat. He stopped a passing orderly and asked: 'Where's your chief?'

'On the left there, sir,' the orderly stuttered nervously, staring at the officer as if he were an apparition from another planet. Oberst Tollsdorf was clean-shaven, oblivious of the cold, well-fed, and the orderly could have sworn he caught a whiff of eau-de-cologne.

Senior M.O. Dr Münemann sat by the window with his head in hands when Tollsdorf swung open the door. He looked up slowly, blinked, stared dully at the Oberst and finally whispered: 'What do you want?'

The officer slapped his gloved hands together. 'Two things, my dear fellow. The name's Tollsdorf,' he explained with a courtly inclination of the head, almost a bow. 'I'm in command of a task force . . .'

'And?'

'In this section of the front!'

'So?'

'I intend to round up all the shirkers round here and put them to work transporting the wounded to the airfield . . . and then they can reinforce my bunch . . .'

The doctor's eyes widened to great hollow saucers of astonishment. 'Shirkers?' he said. 'You mean me? Or my assistants? Or . . .'

'Don't talk nonsense!' Tollsdorf boomed. 'But maybe there's the odd malingerer here, and . . .'

'Dear God in heaven!' Dr Münemann's drawn, ghostly-pale features cracked into a hideous smile, and he laughed. Still laughing, he went up to the Oberst and stared straight into the face of the last crazy patriot left in Stalingrad. He clapped him on the shoulder and murmured: 'Please follow me . . .'

He went on ahead with Tollsdorf trailing behind him, then stood and pointed at the long, dimly-lit corridor, shivering in the icy wind. 'Do you mean them?' the M.O. croaked. 'Those shirkers there? Filthy cowards, eh? Just cop themselves a nice little wound and then they get to lie down here on their cosy stretchers and let the other poor bastards do the fighting . . . while they freeze to death!'

Münemann swung round with whiplash suddenness, gazed threateningly at the colonel and bellowed: 'While they freeze!'

'I don't understand,' Tollsdorf said lamely. 'I thought you were a doctor . . .'

The M.O. laughed again, and it was more like a strangled cry of pain. He hobbled off back towards the main ward. 'I treat everyone the same,' he said after several moments. 'The method is quite simple: windows open, doors open, off with the blankets, and then . . .' His head slumped between his boney shoulders. 'So long as the temperature doesn't rise above, say, twenty below . . . all their problems are over.'

The Oberst finally understood, and for the first time since he became a soldier he had no answers. For the first time he had seen something that even his inhuman powers of self-control couldn't cope with. 'Everyone here . . . they . . . ?' he mumbled.

'Exactly,' the doctor retorted harshly.

Tollsdorf turned back and walked through the crowded corridor, the moaning, evil-smelling valley of the dead and those about to die, and he looked briefly at the faces there and turned away from the sight. He stood for a moment with his eyes shut, then straightened up and was his old self, the man who could shrug and smile crookedly and say: 'Sawbones, you're looking at me as if it was my fault.'

Dr Münemann said nothing.

Tollsdorf came back to him without another glance at the horror. 'I'll tell you something,' he said suddenly. 'I've had all this up to here! If I got the chance to get out of here, I swear I'd never put on a uniform again for the rest of my life. If I had children, I'd tan their arses raw if I ever saw them playing with tin soldiers. I'd be the biggest, meanest pacifist the world's ever seen! I wasn't always that way . . . but I've learned, me of all people . . .' He pulled out a cigarette and lit it with a trembling hand that belied the professional hardness of his voice. 'And now I'm here in Stalingrad . . . Sawbones, I'm no angel, but I'm sure as hell not the worst officer in the Wehrmacht. My boys work their butts off for the love of me, understand?'

'Then why don't you just let them go?' said Münemann.

The Oberst took a final hefty drag on his cigarette and handed it to the doctor. 'It's all right for you,' he said defiantly. 'You can still do something useful.' He gestured at the wounded men. 'You've got your work. Your system. You can send those poor swine into the next world as gently and as skilfully as you know how. Those wounded men still believe in something before they go . . .'

The M.O. nodded solemnly.

'I'm trying to do the same with my men, from a different standpoint. A man who's fighting's got no time to think. As long as the fellows are blasting away at something, their minds are occupied. You're a doctor, and I'm just a con-man.' He laughed, and it was full of contempt for the world and the system. 'But we're playing the same game . . .' He took the cigarette back. 'And now you can let me have a few wounded who won't give up the ghost if they're moved, and I'll haul them over to Pitomnik . . . and maybe . . . we can try . . .' He shrugged his shoulders.

Tollsdorf offered the Senior M.O. his hand. He had won Münemann's reluctant admiration, and he had torn the doctor out of his lethargy. Münemann escorted him through the corridor to the double doors.

Suddenly the Oberst stopped and stared, crouched down quickly, then stood up muttering curses under his breath. 'You were going to leave that man to die?' he hissed.

'As hopeless as the rest,' the M.O. explained.

'Do you know who that is? That's Oberleutnant Kleebach, one of the best!'

'I'm sure all those poor bastards have got something good about them,' the doctor said wearily.

'Maybe so,' answered Tollsdorf with a touch of his personal brand of sarcasm. 'But the good thing about Kleebach is that I'm his commander!' He stomped out to where his men were waiting in the cold and ordered them to make sure that Oberleutnant Kleebach got to the airfield, dead or alive . . .

They stood and they waited in their hundreds, their eyes fixed on the skies to the west, their last hope. And it was why, with the insane strength of despair, they held out on the airfield at Pitomnik, the solitary lifeline to home and already under Russian artillery fire. They knew that the runways were so full of potholes that a landing was crazy, that the flying-distance was too great, that the approach run was too steep, that there were far too few transport aircraft. They knew, too, that the numbers of the Junkers was getting smaller as the fuel ran low and the Russians got closer, and that thousands wanted to seize the lifeline that could only take hundreds. None of that mattered a damn.

The worst cases were laid out on stretchers right on the edge of the runway. They had cardboard placards hung round their necks detailing name, unit and their wounds. If the orders were followed, these were the men who would be first to be loaded aboard the aircraft, and that was why the others stared at them with hatred in their eyes, why there was a ripple of celebration in the waiting ranks when the orderlies pulled up the blankets on a stretcher and carried it back to the rear. Another place free on the next plane . . .

There was another group two or three hundred metres away, carefully separated from the stretcher cases, a rabble of walking wounded who would in theory be allowed to board if any places were still free after the others had been loaded. They were herded together like sheep in a pen, guarded by the military police like criminals.

Between the two groups stood German soldiers responsible for keeping 'order', the improvised airfield police, including Achim Kleebach's platoon. Kleebach had been given two flak guns to help him – not against the Russians but against his own comrades, the walking wounded, who were liable to try and rush any transport plane as soon as it landed.

'Right. Everyone got that straight?' said Unteroffizier Hanselmann to the two others who had joined his conspiracy. 'And don't be so frigging mamby-pamby, Herr Kleebach. It all depends on our getting on that plane at just the right moment, not too early, not too late.'

Achim Kleebach nodded like a man in a trance. He wasn't exactly sure what was being discussed, but he was prepared to follow the sergeant into anything. Hanselmann had always been right so far.

'And if we get away with it?' said a private. 'And we get to the other end . . . what do we say?'

Unteroffizier Hanselmann chortled grimly. 'That's a problem I'd like to have,' he snarled. 'Let's get out first; the rest'll be a piece of cake. There'll be so much confusion you'll be able to pick any one of a million excuses.'

Hanselmann's plan was simple and horrifying. In their role as members of the security squad they would be allowed to get right up to the planes to fight off the desperate men trying to board. That was when they would get into the overflowing cargo hold and then, if need be by force, throw out a few of the seriously wounded to make room for themselves. The method was hardly noble or subtle, but it was brutally simple and it would save their hides. The Unteroffizier was not a complicated man, and at the moment the preservation of his own life was the highest ideal he knew.

Achim Kleebach stood watching from between the two flak guns. The sergeant nodded once more to him, and then they looked longingly at the crates that were being tossed down through the hatchways of the Junkers at the same time as the stretcher cases were eased up into the cargo holds.

Then all hell broke loose.

No warning, no hint of any pre-arranged signal. The flock of walking wounded suddenly exploded out of its pen, the hopelessly outnumbered guards were overpowered, and hundreds of men were running, limping, hobbling towards the runway. Some fell, were crushed and trampled under foot, some managed to rise again and stormed on, their crazed faces contorted with the lust to live that overrode any order, any thought of decency, all reason, all other thought. The most ruthless would get there first, and the savages would be the winners.

The horde swarmed on, reaching the edge of the landing-strip close to the nearest plane. All they could see was the hatchway beckoning; all they wanted was to get in there, away, home. Men tripped and kicked, slapped and punched each other, and those who fell grabbed frantically at the legs of running men and let themselves be dragged along, cursing, moaning, weeping. All that counted was getting through, surviving, a few seconds now, into that crate of a Junker and then . . .

'Fire!' murmured Achim Kleebach.

The two gunners nodded, and then the first flames vomited out of the flak emplacement to his left, bang into the middle of the rabble.

The first ones went down, the ones behind pressed on and were mown down and torn apart in their turn, but their bodies protected the others, who stumbled on closer to the aircraft. If they got in, no plane would be able to take off with that weight on board . . .

'Now!' Hanselmann bawled, and grabbed Achim by the arm.

As always, the Unteroffizier had got it absolutely right. The flak couldn't stop them all, and a few dozen had managed to get out of the killing-ground and get close enough to the planes for the flak gunners to hold their fire so as not to endanger the transporters. That was the decisive moment for Hanselmann and his gang.

The Unteroffizier fired from the hip as he ran, short, carefully-aimed bursts. Within moments he was at the hatchway, turned, fired straight into the panic-stricken horde, gained some space, hauled himself up through the gap and stood almost in the belly of the plane, feet planted firmly apart and his machine-pistol at the ready, a terrifying smile on his face. Here was one position he was prepared to defend to the end . . .

Achim had made it too. The sergeant helped him up. At that moment the Russian artillery opened up and shells began to explode on the runway, puffs of flame all around, turning bloody confusion into a foretaste of hell.

The pilots of the Junkers had had enough. They opened their throttles ready for take-off. Others had arrived at the hatchway and were pushing Hanselmann and Achim up into the belly of the plane. They stumbled over wounded men scattered around the floor, and they knew they had to hold out for another ten seconds, fifteen at the most, before the planes moved off and they were safe. They knew too that the hatchway would stay open, because there was no time, and that the undertow would suck them out unless they could find space and something to hang on to during take-off.

So the sergeant bent down and picked up a wounded man, tried to haul him to the hatchway but couldn't manage it alone. Achim stared at him in horror, incapable of helping even though he knew it was vital to their survival.

'Come on!' Hanselmann screamed. 'Lend me a hand!'

At that moment, as the stunned Achim staggered forward to obey, he saw the wounded man's face and recoiled. It was Thomas, his own brother.

He was released from Hanselmann's spell. Just as the pilot began to taxi, at the moment the Unteroffizier, red-faced with exertion, finally reached the hatchway and prepared to throw the unconscious Oberleutnant Kleebach out of the plane, Achim kicked the astonished Hanselmann in the behind and leapt at him, his hands clawing at the man's windpipe, then toppled slowly out of the hatchway and onto the rock-solid concrete of the runway, where the pair of them, still locked in the sudden death-struggle, were pitched towards the tail by the airstream.

Hanselmann tore himself free. Ignoring Achim he leapt for the wing, where there were a dozen men hanging to the fabric like flies. With a brutal swipe he knocked two men from their perches and clawed himself up until he was hanging on to the taxiing Junker. As it picked up speed a few others were shaken off, but Hanselmann hung on grimly, insanely, and was still there when the pilot lifted his heavy-laden craft painfully from the runway. His starboard wing was dangerously sloping, pulled down by the weight of the sergeant. The pilot forced her onto an even keel once again and she was a good seven or eight metres above the ground. It was then that Hanselmann slid down the iced-up surface of the wing and tumbled down to land in a pile of snow in the path of the following Junker. The sergeant staggered to his feet and raised one arm, as if trying to stop the plane, and shortly before it reached him he was hurled to one side by the blast of the port propeller. Then came the third Junker, just about to lift off, and this time the blades of the propeller caught him, slicing his head to pulp before they broke apart. It was too late for the pilot to do anything: the plane was several feet off the ground before he could react, and the power of the remaining engine slammed the machine into crunching nose-over loop on the ground.

The fuel tanks exploded within seconds.

The force of the blast hurled Achim Kleebach to the ground, but even as he fell he was staring up at the first Junker, the one where Thomas lay safe in the cargo hold. The plane was passing into the path of the Soviet flak. And Achim, sprawled bruised and broken on the concrete, kept his eyes on the dark puffs of smoke that erupted round the Junker like ugly, lethal freckles in the sky, saw the plane shake and waver, bank sharply to the left, then begin to climb once more. The pilot made it over the forest to the west with no more than a few metres to spare, then headed on up steeply until he reached the safety of a big, beautiful black cloud and was away.

A cloud had never seemed so wonderful to Achim, and for a few seconds he felt a raging, crazy wave of gratitude that Thomas had made it. Then there was a terrible quiet around Achim Kleebach. He began to feel cold as death, and in that moment he realised that he was absolutely alone.

It was supposed to be a family party, but it bore more resemblance to a wake. The men wore dark suits, the ones they kept for special occasions, but it gave them the look of mourners. The flickering light of the candles in the small Lutheran church added to the gloomy atmosphere.

The man in whose honour this ceremony was taking place could see none of all that. He was blind, condemned to a life of darkness. He no longer needed to wait for them to take off the bandages, because he had known the truth for seven months now. His face was disfigured by burns, and a pair of dark glasses shielded the glass eyes that they had implanted to fill the scorched sockets. He knew that the girl who was going to become his wife today, Marion Kleebach, was marrying him out of a mixture of pity and guilt. He despised himself for accepting her sacrifice, but he was happy – if a man can be happy in the eternal night of the mind. He would never see light, or a flower, a picture or a book, but he had Marion for a wife, the prettiest girl he had ever set eyes on in the days when his eyes could still see. The hands that had already begun to replace his eyes were thoroughly familiar with every contour of his wife-to-be, and they were less cruel than his ears, which were sensitive enough to tell him the scale of the sacrifice that Marion was taking upon herself.

She stood at his side, pale and pathetic. Behind her stood the sad figure of her mother, who was fond of Heinz Böckelmann and ached with pity for him, but who loved her daughter even more passionately. She had told Marion again and again:

'Think of what you're doing. I won't stop you. But remember that you have your whole life ahead of you . . . and that Heinz's condition won't change.'

Now Maria was leaning for support on the arm of her husband, whose thoughts were even more desperate. He knew what it meant to have two sons trapped in the Stalingrad pocket, and his despair was all the greater for having to be hidden from his wife. Until now he had managed to give her some comfort, some hope, though he knew that the situation was hopeless.

Arthur Kleebach kept up the façade through the wedding service and on into the afternoon, feigning enjoyment of the food and drink laid out for the small reception at their apartment, acting the jolly father of the bride. Then suddenly it was all too much for him. He slipped out of the room like a thief in the night and stumbled out onto the street, yearning for solitude, relief from his burdens for just a few moments, for a quiet schnaps alone with his thoughts.

For most of his life he had kept out of bars, and it was only under the intolerable strain of the past few weeks that he had started to become a regular at the little place on the corner. The owner was a friendly enough sort.

There were no more than half-a-dozen customers in the bar, talking quietly for the most part. The exception was a big, red-faced man at the counter, who was holding forth loudly on the subject of the coming relief of Stalingrad. The embarrassed owner tried to silence him by turning on the radio at high volume, hoping that the march music would drown the man's drunken ramblings. He glanced furtively at Arthur Kleebach, who was standing in the corner with his schnaps in his dark suit. The owner shrugged and slipped him a double on the house, motioning for Kleebach to drink it before the other customers noticed.

At that moment the march music came to a sudden halt and an announcer's voice barked: 'In a few minutes there will be a special military report.'

Arthur Kleebach looked up from his schnaps and began to hope, but when he heard the fanfare he realised that it was the one they reserved for glorious victories against the British. No good news from Stalingrad. Maybe some nonsense about sinkings by U-boats. He downed his drink, ignoring the man at the counter, who was pinching his arm to get his attention.

'A whole convoy,' the man droned. 'Seventeen ships ... One hundred and eighty thousand gross register tons! Jesus!'

Arthur Kleebach shook the man's hand away, tossed some money onto the counter and turned to go.

'I tell you, we'll win this war yet,' the man bellowed. 'The Führer's a genius, he'll ...'

Arthur Kleebach turned round and in that instant he forgot that he had always been unpolitical. He thought of Gerd, buried in France under a wooden cross, and of Fritz, waiting for the war's end in a P.O.W. camp in Canada, and of Marion, giving up everything for a man robbed of his sight by Hitler's war, and of Thomas and Achim facing death in Stalingrad. For one brief, unthinking moment he lost his self-control and screamed in the Nazi fanatic's face: 'A genius? As far as I'm concerned he's a swine, a con-man, a ... a criminal!'

All conversation stopped. The bar owner looked down at the floor and shook his head. Someone slipped off to the telephone. Two customers in the corner got out of the place in a hurry.

Before Arthur Kleebach could return to his family party, three uniformed policemen arrived to arrest him.

CHAPTER THIRTEEN

The day came when Achim Kleebach achieved the ambition that had spurred him on from his childhood, long before he had put on a field-grey uniform: he was commissioned, promoted to Leutnant. Stalingrad might be a charnel-house, the Russian front might be collapsing into bloody chaos, but military bureaucracy functioned with perfect precision. If the High Command couldn't send reinforcements, then the Army Personnel Department could radio in promotions by the hundred, fuelling a kind of career inflation in the beleaguered fortress on the Volga. The only slight problem was that the subjects rarely got to know about their new distinctions. By the time the message got through, they were dead of the cold or from starvation, shot to pieces or buried under the rubble somewhere in the ruins of the martyred city.

Even if Achim Kleebach had been informed of his dream-come-true, he wouldn't have given a damn. Since he had encountered Thomas at Pitomnik airfield, about to be tossed off the plane by Unteroffizier Hanselmann, something had snapped inside the boy. Suddenly he had realised that his eldest brother had been right all along. Thomas's 'defeatism' had been no more than realism, a realism that had increased rather than detracted from his effectiveness as a soldier. He had stared after the Junker that carried his brother away from Stalingrad and he had been devastated, and also overjoyed in the knowledge that Thomas at least had a chance to make it home.

The panic at the last airfield in Stalingrad had finally died down, and the victims of the slaughter had been cleared from the runway. Among them had been Hanselmann, so torn and disfigured by the propeller blade that there was nothing left of his face. Achim forced himself to look at the man before they hauled the corpse off for burial, because for him the

Unteroffizier had been more than just a comrade, he had been a symbol. Hanselmann was the complete personification of the system, a man formed and made by the Wehrmacht, with his stubborn, ruthless belief that there was always somewhere to run to, a way out. The sergeant had always known what to do, where to scrounge what you wanted; he had been a master of organisation, a figure of barbaric energy, a leader – the man they admired, even idealised in secret, though often they hated and feared him. But when Achim had looked down at the pathetic corpse on the runway, he was just another soldier, another among the thousands of men who had found death at Stalingrad . . .

It was the end for Achim. The veil fell from his young eyes, and suddenly he was no longer prepared to listen, only to think his own thoughts. There at Pitomnik at twenty-eight below zero, surrounded by a rabble of stinking, ragged, voracious animals that had once been men, the ex-Hitler Youth leader realised the full tragedy of what history and the system had done to him. And because he was still young, and he still needed to believe in something, he substituted a burning hatred for the Führer he had been willing to follow so blindly only days before. A deep, total loathing for the man who had betrayed him and his generation.

His hate, the fervour of the convert, gave him strength. Suddenly he had a reason to live, a weapon he could use against the hunger and the cold. He didn't yet know it, but that strength gave him a chance to survive where other men despaired.

Pitomnik held. Elsewhere, the battle line zig-zagged through the middle of the city of Stalingrad so wildly that no one knew who held what. There were scattered islands of resistance near the airfield where the supplies were dropped. They still called it the 'Square of the Fallen', and the pathos and the cynicism were interchangeable.

The airfield was completely sealed off from the living. The entrances to the 'Square' were barred by barricades and sandbags: broken girders, smashed lamp posts, burned-out panzers, piles of railway sleepers and barbed wire kept out hunger. The military police, the last branch of the service to remain intact, ruled the fortress within a fortress as their private domain. They guarded the last lifeline day and night, occasionally making forays to comb the cellars and drive dying, starving, and shell-shocked men into battle. Legend has it that they even tried to raise the dead.

So it went on, among the corpses, the armies of rats, the raging epidemics. The last shell had been fired long since, at about the time von Paulus had been made up to Field Marshal. For days now the men responsible for the whole tragicomedy had been staging grandiose 'Festivals of Remembrance' throughout the Reich and using the mass slaughter in Stalingrad to justify their proclamation of 'total war'. And the resistance continued. Perhaps only because von Paulus, the hero of the newsreels, was too frightened to surrender his own skin. He was only converted when the Soviets assured him that he would not need to tramp to Siberia with the starving remnants of his army but would drive past them in a closed limousine . . .

Achim was herded together with other survivors of the massacre on the airfield and sent off to join another unit. The cellar he commanded had the luxury of a radio, and a few days later he and his comrades were privileged to hear a crackling voice announcing Berlin's boundless admiration for 'Germany's bravest of the brave, who have held Stalingrad to the last man and the last bullet before giving their lives in ruthless hand-to-hand fighting.'

Achim Kleebach listened, and then he laughed loud, a laughter tinged with hysteria. He roared until the tears ran down and froze on his cheeks. The others nodded, and those who had the strength recognised dully that it was they who were being talked about on the radio. It was like lying there in your coffin, fully conscious, listening to the conversation of the guests at your own funeral.

'That's more than I can take,' said Achim when he regained control of himself. 'I've had enough. Finished. End.'

Two or three of the others looked at him. The rest, too weak to react, lay silently on their beds of rags.

'What do you have in mind?' asked the Unteroffizier.

'Clear off.'

'Where?'

'To the Ivans.'

'They'll shoot you down like a dog.'

'Then at least it'll be quick.'

Most of them were past listening, but a few managed to shake off their lethargy. They had a leader again, and they were ready to follow.

They hunted around, found a filthy piece of white cloth and a stick, and they crept out of the cellar with the applause for the heroes' deaths they were dying still crackling away on the radio and echoing among the ruins.

They didn't bother to go round stiff-frozen corpses of their comrades, just stumbled blindly to where the Russians were supposed to be, trampling over anything in their path. But even desertion turned out to be a problem. Without warning they were faced with a screaming Hauptmann coming towards them through the ruins. They barely had time to hide the white flag.

The officer quietened down a little when he saw Achim's shoulder-flashes and noticed that he was carrying a loaded machine-pistol. 'Glad to see you, my boy,' he said.

It was now that Achim recognised the gorget hanging round the officer's neck, the badge of the military police.

'Caught a few deserters,' the Hauptmann rasped. 'I intend to shoot the bastards as an example to the rest, but I've got no men to do it . . . Have you still got some ammo?'

Achim Kleebach simply stumbled on without another glance at the M.P. The others followed him silently.

The Hauptmann rushed after them and grabbed Achim by the arm. 'Are you deaf and dumb, or what?' he yelled. His starved, skull-like face wore a crazed grin. Fanaticism. Madness. What was the difference? Whatever it was, it had robbed this man of the last vestige of humanity, Achim thought. He tore himself away from the man's grasp and found himself staring over a heap of rubble at the four poor swine that the Hauptmann had condemned to death, standing listlessly in the ruins guarded by a Feldwebel and waiting for the end.

'There you are,' the officer gabbled. 'Kill the bastards!'

'Why?' murmured Achim.

'Orders!'

'Whose orders?'

'Mine.'

'That's what I wanted to know,' Kleebach said, and a slow smile spread over his battered, thin features. 'We've still got a few bullets left, Herr Hauptmann . . . we've been saving them

235

up for something special.' He freed the safety-catch from his weapon and spat out the next words: 'For you, Herr Hauptmann.'

The skull-Hauptmann realised his mistake too late, because a moment later Achim emptied the entire, carefully-hoarded remains of a magazine into his chest, smashing the breastbone and sending a glutinous shower of blood shooting out onto the snow. He would need no more ammo where he was going, and neither would the skull-Hauptmann. Then he looked wildly around for the Feldwebel, but the Hauptmann's sidekick was making himself scarce. Achim shuddered, shouldered his machine-pistol, and said to the four 'deserters': 'Come on, join up with us . . . We've finished with the slaughter!'

Now there were eight men stumbling towards a slim chance of survival, cautiously, keeping a lookout on every side. But they were lucky. A quarter of an hour later they encountered a Russian patrol, put their hands in the air and walked slowly, haltingly towards the enemy. They waited to be scythed down, and they were too exhausted to be surprised when nothing happened. Only Achim Kleebach felt anger – a rage at not having chosen the only way out of Stalingrad a long time ago . . .

The prisoners were given a hard time by their captors, but the Ivans' treatment of them was sheer luxury in comparison with the last few weeks. They slowly regained their senses; even a diet of water and turnip soup was enough to give them back some of their strength. They were herded into central assembly points, where the survivors were gradually brought together: one Field Marshal, twenty-four generals and almost 90,000 officers and men, most of them wounded. Many, even after all they had gone through, would find death in Russia over the next weeks, months, years. But meanwhile the Red Army was busy on the deathly-quiet battlefield, piling up the corpses of 150,000 Germans and burning them to ashes, Stalingrad's funeral pyre.

Achim Kleebach was sent to a P.O.W. camp where the Russian commandant had kept some vestige of humanity, despite everything, and so he was given food as well as hard labour. But the restoration of his strength only increased his capacity for hatred, and when the Soviet-sponsored 'National Committee Free Germany' was founded and began recruiting in the camps, he volunteered. Some joined because it meant better rations and relatively decent treatment, but not Achim: his hatred was so powerful now that it screamed for an outlet. It was hatred for a leader, a party, which had spoken of comradeship and sent hundreds of thousands of comrades to an inhuman death in the frozen city by the Volga . . .

The special session of the People's Court had been in progress since nine a.m. without a pause. Death sentences were sliding off the well-oiled conveyor-belt, because Nazi justice had to be done and heads had to roll for the 'final victory'. The judges who were to hear Arthur Kleebach's case were average time-servers, no better, no worse than the rest of the 'lawyers' who staffed the courts. The men in the dark robes were, after all, expected to justify their jobs by producing material for the executioner, just as the armaments manufacturers had to raise their production figures.

A black-market meat merchant was sentenced to five years in jail, while a man found guilty of listening to enemy radio broadcasts was sent to the guillotine at Plötzensee prison. Now it was Kleebach's turn. The accused was brought up from the cells, undernourished and pale, his skin wrinkled and leathery. His eyes seemed empty, turned inwards, and he showed no interest in the proceedings, as if he had somehow chosen to take whatever came to him.

Arthur Kleebach stared absently out of the window. It was a dull day, and a light drizzle pattered against the grubby window-pane. They should wash those sometime, he thought . . . He was glad that Maria had seen sense and not come to the hearing. Thomas had been sent back to the front – and his father had not even been able to see him. You'd think after three wounds collected for his country, the swine would give him a rest from the slaughter . . . Even Freddy had finally got his come-uppance. They had transferred him without warning, without leave. And still no letter from Achim, with Stalingrad in Russian hands . . . Now they called it 'total war', but maybe a few of them would end up as prisoners. After all, things had looked bad with Fritz at the beginning, and he was sitting pretty in a P.O.W. camp. The main thing was that Maria must be protected to some extent.

Her sons, her weak heart, and now – dear God – the whole thing with him . . .

'The accused will rise,' barked the chief judge.

Arthur Kleebach was jarred rudely out of his private world. He blinked at the man in the robes as if he were seeing him for the first time; he tried to look into his eyes, but the judge was wearing opaque spectacles that reflected back, giving nothing away. He must be very short-sighted, or maybe just cruel.

'Accused, have you understood the significance of the charge?'

'I have,' murmured the little postman.

'The charges against you have been confirmed by witnesses during the course of investigations. Do you dispute their evidence?'

'No,' Arthur Kleebach said calmly.

'You therefore admit that you called the Führer . . .' The judge coughed and read laboriously from the document in front of him, as if to distance himself from such blasphemy. '. . . A swine . . . ah . . . a con-man . . . a criminal?'

The man in the dock said nothing.

'At least you can have the decency to admit your crime!' the judge thundered.

Kleebach hesitated. 'Yes, I said that, but . . .'

'No buts!' the judge roared. 'You have had the temerity to stab the German people in the back as they face a struggle for their very survival as a nation, while our sons offer up their blood-sacrifice on the battlefields of Europe . . .'

Arthur Kleebach understood that part, at least. It was he who had offered up the blood-sacrifice – a fact that even the state prosecutor had mentioned in the charge document, hinting at extenuating circumstances. Maybe some bureaucrat had wanted one less death on his conscience.

Eventually the judge finished his propaganda speech and calmed down slightly. 'So. You had been drinking?' he asked.

'Yes. At home, before I went out.'

'How much?'

'A glass of wine perhaps.'

Arthur Kleebach could not understand the ripple that went through the courtroom. His defence counsel was making desperate signals at him, but Kleebach still failed to accept the lifebelt that was being tossed to him.

'And in the . . . ah . . . bar – how much did you drink there?' said the judge slowly, giving him every chance.

'Two schnapses.'

'Large ones?'

'I can't remember,' answered Kleebach.

The defence lawyer, despairing of his client's sanity, leapt in. 'Herr Kleebach,' he pleaded. 'Think carefully. Wasn't it more than that?'

'No. I'm not a big drinker,' Kleebach countered stubbornly. To lie was alien to him, and he was still too ignorant of the system's operation to realise the danger he was running. In any case, it all seemed so stupid and unimportant. If only Maria's heart were stronger . . .

The defence lawyer and the chief judge looked at each other in weary disbelief. Even the state prosecutor seemed to have given Kleebach up for lost. He had his head down in some other papers, other men's fates.

Just as the judge seemed ready to retire and decide sentence, a bizarre figure rose from the back of the court, a man in the mustard-brown uniform of a minor party official. He announced his intention of giving evidence in mitigation, and his secret wish was to ensure that at least one poor, harmless soul would survive the 'justice' of the system he served. The man was none other than the Ortsgruppenleiter, Party Comrade Rosenblatt.

He gave a brief description of the circumstances surrounding the case and the situation of the Kleebach family, the fate of Arthur's sons and the strain on their father's nerves. Of course, he could not comment on the case itself . . . The judges fiddled nervously with their pens, but they listened.

At first the chief judge seemed unmoved. 'You call yourself a servant of our glorious movement?' he blustered. 'And you can find excuses for such . . . slander . . . of our Führer? That is a strange sort of National Socialist commitment . . .'

Nevertheless, the simple words of the petty official, who long since wished he had never heard of Adolf Hitler, had some effect. The court rose to deliberate, the emaciated prisoner was led out past the tame fanatics who packed the public gallery. The watching ghouls were already eagerly discussing whether he would lose his head or end up with a nice long term in jail. The relative optimists were in the majority, and they were right.

The court came back in session.

The chief judge stood to read the sentence. 'In the name of the German people . . .' he began.

Arthur Kleebach looked down at the floor and found himself wondering if the Russians might not be as bad as the propaganda handouts said, if German P.O.W.s might get decent treatment after all.

'. . . having been found guilty on all charges under the Law for the Elimination of Covert Attacks on People and State, you are condemned to three years' imprisonment . . .'

Three years' jail, thought Arthur Kleebach wonderingly, shaking his grizzled head. Three years for three words? He was naïve, because by the standards of the time he had been let off extremely lightly. The sensationally lenient verdict of the special court was the talk of Berlin legal circles for days afterwards. As for Arthur Kleebach, he found comfort in the fact that by the time his sentence was complete the war would be over and his children would be home . . . the ones that were still alive . . .

This time, Oberleutnant Thomas Kleebach was posted back to active service before being passed as fully fit. The desperate military situation on all fronts outweighed any minor medical considerations. Anyone who could walk could fight . . . No one asked whether a son would be willing to die for a system that had sent his father to prison for the sake of a few despairing, unconsidered words. But then no one asked many questions any more – least of all about the mythical 'final victory', and why sons had to die and mothers cry. The Kleebachs had been hit hard, but then every street, every village, every city had its Kleebachs now.

Thomas still walked with a limp when he reached the Vitebsk front and again took command of a company. Still the old slogans, the slogans of Stalingrad, the order that they would shoot out of hand any man who gave up 'a foot of ground'.

After the fall of Stalingrad, the onset of spring and rains had brought the fighting on the Eastern Front to a halt. The warmer weather brought the mud, making the roads impassable to both sides, preventing large-scale troop movements. The initial effect was to stiffen the German resistance and hold up the Russian advance. But when the autumn of 1943 arrived, the breathing-space came to an end. The Red Army, now no longer a demoralised rabble but a mighty fighting-machine, attacked along a thousand-kilometre front, smashed through and drove the Germans back. On November 6th they took Kiev. Soon the Wehrmacht was in headlong retreat, from Leningrad in the north to the Crimea in the south.

The Russians had weighted their initial attack towards the southern front, sending their spearheads racing to free the Ukraine. But in the north they raised the two-year siege of Leningrad. Only the German Army Group Centre, reinforced by new panzers, managed to hold on and retain the so-called 'Panther-line' on the eastern bank of the Dniepr between Stary Bishov, Orzha and Vitebsk in a grim defensive battle.

The final Russian offensive, the breakthrough that would take them on to Berlin, was launched on June 22nd 1944 with a fine sense of timing. It was the third anniversary of Hitler's attack on the Soviet Union.

Their section of the front was still relatively quiet, and Thomas Kleebach's unit relaxed in the calm before the storm. Supplies were getting through, the mail came regularly, and their losses were modest. Nevertheless, something close to panic was spreading through the lines. The Nazi fanatics kept their mouths shut, and there were very few ordinary soldiers who seriously believed in the 'final victory'.

The Russians were totally superior in weaponry these days, but they had something else: they had refined their psychological techniques to a high degree of sophistication. They dropped planeloads of leaflets promising good treatment to German deserters, and they were installing more and more loudspeaker squads in the front lines, including members of the National Committee Free Germany, recruited from among German P.O.W.s. Their success rate grew.

It was, of course, true that both sides had become so hardened by war that fear of what lay in store on the other side prevented any desertions on a massive scale. Most of the ordinary soldiers were well aware that the Soviet promises were crude propaganda lies. But the constant barrage of words hacked at their nerves and undermined morale.

In the course of the past three weeks, Kleebach's panzer regiment had lost nine men through desertion to the enemy. This was serious enough for the regimental commander to make a report to the High Command and request instructions. Berlin told him to concentrate on knocking out the enemy propaganda squads.

The Oberst was no Nazi, but perhaps he had been required to show proof of success, or he may simply have been driven by an urge to do something before despair at their hopeless situation sent him out of his mind. Whatever his reasons, he decided on a special attack, a coup against the Russian propagandists.

'Gentlemen,' he announced to his officers, pointing to a map on the wall of his dugout. 'Here we have a salient that the Russians have managed to drive into our front. The Ivans, I need hardly tell you, are using their position to hawk this poisonous nonsense of theirs to our men ... I intend, therefore, put an end to their activities forthwith.' He stared along the row of officers, and then fixed a beady eye on Oberleutnant Kleebach. 'You're reckoned to be the hero type,' he continued sardonically. 'Right. You'll take your bunch in hand, and while we play soldiers on the other flank you'll sneak round to the rear and sort the swine out when they're least expecting it. Understood?'

'Yes, Herr Oberst,' Thomas murmured coldly.

'Kindly repeat the order,' said the commander.

'While the other units of the regiment deceive the Russians opposite us by feigned attacks on their positions, I shall endeavour to take my men to the enemy's rear and ...'

'You will not "endeavour",' snapped the Oberst. 'You will succeed.'

'Very well, Herr Oberst.'

He returned to his company and explained the whole plan so provocatively that an observer would have thought he was out to cause a mutiny.

'This is a suicide mission,' he said. 'It'll probably go wrong. If we manage to sort out those boys from the National Committee, the Ivans'll just ship some more in tomorrow, because they've got enough prisoners and enough equipment.

242

But . . .' He tossed away his cigarette and ground it to dust, his face a mirror of fastidious disgust. 'Orders are orders, and anyone who refuses to obey will be shot . . . Is that clear?'

'Yes, sir!' they chorused.

It was early summer. Their uniforms were damp with dew, their minds dulled by a desperate longing for peace. They formed up yet again, ready to go where the military machine ordered. Into the night against a tactical target. Maybe they had already been betrayed to the enemy, maybe not. If not, they might pull off a minor local success, the kind the propagandists in Berlin loved to trumpet when they needed to cover up the disastrous position elsewhere. That, at least, was a formula that hadn't changed from Julius Caesar to Goebbels.

They advanced in single file, keeping within sight of the man in front. They reached the first wire and cut a way through. On the other side of the lines, two or three hundred metres away, someone stepped on an anti-personnel mine and was blown sky-high. The Russian machine-gunners opened up for a few moments, and then the landscape went quiet again, swirling with mists that could hold a company, a battalion, a regiment of waiting Ivans. The company crawled on through no man's land, waiting to be spotted and come under fire.

Suddenly they heard a sound cut into the silence, a voice carried through the lines by the wind.

'Come to us,' the loudspeaker coaxed. 'Throw away your weapons . . . Refuse to die for the gangster Hitler. He has no right to your loyalty . . .'

Oberleutnant Kleebach climbed slowly to his feet, listening with calm concentration. That voice . . . it couldn't be . . . he must be hearing things . . .

Then he heard the next words: 'Come to us. Then your war will be over and you'll be on your way home . . .'

Achim. Achim. Thomas Kleebach hit the dirt and lay with his face pressed to the ground, paralysed with horror.

The shooting started. The other companies were going in to launch their feints, to keep the Russians occupied. The boom of shells, the crackle of small-arms fire drowned the voice. Searchlights probed the terrain. And the Oberst sat in his dugout in the rear, looked at his watch and settled down to wait for the success report that might never come – which he had never really expected to come . . .

Kleebach's company cowered in no man's land, was caught in the beam of a searchlight and hit cover where they could. A wave of concentrated Russian fire swept through the undergrowth, merciless and terrifyingly precise. Some lost their nerve, made a run for it and were mown down by cruel seams of machine-gun bullets before they could put more than a few metres between themselves and the enemy. Those who managed to keep calm chewed the dew-soaked grass and hoped desperately for reinforcements from the rear. And the Russians kept on firing. More than one German soldier dreamed one last dream of getting his hands round the Oberst's windpipe and squeezing, squeezing, before the Russian night-snipers found their mark and turned those hands cold and stiff, put an end to dreams.

There was no time for reinforcements. The Ivans, probably expecting a night-attack, came forward out of their prepared positions once the snipers and machine-gunners had softened up the German resistance. The last survivors regrouped around the Oberleutnant in a shell-crater in no man's land. Thomas Kleebach knew they were lost. All he had to decide was whether they would die going forward to capture his own brother for a German execution-squad, or whether they should sit here and wait to be shot to pieces by Achim's Russian friends . . .

But before he could reach the grimmest, most futile decision of his life, a cone of tracer fire caught him in the chest, hurling him onto his back in the mud. It was his fourth and last wound, and he died instantly. Perhaps, as he died, he was thinking of Luise, the woman who had become his wife a few short months before, because his pale, bloodless face seemed strangely soft and relaxed, as if he had caught the sound of some distant, supernaturally beautiful music, the music of tenderness, love and hope . . .

Then the gunners on both sides of the line opened up, and the patch of no man's land where Kleebach's Third Company had found its weary Golgotha became the target of a vicious artillery duel that ensured a mass-burial without benefit of wooden crosses.

The girl had a pretty, moon-shaped face and a ready, come-hither smile. She was in uniform, perhaps twenty-five years old, eager to live and not slow to seize her opportunities. Freddy Kleebach never missed a chance either, and as he got out of his train at the Anhalter station in Berlin his sharp eyes picked her out.

The uniform suited her. The blue went with her fair hair, and it was cut tight, emphasising the full ripeness of her figure. She was carrying a mock-leather suitcase and having trouble forcing her way through the jostling crowds on the platform.

Freddy, the gigolo, smiled to himself, and within seconds he was at her side and helping her. She glanced at him just for an instant, but that was enough for him to know he had a chance, which for Freddy meant that he was home and dry. He may not have been the most likeable of the Kleebach brothers, but he was the sharpest, which was why he had survived.

He had managed to keep away from the combat zone for four years; then, six months ago, there had been a surprise inspection at the depot in Berlin and he had found himself transferred to the front. The last few months had been disturbing, and he had never given up trying to find ways of getting away from the slaughter. He had hated the war from the start; in his own way, Freddy had always been a convinced pacifist, and what had happened to his own family had done nothing to change his mind.

He had no intention of ending up in a 'hero's grave' like Gerd, or rotting in a Canadian P.O.W. camp like Fritz, or being posted missing like Achim, or ending up in Russia for eternity like Thomas, the eldest. He intended to wangle his way through, escape, survive.

His big chance came, in fact, without his lifting a finger. One day he was summoned to the orderly-room and asked by his commander if he wished to take advantage of a new Führer-order that had just been received. Ever-cautious, the gigolo had read the order through twice, checking for loopholes, then had answered simply: 'Yes indeed, Herr Hauptmann.'

The Führer-order in question was certainly bizarre. The massive toll of blood that the German people was being forced to pay on the battlefields of Europe to prolong Hitler's war conflicted with the Nazi ideologists' commitment to the maintenance of 'good racial stock'. After high-level discussions, Hitler had dictated an edict intended to preserve what was left of the German family. Under its terms, if three sons from one household had been killed, then the head of the family concerned was entitled to request that the fourth be released from the Wehrmacht or at least transferred to non-combatant duties. Freddy could not know that his mother had made such a application on his behalf at the urging of Orstgruppenleiter Rosenblatt, but that did nothing to mar his pleasure and relief. Today he was arriving in Berlin to be formally demobilised, and he could hardly believe his luck.

'Where are you going?' he asked the girl.

'I'm supposed to be reporting to headquarters. To be assigned to a new unit,' she said.

'Surely that can wait until tomorrow?' Freddy said with a smile. 'Do you know Berlin?'

'No. I'm a bird of passage. In today, off somewhere else tomorrow.'

'Then may I have the privilege of showing you the city where I was born?'

She looked at him doubtfully, but she was weakening.

'I know my way around all the best places,' Freddy coaxed. 'And among other things I've got some vitamin B.'

The girl nodded. 'I'm not sure, I . . .'

'My name's Kleebach,' he said, introducing himself as if the matter was settled. He put down the suitcase and they shook hands formally. She smiled.

Now they had some sort of understanding. Both of them knew that in wartime you accepted the good times when you could.

'No one expecting you, privately I mean?' the gigolo asked delicately.

'No.'

'No boyfriend?'

'Curious?' she giggled.

'No, jealous,' said Freddy with a grin.

'I didn't know that still existed these days.'

'Oh, I'm a child of peacetime,' Freddy answered proudly. 'And I reckon that I'm just the boy for you.'

'Maybe so,' the girl said. 'Keep talking like that and you'll have me convinced I've been waiting for you all my life.'

'Wouldn't do any harm . . . anyway, I'm only wearing this damned uniform for form's sake,' he announced. 'Within the next few days I'll be demobbed, out of the pantomime club and back into real life.' The joy showed in his handsome face so clearly that it was almost comical. 'Civilians, my dear girl, are the real élite.'

'Do you always talk so much?'

'Only when I meet a beautiful woman.'

'You think I'm beautiful?'

'Don't you?'

'Not always,' she laughed. 'Particularly when a silver-tongued Romeo like you tells me so. But I suppose you're not so bad . . .'

Freddy could tell she meant it. 'Still in one piece, never wounded . . . all parts fully functioning – except I had my appendix out before the war . . . So make up your mind, lady, and tell me your name.'

'Gerda.'

'You're the sexiest Gerda I ever met, maybe even the first . . . And I know a bar round the corner where you can still get something to drink . . . Then we can find somewhere to spend the day . . . Then maybe a coffee and see what happens.' He winked.

'You seem to have it all sewn up,' the girl murmured.

And he had. He promised her that he could take her to a few night-clubs that still sizzled even in the blackout, and she agreed willingly. These days you never turned down that kind of an offer. Life was, literally, too short . . . They soon began to feel comfortable with each other, and Freddy began to drop his act a fraction.

They wandered over to a nearby restaurant, already arm in arm and dizzy with anticipation. Freddy knew that tonight was going to be good, and his pleasure was only momentarily dulled by the thought of his mother sitting at home and waiting for him. He tossed away the notion like a burned-out cigarette, telling himself that his mother would have him for the rest of his life, but this girl with the long legs and the tempting lips would probably be sent God knows where by her unit come tomorrow.

The cosy living-room of the apartment on the corner of Lietzenburgerstrasse and Wielandstrasse was quiet, though three people were sitting there: Maria Kleebach, her daughter Marion, and her blind son-in-law, Heinz Böckelmann.

They had the radio on, but the only entertainment coming over the airwaves was warning upon warning, report following report of enemy bombers over Germany. One big bomber force was approaching from the south while another, from the west, was heading for North Germany, probably Hamburg. A third, which had just crossed the Reich border, was within equal flying-distance from Cologne or Berlin, and the final target would be known within a few minutes.

'Dear Lord, I wonder where Freddy's got to?' Maria Kleebach said softly. Only her eyes held a spark of life, and even they seemed distant, inward-looking. Her voice was a monotone whisper. The skin she had once been so proud of was leathery and wrinkled; Maria Kleebach had become bent and thin and quiet, and the young people around her wondered if she was still capable of grasping her own suffering. Perhaps it would be a mercy if she wasn't . . .

Maria's mind, the fortress she had withdrawn to, was a ruin. But in that labyrinth of pain and shattered hopes something was still alive: a slim hope that a little of what she loved would be left to her. Arthur Kleebach, the man who had been crushed by the system, would come out of prison one day. Fritz stood a good chance of surviving the war in Canada. And perhaps Achim had not died in Stalingrad after all but been taken prisoner by the Russians. Finally, the last, terrible blow, the news of Thomas's death on the Eastern Front, had been softened slightly: Luise, his widow, was expecting his child, a baby that would never see its father but would have a tender, affectionate grandmother.

Marion, too, was a great support to her mother. It was true that she seemed too old for her age, but the girl did her best to stand by Heinz, her husband, and her mother.

'Perhaps the railway line's been bombed,' she suggested.

Heinz nodded. 'There would have been no point in his sending a telegram,' he said. 'These days you can't rely on them to arrive.'

'With any luck the housing authorities will let us have the spare room back,' Maria murmured. 'And we still have some of those bottles of wine of his in the cellar . . .'

'WARNING! WARNING!' the radio announcer barked.

'The enemy bomber formations have changed direction: expected target now Berlin . . .'

'Not again!' said Heinz wearily.

Marion stood up. 'I'll get some blankets for the shelter.'

'It's a good thing that Freedy hasn't arrived,' Maria Kleebach sighed. 'It wouldn't have been much of a home-coming for him.'

The howl of the air-raid sirens signalled full alert, and the three went calmly down to the cellar beneath the apartment building. Heinz made his own way. The route to the shelter was everyday, familiar, like making for a home from home . . .

Freddy Kleebach sat with Gerda in a black-market night-club when they heard the air-raid sirens. The girl looked nervous, but Freddy smiled knowingly.

'Don't let it spoil the party,' he said. 'Berlin is a big city, and not every bomb goes off.'

'Sorry!' the club owner announced. 'You have to go down to the cellar.'

'Rubbish!' retorted the gigolo.

They could hear the distant sound of anti-aircraft fire. Searchlights were probing the night sky. On the outskirts of the city the British Liberators dropped their first carpet of bombs, with a sound like a train steaming through a tunnel. The first wave passed quickly.

The customers began to swarm out. In this place, if you kept in with the owner, you could still get almost anything, but they had lost their taste for the home-brewed schnaps and the black-market cigarettes. They jostled wildly for places in the queue at the top of the cellar steps. Gerda had got to her feet too, following the herd, but Freddy seized her arm and held her.

Suddenly they were quite alone.

'Come on,' pleaded Gerda.

The gigolo laughed and raised his glass. 'One more drink!'

'Cheers,' she responded, and picked up her own schnaps tumbler.

He put his arm round her and kissed her. Her lips were moist, parted longingly. She was frightened, but she would not leave him. He had switched out the light, leaving only the candle flickering between them, and she could hear no more bombs. There were raids every night, Gerda thought, and you had to go through them alone, but tonight this man was at her side . . . and Berlin was a big city, and not every bomb was a killer, and tomorrow the papers would say: 'There were casualties among the civilian population', but then anyone who read that would have survived for another day, and many of those maimed would regret the moments they had missed.

'Not here,' she said.

'Anywhere with you,' Freddy said, and he laughed again. 'I don't usually like air-raid warnings, but this one couldn't have come at a better time.' He drew her closer.

Gerda freed herself and leaned back in her chair, staring upwards at the ceiling.

'What's the matter? Frightened?'

'No,' she answered. 'Not while you're here.'

'How old are you?'

'Twenty-four.'

'And what do you do?'

'You can see . . . I wear a uniform, but I want to live. And now I've been conscripted . . .'

'That's for tomorrow,' the gigolo muttered. 'Tonight I don't want to hear about it . . .'

The first wave of bombers had dropped its lethal load in the eastern part of the city and was heading for home, towards England, keeping several hundred metres above their comrades of the second wave, who had orders to bomb another area. One Liberator had been destroyed by the flak, and another was limping behind the rest of the squadron with one engine on fire. Four crew members had already baled out, but the pilot was still trying desperately to save his shattered aircraft, even though he knew that the German night-fighters would pounce on him as soon as he was out of the flak.

Freddy held her face between his hands and gently forced her to look at him. They gazed into each other's eyes, and the irises glinted in the flickering light of the candle like points of life. And they pressed closer, oblivious of the plaster falling from the ceiling, knowing nothing of the smell of fear down in the crowded cellar.

They wanted to live, not to die.

They wanted to know joy, not fear. And they didn't give a

hoot for map co-ordinates, bomber tactics, flak defence and night-fighter techniques. They were in the centre of the storm, and they didn't know it. All they wanted was to hold each other close, because tomorrow would tear them apart.

'You . . .' Gerda whispered.

'Can't you stay in Berlin longer?' Freddy said urgently. His breath stroked her face. A strand of hair had fallen across her forehead. He reached out and brushed it away with infinite tenderness, then held her to him again, so hard that it must have caused her pain. But she was grateful to lose herself in him, the rock she could cling to.

The fear was still there, but it was like a distant echo. Gerda could hear a roaring, louder now, and she could see through chinks in the blackout curtains and know that the whole area around them was in flames.

Danger merely drove them closer together. In that moment they felt something like love, though they hardly knew each other. They were human beings, a man and a woman, and for them that experience was more immediate, more important than any enemy bombers. If they never had anything else, they would have had this.

'Will you take me to the station tomorrow?' Gerda asked gently.

'Yes.'

'And will you write to me sometimes?'

'You can rely on it.'

'And besides that . . .' she weighed her words carefully, because they could be cheapened so often. 'Will you think of me now and again?'

'You can rely on that, too, Gerda.'

He believed what he was saying. There was no easy come, easy go about him now, none of the routine promise to get a girl into bed. He felt drawn to this girl as never before. For the first time in his life, the gigolo was fiercely wondering how to hold onto a girl and not how to get rid of her.

Gerda could read his thoughts, and she was overwhelmed by a powerful, irresistible feeling of tenderness that had nothing to do with the hunger for pleasure that she had felt before. They sat and were at one with the experience, the miracle, while walls fell around them, buildings burned, men and women screamed and moaned, wept and prayed and suffered dumbly.

They were both so gripped by the moment, above all fear, blissful, that neither heard the rasping whistle of the bomb as it fell.

They died in each other's arms, at the same instant of time, locked together so tight that even death could never break them apart . . .